BECOMING A GOD MADE EASY

BECOMING A GOD MADE EASY

THEOS BOOK 1

Arthur Wordsmith

Podium

BECOMING A GOD
MADE EASY

CHAPTER 1

An Unexpected End

He pulled his car out of the driveway and onto the road, letting his thoughts wander as he drove through familiar streets. More often than Luke would like to admit, he didn't remember the act of driving to his office. One moment he'd be at some intersection or a red light, and the next he'd be turning the corner a single stop sign away from what promised to be eight hours of mind-numbing work.

He felt today's drive should have been like that.

Instead, a raccoon ran out from under a bush on the opposite side of the street. An inexperienced driver turned her wheel straight into oncoming traffic in a poor attempt to avoid running over the creature and crashed bumper first into Luke's car. The impact crumpled the hoods of both vehicles, creating a malformed mass of metal, plastic, and rubber.

And so it was to the sound of squealing tires that Luke took his last breath on Earth. Surprisingly, that wasn't the end.

He felt his soul leave his body. For a moment, it floated above the wreck, and he saw—or maybe felt, because he didn't have eyes—his former body lying dead halfway out of the windshield.

Unsure of how to act, and surprised by his state, he hovered above the scene of his death in shock and confusion, observing silently as a young woman pulled herself free from the wreckage.

So that's who killed me. I guess it's good that she made it out okay, he thought with feigned cheer.

Not quite sure what to make of the situation, Luke focused on his new and strange state, only to find that he had been reduced to a wispy blue orb that glowed with a gentle inner light. The only logical conclusion, he thought, was that he was perceiving his soul.

Suddenly he felt a tug. The tug turned into a pull, and he was whisked away into the Aether. Neither up, nor down, nor sideways, but *inward.* Inky blackness surrounded him. Hoping he was being taken to heaven, he surrendered himself to the journey—not that he had any say in it to begin with. Suddenly, the direction of his soul's travel changed.

He felt caught, like a fish trapped in a fisherman's net, and he wasn't alone. Hundreds, maybe thousands of other souls, each glowing with their own soft blue light, all with as much agency as him—none—had been captured.

Onward they went, in a direction that to all of them felt *wrong*. To Luke, it felt as if a taxi taking him home had suddenly taken a wrong turn.

He would have complained. Corrected the driver. Yelled, "You missed the exit!" while he stared out the window and gazed longingly at the missed turn. Instead he found himself without the ability to speak. A natural consequence of being dead, and of no longer possessing a mouth.

Their destination came into view not long after—a bubble in the blackness, invisible except for the shine that surrounded it. The closer they got, the larger it became. Suddenly, Luke was squished right up against it. Then, with a jolt, he was inside.

Surprisingly, he landed on his hands and feet. Instead of flesh, blood, and bone, his body seemed to be made up of the same substance as before, merely reshaped to resemble his human form.

Taking in the world around him, he was in awe of—and in greater measure, terrified by—what he saw. The sky was in tatters. The earth cracked. Mountains were ripped from the ground and carried off into dark rents in the air, places where space itself seemed to have been torn. It was raining, but the water would sizzle and evaporate when it touched the black soil. In the distance, a forest full of large, leafy trees had caught fire and was spewing dark smoke. Far off in the sky, where the clouds broke, the sun looked like it was growing larger and larger. He watched, horrified, as it went from yellow to orange, and from orange to red, in the span of seconds.

Aw, shit. This is hell, isn't it? Luke's mind filled with righteous anger. He hadn't been that bad a person. Surely! Looking around him, he saw countless other souls. Forms of men and women of all ages, some children of five or six, and a few even younger.

Are the kids going to hell, too? That . . . seems wrong.

Spying what he thought looked like a personable figure in the sea of souls, an older gentleman with big, round glasses whose back was hunched over a walking stick, he took a step toward him. A question burned inside him, begging to be answered. Maybe, just maybe, this guy knew what was going on.

"COME!" a voice resounded through the realm and stopped Luke in his tracks. "COME!" the voice demanded again, its flat tone betraying the speaker's anger. This time, however, the command was accompanied by an invisible force. It pulled them deeper into the world. Whatever had brought them here wasn't done with them yet.

The remains of a city loomed in the distance and rapidly grew larger as the souls were pulled to a destination somewhere within. It was a scene of disaster. Ruins of once-beautiful structures lay shattered on the ground. Aqueducts spilled steaming water onto streets paved with what had once been perfectly cut marble. White columns that looked like they belonged in front of a museum or in a temple in ancient

Athens littered the ground, charred and broken. In some parts of the ruined city, magma oozed from deep beneath the earth and spilled onto the surface, burning everything in its path.

At the very center of the city, there was a castle. Fashioned from gold, it alone stood unblemished and proud, untouched by the chaos that had overtook the rest of the world.

The souls, caught from the Aether, were funneled through the front gates and into a large open room. Twin staircases led to the higher floors, one pressed against each wall. A narrow red carpet sprawled from the castle's gates all the way to the front of a massive throne.

Sitting atop it was a man. He had no more arm past his right elbow, and no more leg below his left knee. His stumps gushed brilliant red blood that pooled on the floor around him, indistinguishable from the red of the carpet. He had a hole, shaped like a perfect circle, carved out of the middle of his chest, oozing even more blood onto already-wet black robes.

He lifted his one remaining arm, and with grace unbefitting a man who looked as wretched as him, curled his finger.

A single soul flew out of the crowd and into his waiting palm. He squeezed, and he pinched, and he rolled, until the soul that once belonged to an older woman, who Luke thought looked rather like his own grandma—who, thankfully, had outlived him—became a ball. The man inspected it curiously and, nodding to himself in approval, he carelessly tossed it into his mouth and began to chew.

Those souls not paralyzed in fear tried to run. Luke watched one enviously as it managed to escape through the door. Envy swiftly turned into pity as an invisible force dragged it into the monster's waiting hands, where he once again rolled it up and swallowed it.

Luke watched the quiet terror as, one after another, more and more souls succumbed to the same gruesome fate. The purpose of the insanity became clear, as the man's wounds slowly began to heal. The hole in his chest shrank, and the stubs of his limbs began to grow with each additional soul that was consumed.

Maybe he'll finish recovering before it's my turn, Luke thought hopefully.

A soul beside him was summoned into the man's hands.

Maybe not.

"Tsk. Tsk. Tsk. How the mighty have fallen," another voice resounded through the world. Luke watched incredulously as the roof was torn free from the castle's walls.

An angel. Maybe she's come to save us.

"You." The man stood from his throne, on his single leg, and glared at her. His otherwise handsome face twisted ugly with hate.

Her white feathered wings beating softly, she landed between the souls and the man.

"I commend you, Aeolus. To think you had fashioned yourself a demiplane. When you fled to the Aether, I thought my prize was lost. It is fate that you came this close to divinity only to fail at the very last step."

He snarled. A black sword appeared in his hand. He pointed it at the winged woman in challenge.

"Ha." She snorted. "*You* want to fight *me*. Be a good little boy and just hand it over." Her voice rang, full of mockery.

"You know I cannot."

"Of course. It's bound to your soul and all that. How could I forget?" Clearly, thought Luke, who was beginning to suspect that she was here for some purpose other than to save him, she hadn't forgotten. "I suppose I have no choice, then, but to tear the Seed from your soul."

Looking far too cheerful for someone about to kill, she flapped her wings. In a motion faster than Luke could perceive, she was in front of the monster, for what else could a man who feasted upon the souls of the dead be? In her hand a blade of blinding white light formed, locked against Aeolus's own sinister blade. A moment later the world shook as reality caught up with their movements. A shock wave rippled out, flattening each of the castle's walls and exposing Luke to the burning hell that the world outside had become.

The man collapsed onto his throne, and his sword clanked as it fell into a pool of his own blood. Defeated after a single exchange. Not a match for her in the poor condition he was in. The angelic woman's arm blurred, and with a sickening plop, his two remaining limbs fell to the ground.

"There. That makes it more even." She smiled at his limbless figure.

He smiled back at her, blood escaping his mouth as he did. "You may kill me today. Know this, though. I did not come close to divinity. I reached it!"

"Hmm." His head slid off his shoulders. "The death of a god. How quaint." She stepped back, as if she was looking at a particularly thought-provoking painting. "Arke, the God Killer. I do quite like the sound of that." She nodded to herself, satisfied with her self-proclaimed title.

Definitely not here to save us, Luke thought, watching the terrifying display. *Also not an angel. No matter how much she looks like one.*

She turned toward the assembled souls. "You are all quite lucky to have seen this. A god hasn't died in ages. Of course, there hasn't been a god as weak as him in ages, either. Had he finished this construction"—she gestured vaguely to the rapidly disintegrating world—"it may have even been me who . . ." She trailed off and looked at the dead god's corpse.

Its soul separated from its body. Unlike the others, whose souls were blue, his was a resplendent gold, shining like a miniature sun in the room. It looked around before attempting to flee into a crack in space. It was an attempt doomed from its conception, as Arke had been waiting just for that moment.

Aeolus's soul struggled in her grip before smiling. Something unsaid passed between them, as in the next moment Arke let go of his soul and constructed a dome of light around her.

He detonated.

For an instant the world became white. When the light faded, it revealed a gruesome scene. Arke was strewn on the ground, her wings shredded and stained red with her blood, her limbs shattered and bent unnaturally. Despite her condition, though, she smiled. A big, happy, cheerful smile as she stared eagerly toward the charred space the man's soul had occupied. Floating there was a gem. Fist-size and glittering. The prize Arke had killed a god for, the Seed.

Luke watched in horror, questioning reality. *First I die, then the guy captures our souls, then he eats some of us. Only to be killed by that crazy angel lady. All for that?* He looked apprehensively at the floating gem.

He watched as Arke hobbled and crawled toward it, weakened by the explosion. Reverently, she strained her arm and closed her fist around the gem, only to grasp empty air instead.

She stared incomprehensibly at her empty hand.

Luke looked at the gem floating in front of him with trepidation. He glanced toward the other souls, only to see most of them had been sucked into a rent that had formed behind him. He even spotted a few of them flicker out of existence, likely resuming their journey. Finally free with the death of the monster that had brought them here.

"DON'T YOU DARE TOUCH IT!" Arke yelled from across the remains of the now-ruined castle.

Unfortunately for Luke and her, the choice was taken out of his hands. Before he could respond, it plunged into him.

"AGGGHHHHHHH!" Arke screamed as she hobbled toward him using her ruined wings for support, one painful step at a time. Not that Luke noticed. His attention was focused solely on the message that had appeared before him. One that only he could see.

Synchronizing.

Suitable Host Detected.

Requesting permission.

Accept Soul Bond with God Seed

Yes/No

CHAPTER 2

A New World

Don't you dare! Don't you dare! Don't you dare!" Arke shrieked.

Luke ignored her as he considered his options. Whatever his decision, he would have to make it, and fast. On one hand, the last person to possess the Seed had been killed. Right in front of him, for that matter. On the other hand, Luke was already dead. His fate was uncertain no matter what happened next. He had been pulled away from wherever he was going by Aeolus, to be eaten. Would his soul be free to resume the journey it started on with his death if he rejected the bond? Did he even want to find out what was waiting for him out there?

Glancing at the rage-filled expression on the crazy-strong winged woman hobbling toward him, he knew intuitively that if she got to him, he would regret it. Considering she had killed Aeolus and captured his soul, she likely had a way to take the Seed out of his. There was a high chance, Luke felt, that she would do it in a way that wouldn't leave him intact.

God Seed. What did that mean?

He remembered, before he died and blew himself up, the man had claimed to be divine. Even the name of the woman, Arke. It sounded like something he had heard in passing. She was a character in a story. A myth come true. Unfortunately, he didn't have time to think of where or when he had heard her name before.

A seed. You planted it, and it grew. A god seed. Would it grow a god? Was that what the man had meant by his last words? That he was a god?

Yes, Luke decided, making his choice, the first one since he had been pulled into this mess.

Installing.

Installed.

Host in imminent danger.

Would you like to use a charge to escape?

Yes/No

In the distance, Arke seemed to have detected that something had changed.

"NO! If you leave, I will find you. Just like I found Aeolus. The fate that befell him will feel like heaven compared to what I do to you!"

Yes. Luke gave the command, committing to memory the names of the monster that had brought him here and the not-angel whose actions had inadvertently saved him.

<table>
<tr><td>Charges remaining: 9 of 10</td></tr>
<tr><td>Choosing Destination</td></tr>
<tr><td>Analyzing Parameters</td></tr>
<tr><td>Destination Set: Theos</td></tr>
</table>

A golden bubble originated from within him and wrapped around his soul. A now-familiar inky blackness once again surrounded him as he was carried into the Aether.

The journey felt a lot more relaxed this time. The direction of his travel, at the very least, didn't induce the same sense of wrongness and anxiety as it had when Aeolus had hijacked his previous trip.

It helped that this time, instead of the blackness, he also had something to attract his attention. A status screen, like in a video game.

Status | Quests | Inventory
Name: Lukas King
Tier: Mortal
Mana: N/A
Rate: N/A
Strength: N/A
Agility: N/A
Constitution: N/A
Arcana: N/A
Stat Points: N/A
Charges: 9/10

All considered, it was interesting to look at, even with all his stats reading "not applicable," something he correctly attributed to not having a body. A problem he desperately hoped there was a solution to.

His tier being Mortal implied that there was something beyond it, and recalling the terrifying might of Arke and Aeolus, he guessed that was definitely the case. Mana, similarly, implied the existence of magic. Strength, Agility, and Constitution were easy enough to understand, even if Luke didn't know exactly what they meant outside of a game. The function of the Arcana stat likely had an effect on mana. What that effect was, Luke couldn't say, magic being a completely foreign concept to him.

The quests tab was empty, for the moment, at least. His inventory, however, was not.

Status | Quests | **Inventory**

Items:

God Seed (Soul Bound)

Tier—Primordial

An artifact forged from the primal energy of chaos by ⠇⠈⠒⠈ ⠐⠂⠒⠈⠂⠒. Guides wielder in their pursuit of godhood.

It was a sparse description, but useful nonetheless. It confirmed his suspicions about the purpose of the Seed. Arke had likely discovered that Aeolus owned it and had come to take it from him. Reading the description once again, his attention lingered on the black bar that was supposed to be the name of the Seed's creator. He wasn't quite sure what to make of it. He didn't know what the primal energy of chaos was, or what "Primordial tier" meant in the grand scheme of things. Something to look into in the future.

Luke's musings were cut short when something came into view. Unlike the bubble in darkness that was Aeolus's demiplane, the world before him just existed. There was no barrier separating it from the Aether. It was a planet, but calling it such felt like an insult to its sheer size. Orbiting it from a distance were nine large stars, and closer to the surface were nine smaller bodies Luke thought looked like moons. Like a picture of Earth taken from space, it was shrouded by white clouds that shone blindingly with the reflected light of its suns. Continents and islands peeked out of its oceans, barely visible under the cover provided by the clouds.

To his untrained eye, it looked vaguely like one of those old models of the solar system, before they had figured out that the Earth wasn't at the center of the universe. This place, in contrast, was.

Theos. That's what the Seed had called his destination.

Entering Theos.

Environment inhospitable to noncorporeal entities.

Recommended action: Possess recently deceased body.

Cost: 2 Charges

Yes/No

Luke considered what it was asking. So, there was a way for him to get a body. Except he wasn't enthusiastic about taking over some dead person's life.

Are there any other options? He directed his thoughts to the Seed.

A Mortal-tier body can be constructed. Cost: 8 Charges Yes/No

That would leave him with one charge. He'd already used one, and it had been a massive help. It had quite literally saved his life. Spending eight more, while he could get away with spending two, didn't seem wise.

Can I get more charges later?

Negative.

Luke frowned, just now realizing that he could communicate with the Seed with his thoughts alone.

Are you alive?

Negative. The God Seed interfaces with the user's soul and possesses information-processing and scanning abilities. Designed to guide the wielder toward godhood. For more information, contact ⠗⠑⠙⠁ ⠉⠞⠑⠙.

He read over the message carefully, frowning at the pattern of seemingly random dots that was either the identity of the Seed's creator—or was hiding it. Even if he had known their name, there was no way he would go and seek them out. In any case, it was a relief to him that the Seed wasn't alive. He wouldn't quite know how to feel if the Seed had been some strange being that he had to share his soul with. Not that there would be anything he could do about it at this stage.

Do I have any other options besides creating a body or possessing one?

Negative.

Possession it is, Luke decided after mulling over his two options. Not knowing what else he might need the charges for in the future, it was best to conserve them.

Affirmative. Scanning. Compatible bodies found: 1,356,087,873 Analyzing. Defining parameters. Optimal host selected. Rerouting.

Abruptly, the speed he was traveling at increased. The distant world became larger and larger to Luke until it encompassed the entirety of his vision. Then he was there, bursting through the clouds, with a clear view of the world's continents and oceans.

He flew at blistering speeds toward the surface of the planet, to an ocean in between two large continents. A moment later, his destination became visible: an archipelago with each island surrounded by beautiful blue-green water and sandy beaches.

Before he could accurately judge the size or even the shape of the island he landed on, he found himself hovering before a body. It was a kid, maybe fifteen or sixteen years old. Dark hair, pale skinned, and dressed in ratty clothes. A body that was soon to be his.

His vision faded to black as a message appeared in front of him.

Stand by.

Luke rubbed the sleep out of his eyes before abruptly getting to his feet. He stood in a clearing and took in the sight of the leafy trees and the sounds of the forest, taking deep breaths to calm himself.

Sitting back down a moment later with his back pressed against a tree, he closed his eyes to think. He took a moment to just breathe for the first time since he'd landed in this mess.

He wondered how his parents and friends would take the news of his passing. Someone would have rummaged through his belongings. Gotten into his phone. Made the appropriate calls. He smiled lightly as a tear ran down the side of his face. Hopefully his roommate, once he heard the news, would close all the tabs he had left open on his laptop and get rid of everything even remotely embarrassing that he saved on his hard drive. A promise made in jest not long before his untimely demise.

Besides, he thought, *I have a real chance of becoming a god. If those two could move around in that weird space, so can I. Once I get strong enough, I might even be able to go back to Earth. Wouldn't that make a mess?* He smiled as he imagined the looks on everyone's faces once he came back with crazy-strong powers.

Calling up his status, he looked over his attributes.

Status	Quests	Inventory
Name: Lukas King
Tier: Mortal
Mana: 0
Rate: 10% per hour
Strength: 8
Agility: 9
Constitution: 13
Arcana: 0
Stat Points: 0
Bloodline: Locked. Conditions not met.
Charges: 7/10

It had updated when he'd possessed the body, and he was relieved to see he finally had stats. Disappointing as they were, he had plenty of room for improvement. Something that he was looking forward to. The Bloodline was new, though, and he wasn't quite sure what to make of it.

What is a Bloodline, anyway?

It was at that moment disjointed fragments of memories belonging to the body's original owner hit him with all the grace of a bag of bricks. Aside from painfully filling his head with the knowledge of this world's language, they didn't paint a pretty picture. The kid, Max, had been an orphan. When he was younger, five, maybe six years old, a fisherman had found and rescued him. Max himself didn't remember, but he had been told when he was older that they found him alone on a dinghy floating listlessly in the sea, dehydrated and on the verge of death. The old fisherman and his wife had been kind to the original Max and had raised him as if he was their own son.

Things had been good until the fisherman had an accident at sea and perished. Not long after he passed away, Max and the fisherman's wife had been harassed over his debt—a debt that Max was sure didn't exist. The wife, already old, and weakened by the death of her husband, had passed away not long after. The creditors, seeing an opportunity, used the alleged debt as well as the fact that Max wasn't the fisherman's actual son as an excuse and took possession of the couple's property, every single thing they'd owned, from the boat to their small house.

As if that hadn't been enough, the creditors had decided that Max was too much of a nuisance to their claim and had chased him out of town. Without any food, water, or even appropriate clothes, he had succumbed to the environment and died. Moments before Luke's soul had occupied the vacant body.

Which led Luke to his current predicament. The island he was on was big. If the jumbled mess that were Max's memories painted an accurate picture, the island would be the size of a continent, at least, if it was picked up and dropped into one of Earth's oceans. The level of technology on the island also wasn't great. If Luke had to guess, what did exist would be comparable to what was present in the preindustrialization period on Earth. They had trains that ran on steam, but the most common modes of transport were various beasts of burden. Giant four-legged lizards and flightless birds that reminded Luke of ostriches pulled carts and carriages, taking people where they needed to go.

At least the weather is nice year-round.

His stomach grumbled painfully, reminding him that he didn't have the luxury of time. If he just stayed here, he would only succeed in reenacting Max's death.

Luke thumped his head gently against the tree, at a loss for what to do. He didn't know what direction the town he came from was, nor did he particularly want to go back there. Compared to his modern sensibilities, the place might as well be a backward and lawless hellhole.

In this world, it was common for the average person to never leave the place of their birth. Max himself had never been possessed by a desire for knowledge and hardly knew a thing about anything other than his own little part of town. He'd fully planned on inheriting the fisherman's boat and supporting himself the only way he knew how.

Quest Alert: Acquire Bellerophon's Blade

Luke stared at the message. This is what a god had died for, a vague clue? He opened his status.

Status | **Quests** | Inventory

Acquire Bellerophon's Blade:

Over five hundred years have passed since Bellerophon's infamous attempt to reach divinity was thwarted by Zeus. His armaments fell with the rain over all corners of Theos. His blade is on the island of Carim. Found by members of the Luminous Sky Society, it resides in their armory till this day. Ignorant of the treasure they possess, or how to use it, they leave the blade unused, hanging on a wall.

That was better, Luke thought as he carefully read over the description of the quest. There was a sword on the island. The Luminous Sky Society, whatever that was, had it. He just had to find a way to retrieve it, and he'd be well on his way to his own apotheosis. One that hopefully went better than Aeolus's—or Bellerophon's, for that matter.

All he had to do was find a way out of the forest and then find a way to the society. Sorely wishing that Max's memories had provided more context, he got to his feet and looked around. Picking a direction that he thought and hoped led to the town Max came from, he began walking.

A few minutes later, he heard someone sneeze behind him. Jumping two feet in the air at the sudden noise, Luke came face-to-face with a sturdy-looking elderly man dressed in bright-red robes. He was floating lazily above the ground with his legs crossed.

Luke started at him, and he stared at Luke.

"You wouldn't happen to be possessing that body, would you?" the man asked, his hands combing through his long white beard as he stared at Luke, an unreadable expression on his face.

Fuck.

CHAPTER 3

The Old Man

Hmm." He stroked his beard. Uncrossing his legs and landing softly on the ground, he walked in a circle around Luke, poking and prodding his body with his finger as he did a lap around him.

"I, uh . . . I don't . . ." Luke stuttered, not knowing what to say and caught off guard by his sudden appearance. He didn't want to admit to anything, but at the same time he didn't want to lie to someone with abilities he didn't understand, lest he anger him. The old man was capable of flight and had arrived minutes after Luke had possessed the body. Who knew what else he could do? The supernatural was entirely unfamiliar to Luke.

"No. No. No," the old man muttered to himself before lifting one of his legs and folding it across one hip and then the other, once again floating in the air. "Sorry to bother you, young lad. Your body displays no signs of possession. Your soul is stable. More than that, both your soul and body are in perfect sync." Luke allowed himself to relax. So he didn't know. "If I hadn't noticed that same body you're in right now lying dead earlier, I never would have guessed otherwise."

He winked.

Fuck, fuck, fuck.

Luke's thoughts skidded to a halt as he stared, open-mouthed, at the old man, stunned that his secret had been exposed already.

"What do you want?"

"Bah. What I wanted was to be left alone. Instead I have those ruddy Olympians breathing down my neck. Treating me like their servant and expecting us to clean up their mess. Tell me—how is it my problem that a thief, a dead thief at that, escaped them and fled somewhere onto the archipelago? Especially when every sane person knows that a soul has a limited window of time to make its way into the Aether or risk dissolving by staying on Theos, making the search effectively useless."

"It isn't," Luke offered, recalling that the Seed had also mentioned something similar about the environment being inhospitable to noncorporeal entities.

"Precisely! It isn't my problem. Instead, they have us poor folk, trying to live our lives in peace, searching every one of these hundreds of islands. Looking for someone who could steal from them and get away. Let me ask you this: if this alleged thief can run away from the Olympians, what chance do we poor and weak members of a small and feeble organization like the Luminous Sky possibly have of finding him?"

"I imagine the chances are very low," Luke responded evenly.

"Next to none! A complete waste of time, and they know it. The fact that I actually ran into you. Ha!" He smiled broadly, displaying a row of perfect white teeth.

Luke mulled over his words. Luminous Sky—those were the people who had Bellerophon's Blade according to the quest the Seed gave him. The old man just so happened to be a member. What were the odds that he would get a quest and moments later meet someone directly relevant to it? Luke looked at the old man consideringly. Next to none, he decided. The Seed must have foreseen this happening.

For whatever reason, the old man didn't want to help the Olympians—Arke, Zeus, and Bellerophon. It was hard for Luke to even wrap his head around them being real. They were supposed to be myths. Ancient legends conjured by ignorant folk to explain how the world worked. Not people of flesh, blood, and bone. Never would Luke have thought that he'd one day be discussing how they conducted themselves with someone who was genuinely inconvenienced by their existence—and he himself would be inconvenienced by their existence, for that matter. Or that he would get dragged into something far beyond his imagination and make off with a prize they were now combing the world for.

"Right." Luke looked at him warily, still on guard for any unexpected surprises. The lack of response from the Seed, however, put him slightly at ease. It had alerted him of danger when Arke was gunning for him minutes ago and given him a means of escaping. Seeing as he still had plenty of charges stored up in case of emergency, he felt that, for the moment at least, he was safe. Charges, Luke realized, that he didn't understand. Not completely.

The old man's smile slipped from his face. "I have no love for the Olympians, but their power makes them terrible enemies. Overtly disobeying a request made by them is . . . unwise. At least for the likes of me. Look at you—they destroyed your body and recovered what you took from your remains. Still, they exert their power over us, just so they could punish you. Forcing us into this mockery of a hunt."

Luke nodded slowly, his thoughts churning as he tried to make sense of the situation. The old man was clearly missing some pieces of information. Critical information at that. As a consequence, he had drawn the wrong conclusion. Luke recalled the time he'd spent as a soul. As an incorporeal being. In hindsight, it wouldn't make sense for a bodiless soul to physically run away with something. After all, it wasn't like he had arms to carry it. From the old man's perspective, he had failed and fled in a sorry state. Except the Olympians could have claimed that he ran away with a critical piece of knowledge or *something*. Which also ran the risk of whoever captured him also learning what he knew. In a way, by saying that Luke hadn't escaped with anything, they were reducing his value in the eyes of others but still leveraging what power they did have to capture him. A situation that aided both Luke and the Olympians.

It's like when a criminal can't go to the police without risking their own crimes being discovered.

He didn't know what Luke had taken. Or that he was just a random person from a different world. He was imagining Luke as someone capable of going head-to-head with very powerful people and escaping by the skin of his teeth and, in the process, likely attributing his current lack of power to possessing a powerless body.

If he knew Luke had an artifact capable of turning a powerless nobody into a god, they likely wouldn't be having this conversation. It would start a bloodbath. In the chaos that would ensue, there was no guarantee whom the Seed would go to. They had even managed, through some unknown means, to figure out his general location and started a manhunt for him. Unfortunately for them, though, the person to catch him wasn't loyal to them. Which potentially gave Luke an opportunity.

"So . . . what did you steal?" He leaned forward, looking at Luke eagerly.

"What do you plan to do with me?" Luke asked in return. He'd decided the less he said, the better it would be.

The old man sighed as he crossed his arms over his chest. "I don't know. I doubt that there's anything you could do for me as you are." He smiled. "How about this? Come back to the Luminous Sky with me and recover your strength. True allies are hard to come by these days. In exchange for not turning you in, I need your help with something once you pass the mortal threshold."

"My help with what?" Luke asked warily as he considered the offer. He was seriously tempted to accept it. Especially because all evidence seemed to point to the fact that their encounter had been arranged by the Seed.

"That, my new friend, is a secret. Here." A silver ring on his finger briefly flashed before a small pile of clothes appeared in his hands. Black versions of the same robes the old man was wearing.

"What are these?" Luke asked, trying his best not to show his surprise at clothing just appearing.

"Members of Luminous Sky keep to a strict dress code. Those robes are what the Outer Disciples wear," he explained.

"So I just put these on and follow you back to the Luminous Sky? Then, once I'm strong enough, I help you with something and we're even?"

"You got it."

"No one will be surprised if I show up with you?" Luke looked at him skeptically.

"Whatever technique you used to take over that body, it's seamless. I can't even tell that it's not originally yours. Granted, I don't know much about the process, but even if there are signs of possession that I can't detect, they should fade in a day or two anyway. As for you showing up suddenly, the Luminous Sky is always recruiting. My returning with someone I claim has talent won't strike anyone as odd. My position as an Elder guarantees that much."

Luke blinked as he processed the old man's words. He had deduced that he wasn't the only one on the path to godhood from the information that came with his quest, but to learn that there were entire organizations dedicated to it was a shock.

"Okay. I want to know more about what you guys actually do, though," Luke agreed after some thought. Worst-case scenario, a rumor would spread about what he possessed, and the old man might act out of greed. So long as he had a charge or two to spare though he was fine. It also gave him an in to get started with his quest.

"The Luminous Sky is decent at keeping itself on the up and up. At least as far as an organization full of bastards trying to be gods can be. Don't worry, we're not demons or anything."

"Right. That's good." Luke nodded.

Demons?

"I'm Nefkha," the old man said, suddenly introducing himself.

"Luke," he responded, taking the robes from his hands.

Might as well, he thought, awkwardly getting dressed. He was relieved that he could get out of the rags that he was wearing and simultaneously annoyed that he was still dirty underneath them.

"Ah! I forgot how annoying it is to carry mortals around. Here, this should be big enough for you to sit on." Nefkha's ring flashed, and a large circular shield came into existence.

Luke desperately wanted to ask how he was doing that, even though he knew the answer would be magic. Instead he kept his mouth shut and did his best not to be visibly surprised by anything he saw. Breaking his character would result in a bad end for him. If Nefkha thought he wouldn't be able to help him in the future, then he had one reason fewer stopping him from handing Luke over to the Olympians.

Aeolus's fate still fresh in his memory, Luke resolved to do whatever he could to avoid it. He stepped onto the dome of the shield, and they took off into the air. Gripping the leather straps with white knuckles, Luke couldn't help but compare how much better traveling was when the Seed was carrying him. Or when he didn't have bugs flying into his face.

Struggling to breathe with the wind pulling the air out of his lungs, he looked over to Nefkha, who seemed completely unbothered by it. So much so that his robes weren't even flapping. Shaking his head, he adjusted his posture in a semisuccessful attempt to make breathing easier.

They covered ground quickly and in silence, mostly because Luke wasn't able to talk at the speed they were moving. Something that he was grateful for.

A couple hours later, they arrived at their destination.

A small artificial mountain range, with twelve mountains in total arranged in a semicircle, each of them perfectly identical to the next. Luke looked at them with disguised awe. Every mountain had had its peak cut off, leaving a flat plateau, on top of which were castles made of white stone. Located in the center of the range was a city.

"Here. Take this token to the administration building in the city. It's the tall one, next to the arena. You can't miss it. They'll set you up with what you need. The rules prohibit me from showing any undue favor, and it's best that you keep a low profile, at least for a little bit, so we won't have much contact. I'll keep an eye on your progress, though, and once you're strong enough, I'll find you. If you try to run . . . I'm sure the Olympians would like to know that you were here," Nefkha threatened as he landed on a road just outside the town.

"You have my word."

"Hmm. Try not to show off too much, either. I don't know how strong you used to be, but take your time recovering your strength. The timing of your arrival is curious, and I don't want any of the others suspecting anything." He nodded and with a pat on Luke's back flew away. Eyeing the town, Luke began walking toward the buildings, eager for the day to be over.

CHAPTER 4

Luminous Sky Society

Luke took in the sights as he walked toward the administration building. It was impressive, to say the least. The memories he'd inherited from Max had painted a picture of the world that was tinted through the lens of, not poverty, but of a lower-middle-class existence in what he was now realizing was a poorer part of the world.

Luminous Sky City was the polar opposite. Every brick exuded wealth. The streets were clean, the people sharply dressed and well-groomed as they milled about. There wasn't a single piece of trash to be seen, no matter how hard he looked. It even smelled good. Like woodland and flowers. Just breathing the air made him feel refreshed.

Opening the door to the administration building, he blushed as he walked to the front desk. People stared at him, no doubt wondering what smelly hole he had crawled out of. Despite being dressed the same as everyone else, Luke felt out of place, acutely aware of the dead leaves in his hair and the grime covering every inch of his skin. Not to mention the smell coming off him. It was bad.

"Hi. How can I help you today?" a woman in white robes sitting behind the desk asked him.

"I have this." Luke slid the token Nefkha had given him earlier across her desk, idly wondering what the deal was with the robes. In Max's memories, most people dressed simply in pants and shirts—dresses if they were women.

Accepting it gingerly with both hands, she looked at the token and then at him, seeming stunned that he possessed it. "One moment, please. I'll be right back." She got up and disappeared farther into the building.

Luke stood there awkwardly for a minute as he looked around the room. Waiting rooms, he concluded, were the same everywhere in the world.

A few painfully long moments later, she returned with another woman. Unlike the white robes the receptionist was wearing, she was dressed in the same black robes he wore.

"Hi. I'm Arya." She stepped around the desk and shook his hand. "Welcome to the Luminous Sky Society. We're glad to have you join us. If you follow me, I can take you to your accommodations and get you properly sorted out."

"Right." Luke nodded as he walked out after her. "So . . . what does the society actually do?"

She looked at him weirdly. "Did the Elder not explain anything to you?"

Scratching the back of his head, he struggled to come up with a response. Nefkha had made incorrect assumptions about who Luke was and what he was capable of. Whatever the society did, he expected Luke to already be aware of it. Instead Luke was completely new to the world and had no idea how anything here worked.

"He mentioned that the dress code is pretty strict?"

She stared at him blankly. "That's it?"

"Um. Yeah. Was he supposed to tell me more?"

Suddenly she stopped and stepped into his personal space. Before he knew what was happening, her hand had snaked through the front of his robes and was resting right over his heart.

"What are you doing?" Luke asked.

"What are you doing here?" she asked in turn.

"Nefkha asked me to join . . ."

She blinked at him owlishly. "I don't sense any mana in your body. You haven't even begun to draw it in. You're as mortals as a mortal can be."

He stepped away from her as he processed her accusation. He was, in fact, as mortal as a mortal could be. Largely on account of the fact that he had no clue how not to be.

"Is that a problem?"

Her cheeks turned red. "It's . . . not a problem. It's just unusual. Typically, those who join outside of the examinations already have a foundation in cultivating mana. That's how they catch the society's attention."

Mana—his status screen had said he had none and that he regenerated none of it every second.

"I don't really know how to do that," Luke confessed, thinking over his words carefully. While Nefkha thought he was a powerful man who had fallen on some hard times, he actually had no idea what he was doing. Seeing as he had no foundation in cultivating mana, now was a good time to get the basics explained to him. If Nefkha looked into his actions, he was likely to assume that he was playing a role—pretending to be an ignorant mortal he had picked up from the outside. While, in fact, an ignorant mortal was exactly who he was.

She opened her mouth and then closed it, before nodding. "Why don't you get settled in, and I'll arrange for someone who can walk you through what you need to know tomorrow," she said, leading him to a house on the outskirts of the city.

"Is this all for me?" Luke walked into an empty living room, fully stocked with tasteful furniture.

"Yes. All members are provided with accommodations and meals. There is a copy of our handbook along with a few other introductory texts already in your house. I'd suggest you acquaint yourself with them. They should answer a lot of your questions. Someone will bring you food later in the evening."

"Thank you."

Exploring the house, he was pleasantly surprised by it. While it wasn't extravagant, all the furniture was of very high quality, and besides lacking a kitchen, everything else in the house was largely what he expected. Peeking his head into the rooms as he went, he nodded at the large washroom, which thankfully possessed all the modern conveniences he was used to. He found a room with a yoga mat in the middle surrounded by shelves, which, save for two books and one scroll, were empty. The last room turned out to be a standard bedroom.

Half an hour and a very thorough shower later, he stepped into the meditation room. Peeling a banana that had been left in a basket full of food on his porch, he eyed the books on the shelf. Picking one at random, he decided to try something he had wanted to do for a while.

Add to inventory. He gave the Seed a mental command and, with a flicker, the book was gone. Excitedly, he called up his status.

Status | Quests | **Inventory**
Capacity: 0.359 kg of 104 kg
Items:
God Seed (Soul Bound)
Tier—Primordial
An artifact forged from the primal energy of chaos by ⠐⠄⠁⠒⠈⠒⠠⠂⠄. Guides wielder in their pursuit of godhood.
Book
Tier—Mortal

Just as expected, an entry, this time lacking a description, appeared under the one for the Seed. His eyes lingered at the top of his inventory page, where a new piece of information had popped up. He frowned as he tried to make sense of the capacity before realizing that it was just his Strength attribute multiplied by his Constitution attribute and converted to kilograms. While it was disappointing that he didn't have a limitless amount of space, he was happy with the current capacity. Being able to carry a little over a hundred kilograms in mass was nothing to scoff at. More than that, the limit should also improve as those two attributes did. Thinking back to Nefkha's flashing ring, he guessed the ability might not be exclusive to him alone.

Leafing through the books, his eyes traced over the foreign letters. Possessing Max's body had come with some welcome side benefits, besides having a body, chief among them the ability to read and write in this world's language.

The first book contained all the rules and duties expected of a member of Luminous Sky and read like those terms and conditions you had to agree to before seemingly doing anything on the internet—contracts Luke had never once bothered reading. Thankfully the book was rather brief.

The society was essentially a gathering of people who all had the common goal of pursuing godhood. There were many challenges to doing so, some of them difficult if not impossible to overcome alone. The society promised its members, among other things, a place where they could exchange resources and learn from those farther along the path, a place to live, and security.

In return, its members were required to contribute to it. All disciples had to fulfill a quota of missions. The minimum required was one a month, but there were provisions for missions that took longer. The society also acted as a police force in the area. All the cities, towns, and even villages in the region sent monthly tributes, and in exchange the society dealt with any supernatural threats.

In retrospect, it seemed obvious to Luke that in a world full of gods, there would also be monsters that mortals were unequipped to handle.

The society was divided into ranks, which determined certain privileges and described a person's power. White robes indicated a person who had attempted to cultivate before being demoted to clerical duties. They took care of the society's more menial tasks. Black robes were one above that. Those that wore them were referred to as Outer Disciples of the society, and from what Luke had seen on his short trip through the town, they were the most populous of the society's members.

The Mortal tier itself was divided into three broad ranks by the society, early, mid-, and late. Outer Disciples belonged to the early and midranks of the tier. Above them were the late-Mortal-tier individuals, who wore blue robes. The divisions inside the Mortal tier, however, weren't actual thresholds, according to the book. Instead, they were meant to signify a difference of ability. Anyone could have their abilities tested, and where you scored within certain parameters informed your rank and progress in the Mortal tier. Those at the Mortal tier ranged anywhere from barely stronger than the average human to having, as the handbook described it, the strength of a hundred men.

If you managed to surpass the Mortal tier and enter the Warrior tier, you would automatically graduate from being a disciple and instead be given red robes and the title of Elder along with an abode on one of the peaks. At the moment, the society only had nine people in the Warrior tier. All of them held considerable influence over the society and had a say in how it operated.

The ability to fly was the hallmark of being in the Warrior tier. Any who demonstrated the ability were instantly promoted to the rank of Elder.

So that's what Nefkha meant by surpassing the threshold.

Having a rough idea of the society's rules, Luke closed the book and looked at the scroll. Smiling at the novelty of it, he unfurled it. His eyes instantly widened at the contents. With the title *Ascending Past Mortality*, it immediately held his interest.

His eyes raked over each word, careful not to miss the slightest detail. After he was done, he put it to the side and sighed. The path of climbing past the Mortal tier was surprisingly simple. All you had to do was exercise.

According to the scroll, the world was full of energy called mana. Living beings, like humans, animals, and even plants, could absorb mana from the environment and learn to manipulate it after accumulating it inside their bodies.

Unfortunately, the ability to gather mana wasn't something that people were born with. Instead, you had to push yourself to your limits, and eventually—how long it actually took depended on something the scroll referred to as talent—your body would develop an affinity for mana, beginning a process of automatic accumulation. It would then use the energy to make your body better and better, until you surpassed the limitations of mortality.

Eventually, you would even gain the ability to sense the mana entering your body and learn to exert influence over it, choosing what you improved and by how much. The ability to sense and direct mana, however, wasn't guaranteed, and you would be eternally stuck at the middle tier of the Mortal realm.

Recalling Arya being able to detect his mana, he concluded that she would likely enter the late stage, if not the Warrior tier itself eventually.

Having learned the rather mundane secret to godhood, Luke stripped out of his robes, down to his underclothes, and started doing push-ups. When he couldn't do any more push-ups, he rolled onto his back and started doing sit-ups. When even those became impossible for him, he stood up and started doing squats until he could barely move. Sweat beaded on his body as he pushed himself further than he had ever pushed himself before. Godhood, a carrot that he couldn't help but chase.

When the sun set over the horizon, Luke quickly rinsed the sweat off his body and stumbled onto his bed.

Waking up sorer than he ever remembered being, he couldn't take the smile off his face.

Status | Quests | Inventory
Name: Lukas King
Tier: Mortal
Mana: 0
Rate: 10% per hour
Strength: 8 > 9
Agility: 9
Constitution: 13
Arcana: 0
Stat Points: 1
Bloodline: Locked. Conditions not met. (0/10,000)
Charges: 7/10

His status had changed. Not only had his strength increased by one, but he had also gained one stat point, along with a counter next to his Bloodline. Eyeing the stat point, he dropped it where he thought he needed it most—the Arcana stat.

Status	Quests	Inventory
Name: Lukas King
Tier: Mortal
Mana: 6.5
Rate: 10% per hour
Strength: 9
Agility: 9
Constitution: 13
Arcana: 1
Stat Points: 0
Bloodline: Locked. Conditions not met. (0/10,000)
Charges: 7/10

Surprisingly, he didn't feel any different, nor could he feel the presence of mana inside him. Frowning, he analyzed the numbers. His total mana was half his Constitution stat, while the regen rate was unchanged at ten percent an hour.

Maybe I don't have enough mana to even notice it? Six and a half is decent for other things, but maybe not much when it comes to mana. I'll have to add more points to the Arcana stat and see if it makes any difference.

Deciding it was what it was, he rolled out of bed and got ready for the day.

Knock! Knock! Knock!

Just in time.

CHAPTER 5

Taking the Tour

Rushing to his door, high on the excitement of finally making some progress, Luke came face-to-face with a middle-aged man dressed in black robes.

"Hey, I'm Xander." He reached out to shake Luke's hand.

"Luke."

"Nice to meet ya. Arya mentioned that you're new around here, so she sent me to give you a tour." He stepped back from the door.

Following him out, Luke locked the door behind him. "Yeah, Nefkha didn't really mention much. I read the books inside, though."

Nodding along as he walked, Xander replied, "That's good. The books tell you practically everything you need to know about the Luminous Sky. Did you have any questions?"

Luke scratched the back of his head as he thought it over, wondering what was safe for him to ask and what wasn't. "None at the moment. The books covered basically everything I can think of," he replied eventually. He wanted to ask him about Bellerophon's Blade but didn't know how to broach the subject. Nor did he want to give anyone any reason to suspect that he wanted it. Without knowing how closely Nefkha was paying attention to him, it was best not to mention anything that might give the old man further leverage over him.

"That's good. I'm assuming you also read the scroll on cultivating mana?"

"I did," Luke replied eagerly.

"Perfect. It's as simple as it seems, so make sure you don't slack off. Reaching a bottleneck at the middle stage of the Mortal tier is one thing, but if you don't even get that far in three years, the society will demote you to wearing white robes or ask you to leave if you're not pulling your weight," he warned.

Luke nodded in response, already aware of the rule.

From what the scroll suggested, it's possible to reach the middle stage with a year or two of dedicated training. A peak Mortal-tier individual is said to have the strength of a hundred men. If I assume that the average person has ten points in the Strength stat, then that means a late-stage mortal will have a thousand. Midstage is about half that. So five hundred points . . . that seems doable. The ceiling on physical gains in this world is a lot higher when I factor in the nourishing effects mana seems to have.

The Seed gave me two points this morning, one automatically in the Strength stat and the other as a stat point. The stat points . . . I'll have to figure out how they work exactly. It seems likely, though, that my increase in Strength is the natural result of exercising, and the free point was from the mana that seeped into my body while I was working out. According to the scroll, early-stage mortals automatically have their bodies transformed by the mana, and the ability to control what the mana improves is supposed to be something that you get when you surpass the middle stage.

With the Seed, though, it's likely I won't experience that boundary. As long as I keep pushing forward, there shouldn't be anything stopping me from powering through.

"All right. That building over there is the Mission Hall. As someone who's just starting out, I'd recommend that you avoid any of the monster hunts, at least until you get a little stronger. Even the ones that seem easy. The Alchemy Hall is always looking for specific herbs that grow in the forests around us. The merits aren't the same, but unless you have terrible luck it's generally safe, and once you get the hang of it, you don't waste a lot of time wandering aimlessly, either."

"Merits?"

"Yep. They're not mentioned in the guidebook, are they? It's a new system—we used to use gold when that book was printed, but mortal currencies aren't really useful to us. Basically, every task you perform for the society, you earn merit points. You can trade them in for medicine, services, instruction from those further along the path, weapons, or even money. You need to pay back ten of them each month for your housing and food. It's how they make sure no one's freeloading."

"Is ten merits a lot?"

"It really depends on what you do and what you want to buy," Xander hedged. "Hunting a monster pays around twenty just for participation, and that's not even counting what the society will pay you for the parts. Of course you have to divide that money among your team, but the price is a lot higher. Risking your life pays pretty well. If you have any talent in refining pills, talismans, or artifacts, then you also don't need to worry a lot about merits. Of course, you need to be able to sense mana to do any of those jobs, so only the Inner Disciples can do them. If you do have some talent, though, you'll practically be rolling in money," he said with a hint of envy. Turning a corner, he continued on. "If you limit yourself to basic tasks like herb picking or patrolling, though, you can expect to make one or two merits a day. It's enough to stay here and buy a low-grade talisman or something, but it's not much."

"I see," Luke responded as he digested the information.

Pills, talismans, and, most importantly, artifacts. I'll have to look into all of them.

". . . and that's the arena," Xander said as he and Luke finished the tour of the town, arriving in front of a large colosseum-like building. Sounds of clashing swords echoed from deep inside.

"Are they fighting inside now?"

"The fighting never stops. In fact, I'd recommend that you go to the arena at least once a week to spar with others. As you cultivate your mana, you get stronger, but if you don't know how to use that strength, even weaker opponents will walk all over you."

"Is there a lot of fighting involved in what we do?" Luke asked, slightly nervous at the prospect.

"It's generally not anyone's first resort, but . . ." He shrugged. "It happens, and it's better to be prepared. If you have any more questions, feel free to drop by the administration building. Oh, I almost forgot. Here." He handed Luke a wristband.

"Thank you . . ." Luke inspected the bracelet curiously, wondering why Xander had given it to him.

"Don't take it the wrong way—it isn't a gift." He smiled knowingly. "That thing is registered to you, and it tracks what missions you do and how many merit points you have."

"Thank you." Luke nodded to him, wondering how the bracelet worked. It was thin and seemed to be made out of leather, of all things. How it could keep track of anything was beyond his current knowledge, although he had a sneaking suspicion that it had something to do with magic.

Watching Xander walk away for a moment, Luke turned his attention to the arena. It was by far the largest building in the town. Circular and many stories tall, it reminded him of the Colosseum in Rome. Curious, he walked in and observed the fighting.

There were twenty battles occurring simultaneously, and a large number of Outer Disciples and a small number of Inner Disciples waited in lines around each battle. In each ring, two disciples fought each other. Half of them were fighting with their fists alone, and the other half used various combinations of wooden swords, spears, and shields. He watched curiously as one of the wrestlers in the ring closest to him was pinned against the ground. A white-robed referee quickly ran onto the platform and pulled the two fighters apart. They shook hands, and the loser walked out of the ring while the winner remained. Catching his breath for a minute, he waved his hand, the disciple at the head of the line entered the ring, and another fight ensued.

"I haven't seen you around here before." Luke heard a voice beside him.

When he turned his head to look at the person, the first thing that came to his mind was *big*. Easily seven feet tall and built like a bull, the other man towered over him. "I'm new here," he replied. Hesitating briefly, he extended his hand. "I'm Luke."

"Ethan." He shook Luke's hand, his gaze locked to a battle. Tracing his eyes, Luke followed them to a fight happening in the fifth ring just in time to witness a black-robed teenager dodge an attack with a backflip. His foot swung out and caught his much larger opponent square in the chin while he was in midair and knocked him unconscious.

Luke suppressed a wince at the brutality, and at the same time he felt his heart speed up in excitement, a thrill born of witnessing a feat of pure skill and technique.

"That kid is growing fast. I remember watching him get knocked around daily when he first started coming around, and now he routinely holds the King for seven or eight battles. There's even chatter that he might be our newest Inner Disciple."

"Really?"

"It's . . . hard to say." A thoughtful look adorned Ethan's face as he looked at the teenager. "Anyone who puts in enough work can eventually reach mid-Mortal tier. Watching that fight, he's already on the cusp of it, if he hasn't already. But developing the ability to sense mana . . . it just comes down to luck. Without it, you reach a limit to how far you can push."

"What about entering the Warrior tier?"

"HA-HA-HA." He laughed out loud and slapped Luke loudly on his back. "Becoming a warrior is hard. The society has thousands of Outer Disciples, hundreds of Inner Disciples, but only nine warriors. Out of all the Inner Disciples, maybe a few dozen are still young enough to even have a shot." He shook his head ruefully. "We're small fish in a small pond. Even though each of us dreams of becoming more, reality is cruel."

"What makes it so hard?" Luke looked at the other man thoughtfully, only to see him shrug.

"I don't know. If I knew the answer to that, I would have become a warrior myself long ago. As it is, I've been stuck at the middle stage for years now. No matter how hard I train, I don't get stronger. My mana sense never developed, so . . ." He shrugged.

"That's . . ." Luke trailed off apologetically, unwittingly having broached a sensitive subject.

"It's fine." He beamed, glancing at Luke. "Even though it's unlikely that I'll progress further, I've still gained strength beyond the vast majority of the world's people. I'm satisfied with what I have. You should fight!" he suddenly suggested.

Luke looked at him blankly. "I'm not sure that's a good idea." Luke rolled his shoulders, feeling the ache in his muscles from pushing them as far as he had the night before.

"All the more reason to. Everyone starts off not knowing." He scanned the crowd. "The first ring is all amateurs and newbies. The second ring is basically the same, but with people who have a little more experience. The tenth ring is basically the best fighters in the society. It's the same concept with the rings where they're using weapons."

Luke watched the fights carefully, and after some observation he could tell exactly what Ethan was referring to. The battles happening in the first ring lacked technique or grace, the fighters simply rushing each other and swinging wildly. More often than not, they would end up rolling on the floor before one of them managed to pin the other. The ones in the tenth ring by contrast, were a lot more agile. Dodging blows gracefully, with small movements. Every attack seemed calculated, precise, and fast. To Luke, the fights in the latter rings looked choreographed in their complexity, as if they were dancing instead of fighting. It seemed more like something he would have seen in an action movie as opposed to the real world.

"Don't think about it too much. Get in there—getting your butt kicked is good for you," Ethan urged as Luke eyed the line.

This is gonna suck.

"All right," Luke agreed, making his way to the first arena. With a plan that amounted to trying his best and tapping out if things got too rough, he was confident that it wouldn't end terribly—if anything, learning what it was like being in combat would only help him in the future. Being a simple office worker in his last life hadn't done much for him when it came to sharpening his instincts for life-or-death struggles.

Paying close attention to the fights as he occupied the second and then the first place in the line, it became clear who he would be fighting. Like most of the others lined up to fight in the first ring, he was young. Luke's guess was that he was of a similar age to his new body, either fifteen or sixteen. Tan skin, brown hair cut close to his scalp, and a thin wiry frame.

Despite his unassuming looks, he had made short work of his last two fights. Luke watched carefully as he started his third, this time against a girl. She wasted no time in engaging him, and with fists raised above her chest, she circled around him slowly before striking out with a quick jab that he dodged by stepping to the side. Before the girl could even pull her arm back, he had closed the distance between them and punched her in the gut with everything he had.

Luke winced along with the rest of the line as she folded instantly and fell knees first onto the ground and started gasping for breath. The society, at least when it came to combat, made no distinction between men and women. While men had a natural physical advantage in the earliest stages of the Mortal tier, it would dwindle rapidly as they progressed. The mana in the air augmented all people equally as they worked their bodies.

As the girl stumbled out of the ring, the referee waved Luke in right after. His opponent had waived the allotted minute of rest granted between battles.

Here we go.

CHAPTER 6

Taking Some Hits

Luke eyed his opponent with caution as he raised his fists in front of him in what he hoped was a stance that would protect his face. Breaking a nose or anything equivalent was bound to be an unpleasant experience, and that was something that he wanted to avoid. From the fights he'd seen up till now, though, none had been particularly vicious, which gave him some hope of getting out of the rings with just some bruises.

Should I be bouncing from foot to foot? That's what they do in those MMA fights . . . No, I'll look stupid if I'm the only one doing it. Why isn't he doing anything, though? Does he want me to make the first move? Fuck it. Might as well get this over with.

Luke stepped forward with his guard still raised, only to step back in order to dodge a sweeping kick. Then he dodged again as his opponent immediately moved in with a jab, pushing Luke to the boundary of the ring.

Luke shuffled to the side in an attempt to get away from the edge, only for his opponent to land a glancing blow on his chest, his knuckles scraping against Luke's skin. Running into the ring, Luke ignored the stinging sensation from the hit as he tried to find an opening in his opponent's guard.

You know what? He can come to me this time.

Growing impatient, the other disciple threw caution to the wind and recklessly closed the distance, swinging his fists wildly. Seeing a punch go wide, Luke repeated his opponent's earlier strategy, stepping in and burying a fist in his stomach with as much force as he could muster. Unexpectedly, the punch was ineffective, and his opponent took it in stride, without showing even a hint of pain. Taking advantage of Luke's compromised position, he moved in even closer and wrapped his arm tightly around Luke's neck.

Gasping for air, Luke knew he should tap and get it over with. Instead, all he wanted to do was *win*. Throwing himself to the ground, Luke used the added momentum to break free of the hold. Rolling on the floor of the arena, they both desperately tried to maneuver the other into a pin until, finally, Luke managed to get behind his opponent and catch him in a choke hold. He attempted to struggle, and after not finding a way out of Luke's hold, he relaxed his body and gently tapped the stage.

Luke won.

Panting, he stumbled to his feet and watched the referee run onto the stage, inspecting both of them for any obvious signs of injury.

"That was good. I thought I had you earlier."

"You almost did—that was a good fight," Luke replied.

"It was fun! I'm Mykonos, by the way." He extended his hand.

"I'm Luke."

"Good luck on the next fight. Back-to-back fights get exhausting fast!" Mykonos walked out of the ring as the next person in line stepped forward.

Oh, right. The winner just keeps going until they lose.

Acutely aware of the sweat dripping down the side of his face and the prickling pain from where Mykonos had hit and choked him, Luke thought he should feel awful. Instead, he found himself looking forward to the next fight.

Locking eyes with his opponent, Luke raised his fists in anticipation and widened his stance. The battle began.

He won his second fight and lost on his third. Then, in a decision that surprised even him, he walked back into the line and started the process over again, sometimes managing to stay in the ring for multiple matches, and sometimes losing after a single one.

Hours later, when the nine suns of Theos sank below the horizon, Luke stumbled home. He had a smile on his face in spite of being covered in bruises and aching in ways he hadn't known he could.

I did not expect fighting to be that fun.

The next morning, he was happy to see that his suffering came with a reward.

Status | Quests | Inventory

Name: Lukas King

Tier: Mortal

Mana: 7

Rate: 10% per hour

Strength: 9 > 10

Agility: 9 > 10

Constitution: 13 > 14

Arcana: 1

Stat Points: 1

Bloodline: Locked. Conditions not met. (0/10,000)

Charges: 7/10

Gaining a point in every attribute except one was a surprise, a very welcome one. Dropping his spare point back into the Arcana stat, he refreshed his status.

Status | Quests | Inventory
Name: Lukas King
Tier: Mortal
Mana: 14
Rate: 10% per hour
Strength: 10
Agility: 10
Constitution: 14
Arcana: 2
Stat Points: 0
Bloodline: Locked. Conditions not met. (0/10,000)
Charges: 7/10

So my total mana is just Arcana multiplied by my Constitution divided by two. My regen rate is still the same. Ten hours to recover a whopping fourteen mana seems pretty crap, though. The fact that it stayed the same, however, is good. No matter how much mana I have, I'll recover all of it in ten hours. Not that I even have a way to use it now. Is it the same for everyone, though, or is a fixed rate something the Seed gives me?

Speaking of, I still can't feel my mana. Maybe when I enter the middle stage of the Mortal tier that'll change. If I keep getting free points like I am now, though, I should have a lot of mana pretty soon, though.

Falling back onto his bed, he was tempted to sleep the day away. Unfortunately, unlike in his last life, he couldn't afford to take it easy. Things seemed calm for the moment, but that could change any second.

If Nefkha suddenly gets cold feet, I'm fucked. I need to get to the next tier as fast as I can, or else I'm just a sitting duck at everyone's mercy. If I can fly, I should be able to hightail it to some random cave and disappear. Hopefully to someplace where no one knows I'm wanted by the Olympians.

Forcing himself out of his funk, he took a quick shower before walking to his next destination.

Back to working for a living.

The Mission Hall reminded Luke of a fast-food joint. There was a row of white-robed people standing behind a counter, with an assortment of mostly black-robed and a small number of blue-robed people in line. All silently gazed at the wall behind the clerks, reading the pinned requests that hung on it, like a menu.

It had more jobs, and a greater variety of them than Luke had imagined there would be: Hunting down dozens of different creatures that were causing trouble in the surrounding areas. Guarding merchant caravans coming in and going out of the society. A few requests for aid in the forges. Hundreds of herb-gathering assignments.

Requests for sparring partners. Repair work and construction. Recruitments for expeditions seeking lands rich in resources and danger. Delivering letters and parcels, and more. There definitely wasn't a lack of options to pick from.

"How can I help you today?" the clerk asked when he finally made it to the counter.

"I want to go on a mission. Preferably a simple herb-gathering one."

"Can I see your bracelet, please?"

"Of course." Luke slid it off his wrist and handed it to him, watching curiously as he dropped it onto a blank sheet of paper and becoming fascinated as words magically appeared in a uniform black ink.

"Just to make sure, you are Luke, yes?" the clerk asked, reading his name off the paper.

"That's me."

"Okay. Welcome to the society! You said you were interested in gathering herbs? That's a good choice—I can't tell you how many of the newer members foolishly choose to hunt a monster on their first missions, only to come back grievously injured if not worse."

"Yeah, someone recommended that I start with a safer mission."

"I'm glad they did. Now, as you can see"—he gestured to the wall full of missions behind him—"we have quite a few of them. Did you have a particular one in mind, or would you like me to choose one for you?"

"If you could, that would be great. Something on the easier end would be nice."

"Of course, let me just . . . aha. This one shouldn't cause you too much trouble. Blue wildflowers are fairly common in the area. The mission is to collect ten of them, and the deadline is tomorrow before noon. If you fail at the mission, and it is determined upon investigation that it was due to lack of professionalism and or poor conduct on your behalf, you will be docked five merits," he recited dryly. "Am I correct in assuming that you haven't collected any herbs before?"

"You would be."

"All right, in that case—" He reached underneath the counter and with a practiced movement pulled out a book. "This is the society's *Compendium of Flora*. It has a lot of information that you'll find useful, as well as instructions on how to harvest the plants correctly. I'd suggest you read the entry on any plant you intend to harvest before you head out into the wilderness."

"Thank you." Luke nodded gratefully.

"It's no problem. We do charge two merit points for the book, though, which will leave you with eight. You will be deducted ten at the end of the month. The mission you're going on will give you one merit, so you have to complete at least one more within two weeks."

"That sounds good to me. Thanks again!" Luke waved before walking out of the building, flipping through the book as he did so.

Finding the section on blue wildflowers, he committed their appearance to memory before reading up on them. The flower, while not rare, wasn't super common in the region. It grew quickly, but only in the wild. According to the book, attempts had been made to cultivate them in greenhouses, but like most other plants useful for alchemical purposes, the properties that made it useful were lost by doing so. The blue wildflower in particular was a common ingredient in many potions, and it needed to be fresh. As such, the society always needed more. Unlike some of the other plants in the book, this one didn't require any particular method to harvest. Only its petals were valuable, so simply tearing the stems was enough.

So I'm basically an errand boy, Luke thought as he walked into the forest on the east side of the society. Finding a trail, he began to hike. He nodded politely as he passed other disciples along the way, many of whom, like him, were also delving into the forest.

"Hey! Luke, right?" He heard a voice calling his name.

"Oh. Hey, Mykonos," said Luke, smiling as Mykonos and two other people walked into the forest behind him. One of them, he recognized as the person Ethan had pointed out in the arena, the one likely to become the society's next Inner Disciple.

"Let me guess, you're gathering herbs?"

"Yup."

"Blue wildflowers?"

"You called it."

"I'm just smart like that. We happen to be looking for them, too. Uh, this is Spiros, he's my cousin, and that's June, who's also my cousin," he introduced. "That's Luke. He kicked my ass in the arena yesterday."

Luke waved at the cousins.

"Why don't you come with us, Luke? Last time we came, we noticed a bunch growing near a small lake."

"Uh . . . yeah, are you sure it's okay for me to tag along? I don't want to intrude."

"Yeah, I'm sure. We're sure, aren't we, guys?" Mykonos turned to his cousins.

"Yeah, it's fine," said Spiros.

"Let's go." Mykonos led the way into the forest.

"So how long have all of you been in the Luminous Sky?" Luke asked, ducking under a branch.

"We joined two months ago with all the other new disciples. Didn't you?" asked June.

"No. I was just kind of minding my business when Nefkha—he's one of the Elders here—asked me to join."

"You're lucky. The test to get in sucked. They made us run laps until there were only five hundred of us left," Mykonos said.

"That sounds brutal."

"Oh, trust me, it was. There was even this one kid who shat his pants while he was running." Luke looked at him with wide disbelieving eyes. "I'm not kidding. I swear on the deities." He grinned.

"That's insane."

"I know, right? You know what's even funnier? You've actually met him alrea . . ." Spiros threw a stone at his cousin.

"Will you ever stop telling that story?" Spiros yelled. "And you know what? I did shit my pants, and I'm proud of it, too. I did what I had to do to get here. I have something called resolve! I have commitment!"

June burst out laughing. "You had poop running down your legs."

"Gggghhhh! You guys are so annoying. Never let yourself slip up with them, Luke. I'm telling you, they will hold everything they can over your head. Right now, it's that I shat myself. Before that it was because Helen turned me down."

"Helen is forty years old."

Luke laughed out loud at the absurdity of the situation.

"Not you, too!" Spiros cried.

"Sorry, I tried really hard not to laugh, it's just . . ."

"Guys! Look." June pointed to a large batch of blue flowers.

"Awesome, there's a bunch of them, too. Enough for all of us." Spiros started walking toward them.

"Wait," Luke called out, pulling him back. "You see it?"

"I do," said Mykonos, running his hands through his hair. "That's one big snake."

"Big is an understatement." Luke took a step back. His eyes locked on the undulating black tube. Just barely visible from behind the trees, its dark scales let it hide near perfectly in the shadows. He didn't know much about the creatures, but he was sure that they weren't supposed to be wider than two humans hugging, or as long as a bus.

"It looks like it's full." Spiros pointed to a large lump halfway through its body.

"It's staring at us awfully hungry-like, though," said June.

"I heard snakes have good noses. Maybe you should poop yourself again and it will just go away?"

"Shut up, and that's not true."

"Move!" Luke shouted, pulling both Mykonos and Spiros back. Just in time, as the snake whipped its tail where they were standing seconds later.

CHAPTER 7

Snakes and Surprises

That was a close call." Luke wiped the sweat off his forehead and crouched behind a decomposing log with the others, a fair distance from the snake. Luckily for them, it hadn't pursued them after striking. Allowing the party of four to retreat to a safe distance.

"I think we should kill it. If I'm right, that's a black-scaled king viper. The society buys them for a lot, and they're not supposed to be all that strong. Just incredibly rare," said Mykonos, rubbing his hands together greedily.

"Are you sure? It looks pretty dangerous . . . and angry, for that matter." Luke eyed the snake carefully, on guard for a surprise attack now that he knew the snake was there.

"It's fine if you don't get hit," Mykonos argued.

"How many merits are we talking about here?" June turned to Mykonos.

"A hundred and fifty merits for every vial of the venom, another hundred for each fang, and twenty per square foot of its skin. I can't remember the price for its organs, but it's not low."

"I'm in!" Spiros raised his hand. "A little risk to not come out here every day is worth it. I've already had enough mosquitoes bite me for a lifetime."

"June?"

"I don't know, Myko. How many talismans did you bring, and are they enough?"

"Five."

"I have three," said Spiros.

"I have five, too."

"Talismans?" Luke asked.

"Right, you're new. Uh, they're basically these slips of paper that explode. Inner Disciples make and sell them for two merits each." Mykonos reached into his pocket and pulled out a small slip of paper with some squiggly lines drawn on it.

"Is thirteen enough to kill that thing, though?" June asked, reaching into her pocket and pulling her own out.

"More than enough."

"If we try, and it doesn't die, I lose at most ten merits. If it does, I make hundreds. If it gets angry, I think we can run away from it, too. Yeah, I'm in." June nodded, satisfied with her assessment.

Mykonos smiled and looked at Luke. "Here." He held out two of his talismans and looked expectantly at June. With clear reluctance, she extended one of her talismans to him, too.

"I, ahh . . ."

"Here's what I'm thinking," said Mykonos, cutting Luke off and taking the tag out of June's hand and forcefully stuffing all three of them into Luke's. "We only really have one shot at killing it. We can't take turns tossing the talismans at the thing. A single nonlethal explosion will spook it, and I really don't want to find out how fast it can move, whether that's in our direction or away from us. I say we circle it and throw them all at once. Four explosions going off in its face should do the job quite well. Like I said, those things are rare, but they don't get too strong. The bestiary said that they concentrate most of their mana in their fangs, leaving the rest of the body fairly weak."

"Sounds good to me." Spiros slapped Mykonos on the back.

"Are you guys sure you want me to participate? You don't have to include me just because I tagged along."

"Luke, Luke, Luke," said Spiros, putting a hand on Luke's shoulder. "Here's the thing. I'm pretty sure killing the snake isn't the hard part. We're spending some easily earned merits and throwing them accurately at a very large snake's equally large face. The hard part is dragging it back to the society. Look how big it is. Do you think me and Myko are strong enough to pull it off?"

"Hey! I'd help pull it, too" June complained.

"Hmm." Both Mykonos and Spiros grunted half-heartedly.

"I hate you guys." She crossed her arms.

"Anyway," Mykonos added, "Spiros is right. We walked for two hours to get here, and dragging the snake out of the forest will be a lot easier if we have you helping us."

"All right, then. If all of you are okay with it. How do we use these, though?" Luke inspected the talisman.

"Super easy. All you do is rip this little bit off"—Spiros pointed to a perforated tab on the bottom of the paper—"and you throw it. It blows after five seconds, so make sure it's a few feet from you at the least. We should probably tie them to rocks or something, though."

This world is insane. They just sell the equivalent of grenades to teenagers in exchange for some cheap labor.

"Right, seems simple enough," Luke responded a moment later, looking at the innocent piece of paper with apprehension and a little bit of doubt. Exploding papers were an entirely foreign concept. At the same time, though, the idea that gods just walked around, actually blew people out of the sky, and that the Olympians were hunting him was equally strange. His standard for what was and wasn't possible had shattered quite a long time ago. Exploding paper was probably one of the tamer things he was going to have to get used to.

Doing his best to move quietly, even though he was fairly certain that snakes primarily perceived the world through their tongues, he got into position. After some planning, they had decided on a horseshoe-shaped formation encircling the snake's head. Reaching into his pocket, he pulled out three rocks, the exploding talisman already attached to them with strips of cloth liberated from his robes.

The plan itself was simple: he and Spiros would aim for the snake's left eye, while June and Mykonos would aim for the right. June would give the signal.

"Now!" he heard her yell, and he instantly tore the perforated edge off the talisman and took aim, already counting down the seconds it would take to explode.

. . . and one!

He flung the rock at the snake, synchronizing near perfectly with the others. Time seemed to slow as he watched with bated breath. The rock sailed through the air—and into the snake's nostril.

BANG. BANG. BANG. BANG. The talismans detonated in quick succession, spewing smoke and small bits of rock and chunks of snake flesh into the air. When the dust cleared, it revealed a brutal and bloody scene.

The snake, mutilated and in pain, was thrashing in the clearing. Its right eye was in tatters, and blood oozed out from the socket. Either June or Mykonos had aimed their attack perfectly. Its nose had likewise been blown to pieces, from where Luke's talisman had entered the cavity, and it had chunks of flesh missing from where the other two paper explosives had struck it along its body, leaving gaping and messy holes on its scaly body.

"Another round?" Spiros shouted.

"No! Let it bleed for a minute. It won't survive those injuries for long. We'll pelt it again if it runs, but let's try not to damage it too much," June shouted back.

After five minutes of watching the snake writhe in pain, Luke was tempted to hit it with another set of talismans just to put the creature out of its misery. Looking at the expressions on the others' faces, he assumed they were, too. Except none of them wanted to damage the snake further and, in the process, devalue it. They, after all, had decided to kill the creature for money. Damaging it more than what was necessary ran counter to the goal.

"Let's just hit it with another one," Spiros broke in, having seen enough of its suffering.

"We can't. It's still moving around too much. If we hit it in the wrong place, the whole thing may as well become worthless. At that point, we would just be killing it for no reason at all," Mykonos said quietly, mirroring Luke's own thoughts on the matter.

"Fine." He turned around and sat behind a tree, facing a direction where he couldn't see the snake.

Ten torturously long minutes after they had launched their attack, the snake finally went limp.

"This is going to be a pain to drag back to the society." June idly ran her hands along the snake's scales. Grimacing as she got some blood on her hand, she pulled out a napkin and wiped it off. "Should we leave it here and put in a request for a mission to move it back to the town?"

"No." Mykonos shook his head. "If we do that, we'll have to leave it here overnight. Scavengers will eat parts of it, and its mana will have evaporated. It'll be worthless by tomorrow."

"Fine. I'll grab the flowers, and you guys can figure out how to move this thing. Luke, your mission was for ten of them as well, right?" she asked sweetly.

"Uh, yeah. It was, thanks."

"Don't thank her!" Spiros raised his hands in protest. "I told you she wouldn't help drag it back."

"You knew I wouldn't anyway," June snapped back while picking up the flowers.

"That's not what you said before." Mykonos looked at her disapprovingly.

"Fine! I'll help you drag the stupid snake back. I swear to the deities, you two are so annoying."

Luke smiled at their banter while simultaneously feeling like he was intruding. Shaking his head, he paced around the snake, trying to figure out how exactly they were going to drag the behemoth back. He had grown stronger, a lot stronger than should have been possible in the scant few days he'd been here, but not strong enough to drag that thing back. Thankfully, he wasn't alone.

"I vote that we drag it from the tail," Luke suggested, looking at the mutilated head. While mostly intact, it was covered in the creature's blood. Not something that Luke wanted on his body. Or something that he wanted to look at for any length of time. Honestly, he was surprised that he hadn't thrown up.

"Smart. Let's get to it," Mykonos agreed. "Hopefully we get back before night falls."

Luke, along with the others, dragged the carcass through the forest. Sweat dripped down their faces and covered their backs. The hike into the forest had been pleasant. The trek out, not so much. Luke's feet constantly dug into the ground as he was repeatedly forced to step into mud and softer dirt, something he normally would have avoided. With the snake, however, watching where he stepped was an exercise in futility.

This is torture.

"How much longer?" June whined for the umpteenth time. Something that Luke could sympathize with, considering they had been dragging the snake for three hours already.

"June. You're my sister and I love you, but shut up!" Spiros snapped at her.

"What he said," Mykonos parroted, exhausted from the arduous task and in no mood to hear any complaints.

Luke shook his head in amusement, the only one in their impromptu group in a pleasant mood.

As hard as this is, I better get some nice stat points out of this.

The trek, in addition to being uncomfortable, had also been longer than any of them had expected. It would have been even longer if Spiros hadn't surprised Luke with how freakishly strong he was.

Luke estimated that Spiros alone was carrying forty percent of the creature's weight. Apparently he had taken the midstage trials and come out just a little short of qualifying. Luke was curious to know how he had achieved that feat, especially as he had joined the society at the same time as his cousin and sister.

From what Luke had seen of Mykonos and June, while they were both in exceptional shape from their time in the society, they weren't quite what Luke would call ridiculous in terms of strength and were just a little stronger than him—albeit in slightly different ways. Mykonos was durable, while June moved with uncanny grace. Spiros, on the other hand, had clearly stepped into the realm of superhumans, at least by Earth standards. The fact that he was still considered to be a lower-stage mortal on Theos was telling of how powerful actual midstage and beyond individuals were. Especially the beyond. Luke suppressed a shudder, recalling Aeolus's abduction and cannibalization of the souls. An event that he suspected would keep him awake at night if he ever stopped pushing himself to the brink of exhaustion.

An hour later, they finally breached the tree line. What came into view horrified them all and sent currents of fear down Luke's spine.

Flying in the air above the Luminous Sky City was Arke. The nine suns of Theos beautifully descending below the horizon in a line behind her, she sat imperiously on a throne made of light. Her wings folded behind her back, and her white hair fluttered gracefully in the wind. Nine humans, presumably the society's nine warriors, prostrated themselves before her midair, not daring to lift their heads in her presence.

Fuck me. I'm dead, aren't I?

"Kneel!" Spiros barked, dropping face-first into the dirt, quickly followed by the other two.

Threat detected.

Yeah, yeah. I know. Thanks for the warning.

CHAPTER 8

Angels and Warriors

Where is he?" she drawled, her head languidly resting on the palm of her hand. A red-robed figure lifted her head.

"My lady. We scoured the entire province of Yilim, as you commanded, and found no signs of the thief. Our disciples have monitored every fresh corpse in every city and town we have a presence in, and none resurrected. Every warrior in the society flew to even the smallest towns and villages, and there weren't any rumors of the dead rising."

"Humph. As expected of you useless weaklings." The throne evaporated as her wings stretched out behind her. "The thief is on one of these islands, and until he is caught no one will leave or travel between them."

"My lady, that's . . ." The red-robed woman trailed off as Arke suddenly appeared in front of her.

"That's. What?" She cocked her head.

"This lowly warrior seeks only to serve and aid you in finding this terrible thief, and none of us dare defy your will, or that of Olympus . . . but Atlantis claims dominion over the seas, and this island."

Arke blinked, and then blinked again. "Do you think I'm unaware of Atlantis?"

"Of course not. This one will never presume to fathom the extent of your wisdom and knowledge. It is only that if Carim were to suddenly cease all exports, the Atlantians would seek to punish us. Many of us still remember her fury. Even centuries later, we mourn the loss of our hero and pay the price of our arrogance. If Atlantis does not get her tithe, they will call us traitors. Her armies will destroy us."

"If the thief is not found—" Arke loomed over her. "Then it will not be Atlantis you need to worry about."

"My lady . . . I'm afraid finding this thief will be impossible. What if his soul already dissipated, or he allowed himself to be pulled into the Aether? Or if . . ."

"Enough!" she shrieked, rattling the world with her voice alone. "I will not abide by your excuses. See that my will be done. As for the Atlantians, do not concern yourself with them."

"How do we find this thief, my lady? If he has already possessed a body, then how do we know who he is?"

She didn't answer and disappeared with a single beat of her wings. The nine warriors shared nervous glances before flying back to their respective mountains, leaving only Nefkha and Irila, the woman who had spoken to her, floating in the air.

"What a bitch," said Nefkha, stroking his beard.

"Indeed. She should know that no one's going to find this thief of hers. He's probably dead, and even if he isn't, how are we meant to find him among billions of people? If he isn't dead already, he could be anyone, anywhere."

"Ha. We don't, that's how," Nefkha lied effortlessly. "She's strong-arming us right now, but the archipelago is too useful for trade, and not just to the Atlantians. Maybe if she knew what island the thief was on, things would be different, but as it is, there's no chance. Besides, Carim is weak, and we're weak. We have no choice but to obey whatever law she lays down. The other islands don't necessarily have the same restriction."

"You mean Sylcra?"

"Mmm-hmm. There's rumors that the hero ascended to the next tier."

Irila's eyes widened before she shook her head lightly. "Even then, angering Olympus isn't worth it."

"Maybe so . . . but Olympus isn't the only faction helmed by gods, and if the rumor is true, the damage that someone at that tier could do . . ."

"He'll be slaughtered. The gods don't look favorably on those who threaten them."

"You're right." Nefkha turned to the direction where Arke had flown off to. His eyes hardened in hate. "But their cruelty breeds enmity, and there are many who would seek to destroy them, regardless of the cost. To themselves or to the world."

"Is this about . . ."

He put a fake smile on his face. "That's enough of that. Dealing with her stressed me out. I have some bottles of Nepthian beer if you would care to join me?"

She raised her eyebrows. "I didn't know you had such expensive tastes."

On the ground outside the forest, Luke and his companions knelt on the ground.

"I think she's gone," said Spiros a minute or two after she had left.

The Seed sent Luke a message.

Threat averted.

He sighed in relief as he stood up. "Does she come here often?"

"Second time, actually. She came here a week ago, and the society was in shambles. Apparently some thief got away from her, and she's searching for him," said June.

"That's crazy. She seemed so strong." Luke did his best not to give anything away.

"Yeah, the society went crazy, and all the Elders even went searching for him . . . Is that when Elder Nefkha found you?" asked Mykonos, squatting down and gripping the snake's tail.

My timing really is suspicious.

"Yeah. I was lost in a forest outside my town, and he must have felt bad for me or something, because he offered to let me join the society." Luke also gripped the snake.

"That was nice of him. Isn't your family worried about you, though?" June frowned.

"No . . . they, uh—" Luke recounted Max's sad tale as they dragged the carcass back to the city, omitting anything to do with the Seed and how he wasn't actually Max.

Thankfully, Nefkha didn't turn me in. Arke seemed to have healed from whatever damage Aeolus did to her, and as fast as she moves, I don't even know if I could have used a charge fast enough to get away. At least I know she can't sense the Seed inside me now, though. She really has no idea who I am. It's surprising that she's still lurking around, though. What's her plan?

Luke shook the thoughts out of his head. It didn't matter why she was around. Nefkha hadn't turned him in, and Arke couldn't recognize him even when he was standing right under her nose. He was safe for the time being.

"Hmm." An Inner Disciple inspected their snake, walking around it with his arms crossed, poking and prodding it as he went. Prying its mouth open, he peeked inside, unbothered by the blood dripping onto his robes. "Thirteen hundred merits."

"What! Come on," Mykonos protested. "You might as well rob us for that price. Look at this." He reached into his robe and pulled out a handbook. "It says right here, one-fifty for each vial of the venom. In a snake this big, there's at least ten vials of it!"

The Inner Disciple started at Mykonos. "It seems you know your stuff, kid."

"How about you give us a fair price?" Mykonos crossed his arms. The Inner Disciple grinned at him.

"I like you. Let me see. You have both fangs, so that's two hundred. It's thirty feet long, and let's say three feet thick"—he cupped his chin thoughtfully—"that's basically three hundred square feet of skin, which amounts to another six hundred merits. Two hundred for the heart, fifty for each kidney, and two hundred for everything else. Altogether, that's two thousand, eight hundred."

"That's bet—"

"Minus two hundred for the butchering fee, minus another one-fifty for the poor shape of its skin, and another four-fifty for the lack of freshness, altogether that'll be two thousand merits. Better?"

"Deal!" Mykonos shook his hand. Beside him, both June and Spiros cheered.

"We're rich! We're rich, Luke!" Spiros slung his arm around Luke's shoulder.

"Tsk. Don't get too excited, you little brats. Lucky breaks like this don't come too often. If I were you, I'd use the merits to buy lessons. Exploding talismans worked on the snake, but to most monsters, those papers might as well be pebbles. Same with anyone beyond the midstage of the Mortal tier. I could have one of those tiny papers burst off in my mouth and I'd still be fine," the Inner Disciple boasted, puffing out his chest. "Now, let me see your wristbands. We're doing an even spread, right?" he asked.

"Yup!" Spiros nodded.

Later, after submitting his portion of the blue wildflowers, and with an excess of merits, Luke walked into the armory.

He had been looking forward to doing so since he'd realized it existed. Entering the building, he was amazed to see it littered with an assortment of swords, shields, spears, halberds, knives, and even knuckle-dusters. Each and every one of them was polished to a shine and gleaming in the light of the gas lamps that were common to Carim.

His eyes raked over the walls, and to his surprise a sword lit up in his vision.

Bellerophon's Blade

The words appeared in front of it.

Is it that easy? he asked himself, staring dumbly at the sword. It was a beautiful thing. A three-foot-long blade, lacking a cross guard unlike most of the other swords in the room. It was forged from pure gold and lacked any seams, as if it had been created from a single bar of the metal. A pommel, encrusted with a large blue gem and a tassel, narrowed into a leather-wrapped grip, which flattened into a wicked double-edged blade, forming a lethal point.

"An eye for the fancy!" a voice echoed through the room. "Can't say I blame ya. Who wouldn't want a golden sword, and a xiphos at that. If nothing else, the Olympians make some fine-looking weapons. What can I get for ya, lad?"

"How much for that one?" Luke asked the shopkeeper, slightly surprised by his massive frame and bulging muscles, barely hidden beneath his blue robes.

"Hmm. That one is three hundred merits." He looked at Luke, a wry smile on his face that just screamed his doubt at Luke being able to afford it.

"I'll take it!" Luke answered as soon as the words came out of his mouth. Sliding his bracelet off his wrist, he held it out to him.

"You're quite decisive." He looked surprised but pulled the sword free of its mount nonetheless. "Are you sure you want this one, though? Don't let the gold fool you—it's not the best sword we have here. Actually, the price is so high precisely because it's gold. Whoever made it possessed more vanity than sense, in my opinion."

"I'm sure. I, uh, I always wanted a gold sword," Luke answered weakly. He remembered that the society didn't know its history, and he didn't want to clue them into its true value, either. Whatever that was.

"Are you sure I can't convince you otherwise? The artificer who made it enchanted it with increased durability just to make use of the gold. Most of the other swords I have in that price range are made from sturdier stuff and have better enchantments. I got swords that shock people, swords that are sharper than they should be, swords that vibrate . . . all for a similar price."

"Thank you, but I'm sure."

"All right. They're your merits." He shrugged and took the wristband. Dropping it on a paper, his eyebrows lifted in surprise. "No wonder you're so eager to waste your money. I thought those vipers went extinct," he muttered as his eyes raked over the paper. After deducting the merits, he slid the sword over to Luke. "You'll want a sheath with that, too. Three merits."

"I'll take one," said Luke, gingerly placing his hand on the hilt. He felt the Seed stir in the recesses of his soul. A tendril of energy traveled from it, down to his arm, and into the blade.

> Quest complete.
>
> Bonding.
>
> Connection formed with item: Xiphos

That was way easier than I thought it would be.

Sitting on the mat in his meditation room, Luke withdrew the sword from its sheath. Then, with a mental command, added it to his inventory.

> Status | Quests | **Inventory**
>
> Capacity: 4.5 kg of 140 kg
>
> Items:
>
> Xiphos (Bound)
>
> Tier—Mortal (Upgradable)
>
> A xiphos gifted to Bellerophon. Although not his primary weapon, after centuries of exposure to mana of a higher tier, it has gained abilities atypical of a mortal artifact. The blade will repair any damage when provided with sufficient mana. The blade will siphon mana from those it cuts, strengthening its wielder every time a foe is slain.
>
> Upgrade—Weakened by its wielder's battle against Zeus and from the centuries of disuse that followed, the mana in the sword has dwindled away, resulting in its decline to the Mortal tier. It can be returned to its previous glory, and perhaps even beyond.
>
> To advance the sword to the next tier, it must feast on the blood of a hundred Warrior-tier entities. (0/100)

Hmm. Not bad, although I'm a long ways from killing a hundred warriors. Hell, I only know nine that exist. If I'm reading it right, though, the sword will take mana from those I cut with it and make it available to me. Essentially, free stat points for killing stuff. I sense some murder-hoboing in the future.

Luke called the sword back from his inventory and stared at the blade. It really was beautiful.

Returning it to its sheath, he put it beside his bed. His inventory, while useful, wasn't something he could explain.

I should probably fill it up on some food and other camping supplies, though. Some talismans, too. Those were useful.

CHAPTER 9

Monsters and Mortals

Status	Quests	Inventory
Name: Lukas King
Tier: Mortal
Mana: 168
Rate: 10% per hour
Strength: 10 > 22
Agility: 10 > 16
Constitution: 14 > 21
Arcana: 2 > 16
Stat Points: 0
Bloodline: Locked. Conditions not met. (1/10,000)
Charges: 7/10

Luke inspected his status, satisfied with his progress over the past two weeks. An exhausting two weeks. With merits to spare, he had spent every moment exercising or sparring, on average, gaining three points a day. All his free stat points, with the exception of one, which had gone to his Bloodline to see what happened (nothing), had gone to the Arcana stat.

Something he was considering to be a bit of a waste the more he invested in it. It was the only stat that hadn't grown naturally, and he still couldn't feel his mana, nor did he have a way to use it. Something he hoped would change after the attribute crossed into triple digits.

Dismissing it, he got ready for the day. Breathing in the fresh air, he made his way to the Mission Hall for the first time since his unexpected windfall. He scanned the missions on the board for something that might catch his eye.

"How can I help you today?" asked the clerk as soon as Luke made it to the front of the line.

"I would like to go on a hunt. An easier one, if that's okay."

"Very well. Can I see your wristband, please?" He extended his hand.

Luke slid it over and watched with amusement as the man's polite smile slipped from his face. He looked between Luke and the paper, and then at Luke again.

"Is there a problem?"

The clerk's mouth opened and closed, not unlike that of a fish. "There is no problem. It's just that . . . a hunt is dangerous."

"I'm aware." Luke crossed his arms.

"There are other considerations."

Luke lifted an eyebrow, wondering what the man was getting at.

"You see, a standard monster-extermination mission groups five people together. Most that participate in them are seasoned members of the society. While I can add you to a team, not many will be happy with the addition of a fresh recruit."

Luke nodded as he mulled over the words. "I see."

"Might I suggest a guard posting instead?" he offered with a strained smile.

"Hmm. No, I'll stick with a monster hunt."

Pursing his lips, the other man nodded. "Very well." He pulled out a binder and began flipping through it. "All right, I've added you to a team. You'll be exterminating a flock of harpies down south. They've been harassing a town, stealing food, and abducting men. Your team is scheduled to depart at noon, from the south gate. Please ensure you have enough supplies to last you for the three days it will take you to get there and the three it will take you to return. The pay is twenty merits, and the society purchases the harpies' wings at ten merits a pair. If you fail at the mission, and it is determined upon investigation that it was due to lack of professionalism and or poor conduct on your behalf, you will be docked five merits."

"Thank you," said Luke, nodding politely while collecting his wristband, amused by the situation. Just two weeks ago, a clerk had been commending him for taking it easy and gathering herbs, and now one was looking down on him for hunting monsters.

Not that it could be helped. Luke would have liked to keep gathering herbs, and he likely could—except he had a sword. One that he very much wanted to use. If siphoning mana actually translated into stat points, then sitting around the society was a massive waste of his time. At least until he learned how much mana, in terms of stat points, the sword actually siphoned from the things he killed. If it eclipsed what he earned in safety by a substantial margin, then it was worth the risk.

Ideally, he'd want to make it to the Warrior tier, and fast, before hightailing it off the island. He'd also need to work something out with Nefkha. The fact that he knew that Luke was the one Arke was looking for felt uncomfortably like a sword dangling over his head.

A single hint from Arke about what it was that he possessed could change their relationship in a heartbeat, and Luke couldn't take the risk that Nefkha wouldn't kill him for the Seed.

What are charges? Luke directed his thoughts to the Seed. A question he had asked it days before, and it was one of the few it had answered, ignoring the rest.

A charge is a unit of primordial energy. The God Seed generates ten instances of this energy every time it transfers to a new host. A charge can be consumed to perform a wide array of tasks, depending on the user's needs. Past users have often used the charges to escape death.

Warning: use of a charge is detectable by beings sensitive to primordial energies within a certain radius.

The first part was great, and Luke was happy to know he had seven aces up his sleeve. The last part, however, had bothered him since he'd learned of it. It hadn't come as a surprise that Arke had a way to track him. She had known he was on the archipelago, after all. It was the knowledge that using his aces would tell her exactly where he was that was unnerving.

Using a charge, then, was tantamount to a death sentence so long as she was around. Even then, there was no telling who or what could detect primordial energy. The last thing Luke wanted was another monstrous being hunting him.

Suddenly, it made a lot of sense why the God Seed was still in circulation. Whoever had it ended up dead before they got strong enough to protect it from people who wanted it more. Luke could already envision them using a charge to escape from a monster, only to end up face-to-face with someone of Arke's caliber, or maybe even stronger.

Shaking the thoughts free from his head, Luke went from shop to shop and grabbed a host of supplies. Enough food and water to last him a couple of weeks. A seemly number of the society's black robes. A decent shield to go with his sword. A handful of talismans, and even some potions. The society's more arcane goods were of great interest to Luke.

He'd found that talismans weren't limited to just the explodey kind. There were other, more expensive ones that acted as makeshift shields. According to the Inner Disciple who had sold them to him, they could block one good hit from basically any monster that he was likely to run into. The caveat was that they were hard to use. Just like the ones he'd used before, they had a perforated tab that needed to be ripped to activate them—a tab that was hard to rip when you had something trying to kill you.

Potions were also handy, although Luke wasn't convinced of their efficacy. Supposedly, spilling them on a wound would help it heal faster, but he hadn't had the opportunity to try it.

After he walked home with his hands full of food, pockets full of talismans, and a newly purchased shield on his back, he settled onto a chair before loading it all—with the exception of his shield and some food that he planned to carry, for the sake of appearances—into his inventory.

Status	Quests	**Inventory**
Capacity: 84.6 kg of 462 kg

He'd dropped a banana in it a week ago and was pleasantly surprised to see it hadn't spoiled at all during that time.

Since then, he had slowly been filling the inventory with food, about an extra meal or two every day. The society gave him three meals a day, delivered to his house at regular intervals, but those who wanted to eat more were free to buy as much food as they pleased.

Everything purchased in the society was bought by merits, and every merit was tracked. With that in mind, he had been careful and perhaps a bit paranoid about what he bought and when he bought it. Paranoia he felt was justified. It wouldn't end well if Nefkha was keeping an eye on his purchases and decided that he didn't like Luke buying more food than was reasonable for him to eat and called Arke down on him.

Sitting on a chair, at a loss for how to spend the last two hours before he left to meet his monster-hunting team, Luke had an idea. Fishing out a protective talisman, Luke ripped off the perforated edge and, a moment later, just as a bubble of blue energy surrounded him, he moved the talisman into his inventory.

Smiling, he brought it back out thirty seconds later. Twenty-five seconds after it should have fizzled out.

Now, this is nice, Luke thought, grinning at the protective bubble around him. *With this, I won't have to fumble around with it midfight. Instant energy shield, a thought away.*

With the initial success, he tore the perforated edge off three of his remaining five talismans and moved them to his inventory. He kept two on his person in case someone else needed to use them.

Watching a clock tick, he stripped out of his outer clothes and started doing push-ups.

Might as well get a workout in while I wait. What I wouldn't do for a phone right now, though. I never thought I would miss doomscrolling this much.

When he arrived at the city's gate, it didn't take him long to find his group. Four people, sitting on a large carriage tied to two bipedal, raptor-like lizards called raphta. Each was the size of a horse and covered in dark-blue and purple scales.

Once he got closer, Luke was surprised to see he actually recognized two of the people on it. One of them was Arya, except she had swapped out her black robes for blue ones. The other was Ethan, his hulking frame easily recognizable. He hadn't seen either since his first days in the society.

"Hi. You guys are hunting the harpies, right?" he asked, approaching the carriage from behind, not scared of the lizards but not wanting to get close to them, either.

"Luke?" said Arya, her face settling into a frown. Clearly, she was unhappy to see him.

"Hi, Arya. Congratulations on becoming an Inner Disciple," he answered, ignoring the look on her face—he could already guess why she wasn't happy to see him.

"What are you doing going on a hunt?" she asked. "I specifically told Xander to warn you against them."

"You know this kid, Arya?" asked the other Inner Disciple, leaning in curiously.

"I've met him before. He joined the society a little over two weeks ago."

"That's fine, right? If he was recruited off-season, he should be decently strong." He shrugged and looked between Luke and Arya, clearly not seeing the big deal.

"And he hadn't started cultivating until then, either."

"So let me get this straight. You've been cultivating for two weeks?"

"Basically."

"You're going to die." He leaned back and crossed his arms, a smile playing across his lips.

"Laxas!" Arya looked at the other Inner Disciple disapprovingly. She turned to Luke. "You're not going to die."

"Is it really that dangerous?"

"It's not as bad as Laxas is making it out to be," Ethan cut in. "Harpies are pretty stupid. If we play our cards right, we can get rid of them fairly easily. Normally, we just fill them with arrows from a distance." Ethan pointed to a large pile of wooden arrows with metal heads and an assortment of bows on the back of the carriage.

"What Ethan isn't telling you is that there are usually hundreds of harpies in a single nest, and if they spot you, they will rip you apart," the other Outer Disciple chimed in.

Ethan glared at him. "Don't worry too much about that. What Arn isn't telling you"—he jabbed his thumb in Arn's direction—"is that harpies are basically blind. They never see where the arrows are coming from. Just stick with Arya or Laxas and you'll be okay. Isn't that right, guys?"

"You think I haven't seen that happen before?" Arn got to his feet and glared at Ethan.

"That's enough. Luke, get on, we're wasting time. And you two"—Arya glanced between Ethan and Arn—"if we're careful, then the harpies won't even know we're there, because we hunt them while they sleep, and if they do see us—" She reached behind her and pulled out a wire net with gaps big enough that Luke was confident he could poke his neck through them. "We have these. We'll set them up before we attack and fire our arrows through them. If they crowd around us, we'll still be fine."

"Yeah, don't stress too much about it. Like Ethan said, just stick with me or Arya, and we'll be all right. I was joking about the dying thing. Mostly," said Laxas, climbing to the front of the carriage and taking the reins.

CHAPTER 10

The Harpy Slayer

That's an awfully fancy sword you have there." Ethan eyed Luke's shiny golden blade. "That's the one that was hanging in the armory, right?"

"Mmm-hmm." Luke grunted, holding it parallel to his nose, inspecting the blade for what must have been the hundredth time since he'd bought it.

Arya looked at the blade curiously. "How did you get the merits for it so fast? I wanted to buy it myself, but wasting three hundred merits to satisfy my vanity wasn't something that I could do."

"I went herb picking, and we ran into a black-scaled king viper. Bit of an unexpected windfall."

"Explosive talismans?" Laxas asked from the front of the carriage, his eyes focused on the road as the lizards pulled the carriage along at blistering speeds under his guidance. He seemed to enjoy the task, almost unreasonably so.

"Yup."

He nodded approvingly. "Not a bad strategy. Anyway, we're almost to the town. Luke, since this is your first time, there are some ground rules. One, don't mess with the locals. I'd go so far as to say don't even talk to them. If you do run into them, they will ask you how to cultivate. Do. Not. Tell. Them." Laxas looked over his shoulder and straight into Luke's eyes. "That's rule two."

Luke frowned. "How come?"

"It's . . . not wise," Arya chipped in. "If everyone is aware that all you need to do to surpass the limits of mortality is exercise, at least to get to the middle of the Mortal tier, it makes people harder to control."

"Why is that a bad thing?" Luke asked, not understanding where she was coming from.

"Well, every time some town or village figures out the 'big secret,'" said Ethan, "it always ends in bloodshed."

"Huh?"

"Some lunatics always end up thinking that because they're strong enough to do something, they have the right to do it. After all, if they get stronger than everyone around them, then who's going to stop them?" he elaborated.

"But how is that different from cultivating in the society?" Luke asked.

"It's not. You saw the Winged Woman earlier—she strolled right in, and the Elders had no choice but to kneel at the foot of her throne. Really, there's just less chaos, the fewer of us there are. Besides, between you and me, all those people who don't walk the path aren't exactly losing out on much. Out of a thousand, maybe ten people can get past the midstage boundary, and the number of people who ascend to the Warrior tier is even smaller than that."

"Right." Luke nodded along, not really satisfied with the reasoning, but at the same time not wanting to argue the pros and cons of the masses cultivating mana. If doing so got him in trouble with the Luminous Sky, it wasn't worth it. He could explore the subject once he wasn't worried about Arke cracking his soul apart like he had a toy inside him.

"Rule three is also pretty simple," said Laxas, pulling the carriage over and stopping just outside a town's gates. "Don't sell anything from the society to those not in the society. Not talismans, not weapons, not potions, nothing. Not all mortals know that becoming a god is possible, and of those that do, we keep the number small, and we maintain an aura of mystery. Selling our stuff to mortals breaks that illusion. As far as they know, everything they can offer us is worthless. Which is true anyway, so don't bother."

"I will not."

"Good. I'd hate to kill you." He looked Luke dead in the eye before bursting out laughing. "I'm just joking. Mostly. Anyway"—he climbed out of the carriage—"you four wait here. I'll go talk to the leader of the place, and we can figure out our game plan," Laxas said, walking off. "Someone wake Arn up, too."

"So, Luke, you know how to use a bow right?" Ethan asked, pulling one free from the pile and loading a quiver with arrows.

"I know the general gist of it, yeah."

"Let's see what you got." He nocked an arrow on a bow and handed it to Luke. "Hmm. Aim for the knot on that tree." He pointed to a leafy tree twenty paces away.

Luke accepted the bow, taking a moment to get used to its weight. When he turned toward the tree, he was surprised by the amount of force required to actually draw the arrow. Wincing in pain as the string dug uncomfortably deep into his fingers, he only managed to draw it back a quarter of the way before letting it loose.

It missed the tree he was aiming at completely and sank a quarter of the way into a tree to the left of it. He frowned in annoyance.

Am I really that weak? I can't even draw a bow.

"Try this one instead." Ethan handed him another bow, an arrow already nocked.

Eyebrows furrowed, Luke did just that. Squinting with one eye, he drew the string back and aimed it at the knot, and thankfully, while it still wasn't easy, he was able to pull it all the way back. Adjusting his aim, he let the string go, and this time he managed to hit the right tree, the arrow sinking in a quarter of the way through with a satisfying thunk—although that still wasn't where he was aiming.

"This one is better. Thank you," said Luke. Reaching for another arrow, he took another inaccurate shot.

"You're welcome—just make sure you don't shoot any of us. That bow should be powerful enough to kill the weaker harpies, so aim for the small, skinny ones. Don't waste arrows on the bigger ones."

"Luke," Arya called out. "Are you going to be able to handle killing them?"

"What do you mean?"

"Well, they look like women, with wings for arms. and talons for feet. They're not, but they do look like people. You're not going to freak out when you see them die, right?"

Luke frowned as he thought about her question. He knew they looked like people, having flipped through a bestiary after killing the snake. Even that had made him queasy—at least, watching it suffer had. Would this be worse because they looked more human?

A few weeks ago, he knew the answer would have been yes. He hated blood. Even in movies, it bothered him. Except he had changed. Dying, witnessing souls being eaten by a dying god. Coming to this world. Possessing Max's body and inheriting his memories. Memories he was just now realizing may have had an effect on who he was. Because while Luke wasn't fond of blood, Max had been gutting fish and chopping heads off chickens for as long as he could remember.

Would this be the same?

"I'll be fine," he answered after a moment. He'd have to be fine—it wasn't like he had a choice. If not now, then in the future, he'd have to be. Otherwise, he might as well have rejected the Seed and left himself to the whims of fate.

The Seed, which had guided him toward Bellerophon's Blade. It had probably even picked this island, and Max's body, just to give Luke access to it. A sword that just so happened to siphon mana from those it cut. The message was fairly clear.

Besides, he thought, *these harpies are kidnapping men and killing people. They need to go. This is a public service.*

"That's good. I know killing can be rough for some people," said Arn, yawning as he hopped off the carriage. "I'll be back." He walked into the forest.

"I swear, that man relieves himself every hour. I've seen him piss more in three days than I have in three weeks," Ethan grumbled, sorting through the arrows.

Arya crinkled her nose in disgust as she tied her dark hair in a bun. "Gross."

"It's weird." Ethan grinned at her.

"It's not that weird. He just drinks a lot of water. Stays hydrated, you know." Luke defended him, suddenly conscious about the fact that he, too, drank a lot of water and had joined Arn on his pit stops more often than not.

"Oh, look. Laxas is back," Arya pointed out, eager to change the subject.

"Okay! So, here's the situation: there's a nest on the other side of the town. They said it's easy to see if we just stick to the river. The birds sleep during the day, and it's getting kind of late. I say we camp out here tonight and attack the nest tomorrow afternoon," Laxas said. "Are we all okay with that?"

"Works for me." Luke ran his fingers over the bow's sinewy string, planning to practice his skills with the weapon.

"Same. Why don't we just sleep at an inn in town, though?" asked Ethan.

"Well, I wanted to give our newest member here a taste of what he can expect tomorrow. We're far enough away from the nest that we'll only attract a handful of strays. It should be good practice for him."

Night fell over their makeshift campsite not long after. They sat around a roaring campfire, which, Laxas claimed, would draw the harpies right to them.

Luke kept his hand on the pommel of his sword in preparation. His eyes constantly darted through the darkness in search of their would-be foe.

"Take it easy, Luke," said Arn, lying back to watch the star-filled sky. "You'll hear them coming. They make these loud clicking noises when they move."

"He's right. They're not stealthy. It's also not good to be so tense before a battle—that's how you make mistakes. Take some deep breaths and relax." Ethan was roasting a rabbit he had caught earlier over the flame. "How's fighting in the ring going? I've seen you going there pretty regularly over the past week or two. Second ring now, right?"

"It's going well. The first ring was getting too easy. I would get weird looks after winning five or six fights in a row."

"That's good." He took a bite out of the rabbit before spitting it out. "Awgh. It's still raw. The first ring is all the people who're gonna get the boot."

"That's not true. Stop filling the newbie's mind with nonsense."

"You still fight in the first ring, Arn?" Ethan turned toward him.

"No, I stopped after my first two or three weeks, but"—he climbed onto his elbows—"I know people who made it to the midrank without ever fighting someone at the arena."

"And how many others did you know that never fought in the arena, that ended up in white robes—or worse, got expelled from the society? What even happens to those people anyway?"

"They get sent to the mines," said Laxas.

"Fuck. Really?" Ethan stared at him, horrified.

"It's not that bad."

"The mines?" Luke glanced between the two, not having heard of the term before.

"Mana-crystal mines," Ethan answered. "The society manages a few, but it's dangerous work. A lot of the people who work there end up dead."

"Ethan is exaggerating. I got sent to the mines myself. It's hard work, but it pays well, and if you can reach the midstage or higher, they let you return to the society," said Laxas.

"I've done guard duty there. It's miserable," Ethan argued.

"I suppose." Laxas shrugged. "It's not as fun as being in the society, but it's the same premise—you work, they feed you, and you cultivate. Besides, if you ever end up there, it's because you pissed away three years in the society, living in the lap of luxury and not giving anything back."

"Do you hear that?" asked Arya, reaching for her bow and nocking an arrow.

Luke jumped to his feet and strapped his shield to his arm before drawing his sword. Its blade shone dimly in the light of the fire. Straining his eyes in the dark, he felt his heart beat in anticipation as he heard them come. A wet clicking sound reverberated through the night.

Arya fired two arrows in quick succession. A moment later, Luke heard two heavy thuds as two harpies dropped to the ground. Dead.

"Nice shot," Laxas praised.

"You two can see them?" Arn asked, drawing his own sword with a swish.

"Perks of being in the late stage," Laxas answered smugly. "Luke. Arya left one for you. Be ready. The rest of you, don't interfere," he warned.

Luke tensed his grip on his sword.

It came into view seconds later. A hideous creature. Every surface of its vaguely feminine body was covered in dirty black fuzz. A humanoid torso, with large, feathered wings for arms, and humanlike thighs that turned to bird legs at the knees. Instead of feet, the creature had wicked talons. Its face lacked ears, a nose, and a mouth, instead possessing a large pointy beak, above which were two small and beady eyes. They met Luke's gaze with animalistic frenzy.

She circled the air above Luke and swiped at him with her talons. He warded her off with a swipe of his sword, and she screeched in pain as the golden blade bit into the flesh of her leg. Beating her wings rapidly, she flew back, climbing higher and higher. Seemingly, she'd decided her target wasn't prey after all.

Thwip. Thwip. An arrow pierced each of her shoulders, and with her limbs immobilized, she fell to the ground.

"Kill it," Laxas said, a bow in his hand.

Luke raised his shield as he approached her. Realizing that, stranded as she was on the ground, she lacked means of attacking him, her wings making ineffectual weapons.

She watched in fear as Luke approached her, blindly lashing out with her wings as she limped away from him. Luke's prior slash had cut deeper than he expected.

Fuck this. Fuck this. Fuck this.

Luke closed the distance and, with a powerful lunge, stabbed his sword through her chest. He watched miserably as life faded from the creature's eyes.

+2 Stat Points

Luke dismissed the message as soon as it came.

Guess this is my life now.

CHAPTER 11

Destroying the Nest

Luke killed three more harpies that night, gaining a total of eight points from his kills. Even when he worked himself to collapse, he hadn't gained that many. Except he preferred working himself to exhaustion to killing the downed creatures.

Opening his status, he agonized over where to put his points before dropping half of them into the Strength stat and the other half in Agility. Tempted as he was to unlock the secrets of Arcana, the stat was a void. Recalling the difficulty with which he pulled the bow, he figured it was better, at least for now, if he increased a stat he could actually use.

Status │ Quests │ Inventory
Name: Lukas King
Tier: Mortal
Mana: 144
Rate: 10% per hour
Strength: 22 > 26
Agility: 16 > 20
Constitution: 21
Arcana: 16
Stat Points: 0
Bloodline: Locked. Conditions not met. (1/10,000)
Charges: 7/10

He felt the difference immediately. He felt both more limber and stronger. Rolling out of his sleeping bag, he put both fists on the ground with his elbows tight on his body and pushed himself up. Not feeling any pressure, he put his entire weight on one fist and put his other hand behind his back, lowering himself as slowly as he could and then pushing himself back up.

Too easy.

He unfurled his fist so that the weight was on his fingers alone. He pushed himself back up, marveling at the ease of the movement.

So this is what it feels like to be strong, huh.

"Look at you go!"

Quickly climbing to his feet, he turned and saw Laxas watching him from the cart.

"Good morning." He nodded to the older Inner Disciple.

"Are you ready for today?" Laxas asked, his tone growing flatter. "You hid it well, but I noticed you weren't doing too well last night. I get the feeling. Killing isn't fun. But it needs to be done. I've seen what happens to places like these when monsters come knocking. They'll strip this town bare."

"I get it. It's just . . . It feels cruel." Luke ran his hands through his hair, wincing in disgust as he felt the dried and crusty harpy blood caked against his skin. One of his kills had been extra bloody.

"That's because it is," Laxas said, picking an arrow from the carriage and slapping it against the palm of his hand. "The work we do is ugly, but it needs to be done. It's the price we pay. We hide the truth, and in doing so, we make all these people vulnerable. As such, it becomes our duty to protect them."

"You mention you worked in the mines. What was that like?"

"Hmm. I liked it. A lot of the people still working there will probably stab me if they heard me say that, but it's true. I wasted my time in the society, but when I got to the mines, I understood what I had to do. I had a purpose: to leave. They didn't make it a secret that all we had to do to get out of the mines was reach the midstage of the Mortal tier, and they even gave us tools to exercise with to achieve that goal. Most people didn't bother with them. I could never understand why that was. Even now it bothers me. Those people chose indenture, and then they whined about it when their bodies became too frail with age, and they became too weak to progress. It made me not want to stay there. Being surrounded with such sloth."

Luke's eyebrows furrowed as he mulled over his words. "People are dumb."

"Truer words have never been spoken." Laxas glanced at the morning sky, the suns just beginning their ascent. "Wake the others. We should get going."

"How far away is the nest?" Arn asked, only for Arya to tap his shoulder. She held a finger over her mouth, telling him to shut up.

Taking the cue, the group of five walked in silence upstream along the river, careful not to rattle their equipment.

A few minutes later, the harpies became visible. They had built a giant, malformed nest on the ground, spanning across the bases of at least a dozen trees. Men, presumably from the town, could be seen nailed to the trunks of the trees the nest was built around, naked.

Luke winced at the sight. Harpies were all female, and they regularly abducted human men to breed with. It was a gruesome fate. The bestiary claimed that their bodily fluids would put the captured men into a state "conductive to procreation," for as long as their bodies could withstand. The harpies drained them of their vitality until they died. After that, the harpies would feed the men's corpses to the offspring that emerged from the union.

It was easy to forget, with how peaceful life had been the last two weeks, that Theos was dangerous, and that there were threats other than Arke he had to be wary of. Thankfully, the society itself was fairly insulated from them, letting those that resided in it accumulate strength in relative peace.

He watched in silence as Arya and Laxas handed both Ethan and Arn some metal posts and a roll of the wire net that they had brought with them. Splitting up in three groups, with Laxas setting off on his own, each of them chose a spot along the river and set up their defenses, wrapping the wire net firmly around three trees in a tentlike formation—one that was hopefully strong enough to give them some breathing room in case the birds crowded them.

Once they were all set up, Arya fired an arrow into the sky near the harpies. Moments later, both Laxas and Ethan fired arrows from their vantage points. They were ready.

Luke readied an arrow but didn't fire. His aim wasn't good enough to kill them in a single hit. The initial volley instead would be just Arya and Laxas, with the goal of picking off enough of them silently while they slept.

Luke and the other two Outer Disciples would join in when an inevitable non-lethal arrow roused its victim, and with her, the rest of the flock.

It happened after they killed around thirty of them. An arrow glanced off a bird's head, and, waking up to the smell of her dead sisters, she shrieked.

Within moments, the human-bird hybrids took to the sky. They were even uglier in the day. Their battered wings, mottled fuzz, wrinkled skin, and spotted beaks spoke to the harsh lives they lived.

Luke took aim and loosed an arrow, watching its trajectory as it managed to pierce one of them in the shoulder. It fell out of the sky, its flight interrupted, and into the river, where it was carried away by the current.

Under their coordinated attacks, it didn't take long to thin their numbers from hundreds to dozens. A good number of them managed to escape the range of their arrows and fly away.

"It's impossible to get all of them. They always scatter. They'll fly around, attack small villages and travelers until they build their numbers high enough, and then they'll camp out at a town this size again," said Arya. "When that happens, the society will organize another hunting party, and the cycle will repeat."

"On and on, huh."

"Mmm-hmm. Our work isn't done, though. A lot of the ones we shot down should still be alive. We'll have to finish them off. Will you be fine on your own, or do you want to come with me?"

Luke frowned as he considered her words. On one hand, the idea that he needed to be babysat was emasculating, but at the same time, it was also justified. Swallowing his pride, he replied, "I'd appreciate it if you tagged along. Maybe I can practice with my sword more?"

"Very well."

"The guy who gave me the mission also said something about their wings being worth good money. Do we cut them off?"

Her face crinkled in disgust. "No, we have an agreement with the town. We just kill all of them, and their butchers will prepare the wings for us."

"Convenient."

"Very," she agreed.

"I remember hearing something about freshness and mana draining away—won't that be a problem if it takes us three days to get back to the society?"

"We have preservation talismans."

"Oh. That's convenient, too."

"Very. There's a harpy behind the tree." She raised her bow, gesturing for him to get on with it.

Drawing his sword, he did just that.

+2 Stat Points

Dismissing the message, he moved on, not wanting to look at the fruits of his foul deeds. The role of an executioner, while rewarding in terms of strength, was decidedly not something that he enjoyed.

As the points racked up, though, Luke couldn't help but notice how much progress he was making. How much power he was gaining. All at the expense of life.

"It's good that you don't enjoy this," Arya said after studying his expression. "I've known people who find joy in such acts. It's unpleasant to observe."

"I just wish I didn't have to do it."

"Then why did you accept the mission?"

Luke stayed silent. It wasn't like he could tell her that his sword made him stronger after every enemy he killed, and that he knew that because he was the thief Arke was searching for. One who had made off with an incredible prize that was guiding him toward godhood.

"It felt like the right thing to do. If you're not advancing, you're regressing and all that. Staying in the society and picking flowers for chump change was a waste of my time," he answered eventually, mixing elements of the truth with lies.

"It's not a waste of time. When you learn to sense your mana, a lot of doors open up. A lot of the society's easier tasks are meant to give you a foundation in higher fields of study. The skills and knowledge you gain by picking herbs, for example, are useful when refining them into pills and potions. There's a familiarity that's needed with nature, and the environments that the plants grow in, that translates into combining those plants for the purpose of alchemy. An understanding that you can't gain just by flipping through books. There's so much information and nuance to nature that only a small fraction can be learned through study. The smells, how they face the sun, what the light looks like when it reflects off their petals, what the soil feels like, and not just what it's composed of—there's so much that books can't tell you. Or if they do, they only give you a small glimpse of what's actually there."

"So you're an alchemist?"

"I am," she said, her face turning slightly red.

"How come you're out here hunting harpies, then?"

"Plants aren't the only things an alchemist works with. Mana, refined by the bodies of different animals, gains certain properties that can be harnessed. Just like plants, you can learn a lot by directly observing the environment they live in."

"Huh. I guess I was just being narrow-minded."

"Wisdom comes from experience. When I was an Outer Disciple, I thought that what I was doing was a waste of time, too."

"So . . . two weeks ago?" Luke teased.

"I'm very good with a bow, you know." She pulled the string back, the arrow pointing at Luke menacingly. He looked at it cross-eyed. "There's another harpy over there."

Suddenly Luke was back to reality. A smile that he didn't even know he'd been wearing slipped off his face.

Right. We're here to kill stuff. Not talk to pretty girls. It's weird that the two aren't mutually exclusive, though.

After all the harpies were dead, they returned to their makeshift shelter and disassembled it before meeting up with the rest of the team.

"How many?" Ethan asked.

"I counted eighty-nine bodies," said Laxas.

"Eight hundred and ninety merits, then. Not bad. How are we doing the split? Even or standard?" Arn leaned in.

Laxas's and Arya's eyes met as they had a silent conversation.

"Standard," Laxas replied slowly. Both Arn and Ethan deflated slightly at the news.

"What's the difference?" Luke asked.

"Even, we all take an equal share. Standard, it gets sorted by rank. Let's see." Ethan cupped his chin thoughtfully. "Five people, one low, two mid, and two high. Luke, you get ten percent, so eighty-nine merits. Me and Arn will take fifteen percent each, and those two will split the remaining sixty." He looked at the two Inner Disciples.

"Not bad, sounds good." Luke nodded, never having expected to get an even share of the merits in any case. Not when he'd shot down a fraction of the birds the other four of them had. If he was being honest, just Laxas or Arya alone was probably capable of taking out the entire nest. Except for the part where they woke up and scattered. Having more people shooting them down had been useful there.

Besides, he thought, *the real reason I came here was for the mana.*

Status | Quests | Inventory
Stat Points: 32

He had earned a frankly astounding number of stat points in a very small window of time. If he counted the ones from killing four harpies the night before, then he had gained more points in one day than he had in two weeks of ruthless grinding.

Quest Alert: Escape the Island of Carim

He blinked at the sudden appearance of the quest.
Well, look at that. A solution to all my problems.

CHAPTER 12

Game of Gods

<table>
<tr><td colspan="3" align="center">Status | Quests | Inventory</td></tr>
<tr><td colspan="3" align="center">Escape the Island of Carim:</td></tr>
<tr><td colspan="3">Join the expedition to the Hero's Tomb. Activate the portal. Walk through it.</td></tr>
<tr><td colspan="3" align="center">Subquest: A Hero's Disguise</td></tr>
<tr><td colspan="3">Among the hero's treasure there is an artifact called the Mask of a Thousand Faces. It gives whoever wears it a disguise undetectable by the gods themselves.</td></tr>
</table>

Luke scratched his chin as he read over the quest. It gave him a way out of his current predicament, and the subquest was promising. If he could get off Carim and disguise what he looked like, then he was home free. Hopefully.

Depending on where the portal took him. Or if anyone followed him to where he went. Since the quest was coming from the Seed, though, Luke was confident that it wouldn't guide him astray. Mostly confident—it was hard to forget what happened to Aeolus.

If there was one thing to learn from the dead god's example, it was that the Seed wasn't infallible. So far, the path it had laid out had been okay, but Luke wasn't blind to the fact that the Seed was willing to toe the line and put him in danger for the sake of progress.

Just the fact that it had put him in Max's body was a risk. It would have been safer, much safer, if he had possessed a body no one knew was possessed. Not that the gambit hadn't paid off. Bellerophon's Blade was a game changer, and it seemed that Nefkha had no intention of turning him in. A win-win scenario.

Honestly, at this point it's been long enough that even if he does turn me in to Arke, he would have to answer some uncomfortable questions.

"Are you thinking about how you're going to spend all those merits? What is it, a hundred and nine of them all together?" Arn asked while they were sitting in a circle around the campfire. They'd retreated there while Laxas went back into town to get the harpy wings sorted out.

"No, just life in general," said Luke.

"You're a lucky kid. When I was a newbie, I barely had two pebbles to rub together. At the rate you're earning merits, you'll practically be swimming in them."

"Earning merits seems to be pretty easy so far."

Ethan and Arn shared amused glances.

"Nah, you're just lucky. You should kiss the person who put you on this mission—two Inner Disciples, and one as prepared as Laxas. It's rare. Most of the time we go on these hunts, we scratch our asses the first day, just figuring out all the details. Laxas had everything ready, though. The wire fence, the arrows, the carriage—it couldn't have been a smoother trip. And no one got hurt . . . or worse. There's always a chance of that happening," Arn said, tossing another log into the flame.

Luke nodded. It had been smooth sailing for the most part.

"I'm going to turn in." Ethan covered his yawn.

"Me, too," said Arya, walking over to the carriage and grabbing a sleeping bag and tossing one to Ethan.

"I'll take one, too," Luke said, catching her eye. He had points to spend, and he needed to think about what he needed to spend them on.

With thirty-two points burning a hole in his pocket, he could practically double one of his stats. Not that he would. Maximizing one attribute at the expense of another might work in games, but with his life on the line, it was better to have a more even spread.

A jack-of-all-trades is a master of none, but oftentimes better than a master of one. Especially when I don't know what I need to be better at. Saving the points is a no-go as well—no point in being weaker than I need to be at any given moment.

Status | Quests | Inventory
Name: Lukas King
Tier: Mortal
Mana: 375
Rate: 10% per hour
Strength: 26 > 30
Agility: 20 > 30
Constitution: 21 > 30
Arcana: 16 > 25
Stat Points: 0
Bloodline: Locked. Conditions not met. (1/10,000)
Charges: 7/10

Hesitating over his choices, he finalized his decision. He enjoyed the feeling of his muscles becoming both stronger and more limber. This time he also experienced a new, heady feeling of his entire body becoming more robust that came with increasing his Constitution.

Still nothing with the mana, but I can't let it lag behind, either. It would really suck if I finally start to sense it, only to find out that I don't have enough to do anything with it.

I should probably start working on the Bloodline stuff, too. It's got to be amazing if it needs a whole ten thousand points just to activate it. I wish it would tell me more about it, though. Not that anyone's ever mentioned anything about bloodlines for as long as I've been here.

Bellerophon was the son of a god, if I'm remembering his myth right. A son of Poseidon. Max was found at sea, and the Seed led me to Bellerophon's Blade. Is it a coincidence?

Luke got comfortable in his sleeping bag, knowing that he would have to wait, and wait quite a while, to find out the truth of the matter.

Laxas returned to the camp early the next morning with a massive bundle of harpy wings secured firmly to a cart. He'd stayed in town overnight to watch over the butchering work. The group packed up and began the three-day journey back to the society, arriving in the middle of the night. Once everyone had received their merits, they separated.

The next day saw Luke once again lined up at the Mission Hall. This time he was scanning for expeditions leading to Hero's Tomb. Surprisingly, he found one on the top right corner of the board, printed in bold text.

"Hi, how can I help you today?" the mission hall clerk asked.

"I'd like to sign up for Elder Irila's expedition."

"Of course." The clerk held out her hand. Luke stared at it, confused, before realizing that she was asking for his wristband. Handing it to her, she dropped it on the magic paper before handing it back to him.

"I've added you to it. The Elder is holding a meeting a week from now at her palace; the expedition will depart then. Please ensure you bring suitable rations. Keep in mind, Elder Irila has final say in who joins her expedition, and if she decides that you don't meet her criteria, she can and will leave without you. However, she explicitly left applications open to all disciples of the society. Anything else I can do for you today?" The clerk smiled at him, sliding a pamphlet across the desk.

"No, that would be everything. Thank you." Luke walked out of the building, flipping through the pamphlet. It contained basic information that all those going on the trip were expected to know.

It provided information on what they needed to bring with them, a small list of formal robes and their weapons. That was it. Apparently, they would be given enough provisions in Arlym, the island's capital, to last them the duration of the expedition. What was surprising to Luke was that it gave them a brief rundown of the island's history.

In the past, Carim had been ruled by an empress, a cultivator at the Hero tier. She had apparently offended the Atlantians, who in their fury had threatened to sink the island. Appalled and horrified, she instead bargained with them. In exchange for her life, and a tribute to be paid every year for three hundred years, the Atlantians would forgive her offense. Before her execution, she had created her own tomb and filled it with her treasures, to be opened a year before the debt was paid. Which was a few days from the present.

Reading it, Luke was horrified.

Does everyone here just live at the mercy of those stronger than them? What did she even do to piss off someone that powerful? Luke shook his head. He sorely missed civilized society, rather than the paper-thin visage of it that was present in this world. *Is this what life was like in the Cold War? Just living with the knowledge that at any moment the world could turn to ash, at the whim of some dumbass with a button who lacked the sense not to press it? Except—* He felt the presence of the Seed in his soul. *I have a way to become a player in this game of gods.*

Stowing the pamphlet away in his pocket, he made his way to the arena. He sorely needed to alleviate some stress. Having it beaten out of him in the ring had proven to be a good method to do so, and a way to get stronger at the same time. Punching people was also surprisingly fun.

I should also spend all my merits. If everything works out, I won't need to save up anymore. Some more protective talismans are a must. I should also stock up on anything I might need to survive out in the wilderness. Who knows where the portal is going to take me?

Luke walked up the wooden steps leading to the Elder's palace atop the artificially flattened mountain peak, just one body in a vast throng of people. He had underestimated the buzz the event had generated. Usually expeditions were led by Inner Disciples, and most of them didn't pan out, ultimately wasting the time of whoever was hopeful enough to join.

One organized by an Elder, however, came with a degree of confidence among those attending that it wouldn't be a waste of everyone's time.

Reaching the plateau, he took in the sight of the Grecian palace right in the middle. He had seen it before, from a distance when Nefkha flew him to the society, but it was a lot more impressive up close—even if it did feel lacking compared to the golden splendor and easy grace of Aeolus's castle.

Joining the other disciples, he stood among the crowd, in front of a stage, and waited for the Elder to kick off the campaign. Idly, he looked through the crowd for any familiar faces—a futile effort considering there were hundreds of people. Most of the society's disciples shared the same brown or black hair and lightly tanned complexion, and they all dressed the same, too, making finding faces in the crowd a doomed effort. For a moment, Luke thought he saw Spiros milling around, but when he looked for him again, he wasn't to be seen. Shrugging, he moved closer to the stage. If he was here, then Luke would see him eventually.

She arrived exactly at noon, her long black hair braided in a complex pattern, falling almost artistically around her face, down the front of her red robes.

She's . . . hot, Luke thought, poorly masking the look of surprise on his face. He'd assumed, incorrectly, that all the Elders would look like Nefkha—old and sturdy.

"Thank you all for joining this expedition. As most of you know, I'm Elder Irila. I'll be the one leading you to the tomb. I'm sure all of you read the pamphlet before coming here, so I'll keep this brief. The Hero's Tomb is opening, and in it resides her inheritance. In her will, she wrote that all mortals are welcome to test themselves and, if they succeed at the trials within, earn her treasures. Treasures that can take you to past the limits of mortality. The Luminous Sky Society will not be the only organization attempting the trials within. So will the Crimson Night Sect and the Brotherhood of Dawn. For those of you who are unaware, they respectively manage the provinces of Castor and Crevin, similar to how the Luminous Sky presides over Yilim. Due to the restrictions placed over the tomb, no warriors are able to enter. What this means for those of you that chose to participate is that you will be in a tomb, competing for priceless treasures, with people desperate for them, some of which are standing at the peak of mortality. You will not be safe. There will be no laws to protect you, and if you lack the ability to protect yourself, you may be killed. There will be no justice for you if you die. Not from us. Or from anyone."

Luke mulled over her speech.

Basically, anyone can go, but at our own risk. The warriors can't enter, so there's no one to ensure our safety. If anyone dies, it's their fault for being weak and attempting something they weren't ready for. What she's not saying, but implying, is that we, too, are free to act however we want. There won't be any consequences for what we do, just like there won't be any consequences for what's done to us. Serious Purge vibes.

The crowd broke into chatter, but as Luke looked around, he spotted more than one greedy expression. A chill ran down his spine as he realized that he wouldn't just be competing with the other two organizations, but with his own allies as well.

There was no predicting the kind of treasures that were present in the tomb, but they belonged to a Hero—someone an entire realm above the strongest people in the society. Putting his hand on the hilt of his sword, Luke realized that with the right treasure, some of these people who had been stuck at the middle stage, or perhaps even the peak of the late stage, could perhaps break through and become warriors. Tangible, tempting power awaited them in the tomb.

"For those of you who are unwilling to risk your life, you may leave now. Those of you who are, step forward."

Without hesitation, Luke did just that.

Getting off the island is worth a little risk.

CHAPTER 13

A Paragon's Path

The ones who stayed watched the ones who left with mixed emotions. Some brief whispered arguments broke out as cliques broke apart. The prevailing emotions, however, were a strange mix of derision, relief, and, surprisingly, envy. Those who remained were simultaneously looking down on the people leaving, happy about the lack of competition, and jealous that the people leaving were able to walk away from the opportunity. After all, how could those leaving be content with remaining as weak as they were, or were they confident enough in their ability that they didn't feel the need to risk their lives in the tomb?

Luke winced as he took in the sight of those that remained. Many of them looked to be in their late teens to their midtwenties, and a quarter of them were wearing blue robes. He wasn't quite sure how strong Inner Disciples were, but he remembered the ease with which Laxas and Arya had culled the harpies. Their arrows flew both true and with power as they struck down one bird-woman after the other. Now he was their competition, if not their enemy.

"All right." Irila waved her hand, and with a flash of a ring on her finger, a large red carpet appeared on the stage behind her. "I'll carry everyone on this." She looked over at the crowd. "Try not to fall off."

All right. Aladdin *style. I kinda like it.*

Luke ambled onto it with the rest of the crowd, slightly enjoying the looks of confusion on their faces. For once, he knew what was going on and they didn't. Settling into a spot near the middle, he sat down, crossing his legs as he did so. Idly, he adjusted his sack full of supplies.

"Why am I not surprised to see you here?" Turning around, he was surprised to see Arya.

"I'm not sure." He looked at her strangely as she sat down next to him. "Are you looking forward to the tomb?"

"Not particularly. I didn't plan on joining the expedition. These kinds of things tend to pay off, but not many return from them."

"These kinds of things?"

"Inheritances," she clarified. "Cultivators tend to die without families, so they leave their belongings trapped within tombs."

"And that's common?" Luke raised his eyebrow.

"More than you'd think. Normally it's a warrior's tomb. There are hundreds of them scattered around just in the province, and some disciples make it their mission to find them and get their hands on the treasures within. There's always some buzz about one every year or so, although I've never participated."

"Why now then?"

"A hero's tomb is much, much more tempting than a warrior's tomb. Besides, I'm strong enough now that I feel I won't be cannon fodder." She looked at him disapprovingly.

Luke shrugged his shoulders. "No risk, no reward."

"Well, for what it's worth, I hope you don't die."

"Me, too." Luke frowned. "This might sound dumb, but what would you say to teaming up? Having someone watch your back has got to be worth something, even if it's me."

"I'm not against it, but . . ." She trailed off.

"Am I too weak?"

"It's not just that. How would we split what we find?"

Luke rubbed his chin. He only really needed one thing, and that was the mask, but he couldn't say that to her—at least not without clueing her in to the knowledge that he knew more about what was coming than he should. Even if it was barely more than she herself did.

"I'm mostly here for the experience. If there's anything useful to developing my mana-sense faster, then I would like to have that, but aside from that, you can have first pick on anything we find . . . but I get first call on one thing. If there's any monsters, I wanna fight them, too," he added hastily. "Like we did the harpies. Unless they're too strong for me."

She looked surprised.

"And you would trust me to keep to these terms? I'm stronger than you, so if I decide to rob you or worse, what will you do?"

"We're both still in the Mortal tier. I don't believe you can kill me that easily." Luke hedged, ". . . and I don't think you're that kind of person."

"You're underestimating the difference between us. Maybe you could take on someone at the midstage, and win, if you don't make any mistakes. At my level, I might even be too durable for you to cut."

"I guess it's just a risk I'll have to take, then, won't I?"

She shrugged. "Very well. Consider our alliance forged."

Luke grinned at her. "How much more durable are Inner Disciples, anyway?"

"It's hard to say." She looked at him out of the corner of her eye. "We're not really supposed to talk about it, but it depends what you focus on more. Toughness, strength, speed . . . There's a threshold. Once you cross it on any one of those things, you advance past the Mortal tier."

That sounds a lot like the attributes I have—minus the Arcana stat.

"So everyone just focuses on that one thing, then. To get past the limit as fast as they can?"

"Kind of. It's not like any of them exist in a vacuum. You need to improve all of them, but one needs to be the focus."

Luke frowned. "Why not improve all of them equally?"

"Time. You need to be young. It's different for different people, but the general rule is that if you don't become a warrior before you turn thirty, you never will. After thirty, it becomes much harder to even grow a little bit stronger. It's also a lot quicker going from nothing to the midstage than it is going from the midstage to late stage. So it's better to focus on one thing to get you past the threshold. Besides, it's not like you can't improve the other aspects once you become a Warrior," she explained, looking uncertain at the last part.

"Is that why all the Inner Disciples here look so young? The older ones know they don't have a chance."

"That's right. A lot of the society's Inner Disciples have already passed the age where they can improve."

Before Luke could respond, the carpet gently lifted off into the air and began cutting through the wind. He gasped and stared enviously at the red-robed Elder who, unlike the rest of them, was unbothered by the wind.

I forgot how much it sucks flying like this.

"We're moving so fast," Arya said beside him. Luke opened his mouth to respond, only for the wind to steal his breath the next moment.

Avoiding the impulse to gasp, Luke adjusted his posture and looked at her, ignoring the wind biting at his rapidly drying eyes.

"How . . . are . . . you . . . able . . . to . . . talk?" He struggled to get each word out.

"My lungs are just stronger than yours." She grinned at him.

He gave her an angry thumbs-up. Luckily for him, the flight this time around went by a lot quicker. An hour after they departed, the capital was in sight.

Floating above the city, Irila turned toward them and stopped the rug in midair.

"While we will stay in the city overnight, and our accommodations have been secured, limit contact with mortals as much as you are able. Do not, under any circumstance, divulge the details of cultivation to them. Am I understood?"

A chorus of yeses rang out from the crowd.

"Good. Once you are settled in, get dressed in your formal attire. We will be introducing ourselves to the others shortly," she said, directing the carpet onto the roof of a large multistory building.

"It feels so good to be on land again." Luke stretched his arms as he stood up.

"Speak for yourself. I quite enjoyed it. The freedom of the air . . ." Arya looked to the sky and sighed.

"I'll enjoy it a lot more once I can fly under my own power."

"When?" She lifted an eyebrow.

"When."

"Ha-ha. Little Outer Disciple wants to fly?" Luke felt someone put an arm around him. He winced in pain as fingers dug uncomfortably into his skin. He tried to shift out of the grip, only to find that he couldn't. It was iron. Turning around, he came face-to-face with a bearded Inner Disciple. An unpleasant smile was stretched across his face as he stared intently at Arya.

"Yjarn." Arya stepped forward. "Now isn't the time for your games."

"It isn't?" He looked surprised. "Of course, that's totally my fault."

He stared at her a moment longer before Luke felt the other man slide his arm off his shoulder. Luke tracked his footsteps as he walked away without saying anything.

"A friend of yours?" Luke massaged his aching shoulder, relieved that whatever that was, was over, and over quickly.

"In a way. We joined the society at the same time, but he's been an Inner Disciple a few months longer than I have. He was the first from our group to get there."

"Let me guess. He has a crush on you or something?"

She frowned at the question. "No. Nothing like that."

"Should we be concerned about him when we go to the tomb?"

"His brother died on a hunt. I was the only survivor." She watched Yjarn walk into the building. "It's unlikely but not impossible."

"Fun. Any other enemies I should know about?" Luke started walking inside.

"No. And Yjarn isn't an enemy. He just hasn't dealt with his brother's death." She looked unconvinced.

"We'll see. If he does try anything, you can take him, right?"

She nodded slowly. "If he does try something, he won't find us to be easy prey."

"That's reassuring," Luke said, holding the door open for her as they entered the building. "So what do you know about these other . . . organizations?"

"Not much. I've heard that some of our disciples have run into them on occasion. Not much more than that, though."

They walked down the stairs together before an attendant led them to their own rooms, leaving them with instructions to gather at the lobby in half an hour.

Luke stood in front of the mirror and got dressed in his formal robes, still predominantly black but embroidered with patterns and red accents. The society really took rank seriously.

They look nice, but what a waste of merits. I could have bought some more talismans. Those would be useful, at least.

Running a comb through his hair, he slicked it all to the back and tied it with a loose string in an attempt to stop it from scattering.

I think it's long enough that I could grow a man bun . . . He shuddered. *This world is changing me. To think I contemplated that. Ew.*

Still having ten minutes before he needed to show up at the meeting, he brought up his status.

<table>
<tr><td colspan="1" align="center">Status | Quests | Inventory</td></tr>
<tr><td align="center">Name: Lukas King
Tier: Mortal
Mana: 528
Rate: 10% per hour
Strength: 30 > 37
Agility: 30 > 34
Constitution: 30 > 33
Arcana: 25 > 32
Stat Points: 0
Bloodline: Locked. Conditions not met. (1/10,000)
Charges: 7/10</td></tr>
</table>

He sighed as he read over it. He had gained twenty-one points in seven days. It was solid progress, but the work involved in it when weighed against the return felt too low. Seven days of waking up at dawn and pushing his body well past his ever-increasing limits, for fewer points than he'd gained in a single night of hunting harpies.

Clenching his fist, he felt powerful. He was easily stronger and faster than even the best athletes on Earth, but he felt weaker than ever. Remembering Yjarn's fingers digging into his shoulder, he felt anger and rage boil inside him, begging to be released. His knuckles turned white, and the comb crumbled in his grip.

I can't believe I just stood there and let him do that to me. Even with all the work I've put in, a random guy just casually reminds me how weak I am. For fuck's sake, some dude I don't even know just grabbed me to make a point to someone else.

How strong is Arke? Or even a hero? How strong is a god? Does their strength give them the freedom to do anything they want to me? Am I that powerless? So weak that I have no choice but to suffer in silence? I was like an ant in his hands.

Luke fell down onto a chair and watched the townsfolk mill about their lives outside his window. Forcefully, he calmed himself down, knowing that mindless anger wasn't useful to him. It had never been.

It's fine. It's fine. I have the Seed. I'll keep getting stronger until no one can walk over me like that again. Until Arke is the one scared at the mere thought of what she will do if I find her. I won't need to rely on Arya to keep me safe on a hunt. I won't need to make alliances to ward off greater threats. I won't stop until there's no one in this world strong enough to make me bend.

Suddenly he felt *it*. The world grew dim and quiet. *Something* was asking him to choose. Choose if he really wanted to be the strongest. It promised strength, but it demanded a price. To see it through, or to lose it all.

Quest Alert: A Paragon's Path

Luke blinked in confusion.

This is new. Since when do quests do this?

Quest Alert: A Paragon's Path

Luke blinked in confusion.

This is new. Since when do quests do this?

CHAPTER 14

Into the Tomb

Status | **Quests** | Inventory

A Paragon's Path:

Over the eons, many gods have arisen, but few have trod the Path of Paragons, and fewer have succeeded.

Requirements: Raise all attributes to 1,000 at the same time for a perfect ascent to the Warrior tier. Unlock your Bloodline before ascending to the Warrior tier.

*If accepted, all attribute gains over 999 will be redirected as Stat Points until all conditions are met.

Accept

Yes/No

Luke mulled over the text. It explained what was happening. The world, it seemed, had more layers than he thought it did. More than that, it offered him a path to becoming stronger—stronger than he would otherwise be, but in return, he had to ascend perfectly or not at all.

He read it again. The prompt inadvertently revealed a lot about Theos, and cultivation in general. Confirming some of what he knew and spawning even more questions in its wake.

So even if I raise just one attribute past one thousand, I'll enter the Warrior tier. Arya said as much on the way over here. In vague terms.

The quest is weird, though. It's not coming from the Seed. At least not entirely. It's more like the Seed is contextualizing it for me. Which means the very act of cultivating is baked into this reality. Nice.

He tried to stand up but found he couldn't.

It's like my limbs lost connection. Freaky, but I'm not freaked out. I just have to accept or deny, and the world will go back to normal. This pause . . . It's giving me time to decide. Interesting.

Let's think this over. The Seed is giving me the option to refuse, implying that I don't have to do this. It's not like the normal quests it gives me. Those just seem to be things that

I need to do, either to survive or become a god. Likely both. I can't reject them. Don't know what happens if I fail at them, though.

An image of Arke ripping his soul from his body and removing the Seed that was implanted in his soul flashed through his mind.

Death. That seems likely if I fail.

Do I want to accept this one in particular? Locking myself in the Mortal tier until I unlock my Bloodline is going to take a lot of time. The fact that I can refuse it is interesting, though. It means, or should mean, that I don't strictly need to do this. I can still become a god without it. Except . . . not all gods are equal. This . . . It's promising me the strength needed to be unparalleled. A paragon. But not really. It's promising to let me stand at the precipice. I still need to get there, though. Accepting this won't make me any stronger right now. I may not even be that much stronger when I ascend to the Warrior tier. Except I'll always be the strongest I could possibly be at the peak of every tier. Even when I become a god.

Curious, he directed his thoughts toward the Seed, and his thoughts reeled in surprise when it actually answered. He had gotten used to it ignoring his inquiries.

Sweet.

Let's see what it says.

—The Path of the Paragon emerged from the primordial order, manifesting alongside the creation of Theos. The path demands that all who tread it do so without hesitation. Once embarked upon, it cannot be abandoned. If rejected, it is lost forever.

—Quests given by the God Seed guide the host through danger and opportunity, directing the host through the eddies of fate toward the ultimate pursuit of divinity.

He read it, then read it again. Just to make sure he wasn't missing anything.

If I didn't have the Seed, or the sword, I'd be locking myself at the Mortal tier, perhaps forever. I might not even have known if I had a Bloodline. With it, though . . . I know exactly how far away I am from my goal, and exactly what I need to do to get there. Just killing monsters will be enough.

More than that, if Aeolus had chosen the Path of the Paragon, would he have been killed by Arke, even after he reached godhood? It's clear that the Seed will guide me, but it won't make me the best version of what I could be. That—that is what this quest is about. Perfection. A paragon is perfect.

So, really, the question is, can I afford to be lazy? No. Not now, and not ever.

Yes. Luke directed his thoughts to the Seed, accepting the quests. A feeling of heaviness overcame him as color and sound returned to the world.

Immediately, he felt something in his status change.

Status | Quests | Inventory
Name: Lukas King
Mana: 528
Rate: 15% per hour

So there was an immediate benefit. My mana recovers a little faster now. Five percent doesn't seem like a lot, but . . . let's see. He closed his eyes, struggling to do the math in his head. *Instead of taking ten hours for me to get all my mana back, it'll take me just under seven hours now. Not bad.*

Not exactly immediate, considering I don't have any way to actually use my mana yet, but I can see that being very useful.

Picking up the shattered pieces of his comb off the floor, he threw them away as he ran through the numbers for his quest.

I need ten thousand points just for my Bloodline, and then basically four thousand for all the attributes. A little under, with the stats I already have. Still fourteen thousand points. I can earn three a day just from exercising, so not counting anything else, that's . . . more than a decade.

Fuck. He paced back and forth. *This may have been a mistake. No. It's not. All that means is that I can't go hermit mode.*

His mouth set into a frown as he realized all the things he'd need to kill to get to his goal. *I can do it*, he told himself before glancing at the clock. It was time to meet the rest of the competition.

The scene he walked into wasn't quite what he was expecting. He thought there would be a tense crowd listening to one of the warriors talk. Instead, music played in the background, and people were dancing in the middle of a large auditorium. A bar was in one corner, and there were tables loaded with steaming food beside it.

Elder Irila, now dressed in glittering red robes, was sitting next to two other warriors, one from the Brotherhood and the other from the Crimson Night. Each of them wore fancy red robes. To the left of her was a severe-looking old man, his head bald and his face completely covered in liver spots and wrinkles. To her right was the complete opposite. He didn't look older than twenty and was built powerfully. He looked handsome, with high cheekbones, long hair, and a beard just messy enough to look natural and just neat enough to avoid looking bad.

Luke observed the pair in amusement as the younger of the two regaled Irila with some story, wearing an expression that Luke would recognize anywhere—one of a man desperately trying to impress a woman.

"Jealous? I know I am. If I could talk to Helen like that, that would be so awesome."

"Spiros! I thought I saw you earlier," Luke greeted him with surprise. Absently, he noted the empty bottle in his hand and the characteristic sway of a good buzz in his step.

"And I definitely saw you." He wiggled his eyebrows. "An Inner Disciple."

"It's not like that," Luke said, keeping his voice carefully even. "Besides, she's a little older than I am. I don't think she'll see me that way." *More like I'm older than her. Not by a lot, but if I was in my twenties, I wouldn't look at a fifteen-year-old kid like that. Stupid body. Why couldn't the Seed keep me at twenty-six?*

"Never say never. Besides, I've heard warriors live for centuries. If you can both make it that far, five, six years will seem like nothing. Even decades won't be that far off."

He stepped closer to Luke and whispered in his ear, "The woman I love is forty." Spiros stepped back and nodded to him as if he had told him a secret of great importance.

Luke blinked at him. ". . . I thought she turned you down?"

"She did"—he nodded—"but she's a Warrior. I may be too young now, but what about in twenty years? Or thirty? We'll both be older, but with centuries of life still ahead of us. If I can make it."

"You have a point. After a while, age is nothing but a number."

"That's right. You know, Myko and June make fun of me for it, but I'll get there. I'll become a warrior and ask her to marry me. They don't understand. You know"—he wrapped his arm around Luke's shoulder—"I was the last person to stop running. They let the last five hundred people still running join, but they didn't stop those of us who could keep going, either. Those bastards. I ran for three hours longer than the second-to-last guy. I didn't even stop to shit! Did you know that, Luke? I love her enough to shit my pants! She wasn't even there!"

Luke patted him on the back. "Love makes us do stupid things sometimes. Why don't we get something to eat? The food looks delicious."

"I knew you'd understand," Spiros said, wrapping his other arm around Luke in a drunken hug.

Luke awkwardly smiled at the people staring at them as they walked by. Peeling Spiros off him, Luke led him toward a table and, after dropping Spiros on the chair, sat down himself, observing the crowd as they mingled, seemingly unaware that in a few hours, they would all be competing with each other. Perhaps even fighting to the death in order to sate their greed.

"They're doing this so we'll be nicer to each other tomorrow. You missed the speech they gave earlier," Spiros said, his mouth full of cake.

"Did they say anything else? Anything important?"

"Mmm. No. Just some stuff about trying to stay friendly. Maybe some people will listen, but some won't. You know how it is . . ." He trailed off, shoving another slice of cake down his throat.

"I can guess."

After eating his fill, Luke left the party, having unsuccessfully and half-heartedly tried and failed to find any other familiar faces in the crowd. A futile task considering how many people were gathered.

The next morning saw all the cultivators assemble on the roof of the building before their respective Elders flew them out of the city and toward a large lake.

The assembled cultivators stood around patiently as the three warriors walked up to a seemingly random spot. Three rings flashed, and in each of their hands three identical keys appeared. They walked toward the edge of the water, close enough to risk their feet getting wet in the lake's shallow waves. In unison, they stabbed the keys forward and turned them.

Gasps of awe proliferated through the assembled crowd as a wide stone bridge appeared. It led to the center of the lake, where it cut off randomly.

The oldest of the three warriors flew a dozen feet into the air.

"Walk along this path and complete the trials within. I wish you all the best of luck." He flew back down, and the three warriors stood to the side of the bridge.

The crowd shuffled uncertainly before a blue-robed figure broke away and sprinted along the path. The crowd watched him with bated breath as he ran all the way down to the center before disappearing in a flash of white light, breaking the floodgates. The rest of the cultivators ran forward and started pushing and shoving as they approached the entrance to the bridge.

"Ready?" Arya asked, stepping beside him.

"Yeah," said Luke, watching Spiros break free from the cluster and run down the length of the bridge. "I'm ready. Let's just give it a minute, though. Let that mess sort itself out."

"Agreed."

They waited for a few minutes, letting the crowd thin, before stepping onto the bridge. They watched curiously as the people disappeared once they reached the end of the bridge.

"What do you think the trials are going to be like?" Luke asked nervously as they walked along the cobbled stone of the bridge, quickly approaching the point where people were disappearing.

"I don't know."

"Only one way to find out, then, huh?" They took the final step forward.

Luke covered his eyes with his hand as the world became white. When his vision cleared, he was standing alone in a poorly lit room. Moss grew between the cobblestones, and an array of lanterns led into a dark hallway.

So much for sticking together.

He stepped forward cautiously, only to stumble back a moment later as his foot sank into the ground, and, with a mechanized whir, a wall opened up.

Well, this is going to suck, Luke thought, peering into the cavity.

CHAPTER 15

Taste of Blood

Luke stared into the beady eyes of a scorpion before quickly stepping back, unsheathing his sword as he did so. A few long seconds later, it clambered out of its chamber, the wall closing behind it with the same mechanized whir with which it had opened. Leaving Luke alone with the bug.

It was a translucent white that seemed to glow in the dim light of the torches along the wall. Luke would have thought that it looked cool if it weren't for the fact that it was the size of a large dog. Or if it wasn't staring at him from a few feet away.

Luke's eyes darted between its crablike claws and its large stinger poised for attack and already dripping a sickly orange venom that sizzled when it fell onto the ground.

Gulping, Luke strapped his shield onto his arm in preparation for what was to come. For the moment, at least, the creature seemed content to just stare at him. Not one to waste an opportunity, Luke pulled an explosive talisman from his inventory, already primed and attached to a rock for easy use. He counted down the seconds in his head, and right when it was about to blow, he rolled it under the scorpion, hoping for a repeat of how he and the others had killed the snake oh so long ago.

It exploded with a bang that echoed throughout the hall, temporarily blinding him with a flash of light and obscuring the creature in smoke. When the smoke cleared, Luke was dismayed by what he saw. The scorpion, other than having been pushed slightly back and flipped over, was unaffected. The explosive talisman had proved incapable of damaging its chitinous armor.

This just got a lot harder.

Luke shivered at the sound of its eerie hiss and watched it struggle to right itself before he decided to attack while it was off-balance, realizing that just standing there and letting it recover was a bad idea. Shield raised, Luke advanced carefully before slashing at the thing with his sword. His blade bit into its armored claw, but the cut was a mild inconvenience to the creature at best. Not deep enough to hinder its mobility.

I need to aim for its weak spots.

Luke struck again, this time aiming for the connective tissue between its main body and its arm, only to stagger back as the stinger sank into his shield with a thunk. He blinked in surprise as the sharp point of the stinger managed to poke through the metal of the shield completely, barely missing his arm. Watching a single drop of venom ooze out of the stinger, he vanished the shield, returning it to his inventory. Free of its weight, he gripped the hilt of his sword with both hands and swung it with all his strength. He grinned in satisfaction as the scorpion's thin tail fell to the ground with a meaty thump. The creature had been too slow to retract it, giving him the opportunity to destroy its stronger weapon.

"Yeah, that's right!" Luke yelled out in excitement as it hissed again, this time in pain.

Stepping forward confidently, now that his foe was unarmed and considerably less dangerous, he stood just outside the range of its claws and stabbed his golden blade straight through its head, executing the creature without an ounce of sympathy. Its monstrous nature failed to evoke even a shred of sympathy in Luke.

+4 Stat Points

All right! Four whole points for that thing. It must have been stronger than those harpies. Twice as strong if the points that I got from it are to be believed.

Luke stared at the monster's corpse before collecting its tail and dropping the entirety of the scorpion's corpse into his inventory.

Who knows—might come in useful. Just the venom seems handy to have in this fucked-up world. If not, I might be able to sell it somewhere. If cultivators will pay for harpy wings, then they'll pay for this.

Resting for a moment longer, Luke retrieved the shield from his inventory and did his best to clean the venom off with a rag he'd sneaked into his inventory. Knowing that he'd probably need to use the shield again, and likely soon, it was better to make it serviceable in advance. Luckily, whatever the venom was, it apparently wasn't strong enough to eat through metal, and it wiped off without too much effort.

I should have bought a better shield, though, Luke thought, looking through the hole the scorpion had made. The one he had purchased was decent, but it lacked any enchantments that would let it withstand the enhanced strength of cultivators and monsters.

He sighed as he distributed the stat points. One into Strength, one into Agility, with the remaining two going into Constitution.

I'll get the Arcana stat next time. Spending points on it right now will make me weaker in the short term. I have a feeling that I'll need all the athleticism I can get. He clenched his fists. *I keep forgetting how good it feels to add points to my physical stats. Really beats getting them by working myself to the bone all day, that's for sure.*

All right. Enough waiting around. Let's get this over with.

Luke walked forward, watching his step carefully in case he triggered another trap. Perhaps one that was immediately deadly, unlike the scorpion. He felt that was unlikely, considering that this was supposed to be an inheritance, but it was better to be safe than dead.

Eventually, he reached the end of the corridor and walked into a large circular room. Hearing another whirring noise, he raised his sword and shield in preparation of an attack, only to see that the path he came from had closed behind him.

Well, this is ominous, Luke thought, frowning as he stepped onto sand. He took in the view around him. It made him nervous, as there was no way to get into or out of the place. Relaxing his guard slightly, he paced around the room looking for clues.

There's no way I'm just trapped in here, is there?

Avoiding panicking as best as he could, he walked around the room, his steps muffled by the sand on the ground. Frowning, he dug his foot into it, wondering if the way out was down. He found the same cobblestone as earlier, an inch or two deep.

Five minutes later, when Luke was really starting to panic, he heard another whirring noise. Thinking it was another monster, he readied himself for combat, only to blink in confusion as another person walked into the room. The second he was fully in, the wall shut behind him.

"Hi," Luke said, looking at the person who came in with curiosity, carefully noting his drawn blade and black robes.

He looks vaguely familiar. Probably an Outer Disciple from the society.

"Hey," the Outer Disciple responded, looking surprised to see Luke. "I'm Nafik." He started walking forward, sword lowered, but not sheathed, only to stop when Luke stepped away from him. Irila's warning played over and over inside his head.

"Luke," he eventually responded.

"It's nice—"

Whatever he was going to say was interrupted as a metal plate fell from the ceiling right at his feet. Luke watched him lean over it, reading something inscribed on it, before peering over and attempting to read it himself. Only for Nafik to step on it, stopping him from doing so.

"What are you doing?" Luke asked, stepping away the next moment. The other disciple rapidly closed the distance between them and slashed his sword, aiming right at Luke's neck.

Tanking the attack with his shield, Luke's arm shook under the strain. Nafik was a lot stronger than he was.

He stepped back, and the two of them stared at each other with caution, their weapons raised defensively.

Either he's insane, or the thing said something about one of us killing the other. Likely the latter—he seemed inclined to play nice before it fell. Either way, I'm at a disadvantage. He isn't at the late stage, unless he changed out of his robes, but he's still a lot stronger than me. If I'm going to win this, I'll have to be clever. One mistake, though, and I'm dead.

The thought sent chills down Luke's spine. He'd been in a hundred fights at the society's arena up till now and had even fought monsters straight out of legend. He'd never been in mortal danger, though. The fights in the arena were as civil as a fight could be, and when he had fought monsters, it had been with confidence— confidence that he was safe. With the benefit of having allies more experienced than himself watching over him.

If he lost here, though, he was dead. Using a charge would call Arke down, and he wasn't sure it would be enough to get away from her. Not that he wanted to use a charge in the first place. To Luke, those were his largest aces, and he was beyond reluctant to waste them on someone who, while stronger than him, didn't hold a candle to his real enemies.

Their standoff lasted a moment longer before Nafik started probing for weaknesses in Luke's stance. Circling him slowly, occasionally shuffling forward in what Luke thought was meant to be a feint before stepping back when Luke didn't take the bait.

After a few attempts, Luke's opponent decided that his strategy of trying to lure Luke in wasn't working and instead backed up, leaving ample room between the two.

He's strong, but not a fighter. He also looks like he's in his early twenties. Probably one of those people who couldn't develop his mana sense.

"All right, let's talk." Nafik lowered his sword.

"Why?"

Luke enjoyed the flabbergasted look on Nafik's face as he struggled to come up with a response.

"You don't want to know what the plate said?"

Luke peered at it lying on the ground.

"I think I can guess."

His opponent frowned before reaching into his pocket and pulling out an explosive talisman. He ripped it carelessly and crumpled it in his grip.

Luke blinked in surprise, taken aback by the reckless action, as his opponent held on to the slip of paper, clearly waiting to run down the time on its countdown before throwing it at Luke.

This would be bad . . . if I didn't have an already activated protective talisman in my inventory. How should I play this?

Luke grinned at him. When the talisman was two seconds away from bursting, he retrieved his protective talisman from his inventory and ran toward his opponent. He savored the look of shock on Nafik's face as the distance between them shrank.

This guy really is an idiot. Did he really think I would just stand there and take the hit? Whatever he is, he's not a good fighter, though. I should be grateful for that, at least.

He slung the crumpled talisman at Luke, only to have it bounce off the blue bubble surrounding him with unexpected force and ricochet back where it came from.

Nafik raised his arm to slap it away—

BANG!

Luke blinked the spots of color out of his eyes before realizing that his protective bubble had vanished just in time to deflect a crude attack from Nafik, who had survived the detonation. Not unscathed, though. He was missing half the fingers on his left hand, and blood dripped out of every orifice on his head.

Gross.

Luke stepped back to avoid another poorly executed attack and watched as his opponent stumbled and fell to his knees a moment later, dropping his sword and grabbing his mangled and bloody left hand with his right. He squeezed tightly in an attempt to stem the bleeding.

"Arghhh!" he screamed.

Wincing in sympathy, Luke stepped forward and kicked his sword away, watching Nafik carefully as he inched toward the plate.

It read: "Amid the chaos, a victor emerges strong. Loser fades away, dead."

A pretty rosy way of saying "kill each other." Luke frowned.

It would be easy to do it. Luke had learned, firsthand, what death was like. Having experienced it personally, and by killing other things. Monsters, but still. To Luke, it counted.

Killing another human, though, wasn't something he was sure about. He'd thought that it might happen eventually. It was hard not to, after he heard Irila's little speech. Except, now that it was actually happening, he found himself frozen.

Frozen and angry.

Why couldn't he have just died in the explosion? Or kept fighting. At least then it would be in the heat of the moment, and not a fucking execution.

He paced in front of his defeated opponent.

"You don't have to kill me," Nafik pleaded, having regained some composure under the looming threat of death.

Luke glared at him but didn't say anything. Finally, he sighed and walked up to him, his sword glinting ominously in the light of the torches.

CHAPTER 16

A Life's Worth

Empty your pockets," said Luke, his sword pressed lightly against his Nafik's throat. A request he regretted immediately, as Nafik rummaged around in his pockets with his undamaged hand. Watching him carefully in case he pulled any last-minute tricks while trying to stay as level-headed as he could under the circumstance. He trampled his irritation as what should have been a simple task took the wounded man way too long to complete. Irritation founded in the guilt he was already feeling for what he was about to do.

"That's everything." Nafik laid out all his possessions. It wasn't much. A few vials of pills, a few more talismans, and a sack full of coins.

"Is it?"

"It is." He nodded frantically.

Luke stepped on each item, sending it into his inventory as he did so, careless of the fact that it was a power he shouldn't have. Nafik's eyes widened.

"I thought only warriors could use storage rings? Is that how y—" Luke stuck his blade into his heart. Staring into his eyes, his gaze locked with Nafik's.

"I'm sorry," he said, watching death's grip get stronger on his foe. "If it's any consolation, death isn't the end. I never really found out what was supposed to happen, but I hope you find peace."

"Ghk. Ghhh," he wheezed.

+5 Stat Points

I just killed him.

Luke dismissed the message as soon as it came, stumbled away from the body, and puked his guts out on the wall farthest away from the corpse. Idly, he noted the mechanical noise of another passage opening as he heaved, confirming his suspicions about the nature of their battle.

He couldn't just leave, though. Something about it felt disrespectful. Kneeling by the body, he used his shield as a makeshift shovel and covered the remains with sand. Then, collecting Nafik's sword, he laid it on his buried body.

"Try not to get eaten on the way," he said, standing over the body. He gave it a final nod and walked away without looking back, calling up his status as he did so.

Status	Quests	Inventory

Name: Lukas King

Tier: Mortal

Mana: 608

Rate: 15% per hour

Strength: 38 > 40

Agility: 35

Constitution: 35 > 38

Arcana: 32

Stat Points: 0

Bloodline: Locked. Conditions not met. (1/10,000)

Charges: 7/10

He dumped three points into Constitution and the remaining two in Strength. It felt like a good compromise for the moment. The Strength stat, he felt, was the most useful, at least when it came to short-term gains. Being more durable was also bound to come in handy. More than that, increasing his Constitution came with the benefit of increasing his total available mana. Which, while he still couldn't use it, was bound to be useful when he unlocked the ability.

He tried not to let the guilt of his actions weigh on him as he walked down the long, narrow corridor. Watching out for traps helped at first, but as the time spent walking down the corridor increased from seconds to minutes and then to hours, all with nothing happening, his mind kept returning to the fact that he had killed someone.

That he was now a murderer. That the person he'd killed had had a mother and a father. That they would spend the rest of their lives not knowing what happened to their son. That the person he'd killed had had friends that cared for him. Maybe he even had a child, or a lover.

It weighed on him, that he'd robbed someone of their life.

I would do it again, too. I'm not going to let someone kill me, even if it means that I'll have to kill them. It's just nature. Survival of the fittest. He tried to console himself.

Is that what this test is about? Understanding that I have to kill?

He sighed as he stopped walking for a moment. Pulling some food out of his inventory, he began to chew on it as he resumed his journey at a more sedate pace. It tasted like ash on his tongue, but he forced it down anyway.

I can't let this break me. I'll have to kill again, and likely for dumber reasons than this. Whether it's to protect my secrets, or because showing mercy would mean trouble down the road. Or even if it's just to get stronger. I don't think I'll be able to get away from it.

That's that, then, he thought, grasping for straws as he tried to make sense of the situation. *Kill when I need to, try not to when I can get away with it . . . Maybe the other way around.*

He finished up his meal and started walking again.

What's going on? Am I supposed to do something other than just keep moving forward? Or is this another test?

He remembered Spiros telling him about the test he'd undergone to join the society.

Is that what this is? A test of determination? See who has the resolve to just keep on pushing, even without an end in sight. Just a way to cull the numbers as we go through.

It makes sense if that's what this is about. First we fought the scorpion, and I bet there were some who died from that thing. Especially if the one they fought hadn't been as lethargic as mine and attacked right away. Then we faced off against each other in a one v. one. That cuts the number down to half by itself.

Either way, it's not like I have a choice but to keep going. In fact, I have an advantage. I can keep going longer than probably anyone in the trial. None of us were allowed to bring food or water in here, and it's been at least five hours. The longer this goes on, the larger my advantage gets. Simply because I'm the only one who can eat and drink.

A few more hours of mindless walking later, the corridor finally gave way to a large, open cavern, glowing ominously with bright orange-red light.

Luke inched forward cautiously, his shield raised and his sword ready, wary of a surprise attack. This time, however, that didn't seem to be the case.

Walking out of the hall and onto a protruding ledge, Luke observed the scene of the next trial.

There was a giant obelisk, a hundred meters tall, in the middle of a lake of lava. From its tip, even more lava oozed out and dribbled into the pool of bright molten rock at its base. Stones jutted out from it in a helical pattern, leading to a large, shadowy entrance a quarter of the way up.

How are we supposed to get there, though? Luke thought as he inched toward the edge.

"ONLY TEN MAY PASS." An angry but distinctly female voice rang out in the room. At her proclamation, large metallic blocks rose to the surface of the lake. They were irregularly spaced and just far enough apart to allow Luke to jump from one to the other. All led to the center of the room where the obelisk stood.

Luke frowned. *This is going to suck. A lot.* He glanced at the walls encircling the tower, unsurprised to see shadowy figures emerging onto protruding ledges, positioned at regularly spaced intervals. Some of them were already dropping onto the metal platforms. Glancing below, he was glad to see a metal platform just under it, making the first jump easy.

Sighing in resignation at the ridiculous nature of the trial, Luke jumped onto it, wincing as he felt the heat underneath his feet.

Okay, it's pretty hot, but not burning. Thank go— Actually, fuck the gods; this is insane. Why couldn't the hero just give us a written exam, or do a raffle, or anything less lethal for her treasure?

No, that's not fair. We're all idiots who signed up for this death trap of a trial. I knew it was going to be bull. I did it anyway. I just have to live with it now. I chose to take the

Seed. I could have said no. I could have said no to possessing this body. I could have never bought the blade. I could have ignored every quest I received. I didn't.

This is the price. Some dead asshole who loves Floor Is Lava *way too much is making us kill each other for her treasures. Sure, I could never have guessed this would be my life after I died, but Aeolus was eating souls, for fuck's sake. I knew what I was getting into. I knew it wouldn't be peaches and cream.*

I can't cry about it now. I can't cry about it ever. *It's useless. Either I die, and move the fuck on, or I keep going. Keep doing every one of these dumb quests until I'm a god. Then I'll go back to Earth and finally figure out what the One Piece is. Maybe troll some people. It would be so awesome to show up in a flying saucer.*

That's it, Luke. Remember why you're killing all these people.

Hyping himself up as best as he could, he leaped to the next platform, and then the next, and then the next. Ignoring the burning heat on his feet while keeping an eye out for all the others doing the same. So far none of them were close enough to target each other, but that was bound to change, and change soon.

Three platforms later, it finally happened.

Just as he was about to jump, Luke spotted something fly through the air and land on the platform he was about to land on. Luke frowned as he staggered back, covering his eyes as bits of lava splattered at his feet from the exploding talisman.

"Seriously!" Luke shouted at the figure, more than a dozen meters away. Snarling, he pulled out two of his own exploding talismans. Counting down, he tossed one near the foot of the platform the guy was standing on, and one near the platform closest to him. Aiming for the lava instead of the actual person with both of them.

The figure howled as the molten rock splashed on to him, immediately setting his robes on fire. Luke watched dispassionately as he stumbled into the lava and died, too angry to feel guilty for killing another man.

The rest of the figures watched quietly as they processed what had just happened. Some of them reached into their robes and pulled out their own talismans.

"Wait," Luke shouted. "How about we all agree not to go crazy with the explosions? All right? Whoever throws one next gets bombarded by everyone else. Deal? Trust me, I brought a lot of them with me, and I doubt I'm the only one. I don't care how strong you are—all of us will burn to death just like that guy if we go that route."

"Deal. We fight on the steps, or if we need to use the same platform," someone shouted.

"Agreed!"

Luke allowed himself to relax, just a little, as a chorus of voices rang out in agreement. He'd averted his fear of all of them going down in a hail of explosions and splatters of magma.

Mutually assured destruction for the win, I guess.

Focusing on the next platform, he jumped over and, looking at his competition, realized that things would be getting tight and soon.

They had all started quite far from each other, but as they closed in on the structure at the center, the area they were concentrated in kept on getting smaller and smaller.

To his right, two cultivators landed on adjacent platforms, with the only way forward being a platform they would have to share.

Luke jumped onto the next platform, watching them to see how it would play out.

It wasn't pretty. Both of them stared at each other before launching themselves at the platforms at the same time. It would have been smarter to not risk a fight, or maybe even come to an agreement and work together, but instead, as soon as they landed, they fought.

The girl caught her opponent's sword on her shield, and before she could react, her opponent stepped back and kicked, striking the large, circular surface of her shield powerfully. Staggering back, she almost fell into the lava then and there, just barely managing to stop herself from falling. Grunting, she chucked her shield at him as hard as she could.

He knocked it into the lava with ease and was caught off guard when she charged forward and pierced his sword hand.

He watched in despair as his only weapon fell into the lava, seemingly not even registering the pain of having a sword stabbing into him

Disarmed and lacking a shield, her opponent, realizing that he was going to lose, forwent even an attempt at battle and rushed her—impaling himself on her sword as he did so, and tackling them both into the lava.

Luke shook his head at that and kept advancing leap by leap. Until both he and a large, black-robed figure were primed to leap onto a single platform. Just a few hops away from the tower.

I have a bad feeling about this.

CHAPTER 17

Suing for Peace

L et's not fight!" Luke yelled to his would-be opponent, still a few platforms away from where they would inevitably meet. "Fuck," he muttered under his breath as the black-robed man ignored him and leaped to the next platform.

Does he not see how all the fights are turning out? So far, I'm the only person who successfully managed to kill someone who attacked me. The rest all died together. The platforms are way too dangerous of an arena.

Shaking his head, Luke jumped to the next one as well. The only two ways he could imagine surviving were by agreeing not to fight, or by being so fast that fighting became unnecessary. The latter of which ran the risk of an attack from behind.

Is that what he's afraid of? That he can't trust me with his back? Fair, but it makes things a lot harder for both of us.

As he zeroed in onto the platform, though, he realized that both options were becoming increasingly unlikely. Despite the giant man's large frame, he was very nimble. He leaped from one platform to the next with hardly any pause as he moved closer and closer to the obelisk.

As he wiped the sweat off his brow, a feeling of despair manifested in Luke. His opponent had reached the next platform before him.

Cursing under his breath, Luke leaped to the platform just before the occupied one and stared at his opponent, who had drawn his shield and was waiting with a spear leveled at Luke, blocking him from leaping forward.

Luke watched the others as they got closer and closer to the tower. If he wasted too much time with him, he risked not being able to make it before the ten-person limit.

"Look, you can't stand there and expect me to impale myself on your spear."

"I can," the other man replied stubbornly.

"No, you can't, you oaf. If we both stay here, neither of us will make it." Luke tried to explain the situation to him.

"Or you can go the long way around," the other man offered.

Luke lifted his arms in exasperation.

"Are you serious? I won't make it at all, then. I'd rather take my chances with you."

He shrugged and steadied his spear. "So be it."

"Aggg," Luke groaned, snarling in frustration. "Fine, then!" He jumped, activating a protective talisman in midair.

The bubble that surrounded him clashed with the man's spear, and for a moment Luke thought he would bounce off the spear's tip and land in the lava, burning to death as his gambit failed. Instead, the spear ripped free from the giant's hands and rolled into the lava. Luke's bubble dissipated at the same time, and he fell straight onto him.

Before the large man could rip him off and throw him into the lava, Luke wrapped his arms around his neck and swung his body around, pulling them both onto the searing metallic surface of the platform. Sending his sword into his inventory to get a better grip, he ignored the burning pain on his back and did his best to suffocate his enemy.

An attempt that failed right away. His opponent was too strong. With almost casual ease, he pried Luke's arms free from his throat.

This is bad. Think. Think. Think.

Luke summoned an already-activated explosive talisman into his mouth, desperately trying to keep a hold on the man as the timer ticked down in his mind.

With three seconds to go, the man finally managed to free himself. Hastily getting to his feet, he stood over Luke's exhausted form, his shield raised over his head, ready to bludgeon him to death. Luke would have died then and there had his opponent not taken a second to catch his breath.

One second to go.

Luke spit out the explosive talisman, calling forth another protective talisman as he did. The bubble came to life around him milliseconds before the detonation.

I love talismans, he thought with a grin.

Watching the man stagger back, Luke was disappointed that he had managed to block most of the explosion's force with his shield. Recalling his sword into his hand, Luke leaped forward, his blade snaking between his opponent's legs, biting into his flesh. With a flex of his wrist, Luke changed the angle of his blade, hooking it just over his opponent's knee as he did, and with all the force he could muster, he pulled it toward him.

Blinking blood out of his eyes, he flashed a savage grin as his opponent's leg came clean off. Scrambling to his feet, he kicked out his other leg and, with the giant man down, stuck his blade into his throat.

+7 Stat Points

He put all the points into Agility as he struggled to regain his breath.

Fuck. That's three bodies in one day. If I keep going at this rate, my body count is going to surpass my actual body count, he thought sardonically.

Leaning down, he collected his opponent's shield, slinging his own on his back, and quickly riffled through his pockets, just in case he had anything useful. He was rapidly running out of protective talismans and was already regretting not buying even more of them.

"Sorry about this, but you don't need anything you own anymore. Sorry for killing you, too, and if you're still lingering around, I hope no one tries to eat your soul. Also, I tried to do this peacefully, so really, this is all on you," Luke muttered under his breath. "Also, why are you so poor?" He finally managed to find a single explosive talisman and a bottle of cherry-colored pills in the giant's pockets, discreetly storing them into his inventory, not even bothering to read the description on the bottle of pills as he did. He'd already wasted too much time.

Kicking the body into the lava, he resumed his journey, hopping from platform to platform.

Okay, just five more to go.

"No fighting!" Luke yelled at the top of his lungs as he and a lithe woman began closing in on the same platform, just three jumps away from the obelisk.

"Okay. But I'm watching you. Try something, and I'll throw every talisman I have at you."

"Same," Luke responded, marveling at the ease with which he could now move. The benefits of having forty-two points in Agility, now officially his highest attribute, were readily apparent.

In the past, he hadn't found much use for Agility; sparring in a ring was a constrained affair, and while being a little faster and a little more limber with each increase was nice, Luke was still far from being fast or skilled enough to leverage that increased capacity in an actual fight. His rudimentary fighting style defaulted to punching hard and tackling his opponents to the ground and wrestling them when the punching failed him.

Leaping from platform to platform, though, was a different feeling entirely; he could feel the increase like night and day.

Surveying the competition, he was relieved to see that no one had made it to the center yet. Not that he would envy the first person to make it there. They would immediately draw the attention of everyone who was still on the platforms, and the tower was in perfect view of everyone participating.

Whoever tries to climb it first is not going to be in for a fun time. They're going to get pelted with talismans. Actually— Luke stopped four platforms away from the tower. *It's better to let people exhaust their talismans before I give it a try. I'd rather risk a sword fight than be blown off and fall into the lava.*

"What are you doing?" the woman yelled at him, rapidly leaping from the third platform to the second, then the last. She didn't even wait a second before hopping on to the helical staircase.

She made it two steps before an arrow pierced her neck. Her hands clutched her throat in shock, and she fell into the lava.

Avoiding that.

Luke's eyes narrowed as he mapped the trajectory of the arrow, following it back to a black-robed figure to his right. His eyes briefly met the other man's before he positioned his shield in that general direction.

That's really not good. I'll need to activate another protective talisman, but those things give way after a single solid hit.

I could double-wield shields, too. No. One on my back, and one facing my side, and my sword in my left hand facing the tower. That way I'm covering both my blind spot and protecting my biggest openings. It'll stop an instant kill shot, but getting my leg blown off, or an arrow through my ankle, is just as bad.

Think. Think. Think.

There's no way to sneak up there, not with everyone watching the way like a hawk.

I have . . . six more of those protective talismans left. Should I just spam them? No . . . they'll chew through them. I'll use 'em if I need to, but with how crazy this is, I need to conserve my resources.

Luke watched another person start climbing the tower. This time, he managed to catch the arrow with his shield but then fell into the lava when a talisman exploded by his head a moment later. One carried by another arrow that came from a different direction.

Not looking good. Not at all. At least two snipers I'll have to watch out for.

Luke hopped foot to foot, frowning as he did so. *Are the platforms getting hotter?*

They were.

Just what I needed, a shrinking field of play. I can use this, though. If they get too hot to stand on, then that means less people to snipe anyone who tries to break away.

He looked around the cavern again, noticing a few dozen people all standing on platforms two to three jumps away from the obelisk. Having seen what had happened to the last two people who had attempted to climb the tower, they were understandably cautious of meeting a similar fate.

Not that Luke could blame them—the tomb had turned out to be far more lethal than he, or anyone for that matter, had expected. Save perhaps the Elders who had sent them here in the first place.

Something's gotta give, though. We can't just stand around here forever.

He winced in pain as the platform suddenly became hotter.

At this rate, we'll burn alive before someone moves.

A moment later, half the platforms suddenly sank beneath the lava. Those unfortunate enough to stand on them went with them.

Okay, that's it.

Luke activated a protective talisman and leaped into action, and he wasn't the only one, either. With the threat of random death if they delayed too long, it suddenly wasn't worth staying and waiting for an opportune time.

With everyone rushing in, it suddenly made more sense to bull-rush the staircase and seek protection in chaos.

An arrow struck Luke's barrier, and another whizzed by his head as he leaped onto the final platform. Reapplying his bubble, Luke leaped onto the first of the helical steps leading to the cavern inside the obelisk, then the second, before his barrier timed out. He frowned as he applied another one the same instant, counting the five-second timers in his head.

I need to be more careful with how I use my inventory. I doubt anyone will guess what I'm actually doing right away, but that's still no reason to be careless.

He leaped onto the second step as he counted the people ahead of him. He sighed in relief when he counted seven. Relief instantly turned to shock as a handful of explosive talismans sailed over his head and knocked five of those seven into the lava.

That's it.

Luke pulled out all twenty of his preactivated explosive talismans and tossed them into the crowd behind him, doubling up on his protective talismans as he did so. Then, without looking at the devastation he had wrought, he rapidly climbed to the third, fourth, and fifth step. The talismans didn't last long.

An arrow bounced off the shield on his back, and Luke activated another protective talisman.

Just a little more.

Pushing himself as far as he could, he rapidly ascended the three more steps before his talisman fizzled out.

He mentally prodded his inventory to activate another one, only to frown as none came. He was out.

Fuck, fuck, FUCK!

He climbed one more step before risking a glance behind him, batting away an arrow aimed directly at him as he did so.

Luck seemed to be on his side, though, as in the next moment another series of explosive talismans burst in the middle of the crowd, knocking the vast majority of them into the lava.

This is brutal.

Luke raced up another three steps, feeling naked with the lacking state of his defenses.

Just two more steps, and I'm there.

A talisman landed on the step in front of him. He gritted his teeth and leaped onto the step anyway, extracting every ounce of value from his Agility attribute he could to make sure his foot landed on it, sending the explosive talisman straight to his inventory milliseconds before it blew.

One more step.

He scrambled forward and dived onto the last step. An arrow sank into the flesh of his thigh. Wincing in pain, he stumbled into the cavern. A bright flash of light surrounded him.

I can't believe I made it.

CHAPTER 18

Isolated and Alone

Luke groaned in pain as he stumbled to his feet. Desperately scanning the room for threats, and for the moment ignoring the arrow lodged firmly in his thigh through sheer effort of will, he gritted his teeth in pain as he raised his sword, on guard against a potential enemy.

He sagged in relief when he found none. His vision swimming, he collapsed to his knees as adrenaline left his body.

Fuck yeah! I made it!

That was . . . insane, though. A current of pain surged through his body. *And I'm mostly intact, too.* He strained his neck in an effort to look at the wound, grimacing in disgust as he saw the arrow's shaft sticking out of him.

He gripped it as gently as he could and cussed in pain when it moved, just slightly, in response to his touch. With a flex of his will, he sent it to his inventory. He blinked away tears as the now-empty hole in his thigh flared with heat, and hot blood oozed out of it.

Another benefit of the Seed. It's a pro at surgery, he thought morbidly, blinking even more tears out of his eyes as he did. *Let's see what I have, though.*

Summoning a strip of cloth from his inventory, he wrapped it around his wound tightly, using it as a makeshift bandage, and scrolled through every item he had stored away. Most of it was food and water. He'd stocked even more of it in the week since he got his current quest, packing enough to survive even months in the wilderness.

Status | Quests | **Inventory**
Capacity: 278.3 kg of 1,520 kg
Items:
Healing Potion (x 6)
Tier—Mortal
Aid in recovery
Healing Pill (x 7)

Tier—Mortal

Aid in recovery

Blood Pills (x 6)

Tier—Mortal

Replenish blood

Stamina Pills (x 5)

Tier—Mortal

Replenish stamina

He was happy to see his capacity had increased to well over a thousand kilograms. At this point in time, it was more than he needed, and it would continue to scale rapidly, far beyond what he ever imagined using.

Reading over the description of the various medicines he'd accumulated, some purchased and others pillaged, he withdrew a vial of the healing potion and one of each pill. A grin came over his face as he pinched one between his fingers.

Popping pills and dropping bodies. I should write a rap song about it when I have the time. Or when I'm not cleaning out a wound, bleeding to death in a tomb.

Errantly, he tossed the pills in his mouth and washed them down with water. Undoing the hastily done bandage on his leg, he cleaned the wound as best as he could with a wet cloth, making faces of disgust every time the blood-soaked rag came into his sight.

This is exactly why I didn't want to be a doctor. I hate blood. Well, blood and the thought of performing prostate exams. Mostly the latter.

Uncorking the vial of healing potion, he spilled it all onto a fresh piece of cloth and fastened it around his wound.

A sigh of relief immediately slipped through his mouth as the efficacy of the medicine became apparent. The pain leveled off to tolerable levels moments after the bandage was applied. And a few seconds later, his whole leg started to feel numb, providing even more comfort.

Why did I ever doubt honest-to-god magic medicine?

. . . Probably because it was so cheap. Still, this is amazing. Nothing on Earth comes this close. Wait? Am I high? Why can't I feel my leg? Should I amputate it . . .

No! What's going on? Why is everything so colorful?

He waved his hand in front of his face.

Has my hand always been this pretty? So many lines. Evolution really is—

He blinked.

Why are my eyes getting so heavy?

Slumping against the wall, he fell asleep. The toll of the day mixed with the effects of the medicine knocked him out instantly.

• • •

Groggily rubbing the sleep out of his eyes, Luke leaped to his feet when he realized that he wasn't at his house in the society. The events of the previous day came rushing back.

Taking a deep breath, he sat back down as he processed all that had happened.

I killed so many people. Shaking his head, he suddenly slapped himself. Hard. *No. There's no time for that right now. Just falling asleep in this place was dumb—I can't let myself fall apart on top of that. I just need to remember why I'm doing this. To live. To go back. To . . . No, that's about it, and that's enough of a reason.*

Ignoring the sorry state of his mental health, he looked around the room again. He was surprised to see a bed in the corner and on a small table beside it, food and a pitcher of water.

Getting back to his feet, he hobbled forward, ignoring the throbbing pain in his leg as he stumbled toward his destination. Collapsing heavily on the bed, he raked his eyes over the food, frowning in distaste at the cold chicken and rice before his eyes landed on the other contents of the table.

A vial of glowing blue liquid, resting atop a letter. Moving the vial aside for the moment, he read through the note.

Congratulations.

You have proved effective against beast, man, and chaos. You have proven your destiny and earned the right to advance to the next stage.

In the vial is a Warrior-tier healing potion. Drinking it will restore you to optimal health; if it does not, your wounds are too severe, and you are not fated to continue living.

You are not alone in this—death comes for nearly all of us that chase divinity, and only those who can escape its grasp are worthy of divine power. I'd suggest you take the time until your inevitable passing to appreciate the life you lived and the bonds you made.

If the potion has healed you fully, the next stage will begin in:

14 hours, 43 minutes, and 12 seconds.

14 hours, 43 minutes, and 11 seconds.

. . .

What the . . . Luke blinked in surprise as the seconds ticked down on the page. *Magic really is something. Well, not quite smartphone level, but still pretty cool.* He continued reading.

Be warned. All those who have survived, I deem worthy. Killing will not be permitted any longer, on the pain of death.

Alexia Xancrest

Empress and Hero of Carim

. . . That's good? Really good, actually.

Luke folded up the letter and held up the vial of potion, sending it to his inventory as he did.

<table>
<tr><td align="center">Status | Quests | Inventory</td></tr>
<tr><td align="center">Capacity: 278.3 kg of 1,640 kg

Items:

Healing Potion

Tier—Warrior

Heals all nonfatal wounds for Mortal-tier beings. Efficacy decreases as the tier of the consumer increases.</td></tr>
</table>

Basically what the letter said. It seems like she expected a lot of people to die in the lava and those that did survive to be injured.

. . . Crazy asshole.

Luke folded the letter in half and sent the food to his inventory. He pulled out a fresh and steaming-hot meal instead, and after a moment of deliberation, selected one of his Mortal-tier healing potions as well.

He decided that his injury, while severe, didn't demand the use of a Warrior-tier potion. *Saving it for later is the move for now.*

I should eat first, he thought, bringing the food to his mouth. *I'm definitely not going to have an appetite once I start poking around with my bandages.*

Of course it has to be sticky. Why would it not be sticky? Luke complained to himself, sweat dripping down his face as he tried to pry apart his bandage.

I'm dumb. Why am I even trying to peel it off?

Concentrating briefly, he sent the bandage to his inventory and sighed in pleasure when the crusty strip of cloth was replaced by fresh air, letting his sweaty skin of his thigh breathe. *That's it*, he thought. *Just having an inventory alone is worth all of this. Maybe not all of it, but some of it for sure.*

It healed a lot better than I thought it would. I wonder how much of that is the medicine and how much of it is my Constitution? I've almost tripled it since I possessed Max's body. It was, what, thirteen when I started.

He opened his status.

<table>
<tr><td align="center">Status | Quests | Inventory</td></tr>
<tr><td align="center">Name: Lukas King

Tier: Mortal

Mana: 640

Rate: 15% per hour

Strength: 40 > 41

Agility: 35 > 44</td></tr>
</table>

Constitution: 38 > 40

Arcana: 32

Stat Points: 3

Bloodline: Locked. Conditions not met. (1/10,000)

Charges: 7/10

That's . . . wow. He tallied up all the points he'd gained. *That's definitely more than I was expecting. Three free stat points—that's more than I ever got before. Unless I got them from killing stuff, but I already spent those particular ones. Which means that I got these points the normal way. Except, why so many? My other stats went up a lot, too. Five points altogether, if I don't count the points I put into Agility after killing that guy, and combined with the free points, that's eight in total.*

Which is nearly double what I usually get by working out and sparring to exhaustion every day. I shouldn't have that many—but I do. So, there's definitely something that I'm missing. All the fighting was exhausting, but I was only really exerting myself in short bursts. It was intense, no doubt about it, but nowhere close to how hard I pushed myself in the society.

He shook his head.

I'll put the free points in my Constitution stat for now. More points in there should help me heal a bit better. He prompted the Seed. *Fuck, that feels good,* he thought, as the added points took effect. *That feeling is never going to get old.*

Whatever the mystery behind the extra points is, I'll save it for another day.

His wound throbbed with pain once again, pulling him from his musings. Cleaning it out again, he soaked another piece of cloth with a healing potion and wrapped it around his thigh. Then for good measure, he popped another set of healing and blood pills.

Can't hurt, and who the fuck knows what's next? The medicine will be hard to replace now that I'm not returning to the society, but it's better than dying because I can't walk straight. The note said we can't kill each other, but with how loony these trials have been, I shouldn't bet on it.

He picked up the note once again.

14 hours, 29 minutes, and 52 seconds.

So much time to kill.

"ARGGGGG!"

Would it have been too much to have a puzzle or a magazine? Oh, great hero and empress. He tossed and turned in the bed.

Hey, Seed. What can you tell me about this trial? What's coming next?

He frowned when it didn't answer. *I should have expected that.*

Getting up from his bed, he paced around the room. *Is there really no washroom? Really, empress and hero, you can make insane and deadly obstacle courses, but you can't put a bucket in a room? Asshole.*

I wonder, though . . . He focused, and his eyes widened in a mixture of surprise and relief. *Okay, that is wild! I never would have guessed that I would be able to send shit and piss straight into my inventory. Best feature ever.*

Luke stared at the countdown on the note, watching it impatiently as the seconds ticked down, one excruciating second at a time.

He was grateful for the downtime. He really was. Another set of pills, and another potion-soaked bandage had seen him make a speedy, bordering on miraculous, recovery. The hole had, at some point over the hours, sealed over, leaving only a faint scar in its place.

It still hurt when he placed some pressure on it, but since he could walk and even jump with little to no discomfort, Luke was confident that it wouldn't hamper him going forward. And even if it did, he was sure that it wouldn't be more than a minor inconvenience.

All that aside, sitting alone in a quiet room with nothing to do had been torture. So when the walls finally opened up with the oh-so-familiar mechanized whir as the timer on the note hit zero, he grinned in anticipation.

He drew his sword and raised his shield, ready for any surprises that might come his way, carefully making his way down the torchlit corridor.

Making it to the end, he was surprised when it opened up and, instead of a monster, what greeted him was a small crowd of people. Haggard, with tousled hair and torn robes, they emerged into the same room. Most of them were dressed in blue robes, marking them as Inner Disciples and at the late-stage Mortal tier, with a smattering of black-robed individuals.

"Luke! You made it! I was worried about you."

CHAPTER 19

Meeting with Friends

Spiros!" Luke looked at the familiar figure making his way through the crowd. He frowned as he saw the sorry state his friend was in.

His clothes were full of holes, singed, and stained with blood. His hair caked with dirt, blood, and what looked like the remains of an eyeball. His eyes were bloodshot and had deep black bags underneath them, as if he hadn't slept in days. Looking at the blood-covered spear he was carrying with him, Luke had a pretty good idea of what had kept him up at night.

I guess I should be happy that the medicine knocked me out for a few hours. I can't imagine I'd have slept well, or at all, if it didn't.

"That was hell," Spiros said, wearing a fake smile. Then, leaning the spear against the wall behind him, he leaned forward and hugged him.

"It was hell." Luke patted his back. A knot built up in his throat.

It sucked for me, but I'm a grown-ass man. Spiros is, what, sixteen at best. Fuck, I can't even imagine how fucked-up I'm going to be because of this now. Having to do what we just did when I was his age, it would probably have shattered me.

"Sorry." Spiros stepped back. A single tear fell down his face, which he rubbed away quickly.

"Nah, it's okay. That was . . . It was hell. Like you said. I'm just glad that it's over. I'm glad you made it out okay, and I'm even more glad you and I didn't see each other."

"Me, too." He sniffed, rubbing the snot out of his nose with the back of his hand. "Ahem."

Luke heard a woman clear her throat. "Arya!" He grinned at her, trying not to wince as he took in her less than picture-perfect appearance. She didn't look quite as bad as Spiros did, but she had clearly seen better days. Then, stepping forward, he gave her a hug. Feeling her tense up, he feared he might have overstepped, but a moment later she relaxed into it.

With how often Spiros hugs me, I forgot that it isn't actually casual behavior. It is nice, though.

"Hey, Luke. You made it, huh? I had a feeling you would."

"I do inspire confidence in others, don't I?" He grinned at her. "Arya, this is Spiros. Spiros, this is Arya. We, uh, we're all in the society together." Luke scratched the back of his head awkwardly.

Arya looked at Spiros with surprise. "So, you're Spiros. I've heard a lot about you."

Luke blinked in confusion before looking over to Spiros, only to see an equally confused expression on his face as well.

"You have? And what?" he asked rapidly, looking increasingly stressed. "What have you heard?"

"You're the youngest person in the society's history to make it to the midstage. People talk about it all the time. You're kind of famous because of it."

"Oh. Yeah? I only talk to my cousins in the society, so I wouldn't really know."

"Now that you mention it, Arya, I heard about Spiros on my first day in the society, too. Ethan was singing praises about him."

"See, even Luke knows you're famous."

They grinned as the spear-wielder suddenly blushed red, opening and closing his mouth like a fish as he scratched the back of his head.

"Wait." Arya suddenly leaned forward. "Is the rumor true? In the entrance exam did you really—"

"SO!" Luke interrupted her. "What do you think is going to happen next?" he asked, ignoring Spiros's sigh of relief.

That kind of gave it away, buddy. She knows you shat your pants now.

She looked at the two of them oddly. "I don't know. I really don't know what to expect anymore. This isn't anything like I imagined. I never would have thought the hero would make us fight to the death like this."

Luke cocked his head in confusion. "Why do you seem excited about that?"

"I'm not!" She visibly recoiled, adjusting the quiver of arrows on her back. "It's just that . . . Look, if the hero went to such lengths to get rid of the chaff—"

"The chaff?" Spiros interrupted her.

I'm with you, buddy, Luke thought.

"The note said 'beast, man, and chaos.' I've heard that before," she continued, ignoring Spiros's interruption. "It's an old adage about . . ." She shook her head. "Anyway, she wouldn't do what she did for no reason. All of the society's history books describe her as this kind and generous figure. An empress who ruled both fairly and justly."

"I don't get your point," Luke said.

"My point is that whatever her inheritance is, it has to justify what we had to get through to get here." Her eyes glimmered with greed. "A treasure belonging to a Hero, one open to all the mortals on the island. It has to be something of immense value. At the very least, it's something that can pave the way to Warrior. If not to Hero."

I have something that paves the way to God. Yet, I'm still here bumming around with everyone else here for what essentially amounts to scraps. C'est la vie, as they say.

"Wow." Luke tried his best to seem impressed at the prospect.

"What do you think it is, though?" Spiros asked.

"I . . . I don't know. It could be anything. I don't know enough about the higher stages to even begin to speculate."

"It shouldn't be long now. I think we're just waiting for everyone to come out of their rooms at this point." Luke nodded, gesturing at the walls. Like the room with the obelisk, the room they were in now was circular as well, if a lot smaller.

On seemingly random parts of the wall, entrances had opened, out of which each person had come. As they watched, another entrance opened up between two existing ones, and out of it another blue-robed cultivator walked out. Surveying the room with his sword raised, he lowered it when he realized that no one was fighting. A moment later, another blue-robed cultivator shouted at him from across the room.

"See how that path opened perfectly in the middle of those two, and now they're evenly spaced? I think every bit of wall bigger than"—Luke lifted his hands and spaced so that they were about three feet apart—"is actually a closed door. There's probably some people still sleeping in them."

Looks of understanding dawned on their faces.

"I would have figured that the freaky voice from the lava room would wake everyone up or something." Spiros ran a hand through his hair, pulling it back immediately when he realized just how icky his hair was.

"Or that they would know not to oversleep when something so important is on the line. All of you saw the letter, too, right, with the countdown?" Arya asked.

Luke shrugged his shoulder, leaning against an empty bit of wall as he settled in for what he suspected would be a rather lengthy wait. "It's possible that they're just taking their time walking down the hallway. With how it turned out last time, I wouldn't blame them for being anxious."

"We had a day," Arya deadpanned.

Luke raised his eyebrow.

"What?"

"Nothing."

"He's surprised that you're so callous." Spiros grinned at her.

"I'm surprised you shat your pants. You're a little old for that, don't you think?" She glared at him.

"That's a low blow."

"That was some lowly behavior."

"All right. Enough, you two," Luke interjected.

Poor kid. No one is ever going to let him live that down. Ever. At least he's out of his funk, though.

Two hours later, everyone in the chamber was staring at a single bit of wall between two entryways, waiting in heavy silence for the last person in the trial to show up, growing more and more impatient with every second that passed.

When it did finally open, Luke was surprised to see he recognized the person who walked out.

"That's, uh . . . Yarn, right?" Luke asked, looking at his immaculate blue robes and perfectly combed hair. "Why does he look so together?"

"Yjarn," Arya corrected him, "and I don't know. Maybe he got lucky and was in a group where no one could challenge him."

"Is he also from the society?" Spiros whispered, his eyes tracking the bearded figure walking into the room.

"Yeah, Arya and him have some history."

"Oh. I'm sorry, Luke," Spiros said while patting him on the shoulder consolingly.

What did he just say? Luke's mouth opened and closed in shock.

"Not that kind of history." Arya looked between the pair oddly. "Don't worry about it—if anything happens, I'll take care of it."

"I have your back, too, Luke." Spiros nodded at him solemnly. "I don't know how useful I'll be against an Inner Disciple, but I'll—"

How do I turn him off?

Luke palmed his face. "It's not like that. He and Arya have bad blood."

A look of comprehension finally dawned on the boy's face.

Moments later, all the torches lighting up the room turned dim. The floor shook, and three podiums emerged from the ground in the middle of the room. The people standing near them stumbled back in shock.

The air above them shimmered, like a mirage on a hot day, before condensing into a vague apparition of a blonde-haired woman, one that became clearer and clearer until it looked like she was actually floating in the room.

"She's beautiful," Spiros muttered underneath his breath. Luke nodded slightly. She really was.

"Greetings." Her lips moved, and sound rang throughout the room, echoing from the walls instead of her lips.

She sounds like a bell. It's haunting. Luke looked at her, transfixed.

"I apologize for the pain you suffered and inflicted to get here. I did not create these trials lightly, and while the price is high, so is the value of what you seek." She gestured vaguely to the three podiums, and on each one, a miniature hologram of her appeared. One wielding a sword, another a spear, and the last a shield.

Each of the three holograms leaped into action, moving gracefully from one stance into the next, each of them in a way that felt *right*.

Poetry through action.

Luke stared, compelled, at the version of her swinging the sword, moving seamlessly between different forms. Each was designed for a singular purpose, but they all flowed together into an intricate dance. One that seemed as natural as a drop of rain falling from the sky, or a leaf drifting in the wind. She was tapping into a rhythm Luke didn't even know existed.

As suddenly as they started, the holograms went still, flickering away as if they were never there. Leaving Luke with a burning desire to attempt what he had just seen.

I have to do that. I need to do that. I must do that.

Unconsciously he gripped his sword and took it halfway out of his sheath before he caught himself.

What just happened? He stared at his hand, confused, not realizing he had even moved. Looking around the room, he realized that he wasn't the only one, either. The entire crowd looked like they had sunk into a trance and were just now waking up from it.

"What you just witnessed, you must do. Sword, spear, and shield. Those were the weapons I wielded in my life. These techniques, these forms—I created them, or perhaps discovered them, after centuries spent on fields of battle. They came to me in bits and pieces, through moments of revelation, insight, and epiphany." She looked around solemnly.

"To inherit my treasures, you must master these techniques to my satisfaction. All of them." She waved her hand, and a loud, mechanized whir echoed through the room.

Rapidly the room became larger, doubling, then quadrupling in size. The ceiling shimmered, displaying a fake sky above their heads. Arenas appeared on one end, racks full of wooden weapons beside them. The doors leading to their rooms all shifted to one wall. Opposite to them, cages full of all manner of beasts appeared. From the white scorpions from before to tigers, snakes, and bears.

The podiums rearranged themselves into a triangular formation, in the new center of the room. What looked like yoga mats arrayed in front of them.

Whoa.

"Only those who can master the techniques will be allowed to leave. Those who do well will have the opportunity to select a single treasure from my treasury. If you cannot learn, you will stay here as prisoners until you age and die."

What?

CHAPTER 20

It's Training Time

The hero's apparition vanished moments after delivering those ominous words, leaving the crowd alone to process the information.

Surveying the room, Luke wasn't all that surprised to see that most of those present were okay with the situation. They were all confident enough in their skills to come here, after all, and then survive the shit show that resulted from it. None of them truly believed that they wouldn't be able to learn the techniques being displayed—in fact, a significant portion of the people were walking around with excited smiles, seemingly pleased with the arrangement.

This predicament was both a chance to learn some clearly mystical and equally mysterious techniques, and walk away with a treasure at the end. A classic win-win scenario.

I might be a bit pessimistic, but I don't think there's going to be as many smiling faces when some of them inevitably realize that they'll never leave here.

"Luke. Arya. I think I might die here. I think we all might die here," Spiros said, looking more panicked than Luke had ever seen him.

"Why?" Luke asked, suddenly feeling a nervous knot forming in his gut.

"Those techniques. There aren't just motions that we need to imitate. They represent fundamental aspects of reality. It's hard to explain . . . but you'll get it when you try doing them. It's like, the world itself will stop you. It's . . . You'll see," he finished awkwardly.

"What do you know, and how do you know it?" Arya tilted her head, her eyes squinted, as if she was trying to solve a particularly hard problem.

"Well, uh. I've seen them before. I mean, not them"—he pointed to the podiums—"but other techniques like them. My grandpa showed me a few."

"Your grandpa showed you a few?" Luke looked at him incredulously.

"Yeah. He's in the Hero tier, so . . ."

"Huh."

"What?"

Arya suddenly stepped in really close, pulling both Luke and Spiros into a very tight huddle.

"Your grandpa is a Hero?" she whispered as quietly as she could.

Now, isn't that a bombshell. It does explain some things about him, though. Not why he shat his pants, but some things, Luke thought, recalling Spiros's startling strength when they were pulling the snake back into the town. He had meant to ask him about it earlier but had forgotten when he saw Arke not long after.

"Yeah—"

"There aren't any heroes on the island," she interrupted.

"Well, I never said I was from here, did I? My family has this thing where they send us all out when we turn fifteen, and we're not supposed to come back until we become warriors. Me, June, and Myko were all sent here."

". . . so where are you from?" Luke asked.

"You probably haven't heard of it."

"Come on, just tell us. What's the harm?" Arya egged him on, batting her eyelashes.

Luke suppressed a grin when he saw Spiros suddenly turn pink.

He really is a simp.

"Nothing, I guess. We're not really supposed to talk about it, though, so on the off chance that we actually do make it out of here, promise not to tell my sister I told you, okay? She'll kick my ass."

"I promise, I won't."

"Me, too," Luke chipped in.

"Okay. I'm from Troy. It's a kingdom, way north and a little right from the archipelago."

Troy? *The Brad Pitt movie!*

Luke sighed softly. It only made sense that if the gods were real, so were some of the locations that featured in the myths.

Really, I should have figured it all out sooner.

Olympus is real. So is Atlantis. I have Bellerophon's sword attached to my waist; a mythicized city shouldn't really surprise me, but you know what, it still does. He eyed Spiros. *For his sake, I hope his home doesn't get razed to the ground by some Greeks hiding in a fake horse.*

Hmm. Does this mean that Achilles is kicking around somewhere. What about Hercules? Or is it Heracles? Whatever, it's another mystery for when I get Arke off my tail. It would be cool to meet them, though.

"What?" Luke asked as the other two looked at him oddly. Spiros's eyes narrowed.

"You've heard of Troy before?"

Well, duh. Who hasn't? . . . Unfortunately, I don't think I can share why I know about it, or how.

"I've heard about it in passing. A story my . . . The man who raised me told me when I was a kid. Something about it having legendary walls. I thought it was just one of those things they tell kids."

"Oh." Spiros grinned, buying Luke's explanation. "You've heard about those, huh. There aren't really walls—it's more like a"—he made a vague dome shape with his hands—"giant protective talisman that surrounds the kingdom. It's impenetrable. They say Lord Poseidon himself built it. When I become a Warrior, you two should come back with me and see it. The way light reflects off when the suns set and rise it is beautiful."

Luke grinned at him. "Maybe. I don't know about following you there, but I'll come and visit sometime."

"I'll keep an eye out for you in that case. Just ask around for the House of Paris."

Luke's thoughts immediately started churning a hundred miles a second.

Paris. Helen. Troy. He looked at Spiros again, doing his level best to keep his expression neutral. *Is he going to start the Trojan War? Holy fucking shit. No way, that can't be it.*

"Wait. Who is Poseidon?" asked Arya, looking between Luke and Spiros and pulling Luke out of his thoughts.

Fuck. Was I not supposed to know that? Keeping things secret is so much easier when I don't have to talk to anybody.

"You don't know?" Spiros looked at Arya, then at Luke. "He knows."

"Uh, the person who raised me was a fisherman . . . I didn't really think he was real, but when I joined the society, I thought that there might be more to those stories than I thought."

"Oh, makes sense. Lord Poseidon is a god. He rules Atlantis. Kind of like Lord Zeus rules Olympus. I figured with the tomb and everything, everyone would know about him."

"Yeah, they don't really tell mortals too much around here." Luke shrugged.

"Well, yeah. Otherwise everyone would start cultivating." Spiros shrugged, too.

Luke and Arya looked at him curiously before Arya shook her head.

"All right, this is all really fascinating. But let's focus on the techniques for now. We'll talk more later," said Arya, stepping back and looking toward the podiums. "I'm going to start with the shield technique. What about you two?"

Spiros lifted his spear, and Luke touched the hilt of his sword in response.

"Good luck." She walked off.

Sitting down on a mat, with the best view of the podium he could find, Luke joined the others in watching the hologram of the hero's sword technique.

He watched her every move with an intensity that surprised even him. For the moment, he ignored the urge to draw his sword and follow along with her movements. He traced the sword as one movement flowed into the other seamlessly and with inhuman grace.

He imagined himself, standing opposite her, his xiphos in hand, looking for an opening, some way to get past her sword. He waited, and he waited and he waited, not seeing any way to get through her defense. He grew increasingly impatient as the seconds ticked by. Seconds that turned to minutes, then turned to hours, until pangs of hunger gnawed at him from the inside, and his throat grew parched with thirst.

She's not even moving that fast. Why can't I find any way in?

As if in response to his frustration, the image of the hero fully extended her sword and lunged forward. At that moment, Luke was sure. Sure that she had made a fatal mistake. Sure that he could slip past her guard and pierce her heart.

Not hesitating for even a second, he stepped into her guard, sword thrusting forward. A strike poised to pierce her heart.

Luke's head rolled off his shoulder, and he was back in his body. Whatever had sucked him into the illusion had released its hold.

The hero continued her dance. Unfazed and unbothered.

A bead of sweat rolled down his face, and his breath suddenly came in short bursts, as if he had just gone a dozen rounds in the ring. He clutched his hand to his chest and scrunched his robes. His other hand sought support from the ground as he desperately tried not to fall over. Trying not to throw up, he reassured himself that he was alive.

What the fuck was that?

No answer came to his mind. There was clearly something beyond the physical happening. Observing the others watching the recording, he shook his head. They were all still in a trance, likely still having the same out-of-body experience he had.

Quietly getting to his feet, he ducked between the mats, careful not to disturb anyone. A thoughtful but ultimately pointless endeavor. As engrossed as everyone was, he could slice their throats and they wouldn't even realize that they had died.

Finding an open and out-of-the-way space near the arenas, he drew his sword. After spending hours watching the hero go through the same simple but beautiful moves, he was confident in his ability to perform them. Or at least go through the motions.

He lifted his sword, holding it vertically in front of him. The first motion was simple. All he had to do was tilt his sword to the side and slice it down diagonally. A motion he had performed hundreds, if not thousands of times before, since he had bought his sword.

His blade moved a millimeter forward, and immediately he felt resistance. As if there was another sword pressed against his, stopping him from moving forward.

What?

Quietly, Luke started to panic at the strange event. Remembering Spiros's words, he finally realized what they meant.

How am I supposed to learn this if I can't even do the actions?

A prompt from the Seed flashed before his eyes.

Quest Alert: A Paragon's Path

Warning—the technique First Stance of the Sword, if learned, must be fully mastered as per the Paragon's Path. Perfection in all things is required to advance to the Warrior tier.

Create Skill: First Stance of the Sword

Yes/No

Luke eased his grip on his sword and lowered it. Whatever had stopped his movements didn't prevent him from backing away. Blinking in surprise, he read over the warning.

Huh.

Luke opened the status and read through the original quest prompt. It hadn't changed. The only conditions still listed were maxing out his Bloodline and getting all four attributes to one thousand at the same time.

So what's this about, then? If I learn it, I have to master it, and if I can't or don't, I'm stuck as a mortal until I die? I guess that's not too different from being trapped in here, but still. Bummer.

His eyes flashed between the two other podiums.

Chances are, once I attempt to learn those two, I'll also be required to master them completely. I can't leave here until I learn them to the hero's satisfaction, either. Not unless I find a way out of here, but I have the first quest to work through as well.

I need to get the hero's mask, activate the portal, and skedaddle.

Decisions, decisions, decisions.

Navigating back to the quest alert, he read it again.

What does it mean, "create skill"? He directed the query at the Seed and frowned when it didn't answer.

This is bullshit. The Paragon's Path locks me to the Mortal tier unless I do everything perfectly. I thought that was just my attributes—murdering a bunch of stuff is doable, easy even. Even if it ended up taking me years, I was confident I could get there. Mastering a skill, though? There's no guarantee I'll ever be able to do so.

Was accepting the Paragon quest a mistake?

His eyes skimmed through the room, and his gaze locked onto Yjarn, who sat silently in front of the spear podium, enraptured.

Anger bubbled inside him again. He remembered the fear that had overtook him when he saw Arke flying above the society's sky. The terror he felt as he watched Aeolus eat one soul after the other.

I want to be the strongest I can be. I don't want to be helpless in the face of power ever again. I know that. So why am I hesitating?

I have to get out of here. I have to learn the three techniques to do that.

I guess I could use a charge, but then what? I'll just have Arke on my trail again.

He sighed as he ran his hands through his hair.

Yes. He directed his thoughts toward the Seed and immediately sensed a change in his status.

Well, that's new.

CHAPTER 21

The First Stance

A new tab had appeared on his status screen.

Status | **Skills** | Quests | Inventory
First Stance of the Sword   Tier: Mortal   Progress: 0%   An expression of a Mortal-tier truth uncovered by the Hero Alexia Xancrest. Through centuries of battle and meditation, she perfected her understanding of the truth and infused it in the First Stance of the Sword, creating a sword style that draws out its complete potential. A technique that has since received the acknowledgment of the heavens and become permanently entwined within the eternal tapestry.

Luke read the description of the skill over and over again. With every reread, he came away with more and more questions.

Eternal tapestry? Truth? There's even more layers to all this cultivation stuff than I thought. Luke ran his hands through his hair as he watched the rest of the people watch the holographic avatars of the Hero. Even after hours, they were still enraptured by the masterful techniques on display.

Occasionally some of them would break free of the trance, have a mini panic attack, and go right back to watching it.

Shaking his head, Luke raised his sword again. *I don't know why, but something tells me that I could watch that recording replay a million times and I'd get no closer to mastering the technique than if I had only seen it once . . . Still, I should probably watch it again sometime. For now, though, let's see how far I can get on my own.*

Recalling the hero's movements, he pressed his sword down, unsurprised when it didn't budge. The same sense of resistance overcame him and stopped his movements as before. Frowning, he pressed harder until the veins in his arms were bulging with strain and his arms were shaking with stress. Not relenting, he pressed onward still until sweat flowed freely from his body and gathered in a shallow pool underneath him. His arms started to burn with the pain of his exertion, but he would not give up. His palms ripped open where he was gripping the sword, covering the handle with blood and sweat, and even then, the blade did not budge. Not even the tiniest fraction of an inch.

Red-faced and breathing heavily, he collapsed to his knees.

There's something that I'm missing. Brute force clearly isn't the answer. Whatever's stopping me, it isn't something that I can power my way through. There has to be a trick.

Stumbling back up, he slashed his sword down—frowning as it moved easily through the air.

There's no resistance when I'm just slicing through the air. But— He recalled how the hero moved. The rise and fall of her chest. The way her knees were just slightly bent. The position of her shoulders, and how she gripped the sword. He pressed against the empty air, and his sword once again didn't move. *When I try to do it the way she did, something stops me.*

Is it because I'm doing it wrong? He mentally compared his own stance and the hero's. Shaking his head in the negative when he realized the way they stood was identical, at least when accounting for the differences in their bodies.

Truth.

The hero uncovered a truth and built her technique around it, according to the description that the Seed gave me. That's something to work off, at least.

He turned back to the podium displaying the hero's avatar, straining his eyes as he watched it move. This time, he didn't resist the urge to draw his own blade in response.

Imitating her stance, he once again tried to copy the movement of her sword. Once again, that same mysterious force stopped him.

Frowning, he lowered his sword and just watched. A light bulb went off in his head.

Truth. Truth. Truth. That's the key. There's some principle guiding her every movement, and without knowing what that principle, what that truth is, I'll never be able to learn.

How do I find out what it is, though? It's not like she's tracing letters into the air and spelling out the answer. Right? He watched the tip of her sword just in case, smiling in disappointment when no letters became apparent. *That was a long shot anyway.*

Blood oozed from a torn blister on the palm of his hand and traveled in a straight line down the length of his blade, dripping onto his foot.

Ew, he thought, suddenly aware of how gross he was. *I should call it for today. Sleep on it and come back to it with fresh eyes.*

Sheathing his sword, he found Spiros and Arya still sitting in front of their respective podiums, meditating on the technique. Turning to the wall, full of open tunnels, Luke attempted to go through a random one, only to be stopped dead in his tracks.

Great, another invisible force. Just what I need. He walked up the length of the wall, idly pushing against each entrance, until he finally found one that didn't reject him. *Although the privacy is kind of nice,* he thought as he walked through.

The room was mostly as he left it, but he was surprised to see that a door had appeared on a wall opposite the bed, and that a plate full of food had appeared on the table again. Ignoring the food for the moment, he poked his head through the new door and was pleased to see that it was a washroom. *Kinda creepy—torches and stone bricks aren't really what I would call my preferred décor—but it's better than nothing.* His eyes fell over the large tub, equipped with a rectangular showerhead on top. *Definitely better than nothing.*

A few minutes later, he sat down heavily on the mattress, enjoying being clean way more than he'd thought he ever would.

This isn't terrible, to be honest. It sucks that I can't leave, but it isn't terrible.

Idly wrapping his palms with a Band-Aid he found in the cupboard in his washroom, he ate his fill and turned in for the day.

The next morning found him standing a distance from the podium, with his sword drawn and held loosely at his side as he watched the hero once again. He ignored the throng of blue- and black-robed individuals milling about. Most were still seated in front of the podiums, but more than a few were sparring in the rings.

One woman had even managed to release a monster, some kind of large wolf, from its cage, and then found a way to bring it into the arena where she was desperately trying to fend off its attacks. A blue-robed disciple standing just outside the ring with a bow, arrow already nocked, pointed toward the creature, following along with every move it made, with narrowed eyes, in case the woman fighting it needed help.

Now, that's a real spotter, Luke thought when he first saw the spectacle. Idly, he noted that he should still be able to accrue stat points by defeating the caged monsters. *Getting stronger here might even be easier than at the society. The people are a lot stronger on average, monsters on tap, and there are even some mysterious Seed-recognized skills to learn. Not bad at all, actually.*

He raised his sword, focusing on the hero's avatar. This time, he didn't intend to copy her but to fight. Shadow fight.

He blinked deliberately, imagining her standing before him, her sword held over her shoulder, preparing to slash an opponent diagonally across their chest. He lifted his own blade in challenge, intending to meet her, metal with metal—only to find in the next moment, she'd expertly maneuvered herself out of the way.

His blade cut through empty air, and hers wove through his guard and stabbed into his throat. She left him gasping for breath as the vision of his death replayed inside his head again and again. Shaking his head, he gripped his sword with both hands and lifted his blade in challenge once more. Resolving to win.

A guy can dream, right?

Her sword pierced his heart and stuck out of his back.

The next time she stabbed him in the eye.

The time after that, she decapitated him.

All without breaking her rhythm.

I think she's killed me a hundred times by now. It's like, no matter what I do, her sword finds a way through. Always on the first move. How?! It shouldn't even be possible. How am I losing to a juiced-up recording?

Wiping away the sweat dripping into his eyes, he surveyed the room once again.

His eyes found a group of blue-robed people stuck in place with their blades raised. Their limbs shook with exertion as they tried to copy the hero's movements.

It's not going to work. Luke shook his head. Ignoring them, and looking over to the podium where the hero was displaying her spear technique, he easily found Spiros standing a distance away with his spear drawn. From time to time, he'd lunge or swing his weapon, only to shake his head and try again.

It looks like he had the same idea as me.

Walking forward, Luke stood just outside his striking range and waited patiently.

"How's it going?" he asked, grinning with amusement as Spiros suddenly staggered back and clutched his heart. *I wonder how many times he's seen his death.*

"Not good." He smiled, placing the butt of his spear on the ground and leaning against it. "I'm really starting to think we might die here."

Luke shrugged his shoulders. "I hope not."

"Me, too. But it might happen anyway. I was thinking of talking to some of the others and making a pact."

"A pact?"

"Yeah. You know, if you escape, try to come back here as a hero and break out everyone still stuck here, and if I escape, I'll do the same."

"That would be nice, but becoming a Hero—isn't that asking a lot?"

"I don't think so. If anyone can learn not one but all three techniques, I'd say they have a pretty good shot. I bet a lot of us will still be here, too. Maybe for centuries if we manage to break through to the Warrior tier. Besides, being a hero is probably the minimum amount of strength you need to break anyone out of here."

Luke leaned back in surprise. "You're joking, right? You expect people to become warriors but still stay trapped here."

"Yeah. These techniques, they aren't just some moves, Luke. You've felt it by now, right?" He pointed to a group of people straining against an invisible force. "You can't even begin to imitate the moves without understanding their core."

"Their core?"

"Yeah. I don't know a lot about it, but I remember my grandpa mentioning it when he showed us his technique. He used to bait us, say if we managed to find the core and copy his moves, he'd give us candy. None of us ever succeeded." He sighed, putting even more of his weight onto his spear.

"Still. It wouldn't make sense to give us a challenge that's impossible to complete. There's no point to all this, then, is there? Why would the hero set all this up if she intended for us all to die?"

Spiros visibly perked up at that. "You're right. Just because I couldn't do something as a kid doesn't mean it's impossible now, too."

You're still a kid. But that's the spirit! "Right. Now, what's this about a core?"

"I honestly don't know"—he shrugged—"Gramps only mentioned it to me that one time. He said we wouldn't be able to learn what he was teaching us unless we figured out the core of his movements."

"The core, huh?" Luke cupped his chin. *Could the core of the movements be the truth that the technique is built around? It kind of makes sense.*

His eyes were drawn toward the figure of the Hero, dancing with the spear with the same easy grace with which she moved with the sword. Her movements cleanly transitioned from one stance to the next.

Should I try to learn that one, too?

No. Not yet.

Piling more stuff onto my Path is just asking for trouble. There's no guarantee I'll even be able to advance the First Stance of the Sword—adding a spear technique onto that is stupid. I should wait until I make some progress with that first. If I keep adding stuff to the list of what I need to do before advancing to the Warrior tier, I'll never advance.

Spiros broke him out of his musings, excitedly tapping Luke on his shoulders.

"Look." He pointed to Arya. A crowd rapidly formed around her.

Looking over, Luke saw her in a low stance as she held a wooden shield at her side, straining against the same invisible force that the rest of them had experienced before. Before he could ask what the buzz was about, though, he noticed it. While still under immense strain, her arm was moving. Excruciatingly slowly, but inch by inch it moved forward.

"She's figured it out," Spiros whispered. His eyes widened in awe. Suddenly he turned toward Luke. "You really know how to pick them!" He slapped Luke's back in congratulations.

"What?"

CHAPTER 22

What Is True?

For the last time, Spiros, it's not like that," Luke said, eyes focused on Arya as she ever so slowly moved through the motions. He ignored Spiros looking at him out of the corner of his eyes with an expression that could best be described as belonging to someone who thought they were being lied to.

"How do you think she's doing it?" Spiros asked, a teasing grin on his face spreading from ear to ear.

"No clue. You think she figured out the technique's core, like you were saying?"

"It's the only thing that makes sense. Do you think her having access to mana helped her?"

"Possibly." Luke shrugged. *Something like this does seem like it would fit. "Arcane" seems like an apt description of these skills.* "You probably know more about mana than I do, though."

"Not enough. None of the other Inner Disciples have figured it out. So I guess we'll just have to wait and see."

"Yeah," Luke replied. "Did you see what she was doing before she started?"

"I'm pretty sure she was just sitting there."

"Hmm. All right. Let's try and ask her about it later." Luke frowned at the slowly increasing crowd around her. "I don't think we'll get a chance anytime soon. Not with that many people crowding around her."

"Yeah, you're right."

"Do you know how to work the arenas? I'm pretty sure I saw someone fighting a monster earlier," Luke suddenly asked him.

"Are you sure you want to fight one? None of them look weak." Spiros turned to the assorted cages arrayed against the wall, eyeing vicious monsters with apprehension.

"Yeah. The hero probably had some reason to put them in here. Who knows— constantly fighting something might help."

"You think so?"

"I'm willing to try. I'd appreciate it if you spotted me, though?" Luke glanced at him. "Huh?"

Oh, right. There isn't actually a gym culture here. Keep forgetting I have to be careful with how I talk.

"I mean, stand outside the ring with a bow, and let an arrow fly into it if it looks like I'm in trouble. I saw someone else doing it that way and figured it was a good idea—having someone watching in case things do go wrong."

"Oh. Yeah, I'm okay with that. It is a good idea." Spiros nodded.

"Thanks." Luke nodded gratefully, glancing between the cages stocked full of animals and the arenas, wondering how to get a monster from a cage into a ring.

Not seeing any method or mechanism to help him get one of them out of their cages, he made his way to an empty arena. He climbed over the short stone barrier and into the sand-filled pit inside. Sword and shield ready, he spotted a small post sticking out of the ground along the edge of the ring.

Walking toward it, he was surprised to see an image of a large, mean-looking bear, along with a short description underneath it that read "low Mortal tier." A large red button with the word *call* was printed in large white letters beside it.

Could it be?

He slid his finger over the image of the bear and grinned when it changed, becoming a thin, bright-pink snake instead. Its descriptor read "Peak Mortal tier, very fast, extremely venomous."

So it's basically Tinder, but for monsters. Nice. Definitely not swiping right on the snake, though.

Navigating to the next beast, a cute rabbit, he thought it looked rather weak. To his surprise, though, the description identified it as a mid-Warrior-tier monster. Being extra cautious not to accidentally hit the *call* button, he scrolled through the list of monsters, frowning as he realized a fairly large chunk of them were in the Warrior tier.

I can't believe there are actually Warrior-tier monsters in here, let alone this many. Does she really expect us to be here for that long? Or did she just plan for people at the very peak of the Mortal tier to participate and break through during the trial? There are a lot of late-Mortal-tier people here. In fact that's most of the people here. It wouldn't be the craziest thing if a few of them became warriors, I guess.

Whatever—it isn't something I have to worry about at the moment.

Unless some idiot lets one of the monsters loose . . . I'm sure it'll be fine. Hopefully. Worst case, I run to my room, never come out, and pray that whatever barrier stops me from going into other people's rooms works on monsters, too.

After a few more minutes of scrolling, he eventually settled on a large, ugly, ratlike creature that was labeled as being in the early Mortal tier. It was approximately the size of a small dog, but with none of a dog's inherit cuteness.

"You ready?" Luke shouted out to Spiros, seeing him standing there with an arrow already nocked.

"Whenever you are."

"How's your aim with that thing, by the way?" Luke asked, suddenly remembering a very important detail.

I should have asked him that before I asked him to spot me. I just assumed he'd be good with a bow, but there really isn't any guarantee that he is, and I've never seen him use one, either.

"Um. I'm decent with it." Spiros shrugged. "Not the best in the world, but I won't hit you, if that's what you're worried about. Just don't pick something too small or too fast."

"Right." Luke hesitated for a moment and then, with finality, pressed the button.

The monster didn't appear right away. Instead, a warning popped up in place of the monster's picture. It read:

Confirm: **Low Mortal tier**?

Cost: 1 credit

Available Balance: 1 credit(s)

Hmm. Looks like I don't get to fight infinite monsters. He pressed the button again anyway. *And what are these credits about? Can I get more of them?*

A sudden noise snapped him out of his thoughts and drew his attention to the center of the arena.

He lifted his shield as a familiar mechanized whir emanated from underneath the sand-covered ring. The ground split, and out of it emerged a large bronze cage containing his would-be foe.

Luke's heart beat in anticipation as the front of the cage slid back into the ground. A savage grin appeared on his face before he realized that he was, in fact, looking forward to fighting the creature. A lot.

When did I start looking forward to this? Whatever. He shook his head. *I can figure out all the terrible ways Theos has changed me later. Right now, I have a rat to kill. A battle to the death isn't a good place or time for a crisis of identity.*

No, I should save that for when I'm lying awake in the middle of the night, wondering what I did to deserve this. Or if this is a good thing or a bad thing. Not now, though. He squinted at the rat sitting still in its cage, inspecting it for weaknesses.

It looked even uglier in real life compared to its pictures. Luke grinned. *More and more like Tinder.*

Its fur was dirty gray and coarse, stretched tight over its muscle-bound frame. It stepped out of the cage cautiously, sniffing the ground as it took one slow step after another. Its wormlike tail swayed gently behind it.

Luke widened his stance in anticipation, waiting for the moment when the monster's beady eyes would meet his own.

All right. This is the real deal. Just me and my sword against that. No talismans, no tricks.

His motion must have triggered it, because suddenly the creature perked up and then came bounding toward him. Its lips pulled back in a rabid snarl, showing each and every one of its sharklike yellow teeth. It closed the distance between itself and Luke astonishingly fast.

Luke shifted his weight from one foot to the other in anticipation.

What's it going to do? Go for my legs? Jump on my face? Try and get behind me?

It leaped into the air.

Luke stepped forward and swung his sword.

It latched onto the blade.

Snarling in disgust as the creature's putrid smell invaded his nose, Luke whacked his sword with his shield, just barely managing to clip its tail and shake it off him, instants before it climbed up his arm. With all his might, he resisted the urge to drop the blade and throw up in disgust.

Maybe I should have picked something less gross. Like a cat . . . No, it's too cute then. Ugh. Why'd it have to smell like shitty vomit? Yuck.

The rat landed on its feet and immediately attempted to crawl onto Luke's leg. For his part, Luke managed to keep his cool long enough to swing his sword. This time he managed to cut the creature's head clean off with a single swing, slicing through its fur, skin, flesh, and bone with startling ease.

+2 Stat Points

So it's roughly as strong as the harpies, huh? Not as many as I would have wanted, but points are points. Luke dismissed the message as soon as it came. His attention instead focused on the creature's corpse as fresh sand bubbled around it and swallowed it whole, leaving no signs of its death save for a few splatters of blood on Luke's robes.

The hero really pulled out all the stops. I didn't even think about what I was supposed to do with the bodies.

"Whoooo!" Spiros clapped and cheered outside the arena.

Playing along, Luke raised his sword and shield in victory. "You want to go next?"

Spiros visibly perked up and, without wasting a moment, hopped into the ring.

"Yeah, of course." He shrugged off his quiver and handed Luke his bow. "Spot me, will you?" He grinned.

"Wait." Luke pulled back the string, smiling in satisfaction when he was able to do so without too much strain. "All right, it's good. I wasn't sure I'd be able to draw it. Make sure you pick something that you have some confidence in fighting, all right? I'm okay with a bow"—Luke lifted it—"and I'm pretty sure I won't hit you, but treat me like an unreliable last resort."

"Will do. Thanks, Luke." The boy slapped him on the shoulder.

Watching him run to the control console near the end, Luke climbed out of the ring and nocked an arrow in anticipation. He drew it a quarter of the way back and aimed at where the cage had emerged from underneath the sand.

A moment later, it finally did. A glimmer of recognition flashed through Luke's eyes.

Wow. He doesn't take it easy, does he?

Spiros had chosen the low-Mortal-tier bear.

It's a good choice, considering his weapon. I have to use a sword, and a bear seemed like a poor matchup. Low Mortal tier or not, a bear is a bear. One juiced up with mana is bound to be even scarier.

His eyes traced the gleaming tip of Spiros's spear, glinting wickedly in the light of the artificial sky.

I should get a cool spear, too. I doubt I can find anything comparable to my sword, but there's definitely bound to be times where the extra reach would be useful.

He watched the bear leisurely climb out of its cage. Its entire attitude changed, though, the second it laid eyes on Spiros.

The bear barreled toward Spiros with unnatural speed. It was going faster than Luke thought a creature of its size was capable and had all the grace of a ballerina.

This and the rat are in completely different leagues. Even with them both being low Mortal tiers. I guess even with mana, a bear is a bear and a rat is a rat.

Tracking the bear's every move with the tip of his arrow, Luke almost missed it when Spiros moved into action.

Jumping to the side, Spiros held his spear out horizontally, parallel to the ground. Taking five quick but steady steps, he met the bear's charge.

The bear ran shoulder first into the spear and stopped dead in its tracks. Spiros, for his part, casually lunged toward the bear and pushed. Not missing a beat, he drove the spear's tip a foot into the creature's body.

Spiros desperately held on to his weapon as the monster began to thrash, only to suddenly pull it back and, before the creature could even realize that the spear was gone, stab it right in the eye.

Pressing forward until the bear stopped moving, he pulled his spear free. The sand bubbled near its form a second later and swallowed it whole.

Damn, that was quick. Luke looked at Spiros in shock, surprised by how cleanly he had dealt with the monster. Then, a moment later, he lifted his bow in the air and shouted, "Whoooooo!" His face turned red in embarrassment as a few dozen people shot him angry stares.

Wow. I know we're all being quiet, but this isn't a library.

CHAPTER 23

Finding the Way

Luke sat in front of the podium and pretended to pay attention to the hero's movements. To any outside observers, it would seem that he was wholly captivated by her technique when, in fact, he was poring over his status screen.

Status | Skills | Quests | Inventory
Name: Lukas King
Tier: Mortal
Mana: 720
Rate: 15% per hour
Strength: 41 > 43
Agility: 44 > 46
Constitution: 43 > 45
Arcana: 32
Stat Points: 5
Bloodline: Locked. Conditions not met. (1/10,000)
Charges: 7/10

Nine points in one day. Eleven if I include the two points I got for killing the rat a few hours ago. There's definitely something going on there. I never got this many back at the society. Ever.

I can't think of anything I'm doing differently, either. Hell, if anything, I've been taking it easier here than I did at the society. Less spars, less push-ups, less everything.

If it's not me, though, then what is it?

The only thing I can think of that changed is my physical location. Is that it? Is there something different about the tomb that's helping me cultivate?

The manual said that as people exercised, their bodies would build themselves better than before, automatically processing the mana in the environment to improve themselves.

Is there just more mana here than at the society? Is that what's making my progress faster? I guess that explains the extra points. I wonder if anyone else has noticed a change?

I could ask, but with the Seed, I have a few more options than the normal cultivator for tracking this sort of thing.

One, at least some of the mana I get from exercising seems to accumulate as stat points. So instead of my body putting it wherever automatically, I can choose where it goes. Two, every time I kill something or someone with my sword, I absorb some of their mana. Which also manifests in the form of stat points.

That's not even mentioning the fact that the Seed tells me my stats. I know precisely how much stronger I'm getting, and I can track my growth from day to day. Without the Seed, would anyone else even notice that they're getting stronger faster?

Or could it be an influence of the Paragon's Path? I thought nothing changed except for how fast I recover mana on my status, but what if it increases how good I am at taking in mana from the environment?

Mana itself is another mystery I need to solve. Eventually. The Seed says I have seven hundred and twenty of it. Still no idea what that actually means, or how much it really is. It's clearly not the same kind that accumulates as stat points.

Otherwise, it would take maybe a few days to completely max out my Bloodline and attributes. All without ever lifting a finger.

He felt a headache forming as he tried to figure out how everything worked.

Does any of it really matter, though? I mean, it does, but not right now. The only thing I have to worry about is learning the First Stance of the Sword and then hightailing it off this island. Preferably before the status quo changes on me.

Escape and a stress-free life are so close, too. I just need to learn three techniques, grab the mask, and figure out how this portal is supposed to work, and then I'm home free.

I can start over somewhere, with a fresh face and, most importantly, without the stress of Nefkha and Arke ripping my soul open.

All right, that's enough dreaming for the moment.

Stat points. I have five of them burning a hole in my pocket, but spending them right now isn't the wisest choice. I will be weaker in the short term, sure, but I don't know which attribute is going to end up being the most important.

The way things are going, I'm just as likely to need to be faster as I am to be sturdier as I am to be stronger. With the exception of Arcana, which only seems to raise the amount of mana I have. Mana I have no way of using. Should I stop investing in it for the moment? At least until the situation becomes a little less threatening?

I didn't mind putting some of my free points into Arcana when I was at the society and just working out, but dying because I'm just a little weaker or a little slower is a real risk now. Especially when I'm not just working out all the time.

His mind flashed back to the last trial and how close he had come to death.

Yeah. No more raising Arcana for the moment, unless I find a way to actually leverage my mana. I've already spent thirty-two stat points on it, and frankly, increasing every other attribute by ten points instead would have made a world of difference. Every fight would have been easier. Even if only marginally.

He looked away from the podium and found Spiros and Arya in the crowd. Spiros was standing in a corner, every muscle on his body bulging with strain and sweat forming a puddle at his feet as he tried to move his spear. This rather strange sight was becoming increasingly common in the chamber as more and more people attempted to imitate the hero's movements.

Arya was still standing at the same place as before.

It looks like she's moving in slow motion. Super slow motion. It's actually kind of boring to look at, Luke thought, watching her move her limbs less than an inch every minute as she slowly shifted from one stance to the other. She had been doing so for the past few hours.

Initially there had been a buzz of activity around her, but the crowd had naturally dissipated when it became obvious that it would take her quite a while to finish up and answer any questions.

None of the people present, it seemed, were impatient enough to interrupt her, either. Luke had spotted a few people who looked like they wanted to grab her and demand answers, but none had acted so far.

I don't envy the position she's going to be in once she finally takes a breather.

Turning back toward the podium, he focused on the Hero, observing her every motion with the entirety of his focus. He let every other thought slip from his mind, not thinking about the position of her blade, nor about how he would get past her guard. For the moment at least, he just watched.

Every swing of her blade is a killing blow. Every shift in her posture is to optimize her attack. To get every ounce of reach without compromising stability. To perfectly evade her foe's blade but at the same time make sure she doesn't create a single opening where she could be attacked. In fact—he watched her seemingly overextend her arm, giving her would-be opponent an opportunity to disarm her—*she's mixing in feints. Every opening is just a way to lure an enemy in.*

It's like every single move she makes, she promises death. It's like fighting her is a guarantee of it. As if the outcome is inevitable.

Suddenly it was like a gong had gone off in his head. Scrambling to his feet, he quickly waded through the other mats until he found a quiet spot.

Drawing his sword, he held it vertically in front of him, undaunted when it didn't move even an inch. He stopped trying to move it at all.

I was right earlier. I can struggle all I want, but I don't have the strength to brute force it through the motions.

Closing his eyes, he imagined himself standing beside the Hero, at first just imagining himself following along with her.

Inevitable. That's the key. Whatever I do, however I move, the outcome has to be inevitable. Whatever gets in front of my sword will die.

He applied a small amount of pressure.

His blade began to move. So little and so slowly that Luke would have thought he was imagining it if it weren't for the currents of energy he suddenly felt coming alive in his body. they felt both new and foreign and, at the same time, as if they'd always been there.

Status | **Skills** | Quests | Inventory
First Stance of the Sword
Tier: Mortal
Progress: 0.01%

His Arcana stat suddenly ticked up by one, and his total available mana for the briefest of seconds went down a whole point, before reading as full again.

His sword continued its motion, inching its way through his swing. Another point of mana disappeared from his pool, only to come back a second later. Again.

I'm spending my mana. Huh. Cool.

Status | **Skills** | Quests | Inventory
First Stance of the Sword
Tier: Mortal
Progress: 0.02%

Do I just keep going?

Luke increased the pressure on his blade, urging it to move faster. The same sense of resistance overcame him, but instead of stopping his movements completely like before, it merely prevented him from moving any faster.

He strained his muscles as much as he could; even still, his blade failed to move any faster.

Relaxing his muscles, he stopped trying to force progress, letting the mysterious resistance dictate his pace as he acted out the motions.

Just taking the time to feel the mana move within his body. Mapping its flow within him.

What if . . . ?

He opened his status and added a single stat point to his Arcana stat.

Let's see what this does.

Status | Skills | Quests | Inventory
Name: Lukas King
Tier: Mortal
Mana: 764/765
Rate: 15% per hour
Strength: 43
Agility: 46
Constitution: 45
Arcana: 34

> Stat Points: 4
>
> Bloodline: Locked. Conditions not met. (1/10,000)
>
> Charges: 7/10

He shuddered in pleasure as warmth flowed into every inch of his body. The flow of his mana became a little bit clearer, and he felt a slight pulsing sensation throughout his body as mana practically oozed out of every cell of his being and bolstered the existing flow of energy inside him by a tiny amount.

Now, this is interesting. He suddenly opened his eyes and sheathed his sword. For the moment, he'd lost interest in learning the First Stance of the Sword and wanted to play around with his newly discovered mana.

Looking around, he was happy to see that a crowd hadn't formed around him like it did with Arya.

That's good. Looks like no one saw me. I have no clue how to explain any of this to anyone, anyway.

Rolling his shoulder, he started making his way to his room, doing his best to act as inconspicuous as he possibly could, but at the same time, he found it incredibly difficult to keep a smile off his face.

He felt great. He wasn't sure if it was a side effect of suddenly unlocking his mana or because he had finally made some progress on the technique, giving him hope of finally leaving. Or some combination of both. But he felt giddy, and light. Too giddy, and too light.

He wanted to skip, and dance, and sing.

Why do I feel soooooooooo good? This can't be normal. Just take it easy, Luke. Get yourself to your room, and you can figure it out when you get there. He tried to talk himself into not acting strange.

He took a deep breath, keeping his head down and his footsteps steady.

That's right, Luke. Just one step at a time. One foot and then the other. Nothing funny going on around here. You just have to get to your room. Ignore that bubbly feeling in your stomach. Don't laugh out loud for no reason.

Don't draw attention to yourself. Come on, Luke. You can do it!

Why am I talking to myself in the third person? Second person? Does it matter?

Go to your room, Luke!

"Hey," a girl whispered as she walked up beside him, bumping her elbow into his gently. "I saw your sword move. What did you figure out? Is there some kind of trick?"

Luke stopped in his tracks and looked at her, raking his eyes callously across her figure. Starting at her toes and working his way up her body.

Blue robes. Nice figure. Long black hair. She's really pretty. And those are absolutely massi—

"I'm Trixie." She frowned at him.

"HA-HA-HA-HA-HA-HA-HA-HA-HA." Luke burst out laughing. Dropping to his knees, he laughed uncontrollably.

What the fuck is going on?

CHAPTER 24

Laughing Out Loud

Luke grabbed his ribs as he laughed uncontrollably on the ground. Tears ran down the sides of his face, and his chest ached as he struggled to breathe.

"What's . . ." he heaved, "happening?"

Trixie looked around the room helplessly. "Uh! Anyone know what to do?"

A crowd of people formed around Luke, whispering and pointing fingers. Most were initially annoyed at the commotion before realizing that something strange was happening.

"Why's he laughing so much?" asked a short black-robed man with a shield. "There isn't anything funny going on right now, is there?"

You think I'm doing this for fun?

"No." A blue-robed figure cut his way through the crowd. Kneeling by his side, he stopped Luke's motions and held him down with frightening ease. His hand snaked through the front of Luke's robes. "Huh." He frowned, leaning in and putting his ear to his chest.

"Hey! Get away!" Spiros came running toward the crowd, pushing and shoving people as he made his way toward his friend. "You! You did this!" He leveled his spear toward the blue-robed figure leaning over Luke. "Move or I'll run you through."

Spiros, you idiot. Luke wanted to smack him upside the head but couldn't get any words out of his mouth.

"What?"

"You're the Yarn guy! They warned me about you!"

"What? Who warn—"

"Spiros. Calm down," Arya said, suddenly appearing beside him. She hooked the shaft of the spear with her finger and gently pointed it away from Yjarn. "I doubt he did this."

"How do you know?" He looked at her indignantly.

Such an idiot.

Sighing, she ignored the question and knelt down beside Yjarn, staring at him with a raised eyebrow.

"Right." Yjarn nodded and backed away, leveling Arya with an angry stare as he did so.

Laying her own hand on his chest, she closed her eyes and concentrated. A look of surprise briefly came over her face before she tamped it down, donning an emotionless expression.

"HA-HA-HA," Luke guffawed as they pinned him to the ground.

"He just awakened his mana. The . . . giddiness will fade away in a bit."

Yjarn cocked his head in confusion, opening his mouth as if he wanted to say something, before deciding against it.

Trixie looked at her with surprise. "Really? I remember being a little smiley when I started to sense mine"—she pointed to Luke, still thrashing in silent laughter—"but whatever's happening to him seems a lot more intense. I, uh . . . I saw him move his sword earlier. He figured out the technique. Like you did. Could that be it?"

Arya looked at Luke in surprise. "Did he? Maybe learning the technique and unlocking his mana at the same time made it more extreme."

Trixie looked unconvinced.

"He has a lot of mana for someone who just unlocked it," said Yjarn, looking between Arya and Luke with suspicion.

"Listen, guys. As fascinating as all this is, maybe now isn't the time. Let me take him to his room." Spiros handed his spear to a random guy. Then, kneeling beside Luke, he lifted him onto his shoulder before collecting his spear and walking off, while leveling an angry glare at anyone who looked like they were about to stop him. Or anyone who even looked at him.

Spiros. I love you.

"Which one is yours?"

Luke pointed to his room. He was doing his best to stop shaking but failing miserably. "Thanks . . . Spiros. You're a real frie—"

"Don't mention it. I'm not sure I can go in, so you'll have to make your own way, all right? Do you want to take a minute?"

"No," Luke wheezed, breaking into another laughing fit. "I'll manage."

For fuck's sake, what's going on with me right now?

Spiros lowered him to the ground, and with shaky steps, Luke ambled into his room. He fell heavily down on his mattress as soon as he made it, trying his best to regain his composure, taking deep breaths in between fits of laughter.

This is really something else. Why did no one say cultivating fucks with your head? It's a weird detail to leave out.

He stayed up the rest of the night. Eventually the uncontrollable feeling of giddiness left his body, leaving him to think about what had happened.

It's obvious it happened because I unlocked my mana. I never expected to be able to raise my Arcana attribute naturally, but it did go up.

The timing suggests that it was directly related to advancing with the technique, and I really have no clue what to make of that. But, if having a higher Arcana stat helps with learning the techniques, that's a massive discovery. Maybe not worth the scene I made, but it is something.

Speaking of, that many people being aware of me can't possibly be a good thing. I can't for the life of me imagine anything good coming out of being in the spotlight. At all.

It would have been better if no one knew I had made any progress and I could have just moved under the radar.

It's not terrible, though. At the very least, information won't spread to Arke for as long as we're all trapped here, and even then, it's unlikely. Arya and Spiros are probably the only ones that know I've only been cultivating for a few weeks, and I think they have enough sense not to spread that information around. So most people won't think that it's unusual for me to unlock my mana.

Trixie. Fuck her. Why couldn't she have left me alone? Damn it.

Think. Think. Think. What else is there?

Yjarn.

He's touched me before. Which means he probably sensed my mana then, too.

Luke rolled off his mattress and started pacing at the foot of his bed.

Hmm. Arya has checked my mana twice now. Once when I joined and didn't have any, and now. Back then, not having any mana was somewhat normal, but I've boosted my Arcana since then. A lot. She'll probably have some questions. I'll have to figure out what to say to her.

Yjarn touched me not long before we entered the tomb, and if he thought anything was unusual, he didn't notice it then. Or, at least, he didn't say anything, but is there a way to know if someone can sense their own mana or not? More importantly, does Yjarn know how to tell? He may not have bought Arya's claim about me just awakening it, either. I'll have to deal with that. Somehow.

How much mana is even normal?

All right, let's think this through. What do I know? What are the facts?

My Arcana ticked up naturally. For the first time, and incidentally, I gained aware-ness of it.

Okay.

If I assume that the relationship between Arcana and Constitution is the same for everyone, and that everyone that unlocks their mana starts with a single point in Arcana, then that means that on average, people start with an amount that's exactly half of their Constitution attribute. Unless the Seed is mucking about and the relationship between mana, Arcana, and Constitution doesn't actually exist in anyone but me. I don't think that's the case, nor do I have any way to test that. So, for the moment, at least, I'll assume that I'm not unique in that.

Most people start sensing mana when they reach mid-Mortal tier. Except, I don't really know what that means.

The only person I know who's at the peak of the middle stage is Ethan, and he was pretty strong, unnaturally so, but the distance between him and Yjarn seems to be a lot further than the distance between me and him.

As strong as I've gotten, Yjarn had no problem whatsoever holding me down. Then and now. With Ethan, I'm sure I could struggle a little bit. Maybe even take him if I catch him off guard. With Yjarn, it's like I'm helpless.

So basically, If my assumptions are right, then the midstage of the Mortal tier isn't exactly five hundred points in each attribute like I first thought it was.

Actually, based on what Arya said, once someone starts sensing their mana, they usually focus on one aspect and try to push for the Warrior tier as fast as possible. So even they may not have every attribute at five hundred. Depending on when exactly they reach the midstage.

If I had to guess, then Ethan's Strength stat, if he has one, would be in the seventy to eighty range.

Luke thought back, recalling the strength of the bows they'd used when hunting the harpies.

A hundred max. As for his Constitution and Agility, they're probably a fair bit lower, just because it's easier getting stronger than it is getting tougher and faster. Maybe. So far, I haven't noticed any reduced gains, but I'm also pretty far from reaching a point of diminishing returns. If I ever do.

The Seed might be preventing any bottlenecks, too. I've been assuming that my growth, minus the stat points from my sword, is standard, but is it?

Whatever. Long story short, that sucked. Arya and Yjarn may have some questions. I don't know Arya too well, but I don't think she'll screw me over. Yjarn could go either way, but there isn't much I have to worry about so long as we're all in here. If anything, he hasn't made any progress with the techniques yet, and me and Arya are the only ones who can help. So there's that.

Once people start leaving, though, word will spread about what's going on in here. I doubt that word will reach Arke, but if I can swing it such that I'm the first person out of here, I should.

Luke sat back down on his bed.

Can't believe I can actually feel my mana now.

Closing his eyes, he observed its presence in his body. It was ephemeral, but there. Originating from every cell, it spread itself evenly across his body. For the most part, his mana was content to just sit there, but Luke noticed that it pulsating where his heart was.

Not exactly moving, but rippling with every beat of the organ. It felt nice. Warm.

Concentrating, Luke sloshed it around his body.

It's . . . responsive, but doesn't do anything.

He gathered a good chunk of it and sent it to his hand. Then, with a flex of his will, he expelled it, opening his status as he did so and watching his pool deplete one or two points at a time.

Should I? Yeah. He added another point to Arcana.

Status	Skills	Quests	Inventory

Name: Lukas King

Tier: Mortal

> Mana: 718/787.5
>
> Rate: 15% per hour
>
> Strength: 43
>
> Agility: 46
>
> Constitution: 45
>
> Arcana: 34 > 35
>
> Stat Points: 3
>
> Bloodline: Locked. Conditions not met. (1/10,000)
>
> Charges: 7/10

"Phew. Why does that feel so good?" he said to himself. He felt all the cells in his body *stretch and contract* as they released more and more mana into wherever mana was stored. His mental image of it in his body simultaneously became a fraction clearer as well, like a camera suddenly coming into focus.

He stopped expelling mana.

Let's see what improving my Constitution feels like. He added a point, closing his eyes in bliss as *something* left the Seed and massaged its way into every part of his body. Strengthening it. Making it more robust.

That feels different. It always felt good, but this is almost addicting. Better than every high I've ever felt. Might as well finish the package and see what Strength and Agility feel like.

Strength first. He sent the Seed the command. Once again, he felt something leave the Seed. This time, though, it didn't saturate his whole body. Instead, it wormed its way into every fiber of muscle and just stayed there. Still feeling good, but not amazing. Luke clenched his fist, feeling the increased power and smiling in satisfaction.

He added a point to Agility, sensing something once again escaping the Seed. Still too fast for him to follow. This time, the energy burrowed its way into every nerve and tendon. A substantial portion of it made its way into his optic nerves and ears.

Huh. I suppose that makes sense. Although—he blinked, focusing his gaze through the door leading to his washroom. *I haven't really noticed myself seeing better. Maybe it's just been happening gradually? Not like I've been reading a lot. Hmm.*

I wonder what else I can do with mana, though? It's kind of just dissipates when I push it outside my body, and I have no control after that. So probably no fireballs. At least for the moment. Maybe I can figure out how to make talismans?

I'll have to ask Arya. Although I doubt that she knows. Someone probably does, though. Hmm. Maybe I can trade? Tell them how I got the technique working in exchange. Unless Arya's already spilled the beans.

Yawning, he rolled into the bed. *I'll figure it out tomorrow.*

"LUKE. I NEED HELP!"

CHAPTER 25

Friend in Need

Luke rushed out of his bed, briefly stopping to grab his armaments before high-tailing it down the short hallway. He came to a skidding halt when he saw Spiros standing in front of the door, waving, a cheeky grin plastered across his face. Cleary not in need of any help. Taking a deep breath, he walked the rest of the way.

"What is it?" Luke asked, tiredly rubbing his face.

"Just wanted to see how you were doing. You've been in there for almost an entire day. So, are you okay?"

"Yeah, I'm fine. How's the situation out there?"

"Not bad. After you left, people started hounding Arya. She tried explaining what she figured out but couldn't really get anything across." He shrugged. "I don't know why people thought a mortal would be able to help them learn a hero's technique when the hero herself can't get it through their skulls. Can you imagine? Idiots."

". . . that actually makes some sense. I think." Luke looked at him appraisingly.

"Of course it does." He leaned against his ever-present spear. "Did you really figure it out, though?"

Luke navigated to the skill tab on his status and looked at the percentage, cupping his chin thoughtfully as he stared at the number.

I learned exactly point-zero-two percent of it. So, yeah?

"What are you doing?"

"I'm thinking. I guess you could say that I got my toe through the door." Luke nodded. "Yeah, that's a good way of putting it."

"You have the strangest expressions. That's not bad, though. It's more than most of these people have." Spiros grinned at him.

"Most?"

Spiros preened. "You didn't think you and Arya were the only geniuses, did you? Me, that prick *Yarn*, and some others figured it out not long after you did. So, yeah."

"Okay! That's really good! Can you sense your mana now, too?" Luke asked. For the moment he ignored the sense of pressure that came with the knowledge that other people were making progress as well.

I have to pick up the pace. It would suck if someone stole the mask out from under me.

"Yeah. I didn't expect it to happen so fast. I never realized that learning a technique would unlock it, either. That said, I didn't cause quite the scene you did. No one did, actually."

"Yeah." Luke frowned. "That was . . . really weird. It didn't affect you?"

"I mean, I felt a little happy. If I hadn't seen what happened to you, I would have chalked it down to just being happy that I could sense it at all, you know? Like, now we're really cultivators. Not just some stronger mortals. It feels good. Carim has pretty low standards, but back home, you're not even considered a cultivator until you can sense mana. I guess it's not too different here. If you don't have a blue robe, you're just a chore boy."

"Yeah, it does feel pretty good. Hey, what was the core of the technique?"

"I don't know. At least, I don't think I do. I just had this realization that no matter what I did, her spear would kill me."

"Like it was Inevitable."

"Yeah. Kind of like that."

"Did Arya say something similar?"

"Um." Spiros turned away and scanned the room. "A little bit. She was saying something like never being able to get past the shield. She's right there, though—let's just go and talk to her."

Luke looked down at his clothes. "Just give me a minute to get less gross. I came running because I thought you were in danger or something."

"Take your time. I was just worried that you fell off your bed and hit your head or something."

"And I appreciate you checking up on me. Thank you."

"Don't mention it." He slapped Luke lightly on the shoulder.

Grinning, Luke leisurely made his way back to his room. *I forgot how nice it is to have friends. Even if he's a kid.* The smile slipped off his face. *A kid who has had to kill. It's easy to forget it with how well everyone seems to be holding up, but we went through some shit, didn't we?*

He felt his heart race in panic as he remembered killing Nafik, and that guy he'd fought on the platforms. *I don't even know his name.* He hadn't stuck around long enough to see the aftermath of all the explosive talismans he threw, but he wasn't naive enough to think that they had made it out alive.

Mood successfully ruined. Great. Sending everything he was wearing to his inventory, he slapped his cheeks lightly in an attempt to shake the negative thoughts out of his head.

Taking a quick shower, he practically inhaled the food left on his table and walked back out into the training room, wondering who or what was making the food, and how they were leaving it for him—without him ever actually seeing them, to boot.

Now that I think about it, there's a lot about this place that doesn't make sense. Is every hero capable of making something like this, or was the empress special? I guess she'd have practically the entire island to help her with it, and who knows what mana can actually do?

The God Seed. Possession. Flying. Talismans. Potions. Random rooms full of lava. Hell, she just casually teleports people around, and she's dead. Allegedly. This building doesn't even make any sense. One moment we were walking down a bridge, and now we're here. Wherever here is.

For a brief moment, he entertained the idea of her being alive and personally managing every aspect of the trials. Handwriting every note, cooking the food, making the potions, keeping the monsters fed and alive.

Honestly, if I came back to life, is it too much of a stretch to say someone else can't do it? Now that I think about it, Nefkha clearly didn't think the idea was strange.

I kind of like it, though. Theos, the world where everything is possible. Where not even death is the end.

Of course, now I have to be worried about someone possessing me.

Eh, the Seed will take care of it. Won't you? He directed his thoughts to it, only for it to ignore him. *Should have expected that.*

He stepped out of the hallway and into the open chamber, enjoying the feeling of the artificial sunlight on his skin.

Spotting Spiros fighting a monster in one of the arenas, he went over to spectate. He was only mildly surprised to see Arya standing outside, with a bow, arrow nocked and aimed at a large, white-scaled kangaroo-esque creature.

It's kinda cute.

It jumped rapidly from one end of the arena to the other, occasionally trying to land a kick on Spiros, only to be rebuffed every time. Spiros was too good with his spear to let the creature into his guard, and the creature was too quick for Spiros to land a decisive hit.

"Hey."

Arya glanced at him briefly before returning her attention to the ongoing fight. "Hi."

"Has he been fighting long?"

"He has. They're at a stalemate. From what I've seen of Spiros, though, the alburopod will tire faster than he does."

"I don't think Spiros gets tired."

"Agreed. You know, there's been a lot of talk about you."

Of course. I did make quite the spectacle out of myself, didn't I?

"What are they saying?"

She shrugged her shoulders. "Nothing too crazy. Well, it's a little crazy. Mostly just trying to figure out what happened to you, and why it happened to you. Some of the theories are kind of interesting, though."

"Really?" Luke asked, trying to seem casual, but a sinking feeling in his chest told him that he wouldn't like what he was about to hear.

"Mmm-hmm. Do you remember Xander?"

"The guy who showed me around?"

"Yes. Well, his little brother is here."

Yup. This could be bad.

"REEEEEEEEE."

Luke and Arya both winced as Spiros grazed the alburopod with his spear, leaving a long, bloody gash in its wake, tracing from the creature's hip all the way to its shoulder.

"And?"

"Well. He told everyone."

Yay.

"Told them what, exactly?"

"Oh, you know. Stuff like, when you joined the society you were a mortal that didn't even know how to cultivate. How Elder Nefkha personally brought you in after being sent on the task by the Olympians outside of normal recruitment. How you have to be the greatest prodigy the society has ever seen. I think he's claiming that you'll be the Carim's next emperor."

Right. Obviously, that's more likely than an Elder housing a wanted man. Emperor, though? Where is he getting that from?

"At least, it started that way. People have been drawing crazier and crazier conclusions. One of the people from the Brotherhood mentioned that he was tasked with standing guard over a town's recently deceased. Apparently the Olympians are looking for a thief. One whose soul escaped somewhere on the archipelago. They say that's who the Winged Woman was looking for," she said quietly, eyes still focused on the fight.

"Huh."

Fuck. Fuck. Fuck. Fuck.

"So, are you?" She turned to Luke.

"I didn't steal anything," Luke replied as nonchalantly as he could.

And that's true. Arke was trying to steal it; I just ended up with it. Even so, I have to get the fuck off this island. Yesterday.

"I know, that would be ridiculous. I've seen the way you fight. The way you move. If you're a thief capable of stealing from literal gods, then Spiros is an alpaca in disguise, and I'm a . . . I'm something equally ridiculous." It took every ounce of Luke's resolve not to sag in relief.

"Even so," she continued, "rumors like that are dangerous. Very dangerous. That woman, she's far beyond the Hero tier, Luke. Stronger than anyone on Carim, and look at what a hero can accomplish."

Trust me, Arya. I've seen what gods can do. I know. Probably better than you. I've seen the destruction of an entire world.

"Power like that has to be respected," Arya said.

So, basically, don't say or do anything that will get her attention. I hear you loud and clear, Arya, loud and clear.

"REEEEEETHHHHH!" the creature screeched in pain. Spiros landed another attack. Sticking his spear into its shoulder, he tore it out with animalistic ferocity, taking the thing's entire arm with it.

"Well, there's nothing I can really do to stop people from talking, is there? Or stop them from having funny ideas. So long as everyone understands that drawing attention from powers that much greater than them is a bad idea."

"I think they do."

"So there's no problem, then."

"You know, you speak very well for someone who was raised by a fisherman."

Luke blinked slowly as he mulled over her words. *She's fishing for information. No pun intended.*

"I was raised by a fisherman and his wife," he corrected her. "She had high standards. Especially of me. I don't mean to be rude, but I don't appreciate whatever this is." He tore his eyes away from Spiros and looked right at her.

"What do you mean?"

"You're digging."

"And what's wrong with wanting some answers?"

"Nothing, really. There's also nothing wrong with me keeping some things quiet. My business is just that. Mine."

"Why did an Elder decide to take you in? What makes you so special? How can you go from being a mortal without the slightest trace of mana in his body to someone who, minutes after awakening it, has more than me? I've been cultivating for more than six years. It's not—it's not normal."

Interesting. So I do have more mana than I should have. Why, though? Is Arcana just hard to improve? I haven't had time to cultivate the normal way, but maybe there's some way to test it.

"I don't know what to tell you. I guess he just noticed something different about me." *Like rising from the dead.*

I wonder, though. I can guess why Nefkha did what he did. At least roughly. Why did the God Seed choose me, though? It wasn't like I was the only soul trapped by Aeolus.

Spiros chose that very moment to stick his spear straight into the heart of his opponent.

That's gnarly, thought Luke, watching Spiros stand over his defeated foe. Splatters of blood littered his face as he grinned in victory.

Lifting his own golden blade, Luke cheered him on silently and with a smile. His eyes were drawn to the sand as it rose up and engulfed the alburopod's body.

The smile slipped from his face moments later as he felt an arm drape itself over his shoulder and a warm body press against his side.

Does no one in this world respect personal space?

CHAPTER 26

Secrets of Mana

Lowering his sword, he stepped away from Trixie. Once there was adequate space between them, he looked at her with a blank face.

"Hi." She grinned at him, tucking a loose strand of her curly hair behind her ear. "Hey."

"Listen, I'm sorry I stopped you the other day. I didn't think there was anything weird going on with you. I just noticed that you had figured something out, and you looked very happy about it, and I wanted to know what that was."

"Right." Luke looked at her blankly. "Is that everything?"

She glanced at Arya and Spiros, who was making his way to their side of the ring. Her grin slipped from her face. "It is, yeah. Like I said, I am sorry."

"Okay." Luke nodded to her and turned toward Spiros. "That was an amazing fight."

Spiros glanced awkwardly at Trixie. "Yeah. You want to go next?"

Do I? Luke eyed the sandy pits with apprehension. "No. I didn't sleep too well, and I don't think fighting a monster would be a good idea. Actually, I was hoping Arya could answer some questions about mana." He turned to look at her. "If that's okay?"

"I can," she said slowly, "but I don't know too much more about it than you do. I've figured out a few things by myself over the weeks, and I've read a few books, but I didn't understand a lot of them." She frowned. "Usually an Elder gives you some guidance when you become an Inner Disciple, but with everything that's been going on, none of them had time. With the thief still not caught, they have to go on regular patrols across the province and check in on all the disciples in case one of them found something."

"Oh," Luke said dumbly. *I forgot they don't have phones here. So if they want to check in on stuff, people really have to send letters. Or, if you have enough pull, I guess you can press warriors into your service and have them act as messengers. They fly around pretty fast.*

"None of the other Inner Disciples said anything?" Spiros asked.

She shook her head slightly. "I asked a few, but none of them would tell me anything. Apparently, it's not allowed."

"That's annoying," Luke said.

"I can teach you!" Trixie suddenly offered. The rest of them looked at her in surprise. "Well, you're all from the Luminous Sky, right? I'm from the Crimson Night Sect, so I doubt word would get back. We're also all technically allies, and I doubt I'll get punished for telling you anything. Not in these circumstances, anyway. We're all in a Hero's Tomb! If any of us can get out, then we'll be too valuable to expel anyways."

Luke looked between Arya and Spiros. "Okay."

She grinned. "You three have to tell me about what you know about the techniques in exchange. Sword, spear, and shield. I feel like we'll all benefit from it, no?"

Spiros sighed. "We can try telling you about the techniques, but it's not that easy. I don't mind sharing what I know, but I seriously doubt that you'll learn anything." He pointed at the podiums. "If the hero can't impart her own knowledge onto you, then I doubt we'll be able to. It's better for you if you just keep at it."

She frowned and tucked away another strand of loose hair. "I've been staring at a podium for a long time now, and I haven't figured out anything. Even if it turns out you can't help me, I still have to try. If I never figure them out, I'll never leave." She looked each of them in the eye. "Even if I don't get anything useful from you, I can't ignore the possibility that I might."

Isn't it a little early for her to lose confidence? It's only been a few days since we've been here.

"It's a deal." Arya stepped forward.

"Perfect." She grinned.

"Well, it's not like I have anything to lose by telling you what I know. I still don't think you'll get anything worthwhile from us, though," said Spiros.

"I'll take that chance. Let's go to my room. I'll get you guys started on the basics there." She turned sharply on her heel and walked toward a random entryway.

"We can go into each other's rooms?" Luke started walking after her. "Since when?"

"Since we got here. Some lovebirds figured out how." She glanced back at them. "Don't worry. It's not like anyone can just wander in."

"Still. It's kind of dangerous."

"What do you mean? This is great!" Spiros said obviously.

Luke stayed silent in response.

What do I actually mean? Luke glanced around the room. *Am I just being paranoid? Even if I am, is that a bad thing? I'm here with virtually all the same people as I was in the society, with counterparts from some other organizations, but it feels different.*

Well. For one, everyone in this room is a murderer. Each and every one of us has blood on our hands. We all killed to be here . . . and you know what, that is a good reason to be paranoid. I'm not going crazy—it's just common sense rearing its head.

"All right, this is me." Trixie stood in front of a random corridor, stepping through with ease. Then, turning back around, she held out her hand. "Take my hand."

"Gladly!" Spiros grabbed a hold of it and followed her.

Once he was in, she held out her hand again. Accepting it gingerly, Luke walked in as well.

It's that easy, huh?

"Do you have to be inside to let the other person in?" Luke asked.

"Yes. Two people can't go in together. Whoever's room it is has to be fully inside, and then you have to pull the other person in. It's pretty secure. I think."

"Hmm," Luke grunted noncommittally.

It does seem foolproof. So long as I don't let anyone I don't trust come into my own room, I should be safe. Unless someone tries to do something in the training room, but there's enough people there that no one should be trying anything.

I'll also have to be careful about entering someone else's room in the future. I feel fairly safe that Trixie won't try anything with Arya and Spiros around, but I can imagine being led into an ambush. Eventually. Who knows what kind of trouble people will get into if we stay trapped for long enough?

The note said killing isn't permitted on the pain of death, but it said nothing about torture. Or cutting off someone's arms and legs. Which, now that I think about it, could be a viable strategy. They'll never get out of here alive. Unless they manage to learn all three techniques without limbs.

As crazy as this world is, I wouldn't actually put that down as impossible. Still, if things get bad, people will start looking for loopholes. I can't possibly be the only one who's realized that while killing isn't an option for getting rid of enemies, perpetual imprisonment is.

Speaking of, will the hero keep us here forever? Is it even possible? What if people break into the Warrior tier or start having babies? Would she keep the babies trapped in here, too?

This is insane.

"So, Arya? What do you know about mana?" Trixie asked, sitting down on her bed softly.

"Not much. I figured out how to cultivate specific attributes. A friend showed me how to imbue mana into things, but I haven't managed to do it yet. That's about it."

"So you know the important bits. That's good. I wouldn't focus too much on any professions yet if I were you. Pick them up when you have no chance of advancing any more. Right now, it's a waste of time. As for you two, have you cultivated at all since you unlocked it?"

Luke shook his head in the negative, and Spiros did the same.

"I only unlocked it a few hours ago."

Although I guess playing around with my stat points could count.

"Okay. It's not super complicated. When you start exercising, you'll notice that mana is entering your body. It will be different from the mana already in there. The Elders call it aethereal mana. How do I put this?" She scratched her chin and looked at the roof.

"If the mana in your body is like water, then the mana that comes in from the outside is like milk. It has water in it, but also a lot of other stuff. It's the other stuff in there that lets you get stronger. Which is why you can't just use your own mana to cultivate. It's missing all the good white stuff." She looked between the two of them.

Spiros turned red and looked at Luke, who just shrugged his shoulders.

It makes sense to me.

"Now, normally, when you start sensing mana, you've been at the midstage for a while, and your body has already become saturated with it. So just exercising isn't enough to get stronger anymore. If the rumors about you two are true, your bodies are nowhere near saturated. What that means is that you can just keep going as normal until you notice that your body isn't absorbing the mana that's accumulating."

"Is that your advice? Just ignore it for now?" Luke looked at her incredulously.

"I mean, yes? I know it's not what you wanted to hear, but it's good advice. At the stage you're at, your body should naturally be able to absorb whatever mana enters it, and it's probably best to just let it do what it does. You'll figure out how to direct the mana you gather into improving certain aspects of yourself almost instantly, but let your body build a good foundation, and then build on top of that."

"Okay, so let's say our bodies get fully saturated? Then what?"

"You'll notice the aethereal mana entering you, and if your bodies don't allocate it, it will evaporate. In that case, what you have to do is draw it to whatever you want to improve. It's hard to explain, but the how will make sense once you have it in you."

"What should I improve, and how should I improve it?" Arya asked suddenly.

"Good question. You have to spread it thin and even. The best thing to improve is just your whole body. Dissolve the aethereal mana in your personal mana and let every part of your body eat it. If you want to improve just your strength, though, focus it all on your muscles. But make sure it's evenly spread throughout all your muscles. Don't make your left leg stronger than your right. Don't give your arms more or less mana than your legs. That sort of thing."

"Why?" Arya tilted her head.

Trixie shrugged her shoulders in response. "Do you really want your legs in the Warrior tier and your arms in the Mortal?"

"No."

"Exactly. What else?" She drummed her fingers on her bed.

This isn't as useful as I thought it would be. I'll probably learn more observing how the Seed is improving my body than from her. Hmm.

"How do I make talismans?" Luke asked. *Might as well get something out of this.*

"You draw a symbol on a piece of paper and then fill it with your mana," she answered simply. "It sounds easier than it is, but it's really quite tricky. You have to make it even and do it in a certain way. It also takes a good chunk of your mana, so you can't make too many. Oh, right, if you expel all your mana, you pass out. So avoid that."

"What kind of symbols?" Luke's eyes lit up.

"I don't know. Like I said, it's not worth spending time learning how to make talismans or brew potions unless you've given up on becoming a Warrior. Which I haven't. Really, we only have until we become thirty or so to try, after which, no matter what we do, our bodies simply won't absorb mana anymore. Until then, even if you don't want to become a Warrior, it's much more worthwhile getting stronger."

"Right. What about improving eyesight or hearing and stuff?"

An uncertain look came over her face. "It's doable, but you have to be careful. Make sure your body can handle the strain, and the best way to do that is just by improving all of it equally. Don't spend too much mana in one spot, either. When I first unlocked my mana, an Elder sent her own into mine and showed me how to improve certain attributes independently without ruining stuff. With your eyes, you can't just do your eyes. I mean you can, but not without problems. There's all these stringy bits going into your brain you have to do at the same time, or things stop working properly. A little is fine, but it really is best to make your whole body better at the same time."

Luke, Arya, and Spiros glanced between themselves.

"Well, I guess we learned something." Luke shrugged. "What do you want to know?"

CHAPTER 27

Three Weeks Later

Luke winced in pain as the wooden butt of Spiros's spear dug itself into his abdomen. A few weeks ago, a hit that powerful would have knocked the breath straight out of his lungs and driven him to his knees. Now? It just stung. A little.

Unfortunately for Luke, though, whatever improvements he had made with his Constitution didn't help him surpass the difference in skill between them. Not when his opponent had been training with a weapon since he was old enough to hold one. Not even when he accounted for the fact that he had an actual sword technique to inform his movements.

Spiros grinned, and before Luke could react, he flicked the spear upward. Hitting Luke lightly on the soft flesh underneath his tongue and grazing his chin. He slowed his strike down just enough that it wouldn't tear skin, but otherwise let it hit, causing Luke to stumble back, dazed, from the hit.

If I had been any weaker, that would have knocked me out and given me some brain damage. It still might have. Luke shook his head clear.

"What is that now? Eighty-five to three?" Spiros withdrew his spear, planting it on the ground and leaning on it. A smug pose if there ever was one.

"Yeah, yeah. Laugh it up while you can. Just because you're better than me now doesn't mean that things will stay that way," he grumbled, cupping his jaw with his hand as he tried to massage the pain away.

"Mmm-hmm," Spiros hummed. "If you say so. You'd have an easier time if you used a spear. Or a shield, for that matter. Everyone knows that a sword loses to a spear. You have no reach." He lunged forward, suddenly stabbing the air with his weapon to demonstrate his point.

"Then I wouldn't improve with the technique." *And I don't get stat points when I kill stuff with a spear, so it doesn't matter if the spear is objectively the better weapon in some cases. I need to get better and better with a sword.*

"How is that going?"

Luke navigated to his status screen.

Status | Skills | Quests | Inventory

First Stance of the Sword

Tier: Mortal

Progress: 4.99%

"Not great. I haven't improved at all in a week," Luke said, walking to the end of the arena. Picking up a towel, he wiped the sweat from his face.

"What about the other two?"

Status | **Skills** | Quests | Inventory

First Stance of the Shield

Tier: Mortal

Progress: 4.99%

First Stance of the Spear

Tier: Mortal

Progress: 4.99%

There's something I'm still missing, he thought, a hint of frustration making its way onto his face as he read the cards.

"Same," he replied curtly. He'd decided to pick up the skills in spite of his initial reservations—a decision that he was beginning to suspect would come back and bite him in the ass, but at the same time, he felt that he didn't have much of a choice in the matter. Not if he wanted to leave any time soon, and not when others had begun outpacing him.

"Well, at least you can do them." Spiros glanced meaningfully at the large assortment of people meditating at the foot of each podium. There had been a surge of people who managed to figure out the techniques in the first few days, which had trickled away since then. Roughly a third of the hundred people who had made it this far into the tomb had picked up at least one of the techniques, but after the end of the first week, no one else had managed.

Luke spotted Trixie, her hair messy and deep bags under her eyes. Even with their best attempts at explaining the techniques, she hadn't been able to learn them.

Seeing as they were going into their third week now, tempers were starting to flare with increasing frequency. Especially among the majority of the people who had made no progress and were fast losing hope of ever making their way out of here.

A fear that was further exacerbated by the fact that nearly all of those who had learned one technique had managed to make progress on the other two, and rather quickly at that. Further stroking the others' fear of being left behind.

"It's not like we're any better off. We're all still stuck in here, aren't we?"

"Come on. It's only a matter of time. And look"—he nodded to the far corner of the room, where Arya was moving through the First Stance of the Sword with what could tentatively be described as a normal speed—"she looks like she almost has it. Barely any resistance. She's just as good with the other two techniques as well."

Luke looked over and shook his head. She was progressing, and fast. Faster than anyone else trapped in the tomb.

Clearly her being the first person to pick up a technique wasn't a fluke. I wonder what percent she's at.

"Yeah, she is. Anyways, I was thinking about fighting a midstage monster later. Spot me?"

"Yeah. Are you sure, though? After what happened to Len, I figured you'd want to wait a little longer."

"He was an idiot. He fought a turtle, and he expected someone with a bow to be able to help him. A turtle! They have shells! I don't know what either of them were thinking. Besides, I've gotten a lot stronger since I've been here. I think I can handle it, and if not, that's what you're there for, right?" Luke grinned at him. "And I'll make sure whatever monster I choose is soft enough for you to pepper it with arrows."

"Pepper?" Spiros grinned. "I like that one. I'm going to steal it," he responded, used to the strange phrases that inadvertently made their way into Luke's sentences. Something Luke had given up on hiding, and instead had taken to blaming any oddities in his speech on the fisherman's wife. She was quickly becoming an urban legend in Spiros's head. A master of idioms and strange expressions.

"If you say you can, I believe you. Have you seen Len, by the way? He hasn't come out of his room since he got bit. Think he died?"

"Maybe. Can't say for sure, though. Not like any of us can check. Even if he's alive, does it matter?" Luke lowered his voice. "He lost an arm. I doubt he's going to be able to get out of here now."

"Yeah . . . that's unfortunate." Spiros scratched his chin. "I really didn't think a turtle would be that fast."

"It wasn't just a turtle, was it? It was a midstage monster. He should have known better than to underestimate it."

"I guess that's true." Spiros stretched out his arms. "I'm going to eat and shower. I'll be back in an hourish," he said, walking away. "Pick a good monster. I don't want to wait hours for you to make up your mind again."

Watching him go, Luke found a quiet spot and drew his sword. He settled into the now-familiar motions of the sword skill while he waited for Spiros to return, moving slowly but gracefully from one stance to the next, aware of every movement his body made.

He could acutely feel his mana expanding and contracting with each breath, slowly draining and replenishing with every second that passed in an endless cycle.

Where is it going, though?

It was a question that he'd asked himself many times over the weeks, but one that he was no closer to finding an answer to.

It's not going into my sword, and it's not escaping through my skin. It's like it just vanishes. But where? Is it just the cost of the technique? But it's not like there's anything magical happening. Is there?

Completing the full range of motions, he picked a wooden training spear from the rack and went through the motions for it as well.

Initially, once he'd been able to move, advancing his progress in the techniques had been simple. All he had to do was imitate the movements, however slowly, and the progress bar would tick up. Something that all three techniques had shared. As the percentage went up, the resistance had decreased, letting him go through the motions slightly faster each time.

It had been exciting, just watching the numbers on his status increase, and surprisingly motivating. Each fraction of a percent released a surge of dopamine in his brain. Awesome, until the progress he'd been making slowed, then eventually came to a halt as he approached the five percent mark. The numbers now haunted him.

Completing the spear stance, he put it away and picked up a shield.

Still four-point-nine-nine. This is fucking bullshit.

He turned to Arya and did his best to ignore the spike of jealousy that ran through him as she flowed from form to form, nearly three times as fast as he had.

She had figured *something* out but hadn't been able to articulate it well enough for Luke to progress his own understanding of the skills. Which was par for the course; Luke's own ramblings had flown over her head, too.

Whatever the truth or core of the skills was, it was clear to him that it was the same for every one of them, or, failing that, very similar. Enough that it translated equally well to the progress of all three techniques.

All right, basically we all understand different aspects of the same thing. And that thing is at the center of each technique. I just don't know what that thing is. Not yet. So all I have to do is figure out what that thing is, or just flesh out my own understanding of that better. Easier said than done, that's for sure.

His eyes were drawn back to Arya. *Whatever she's understood is just taking her further than what I did. That's cool. I just have to keep at it. Unravel the mystery bit by bit. Easy.*

Picking up his sword again, Luke once again began to go through the forms, but then he suddenly stopped himself and picked up his shield.

If I have a sword, I'll have a shield. If I'm holding both, then that means I should be able to use both the First Stance of the Sword and the First Stance of the Shield at the same time.

His eyes darted between the figures of the Hero, one wielding a sword and the other a shield. Analyzing each dance, he tried to puzzle together how he could make them fit.

Awkwardly, he raised his shield, like he was blocking an attack, and immediately followed it with a swing of his sword.

There's no resistance. What if I do this . . .

Just holding the shield at his side, for the moment not doing anything with it, he swung his sword down, falling into a trance as he went through the motions of the sword stance. Ignoring the shield on his arm, he looped through the whole dance once, then again, and then again, wholly immersing himself in the movements.

The fourth time, he just held his sword and instead followed the movements of the shield stance, seamlessly transitioning between them without a pause.

He continued like that, alternating between shield and sword, for hours, ignoring both thirst and hunger as he tried to understand the purpose of the movements.

Every swing of my sword is lethal, and every move I make with the shield blocks an attack and leaves the opponent open to a counterstrike. Just as lethal as my sword, despite my hitting it with a shield instead of a blade. Death is inevitable, after all.

Even though the motions are different, their purpose is the same.

The sword deflects like a shield, and the shield in the absence of a weapon is one. They kill indiscriminately.

Suddenly something clicked in Luke's head. He swung his sword, ducked under an imaginary hit, and raised his shield to ward off the would-be attack. The constant resistance eased away to almost nothing, and he felt the percentages on his status climb faster than they ever had before. His mana drained away, as if it was fueling his inspiration, and he stumbled to his knees a moment later when it hit zero.

The world started to turn black and white, and a buzzing sound echoed through his skull.

Fighting off the dizziness with his will alone, he called up his status and navigated to the skill tab, grinning in excitement as he read the percentages.

Status | **Skills** | Quests | Inventory
First Stance of the Sword
Tier: Mortal
Progress: 49.99%
First Stance of the Shield
Tier: Mortal
Progress: 49.99%

Now, that's progress.

CHAPTER 28

Getting Under It

Luke blinked the spots out of his eyes as he stumbled to his feet. Looking around the room as he did so, he was surprised to see only a handful of people still sitting around the podiums, none of whom had been paying attention to him.

Glad I didn't cause another scene. The guy who's constantly making a fuss isn't really the vibe I'm going for.

He craned his neck to look at the artificial sky above him and was greeted with the nine moons of Theos shining like bulbs, and slowly he came to the realization that he had been practicing the stances for a lot longer than he'd thought.

Time really flew . . . and not just today, either. It's been, what? Two months now, maybe a little over, since I've been here.

Coming to terms with his new life was both a lot easier and harder than he thought it would have been.

It was shocking how easy ignoring everything and living day to day was. The feeling of getting stronger had kept him satisfied, if not happy, and working himself to exhaustion on top of that kept his darker, more intrusive thoughts from surfacing. Still there, but distant. Where they were easy to ignore.

I guess the thing about humans being resilient and adaptable isn't bogus. You just need to have your life constantly in danger, and all the trivial stuff doesn't matter anymore. Add a goal—no, a purpose—onto that and, boom, you wake up every morning brimming with energy. Not really happy, but happiness is fleeting anyway.

Purpose mixed with uncertain survival—the two keys to a content life. All the exercising I've been doing probably helped a lot, too. Nothing like doing push-ups until you think your arms are going to fall off to keep your intrusive thoughts the fuck away.

Not that that works anymore. I guess there are downsides to being in the best shape of my life.

Stretching his arms to his sides, he collected his stuff and languidly started to make his way back to his room, calling up his status as he did so.

Status | Skills | Quests | Inventory
Name: Lukas King

Tier: Mortal

Mana: 11/3,700

Rate: 15% per hour

Strength: 43 > 98

Agility: 46 > 92

Constitution: 45 > 100

Arcana: 35 > 74

Stat Points: 101

Bloodline: Locked. Conditions not met. (1/10,000)

Charges: 7/10

Look at that. My first triple-digit stat. Fuck yeah.

The progress he had made in the last three weeks was nothing short of astounding. Easy access to a monster a day, along with the accelerated gains in attributes that he had been experiencing since he got here, had made for a powerful combination. One that Luke was just now starting to appreciate. It was like this place was tailor-made to enhance his cultivation, without risking his life and away from scrutiny.

Something that wasn't far from the hero's intentions.

If I don't count the Bloodline and the skills, I'm basically a tenth of the way to the Warrior tier. With a hundred and one stat points, I'm also pretty adaptable. If only there wasn't a limit on how many monsters we could fight a day, I could have been even further along. Can't do anything about that, though.

Maybe I can convince someone to let me kill their monster. Or maybe even team up on a late-Mortal-tier monster. So long as I can stab it with my sword, I should get the points.

If I get out of here, I should look into that some more. If I can find a spot where there's a bunch of weak monsters, that would be ideal. A nice and easy grind to the Warrior tier, away from the stress of being found, sounds almost like a vacation.

Life will get a lot harder once I leave, too. Living in the society felt a lot like having a sword over my head, but it was safe. Food, shelter, other people to be around. It felt like I was back in college. Kinda. All in all, it was nice. It's not bad here, either. Spiros is fun to hang around with when he's not being annoying, and the atmosphere, while tense, isn't hostile. The gains are also solid.

Out there, though, I'll likely be slumming for food. Living in the trees, or something equally ridiculous depending on where the portal sends me. Unless I can find a way to control the destination.

"What happened yesterday?" Spiros asked the next day, as soon as Luke made his way out of his room.

"Good morning to you, too."

"Good morning. Now, are you going to tell me or not?"

Should I? I guess I have nothing to lose either way, and he's been good to me.

"I made some progress," Luke said after a while, looking through the crowd. He grinned when he found Arya going through the stances in her usual spot. "I think I figured something out that might be able to help you, too. Let's go. I might as well tell Arya."

"Really?" Spiros followed after him as he navigated through the crowd.

"Yeah. It's like, we've been practicing the techniques separately, but if you can hold a sword and a shield at the same time—"

"Both the techniques can be used together. You're a genius."

"Yes. I, uh, I don't know if it will help you as much as it did me, but both my sword and shield techniques got a lot better. I'm pretty sure if I can combine the spear technique with the shield one, then that will get a lot better, too. I've been thinking of combining the sword and spear ones as well, but it doesn't feel right the same way."

"Yeah, I've never heard of someone wielding a sword in one hand and a spear in the other." Spiros patted him on the back. "That thing with the shield, though . . . it makes a lot of sense."

"I know, right? Everyone's been focused on learning each of the techniques separately; no one tried to do them together."

"Or they did, and it didn't work for them. Not that I remember watching any of them try, but it's not like everyone's watching everyone every second of every day."

"Well, hopefully it'll work for you two," Luke said, coming to a stop beside Arya and waiting patiently for her to notice them.

"Is it just me, or is it weird that if we want to talk to someone, we stand near them and hope they notice us?" Spiros leaned in and whispered as the pair watched her go from form to form.

"Well, no one wants to be interrupted, and everyone still wants to be nice," Luke whispered back, shrugging.

It is a bit ridiculous, but I would have been properly pissed if someone bothered me yesterday when I was in my mojo.

"It's even more annoying when you stand next to someone for over a handful of minutes, and they don't notice you."

"Is this about yesterd—" Arya slapped him on his shoulder with the flat of her blade and glared at him.

"Ow." Luke rubbed his shoulder, entirely out of habit. The hit had been light enough that it felt more like someone gently poking him than anything else, but he felt that adding the sound effect was funny.

"What is it?" she asked.

"Sorry, we didn't mean to interrupt you."

"I did," Spiros chipped in and smiled innocently at both of them as they leveled glares at him. "What? I waited for Luke for half an hour yesterday, and he didn't even notice. I didn't want a repeat."

"Sorry about that. You know how the techniques get. Anyway, I think I figured something out. Something big. Just watch me, okay?" He grabbed his sword's handle before his eyes landed on Spiros's spear. "Actually, let me grab a spear, and I'll be right back. If I can do the same thing again, it might help more than just watching me do what I figured out last night. Spiros, just tell her what I told you while I go and get one," Luke said, making his way toward the weapon rack.

"All right, just watch."

Luke took a deep breath as he adjusted his grip on his spear, realizing that it might not be as easy as he'd thought it would be. The spear, unlike a sword, was both a two-handed weapon and a single-handed weapon when used with a shield, and the way you used it differed widely with and without a shield.

With a shield, what you lost in power and agility you gained in defense. Typically it was what your opponent used that decided if you used a shield or not. For example, if you were fighting an unarmed opponent such as an animal, a shield was often unnecessary, and the extra power that came with both hands on the shaft was much more practical. From what he'd seen of Spiros, both ways had their advantages.

In their spars, however, he favored a two-handed grip, and with neither of them using shields, it tended to give him an advantage. Seeing as how taking hits had the effect of improving his Constitution, Luke figured he was on the winning side of that particular deal—both learning to use his sword better and at the same time getting sturdier. All for the price of some pain.

The few times Luke had won was when he had used a shield himself and managed to get in close to Spiros, turning the excessive length of the boy's weapon into a hindrance.

The Hero, at least in the hologram, used the weapon without a shield, with both hands. Something that momentarily left him at a loss.

If it doesn't work, it doesn't work. I wanted to start off with the spear technique and then add the shield to it, but that won't work. So the other way around it is.

Adjusting his grip on the spear, he ignored it for the moment, just letting it travel where it felt natural while he concentrated on the shield technique.

Immediately, he noticed how easy it was to do now. The resistance was still there, he could tell that much, but it was further away. He'd have to move a lot faster than he was comfortable with to even notice it. Which meant that for the first time, he was able to use the technique properly. Maybe even in an actual fight.

He felt his mana eating away, slowly but steadily, as he shifted from position to position. It seemed that the cost of the skill had finally surpassed his passive regeneration. What that cost was for still remained to be seen.

My mana is draining, but not particularly fast. I can probably keep this up for an hour or two. Not bad, but not great.

He blinked slowly as he fell out of the rhythm of the skill.

No thinking, I need to stay focused. There's only the shield.

Luke took a deep breath and let the stray thoughts fade from his head, thinking about the technique and nothing else.

An imaginary opponent appeared before him. Like him, it wielded a spear. It would strike. Luke would deflect and attack, punishing his foe with his shield every time only to reimagine him into being with every shift of his posture, always in time for his next attack.

Vaguely aware of Arya and Spiros watching him from the sides, he continued on, and on, and on. Repeating the shield stance over and over until time had no meaning.

When it did happen, it was an accident. One that felt right. Unthinkingly, he struck with his spear, seamlessly shifting into its stance, lunging forward and discarding his shield at the same moment. In that moment, the ultimate expression of the truth underlying the techniques was better delivered with a deadly tip.

His shadowy opponent, pierced through the heart, vanished in a burst of golden light.

Luke's mana once again dwindled away, and he sank to his knees in exhaustion. Without even opening his status, he knew that he had broken through to a new level of mastery, for he had felt the telltale resistance fade away into the background the moment he executed his strike.

"See?" Luke turned to Arya and Spiros, stumbling to his feet and smiling widely in elation.

They looked shocked and said something, but all Luke heard was a garbled noise, like they were yelling at him from across a busy street.

"What?" he asked, cupping his ear in his hand and blinking through the dark spots in his vision.

Does having no mana fuck with how I hear, too? I didn't notice it last night, but then again, no one talked to me then, either.

The ground beneath his feet shifted and, before he could react, rose up and engulfed him, covering him in darkness.

CHAPTER 29

Choosing a Reward

Luke fell out of the roof and tumbled head over heels through the air for several minutes before landing roughly in a pit of sand. He just barely managed to avoid impaling himself on his spear as did.

Well, this is weird, he thought, dusting himself off and looking around the room he found himself in. Brilliant red lava flowed down the walls into a thick moat that circled the room, illuminating it with a soft orange-red glow.

Jutting out of the sand pit was a thin, silvery walkway leading to a large statue of the empress. A statue fully cast from gold.

A little pretentious, but I would be tempted to do the same if I had this much gold lying around.

Arrayed along the way at equal distances were hundreds of pedestals, and on top of each one, suspended in the air, was some manner of object—weapons, armor, clothing, jewelry, rocks, jewels, vials of pills and potions, and, strangely enough, a bunch of eggs. Eggs of every color and size that he could imagine.

That's a strange addiction if there ever was one.

Luke's eyes darted from treasure to treasure until he saw it. Floating in the middle of the room, between a sword and a black breast plate, was a wooden mask. Glowing in his vision.

Mask of a Thousand Faces

Huh. I guess forty-nine-point-nine-nine percent mastery was enough for the Hero. A bit sudden, but I'll take it.

Securing his sword on his side, he fixed his shield to his back, sent his spear to inventory, and started down the path, looking at each item with curiosity.

The hero said we can only take one thing, so I should grab the mask first. I'll see if I can manage to get anything else later, but it's better not to tempt fate. It would really suck if the floor falls out under me if she decides I'm too greedy or something.

I'm kind of jealous of how cool this is, though. It's like the ultimate man cave. Or some Minecrafter's trophy room. His eyes darted to the lava along the wall. *A thirteen-year-old one who thinks lava is the coolest thing—hottest thing ever.*

"Is somebody there? I need help! Please!"

Immediately Luke drew his sword from its sheath, unconsciously slipping into the First Stance of the Sword—and regretting it immediately as his already-expended mana was drawn even more, which made his head swim and his knees buckle.

Not good. Luke ended the technique with an effort of his will while he raked the room with his eyes to find the source of the voice. He didn't have to wait long, as a dirty, blue-robed figure clambered out from behind the statue.

Is that—?

"Len?" Luke called out. More than surprised to see him. *I would have put money on him being dead.*

"Yeah," he bit out, clutching the stump of his left arm. He'd lost it fighting a turtle a few days prior—and putting on quite the show as he did.

"I thought you died in your room or something."

"Funny," he rasped. "I had some of the blue healing potion left in my room. It got me through. Just barely. Listen. I think the turtle was poisonous or something. My arm is starting to rot. There's a potion on one of those pedestals—I think it's a Hero-tier healing medicine. I need you to grab it for me."

Luke frowned as he mulled over his request.

I want to help him, but . . .

"Why haven't you grabbed it already?"

"I wanted to, but I got this first"—he fished a small, spherical silver rock out of his pocket—"and it won't let me touch anything else. Please, I'll die," he begged.

It can't ever be easy, can it? Luke thought, feeling a headache coming on.

"Do you think a regular healing potion will work? I have a few of them."

Len shrugged his robe off his shoulder, revealing the stump of his arm. It was hideous. The end was bandaged in a crusty brown bandage, and tracing out from it were thick black and blue lines. Pus-filled boils littered his shoulder and chest.

That's infected for sure. Luke winced as he saw the poor state Len was in.

"You don't know what you're asking me." Luke looked away from him.

I need that mask. I can't let anyone recognize me once I leave. Once other people get out, and they will, word about me will spread. If it reaches Arke, and she finds out what I look like, I can say bye-bye to my soul.

"Here." Len tossed him the rock. "I don't know what it is—it just caught my eye. It was here, though, and it's valuable. Take it and give me the potion. I'm begging you!" He dropped onto his knees. "It's a fair trade."

"Why haven't you left yet? You disappeared days ago."

"I've been trying to! There's this stupid thing here. I've been feeding it my mana for days, but it's still not charged, and the closest place it'll let me go is on the other end of the island. It's too far from anything I know. I don't want to die. Please. Please, help me!"

That must be the teleporter. What to do, what to do.

Luke reached into his pocket and pretended to fish around for something, sending the strange rock to the inventory at the same time.

No sense in turning away free treasure.

He pulled his hand back out, revealing a vial filled to the brim with blue liquid.

"This is the same potion we got earlier. I made it out of the lava without too much damage, so I didn't need to use it . . . The letter said that if we aren't dead, then this should do the trick"—Luke reached back into his pocket, this time coming back with a vial of pills—"and this is all the medicine I have."

"Thank you, thank you, thank you!" Len knelt down in front of him.

. . . awkward.

Luke walked forward slowly, on the lookout for sudden surprises. A few weeks of calm weren't enough for him to forget that he was a killer in the company of other killers. Even with the empress's ban on death, he wouldn't put it above the others to get greedy and do something stupid. Nor did he know how such a thing would be enforced.

His eyes landed on the mask as he walked by it, and after a brief moment of hesitation, he dashed forward and grabbed it before Len could get a word in edgewise.

If the potion doesn't work, he dies. I'll have done what I could. He might even live long enough for someone else to come down and help him.

As much as he didn't want to see the man die, Luke would choose his own life above someone else's. He would give him the potion because he liked to think that despite all he'd done to get here, he was still a good person.

"Here." Luke placed the medicine a few steps away from the kneeling figure, scrunching his nose as the smell of rotting flesh and copper invaded his nose. Then he stepped back as Len crawled toward the vials.

Luke took a moment to check the descriptions for the rock and the mask in his inventory.

Status | Skills | Quests | **Inventory**
Capacity: 325.6 kg of 10,100 kg
Items:
Mask of a Thousand Faces
Tier—Hero
Reconstructs the wearer's skull to alter their appearance. Can permanently alter the pigmentation of skin and hair.
Aethonem Aquilam Egg
Tier—Mortal
An egg of a burning eagle. Descendant of a creature that has feasted on a titan's liver for millennia at the behest of Zeus. If hatched, it will possess strong regenerative abilities in addition to the inherited traits of its genus.
To hatch, soak the egg in the boiling blood of a Warrior.

Oh, wow. Luke read over the description. The mask functioned more or less like Luke thought it would, but he was a little apprehensive learning that it would be rearranging his face.

I can't remember how many times some bully has threatened me with that, and I can't believe it's finally happening. In the weirdest way I could ever imagine it happening, too.

The egg is a little weird, too, and I have no clue what to do with it. I don't remember seeing burning eagles in the society's bestiary, either. I guess that's another thing I have to look into. Still, if the egg's ancestor was choking down titan liver, then it must be fairly strong, and the titan in question is definitely Prometheus. I wonder if the war between titans and gods happened here?

Len pulled the cap off the Warrior-tier potion and downed it in one big gulp, and in the next breath did the same with Mortal-tier medicine.

That really is the stuff. Luke watched him with a hint of regret as his condition improved visibly moments after. His boils shrank rapidly every second before disappearing entirely, while some color returned to his skin. He still looked sickly, but much better off than he was before.

Seems like he'll make it.

"Thanks . . . Luke . . . I . . . O—" Then with a groan, his face planted into the ground as he lost consciousness.

Whatever, no use regretting my decision now. Besides, the egg has to be worth something. If I'm lucky, it'll be worth a lot more. Maybe I can even hatch it and get myself a nice pet.

Stepping over the Inner Disciple's prone form, Luke made his way to the statue before walking past it, barely giving the empress's visage a glance.

Immediately, he came face-to-face with an altar with a map of the archipelago engraved on its surface. Jutting out just in front of it was a post with a button, just like the one he used to call monsters in the arena.

Hmm. Looks like I'm limited to the archipelago. It might have been better to go farther, but pickers can't be choosers, I guess.

He traced his eyes over the map, committing as much of it as he could to memory, not knowing when he would have need of it again. His eyes eventually fell to a red dot on a tiny, nondescript island that he assumed was his current location.

Walking up to the post, he ran his fingers over the surface, only mildly surprised when the map on the altar suddenly zoomed in to a specific point.

Playing around with it, he came to realize what Len was talking about. Even though the entire archipelago was shown on the map, only certain parts, showing as green dots, were available as targets.

There was one on Carim, like Len said, on the northmost tip of the island—the opposite side of the island from where he was currently, and in complete wilderness to boot.

Cities and towns were marked with their own respective symbols, although Luke couldn't be sure that the map was up-to-date. The empress had died three hundred years ago, and a lot could have changed since then.

There are countries on Earth younger than this tomb.

He flicked through from island to island and spot to spot, not knowing what the right choice was. He was hoping that the Seed would give him a quest or some guidance, but it seemed content to let him make a decision without its influence, suggesting that where he went didn't quite matter.

Eventually, Luke's eyes settled onto the largest island in the chain, as well as the one with the most cities.

It's go big or go home right? Now, let's see how this works. I'd prefer to get the fuck out before this guy wakes up, or I'll have to kill him for knowing where I'm going. What a waste of a potion that would be. Or send him through first. Yeah, that seems like a better option if it comes down to it.

Before that, though— Luke removed a few sheets of paper and a pencil from his inventory and scribbled down a copy of the map. His inhuman agility allowed him to draw a near-perfect copy of it. Then, for good measure, he zoomed out all the way and drew a rougher map of the entire archipelago, carefully labeling each island as well as every town.

All right. He navigated back to the island and picked a remote-looking spot a few dozen miles away from a river, along its western edge.

Waiting a second longer to give the Seed time to issue another quest, he pressed down on the button when it didn't.

A message popped up instead of a portal:

Insufficient Mana

Well, that's just great. Forgot about that bit. Nothing ever is easy.

CHAPTER 30

Time to Kill

Luke cupped his hands to his face in frustration as a bar, ninety-nine percent of the way full, appeared underneath the words, with a silhouette of a hand beside it. In blinking red letters underneath the hand was another message, reading,

Estimated time until fully charged: 8 hours, 19 minutes, and 11 seconds
Or insert mana here.

You gotta be kidding me. I barely have any mana right now.

Frowning in annoyance, he put his hand where it wanted him to and concentrated. Immediately he felt a strong suction from the device, which rapidly began to drain his mana. It pulled it effortlessly out of his body and made Luke pull his hand away in surprise before he lost all of it.

Freaky. Looking at it consideringly, he put his hand back on the post and, with an exertion of his will, tightened the grasp he had on his mana. He forcibly lowered the hungry draw to a trickle, then stopped it entirely.

Interesting. I wonder if— Luke eased his mental grip and pulled up his status, keeping a careful eye on his mana levels as did and calibrating the hold he had on his mana until the draw of the machine matched his natural regen so that the level of his own mana stayed constant.

Let's see how much it takes.

Five minutes later, the clock skipped forward one second, and Luke withdrew his hand, shaking his head in disappointment as he did so.

I don't have enough juice to make a real difference. Might as well let it do its thing and keep my mana for myself. Although— He opened his status.

Status	Skills	Quests	Inventory
Name: Lukas King			
Tier: Mortal			
Mana: 112/3,888.5			
Rate: 15% per hour			
Strength: 98 > 100			

> Agility: 92 > 95
>
> Constitution: 100 > 101
>
> Arcana: 74 > 77
>
> Stat Points: 104
>
> Bloodline: Locked. Conditions not met. (1/10,000)
>
> Charges: 7/10

If I spend all my stat points and make my Constitution and Arcana equal so that I get the highest amount of mana possible, then I should more than double my current amount. Let's see.

He pulled out a piece of paper from his inventory and scribbled out the math, mentally cursing his lack of calculator.

Just under ten thousand total mana. He glanced at the altar, sending the paper back to storage. *Maybe that'll chip away five to ten minutes. If that. I'd rather wait and keep my stat points handy. Spending them on those two isn't a waste, but the whole point of saving them at all is to deal with something unexpected.*

He stepped back from the altar and watched curiously as it automatically navigated back to its main screen the moment he did.

I wonder why she's scattering all of us so far from here, he thought, moving back to the walkway with the treasures. *Right, probably so we don't get robbed.*

None of the Elders seem to be thieves or particularly vicious, but if one of them decided that they wanted what I earned, realistically, what could I do about it? Any one of them could leave my body in a ditch for some monster to eat, and I'd be shit out of luck.

As he stepped over Len's body, his eyes locked onto a gold spear, rotating diagonally above a pedestal.

Gold sword, gold spear . . . Hmm. It kind of fits the theme, doesn't it? A greedy smile bloomed on his face. *Nothing wrong with trying, and there's more than enough treasure here for everyone to get something even if I take a handful of it. Besides, it's not like they'll ever know it's me. Not when I'll have a new face pretty soon.*

Walking up to its pedestal, he tried to grab it, only for his hand to bounce off an invisible barrier a foot away from the spear. *Not surprising. It's like the barriers that stopped us from going into each other's rooms. I doubt this thing is going to stick its hand out and let me in, though.*

Stepping back for a moment, he inspected it for any obvious weaknesses. Pulling a rock out of his inventory, he chucked it at the spear from a few feet away, aiming to knock it free. It collided with the barrier in midair and bounced into the lava.

That would have been awesome if it worked. What else can I do? He crossed his arms and tapped his feet in thought.

He continued trying to liberate whatever treasure that caught his eye for the next few hours, trying everything from putting the whole pedestal into his inventory and putting the barrier in his inventory to splashing lava at it with creative use of a shield and his inventory. He even tried climbing the invisible forcefield in case it opened up somewhere along the way.

It didn't, and he gave up eventually when one attempt saw him almost fall to a fiery death. Ultimately, he decided that whatever magic the hero had cast was not something he could get around. Not even with his advantages.

Defeated, he went back to the map and, after playing around with it even more, settled in for a wait. He took an hour to redraw the map of the island he was planning to go to, along with its neighbors, in exceptional detail. Once he was finished, he sat on the ground with his back pressed against the altar, positioning himself in such a way that he could see both Len lying on the ground, still asleep, and the pit of sand he had fallen into earlier. On the lookout in the unlikely event that someone else made their way down.

Speaking of, did Len really figure out the techniques after he fought the turtle? Once he ran into his room and didn't come out, I just figured he died. He must have, though, if he's here. Whatever—I'll ask him if I'm still here when he wakes up.

A few hours later, with just thirty minutes left on the timer, a mechanized whir rang through the chamber, and a blue-robed figure fell out of the ceiling and landed in the sand pit with a dull thump.

Heart racing, Luke quietly drew his sword and hid behind the altar, resisting the urge to curse when he saw exactly who had fallen through.

Yjarn surveyed the room, his eyes darting between the artifacts floating in the air and the lava pouring down the walls before settling onto Len's body.

Come on. Just a little bit longer and I would have been home free. I could finish the quest and finally be off this island.

Taking a deep breath, he steadied his breathing, looking desperately for somewhere to hide and failing to find a place. The large statue was the only thing big enough to hide him, and even then, Yjarn would without a doubt come and check behind it.

Should I just push him into the lava? No. He shook his head. Yjarn was still an Inner Disciple, someone who had been cultivating for years. That, combined with the empress's ban on further killing, was enough for him to discard violence as an option.

If she can pull me through the ground I'm standing on and drop me in here as soon as I figured out her techniques, she can do the same and drop me into lava. I don't care how high my Constitution is, I doubt I'll survive that.

Yjarn started to make his way forward, eyeing each treasure as he passed it, pausing momentarily at the empty spots where Luke and Len had picked theirs, before reaching Len. Then, kneeling down in front him, he checked his pulse before he started riffling through his pockets, kicking aside the empty potion and pill vials.

Not finding anything of value, he nodded to the hero's statue and walked back down the walkway, eventually stopping in front of a pedestal with a pair of simple black leather boots. Picking one up with each hand, he inspected the footwear impassively. Tucking them between his arms, he walked to the next artifact, a jewel-encrusted golden crown. Just as with Luke, when his hands were a foot away from it, they hit an invisible barrier. Looking panicked, he stared at the shoes with pain in his eyes, realizing that he may have wasted a once-in-a-lifetime opportunity to pick out a treasure from a hero's vault on shoes.

They still belonged to a Hero, my guy. It's not like they're going to be useless, Luke thought, still hiding and debating if he should try talking to the Yjarn or not.

Running back to where he found the treasure, the Inner Disciple tried to put them back.

Why didn't I think of that? It didn't work, but it's still clever.

Yjarn cursed softly under his breath, turning on his heel and stepping back onto the walkway.

Luke glanced at the counter that was displaying the time.

Fifteen minutes left. Fuck.

Yjarn started walking toward him and, not seeing any way to hide, he stepped out from behind the altar.

"Hey." He waved with his sword, gripping a shield firmly with his other hand.

"I thought you left," Yjarn replied after a moment. His own hand found its way to the sword at his hip. "After doing what you did to him."

"I didn't do anything to him besides helping. He's just sleeping off a poison from the turtle."

"Hmm. Why do you have your sword out? We're friends, aren't we?"

"No."

"Very well. Why are you still here?"

"I wouldn't be if I could leave."

Yjarn started walking forward, drawing his own sword as he did. He let the pair of shoes he had picked out fall to the ground.

"What are you doing with that?" Luke asked, looking at the steel sword with apprehension.

"You have yours, I have mine. It's only fair," he said casually, continuing walking forward. "You took whatever he chose, right?"

Yes.

"No . . . He gave it to me."

"And you're going to give it to me. Both what he took and what you did."

For fuck's sake. "No." Luke lifted his sword.

"You can't fight me. The distance between us is greater than you can handle."

"And you can't kill me without breaking the hero's rules. Which is what you'll have to do to get your hands on my things."

"You really shouldn't test me like that. I don't have to kill you. Not when I can cut off your arms and your legs and take what I want from your limbless torso. And after I do that, you can also tell me how exactly you have so much mana for someone who hadn't even started cultivating until two months ago."

What an asshole. I knew we weren't friends. Luke glanced at his blade. The orange-red light that permeated the room shone off its silver surface ominously. *He's not entirely wrong, though. I don't like my odds of winning a fight with someone at his level.*

"Why don't you give me those shoes, and I'll forget you said that. The room will let us leave soon, and we can go our separate ways once it does."

He cocked his head to the side. "What do you mean?"

"There's a teleporter behind the statue. It's gathering its power, and once it finishes, we can use it to go wherever we want on the archipelago."

"Will it still work if you don't have any arms and legs?"

This motherfucker. Luke took a deep breath and lifted his sword, choosing not to respond as his thoughts ran wild in his head.

It's pointless talking to him. He thinks since we're in the tomb, and because he's stronger, he can do whatever he wants, and there's nothing I can do to convince him otherwise. Even if I do give him the egg, I can't give him the mask. I could try convincing him that I traded Len the egg for a potion so he could live, but . . . should I even bother?

On the very slim chance that it works and he doesn't attack me for shits and giggles after, am I supposed to just bend over for every asshat that thinks he can bully me? If I wanted to do that, I never would have said yes to the Seed. If Arke can't make me do what she wants, why should he be different?

An amazed expression came over Yjarn's face. "You have some guts. I'm impressed, but guts won't stop me." He grinned. "I wonder how Arya will feel when she walks through here and sees you all cut up, having bled to death?"

"I wonder how she'll feel after I take a dump on your face."

"What?"

Luke looked him dead in the eyes. "I'm not great at trash talk." *But I do have shit and piss in my inventory, and you're going to be covered in it and more holes and bruises than you can possibly imagine.*

Hopefully.

CHAPTER 31

The Inner Disciple

Luke took a deep breath as he settled into the First Stance of the Sword. Yjarn did the same in response before gasping for breath as his knees wobbled. He steadied himself moments later as the shock of overdrawing his mana faded away.

That's right, asshole, you have none.

Luke put on a confident grin as he observed Yjarn in spite of how nervous he was feeling. *Half the battle is mental, right?* he thought, paying careful attention to the position of Yjarn's feet, the angle of his blade, and even where his eyes were looking. Searching for anything and everything that could give him a leg up in the battle.

Blades raised, they both started circling each other. Neither wanted to be the one that attacked.

This is going to be a hard fight, but I have my advantages. I can use the techniques, and he can't. I'm fresh and rested, while he probably spent the last few hours in a trance, not paying attention to his hunger or thirst. Lack of mana isn't debilitating, but it is uncomfortable. I have a shield, and he doesn't. That's a big one, and probably why he's being so cautious. I'm at my best, and he's definitely not.

He has the advantage in strength and experience, and that's undeniable. Something tells me that he isn't like those people I won against in the society's arena. He's not as casual as they were. He's not going to half-ass this fight and give up when it gets painful. He's not going to tap out if I get him into a hold. So when I do win, I'll need to immobilize him. Somehow.

He's calm and he's smart. I can't expect to kill him in the chaos, like I did in the room full of lava. I don't have any protective talismans tucked away, either. It's just me and my sword . . . and my shield, and everything else that's useful in my inventory.

This isn't strictly life or death, but defeat does mean torture and severe maiming, so he'll fight with everything he has. I'll need to as well. Any less, and the outcome will be my death, even if it isn't immediate.

Bad things will probably happen if he lives and spills the beans about me having abilities that I shouldn't, but that cat's almost out of the bag anyway, and if I can escape, no one should be able to track me down.

So it won't be my problem. It might suck for the society if Arke finds out I was the thief and they were harboring me, but I can't do anything about that . . . Unless I can swing it the right way so that he bleeds to death an hour or two after I leave. Or something like that—now isn't the time to think about what I'm going to do when I win. I need to win.

Yjarn twitched forward, itching to attack but holding off.

He's getting impatient. Good. I think.

Seconds later, Yjarn leaped forward, his blade outstretched as he aimed at Luke's arm, seemingly intent on making true on his words and leaving him nothing but a limbless torso.

The draw on Luke's mana surged as he did, the First Stance of the Sword devouring it voraciously. A moment later, it became clear why.

Weaknesses in his opponent's stance became clear. In that moment, he *knew* Yjarn's body like he knew his own. He knew exactly what forces were acting on him and how his enemy would react to them. How a tensing in a muscle on his forearm and a tilt of his wrist would lead to an upward swing, cutting his hand off at the wrist, if he tried to meet the Inner Disciple's sword head-on like he had planned to.

Thoughts that weren't entirely his whispered in the back of his mind and urged him to lunge forward and twist his body to the left. He'd escape the reach of Yjarn's blade while simultaneously driving his own deep into his heart. Delivering instant death.

This is . . . Luke lunged forward, letting the truth buried in the First Stance guide his actions.

Yjarn's sword sailed by his head, cutting a lock of his hair as it did, his momentum not allowing him to adjust his attack in time.

Luke's blade moved unerringly to strike at the Inner Disciple's shoulder, ignoring the instinct to impale his heart like the stance called for. Only to be batted away by Yjarn's open palm when it was inches away from piercing the flesh. Ripped free from his hand, Bellerophon's blade clattered on the ground, dangerously close to falling in the lava.

Wha—

Before Luke could even begin to process what happened, Yjarn drove his knee into his gut, hard. Making him wheeze in pain and his ribs crack and then break.

"Ghk." Luke's bulging and bloodshot eyes met the older cultivator's cold stare. A savage but hollow grin stretched across Yjarn's face as he pulled back his knee and panted.

His shoulder was farther away than his heart.

"If it weren't for Arya, my brother would s—"

Luke summoned his spear into his shield hand and stabbed forward with all his might, slipping its sharp tip straight through Yjarn's ribs and into his lungs.

"Wh—"

Luke rolled his wrist and twisted the tip of his spear, equally uninterested in answering the Inner Disciple's unasked question as he was in his brother's death or whatever had driven him to seek to punish Luke for it.

Fighting through the pain of broken bones, Luke bashed Yjarn's arm with his shield, disarming him. And unlike Luke, Yjarn didn't have an inventory to call upon for an extra weapon.

"How?" he wheezed, just beginning to realize that their battle was over and he had lost.

Luke, once again, didn't answer. Kicking him forward, he ripped his spear free. Then, rotating it over his head, he slapped the cultivator's face with it, mustering every iota of strength that he could manage and leaving a large welt on Yjarn's face.

He's durable.

Twirling his spear again, he stabbed forward, sinking it into the flesh above Yjarn's knee.

Roaring with pain, the Inner Disciple stumbled to the ground, unable to muster any resistance now that he was disarmed, wounded, and with his opponent having the superior reach.

Luke struck again, this time leaving a large gash that traveled from his hip to his shoulder.

"I—"

"Shut up! I don't care." Luke stabbed forward twice in quick succession, leaving deep rends where his arm connected to his shoulder and immobilizing the limbs.

Yjarn screamed in pain.

Uncaring, Luke stepped forward and bashed the back of his skull with his spear, knocking his head to the ground. It bounced.

Luke's ribs protested in pain with every breath he took, but he ignored it. Stepping on the other man's back to keep him down, Luke swiped the spear again and left deep cuts on the bottom of his calves, severing his Achilles tendons and, hopefully, neutralizing him as a threat.

I'm a terrible person. I'm also unusually good at this kind of thing, he thought, standing over the disciple's downed form. *Really not sure I like that.*

Luke glanced to where Len was still lying unconscious and returned his spear to his inventory before walking over and collecting his sword. *I can't believe I almost lost this.* Putting it back in his sheath on his hip, his eyes were drawn to the only other objects in the room.

The pair of shoes that Yjarn had unwittingly chosen as his prize. Walking over to them, he deposited them in his inventory as well.

Then, running out of things to distract himself with, his eyes returned to his foe's defeated and bloody form.

That's not pretty. At all, he thought grimly. Frowning deeply, as he watched Yjarn silently writhe on the ground, struggling to get to his knees, a simple task made impossible with the wounds Luke had inflicted on him.

"I can't kill you in here," said Luke. Walking toward him slowly. "So I guess I have a few options." He knelt beside him. "Either I can take you with me through the portal and kill you on the other side—"

Yjarn screamed and increased his thrashing on the ground.

"OR"—Luke raised his voice—"I can leave you here. Hope you die before you talk to anyone else. It's what I want to do, but I'm not stupid. Someone could come in here and help you, after all."

Luke punched the ground near his head. Anger raced through every cell in his body, and he suppressed the urge to scream his frustrations.

"You know what I wanted to do? Not fight. Fifteen minutes and I would have been gone. That's all. If you hadn't been greedy and hadn't wanted to torture me for my secrets, we could have sat around for a bit and left. But I can't. This world is turning me into a monster, and it's because of people like you that I have to let it."

Luke grabbed Yjarn by his calf and dragged him to the altar. He glanced at the time and nodded as the last five seconds ticked away in front of him. Resting his hand on the control post, he navigated to a random island and selected the remotest destination he could find, far away from any city or town shown on the map and in the middle of a large forest. Not even a stream ran through the area, if what was shown was accurate.

He glanced at Yjarn's twitching form at his feet.

It's not enough. I can't half-ass this. He scrolled through his inventory and sighed when he found something he could use. A scorpion's tail appeared in his hands, dripping with sickly venom. The very same one that he had fought three weeks ago when he entered the tomb.

He hit the enter button on the post, and a large, swirling ring appeared behind the altar. Through it, Luke could see a vast snow-covered forest, needled trees stretching as far as the eye could see, and immense snow-covered mountains in the distance. A gust blew, and flakes of snow whirled into the lava-filled chamber.

Nodding to himself, he knelt beside Yjarn and stabbed him in the side with the poisonous appendage, digging it deep into his skin. Closing his eyes, he sighed softly as Yjarn's body thrashed under him. He'd hoped that by not witnessing his actions and their cruelty, he would be less revolted by his own actions. It didn't work.

What the fuck. What the fuck. What the fuck. I hate this, his thoughts screamed at him. Opening his eyes, he looked at the result of his work. Yjarn was silent—had been since the moment he had told him to shut up.

"Here's what's happening. I've filled you with poison. Maimed you so that you can't walk or lift your arms, and I'm going to throw you through this portal. It's a random spot, so I don't really know what you can expect. It's not worth much, but I'm sorry it came to this. I hope that the afterlife treats you well. For good measure, though"—he bonked him on his head—"I'm going to put you to sleep. Can't have you calling for help . . . I really do regret that things came down to this, though."

Kneeling down, he grabbed Yjarn by his thighs and, working through the pain, chucked him through the portal. He sighed softly as it closed behind him.

Then, navigating back through the maps, he selected his own destination. Taking one last look through the room, his eyes landed on Len.

He had climbed to his feet and was rubbing the sleep out of his eyes.

You know what. Fuck it, I really don't care.

Len's eyes met his and lit up in surprise.

"Oh, hey. Thanks a ton for the potion. You saved my life. I mean it, I can't thank you enough."

"Don't worry about it. Listen. I need you to do me a favor."

"Anything." He nodded earnestly.

Either he's a really good actor, or he has no clue what happened between me and Yjarn. Either way, it looks like he saw nothing. Good.

"Can you stay down here for a few hours and wait for Spiros or Arya to come down? I need you to tell them that I won't be able to return to the society, and tell Spiros that I'll come visit him one day."

"Ah. Sure, that's not a problem. Why not, though?"

"I have some things I need to do. And I can't let you see where I'm going, either. Would you mind standing way back and turning around?"

Len looked at Luke like he'd grown a third head before shrugging his shoulders and walking to the sandpit.

Luke smiled gratefully and opened the portal. Taking in the sight of the tall grass on the other side, he leaped through.

I should have left them a letter. Oh, well.

CHAPTER 32

It's All New

The portal closed behind him, and he landed gently in the tall, knee-high grass of Sylcra, the largest island on the archipelago.

Reaching into his inventory, he pulled out a healing potion before chugging it down whole. He sighed in relief as the pain from the broken ribs eased.

"I'm finally free," he said out loud to himself, feeling the weight of constant discovery lift from his shoulders. At the same time, a sense of heaviness settled in his heart as he once again left behind everything that he knew.

This is becoming a bit of a pattern.

At least I'm better off now than I was the first time around. I have food, water, and a tent. I'm stronger, and I'm not a stranger to this world anymore. Besides, there's no saying I can't visit Spiros and Arya in the future. I'll just have to be careful. Maybe kill Arke first. I'm sure that both of them will become warriors, and once I'm a Hero, I'll go back to the tomb and let anyone that's still there out, he thought, forcing a smile onto his face and blinking unshed tears out of his eyes. *There's no way Spiros will stay in there, and I'll bet everything I have on him simping his way out. If a guy can shit his pants for a girl, he can do anything.*

Using his hands for shade, he surveyed the land. As far as his eyes could see, all that existed was grass. Craning his neck, he noted the positions of Theos's nine identical suns, hanging horizontally in the sky, before he withdrew a map from his inventory.

A largely pointless exercise, as he had spent hours staring at it and plotting his path before coming here. He only looked at it now because he thought it felt appropriate. Nodding to himself, he started walking north. There was a river that cut through the entire island, and nestled along its banks were nearly all of Sylcra's villages, towns, and cities.

Five minutes of walking later, he stopped abruptly, cursing himself as he did.

I'm such an idiot. He took the Mask of a Thousand Faces out his inventory and stared at it apprehensively, noting its soft wooden texture and its two large eye holes as he turned it over in his hand.

It looks so . . . plain. Still, it's a Hero-tier artifact.

"I can't believe I killed people for this dumb thing," he muttered to himself before gingerly holding it over his face.

As soon as he did, it tightened and conformed to the counters of his head. An uncountable number of thin, straw-like wooden tendrils emerged along its edges and wrapped themselves around his skull, snaking around his ears and wrapping thinly across every strand of his hair. They worked their way into every cavity on his face, save for his eyes and mouth. Just when Luke thought it was over, they wrapped themselves down his neck, not stopping until they were covering every inch of his body save for his eyes. Luke squirmed in pain as the strands brushed against his broken ribs, and he fidgeted awkwardly when they wrapped around the more sensitive parts of his anatomy.

Instinctually he brought his hands to his sides, only to pull them back a moment later as the pressure eased.

I can't believe Yjarn broke my ribs so casually. Without the Seed, I really would be fucked. I'll have to be more careful with the stances in the future, so something like this doesn't happen again, either. They're good for instant kills, but using them nonlethally isn't what they're for, and I need to account for that beforehand.

He took a deep breath, wincing slightly as his lungs forced his ribs to expand. *It hurts, but not as much as I would have thought. The potions really are magical. I should figure out a way to get my hands on more. Maybe I can find something like the society here. Whatever*—he shook his head—*that's a problem for future me to figure out once I find civilization.*

Luke lifted his hands to his face and inspected his arm, rotating it slowly as he did.

I'm a wood-themed mummy . . . It's surprisingly comfortable being all wrapped up. Now, how does this work?

Tentatively, he urged some of his mana into the mask. In his vision, a holographic version of his naked body appeared in impeccable detail, from the smallest marks on his skin, to every strand of hair. It was all visible, and Luke cringed a little when he saw it. Max's body was his now, but it hadn't always been.

That's interesting, and . . . Luke felt around the mask with his mana, inadvertently triggering some mechanism, as in the next moment the image the mask was showing him changed. The person he was seeing now was of similar height and build as him, but his skin was a few shades paler. His hair, while the same length and style, had darkened from his previous brown to a raven black. The largest change between him and the person on display, however, was his face. It possessed thicker and darker eyebrows, a smaller and slightly less bulbous nose, higher, more princely cheekbones, and a narrower jaw.

Leaving him reeling in surprise as he took in his prospective appearance.

To Luke, the way he looked was barely worth his attention, and beyond making sure he was well-groomed, his appearance was frivolous to him. Both his original body and Max's were neither ugly nor disfigured and in good physical condition, without any allergies or health concerns, and that's all he cared about.

The one on display, however, looked like it had been chiseled from marble under the careful attention of a world-class artist.

Not supernaturally beautiful or to the level that it would draw attention in a crowd, but if someone were to sit down and look for flaws, it would take them a minute.

Are there no other options? Luke thought, funneling even more of his mana into the mask. Quickly, he came across some manner of built-in controls. He fumbled around for a minute before figuring out what each button did. Cautiously, he pressed down with a wisp of his mana on what he hoped was the next button, panicking slightly as the image changed to display perhaps the ugliest person he had ever laid eyes on. After admiring the sheer hideousness of the form, he hit the button again. The one that came after that looked like a female version of the first, and the one after that had purple skin but otherwise looked the same as the first.

Luke, out of habit, attempted to scratch his head before giving up when he realized that he was still mummified. *You have to be kidding me.* He navigated to the next image, and sure enough, it was a purple version of the extremely ugly option that appeared before. *What kind of options are these? I didn't really know what to expect, but I wanted a character-creation screen. Not this!* he thought, continuing to flip through the various forms.

Eventually giving up on his search and spamming the back button, he navigated back to the very first option it had presented him. He'd discovered that all the other options were the same as the first three it presented him, but in stranger and increasingly unnatural colors.

I'd rather just be handsome than be handsome with bright red, pink, or aqua skin. I'm trying to stay under the radar, not cosplay as a devil or some Star Wars *alt-humanoid that we're supposed to believe is an alien and not a guy painted yellow.*

When he pushed his mana down on the mask's okay button, Luke's world turned white with agony as blood pooled in his mouth. The mask surgically—and mercilessly—had shattered the bones of his skull. At the same time, he could feel straw-like tendrils cutting into his skin and squirming like worms under his flesh as they did their work.

All over his body, the thin strips of wood that had mummified him grew needles as they did *something*. All Luke knew was that it *hurt*. A lot. So much so that he collapsed to his knees as the mask transformed him. Surrendering himself to the worst pain he had ever felt, he lost consciousness.

When he woke up hours later, the suns had set, and the nine moons had taken their place in the sky. An uncountable number of stars glittered around them, in spite of their pale light gently illuminating the night far more than Earth's moon ever did.

Shouldn't the moons make the stars harder to see? Luke rose to his feet, catching the mask as it slid off his face and sending it straight to his inventory. He didn't even want to look at it after all the suffering it had caused him.

The pain he had experienced already felt like a distant memory, but even thinking about it made him wince.

Bringing his hands to his face, he felt around for the changes, fearing that the mask hadn't worked as promised, or he had accidentally become the ugly monstrosity that was the second option, and he sagged in relief when he touched smooth skin.

I'm so grateful I'm not hot pink right now, Luke thought, looking at the pale skin of his hand. *I should have stolen a mirror from the society. I knew I was going to end up with a new face. Whatever. Now, which way is north?*

He looked back at the sky before realizing that he didn't know which way to travel based on the moons, nor did he recognize any of the constellations.

"Fuck it, I'll wait until the morning," he said to himself, accessing his inventory and pulling out a tent he had erected in his house in the Luminous Sky.

I wonder if I can build a tiny cabin now and just bring it out whenever I need it. Like a pocket house. It shouldn't weigh more than ten thousand kilograms, and I wouldn't feel as homeless as I do now if I did, that's for sure.

Wait . . . I almost forgot. Luke opened his status and navigated to inventory, scrolling down all the way until he found what he was looking for: the boots Yjarn had chosen.

Status | Skills | Quests | **Inventory**
Items:
Air-Walking Boots
Tier—Warrior
Enchanted to allow the wearer to walk on air as if it was solid ground.

There's no way! Luke pulled them out immediately. Kicking off his own shoes at the same time and sending them to his inventory, he slid his new shoes onto his feet. He frowned as he realized they were much too large for him.

Maybe I can get them fitted?

Standing up, he sent mana out from his feet and into the soles and grinned as they magically resized, molding themselves to fit perfectly.

They're comfortable!

Lifting one foot into the air, Luke pressed his leg down slowly, increasing the amount of mana he was channeling into them as he did. *Are they broken?* His smile slipped from his face when he felt no resistance.

He fed the shoe more and more mana and opened his status to keep an eye on his consumption at the same time.

Maybe I'm doing it wrong?

Stopping the flow of mana completely for a second, he lifted his foot back into the air, stomping down while sending what he estimated was three hundred points of mana into it at once.

His foot stopped midair, and the momentum of his step sent him into the air briefly before the effects of the boots wore off, making him land roughly on the ground.

"HA-HA-HA-HA." *This is going to be awesome.*

He spent the next few hours practicing with his new shoes, quickly getting the hang of using them while falling onto his face more times than he could count in the process. He would have kept going until the suns rose, but his mana wasn't unlimited, and the rate it replenished didn't keep up with the expenditure.

Each step cost him roughly one hundred mana, and more if he wanted to stand in place in the air.

Crawling into his tent, he sent his new shoes straight back into his inventory. Wanting to keep them in tip-top shape for as long as he could, he did so by putting them in stasis in the safest place he knew.

As he dozed off, he tried his hardest not to remember Yjarn's broken body lying at his feet. Or how he might still be alive out there in the frozen forest. Cold, poisoned, and unable to move. Screaming his throat raw as he called for help. It was something that he was beginning to suspect would haunt him for some time. Just like Nafik and everyone else he had killed. Except at least he had given them the mercy of a quick and painless death.

I hope he passed while he was unconscious.

When he woke up the next morning, though, he had something else to draw his attention.

The Seed had given him a new quest.

CHAPTER 33

Journey to Cyzicus

<table>
<tr><td colspan="4" align="center">Status | Skills | Quests | Inventory</td></tr>
<tr><td colspan="4" align="center">Journey to Cyzicus:</td></tr>
<tr><td colspan="4">Cyzicus is the capital of Sylcra. Every ten years the island is besieged by endless hordes of Gegenees, giant creatures of the Earth, monsters that possess six arms and thick rocklike skin. Whenever they invade, Cyzicus calls to arms all cultivators of the island and rewards them handsomely for their aid.</td></tr>
<tr><td colspan="4" align="center">Travel to Cyzicus and fight the endless hordes of the earthborn.</td></tr>
</table>

Luke read over the quest with a grin on his face.

Now, this is something I can get behind. Endless monsters means endless stat points. If I play my cards right, I can make some solid progress there. If it also helps the people on this island, then that's even better. No, that's great. I should be helping people. I want to be a god. Preferably a nice one. Someone who helps others. Yeah.

After reading through the quest again and making sure he had understood everything properly, he dismissed the screen and rolled out of his sleeping bag, pillows, and blankets. Surprisingly, the temperature, which had been pleasant for most of the day, progressively got colder and colder throughout the night. Cold enough that even with all the improvements to his Constitution, he still felt its bite.

I lost a lot when I came here. Everything really, but I also gained a lot. I'm free now to be who I want to be, and that's not an opportunity people get very often. It's not one I'm going to let go to waste.

There's so much to see and do. So much that's amazing and magical. The entire time I've been here, though, I've been worried that the sky would come crashing down on me. That Arke would find me. That Nefkha would change his mind. That's all gone now.

I'm free. His grin grew even wider.

I did what I had to do to keep myself safe, but that's over and done with. Arke has no way of finding me, and nobody knows where I am or what I look like.

Which leaves me to figure out what I want to do with my life here.

With the Seed, not trying to be a god seems like a massive waste, and honestly, I want to be one. I want to be strong enough never to be bullied by anyone again. I don't want to die again and have my soul almost eaten. I don't want to be an ant for giants to step on as they please. The universe is a lot bigger than I ever dreamed of or even imagined it, and I want to know everything it has to offer. I want to learn about talismans and potions and magic. I want to know who made the Seed and why it picked me. I want to go back to Earth and visit everyone.

He stepped out of his tent and looked across the endless plain. His lips quivered before turning into a full-blown smile.

"And all that is in my reach," he said out loud.

Packing away his stuff—a task made efficient with liberal use of his inventory—Luke donned his new shoes and set off.

Running swiftly through monotonous grasslands, he focused only on putting one foot in front of the other.

His thoughts were blissfully quiet as he bathed in the light of the suns and felt the wind blowing through his hair. Every once in a while, he would channel mana to his shoes and leap through the air. Never too high, lest he fall and injure his still-healing ribs, but high enough and long enough to grow accustomed to using what was fast becoming his favorite artifact.

I'm not even flying, and it's already so much fun. I wonder what that will feel like once I become a Warrior.

His mind flashed back to Nefkha, when he had discovered him. He had been terrified and in awe of the casual disregard with which the old man had treated gravity.

He continued like that for two whole weeks, running all through the day and camping at night. Alone with his thoughts, he dreamed about his place in this world, what he wanted to do with his second life, and what kind of person he wanted to be.

I'm definitely not going back to a desk job, but man, pissing my days away stress-free was super underrated. If a little unsatisfying.

Eventually the scenery started to change. Small copses of leafy trees became more and more frequent, and with them came birds and rabbits. Occasionally he spotted herds of giant, bull-like, elephant-size creatures grazing in the distance. Every time he tried to approach them, though, they would scatter in every direction. So quickly that, even with all the improvements he'd made to his Agility attribute over the past weeks, he was nowhere near quick enough to get close.

Whatever they are, they aren't at the low Mortal tier, he thought after a failed attempt to hunt one, before continuing north.

He hunted rabbits and other small game as often as he could while there were plenty of them around, not knowing when else he would get the chance to stockpile to his heart's content and fully aware that if he hadn't squirreled away the food that he had, he would have starved to death.

It would turn out, however, that his cautiousness wouldn't be needed, as, after a few days, when the nine suns were sinking below the horizon, he finally came face-to-face with the largest river he had ever seen.

Its opposite bank was so far away that not even climbing a hundred feet into the sky was enough to see it, and Luke regretted even attempting it. Coming down from that high up was a lot more harrowing when he knew that a mistake would cost him his life or, failing that, break a few bones.

The next morning, he woke up bright and early with a plan. For the first time in weeks, he deviated from his usual routine. He needed to prepare for the next part of his journey back to civilization. He needed to build a raft.

Pulling out his map, he roughly estimated where he was before nodding to himself.

If I stuck to a mostly straight line on the way here, then I should start running into people so long as I go downstream. That's where most of the towns and cities are supposed to be. He scratched his head as he looked at the map, then back at the river. *There should be people upstream, too, but there aren't any boats going up or down it. That's strange. Either the map isn't accurate anymore, or these people don't use the river for trade.*

Now that I think about it, it's weird how little there actually is on the island. None of the land I passed over seemed like it had anything wrong with it, but all of it's empty.

Is it the Gegenees? I guess that would make sense, depending on how they attack, and I can imagine an infinite horde of just about anything making life pretty hard. An endless horde of giants . . . Seems like it would be impossible to deal with. On top of that, if they come every ten years, I can't imagine what kind of devastation they cause. Then again, even Carim was mostly just woodland outside of a few cities. It could be that the people in this world just aren't as obsessed with building stuff. It's not like cultivators don't keep the monsters in check.

Whatever, I'll find out soon enough, I guess.

For now, I have work to do. He walked down the river's banks until he found a decent set of trees.

His sword wasn't the best tool for cutting them down, but he managed to get a good dozen in a relatively short amount of time. His sword's unnaturally sharp edge, driven by his mana-enhanced physique, made the process relatively painless, especially considering that the trees were just trees, with nothing magical about them.

Stripping the branches off their trunks, he laid them down side by side and then bound them together with rope, impressing himself with how sturdy his construction was.

All that time in woodworking class really did pay off.

Fashioning the leftover wood into a pair of oars, he called it a day and settled in for the night. He spent the rest of the evening fishing in the river and succeeding in pulling out one fish after another with a makeshift pole. Max's memories guided his actions and made the once-foreign task effortless.

The next morning, he pushed his raft into the water and began the last leg of his journey.

He had enjoyed his time by himself. It was helpful in dealing with everything he had experienced, but he was also more than ready for it to be over and to finally have someone to talk to again.

I can't believe some people like just being alone in the wilderness. I think if I stay alone for much longer, I'm going to go insane.

Letting the river carry him downstream, he used his oar to steer and dodge stray logs, keeping an eye out for any water creatures that could be a threat.

A week later, he finally saw the first traces of civilization: a collection of fishing vessels in the middle of the river.

Angling his oar, he maneuvered himself toward them.

Let's hope they're friendly, because if they aren't, this is going to suck.

"Hey!" Luke yelled into the wind, waving his arms wildly as he did. Not that he had to—the fishermen had noticed him almost as soon as he had noticed them.

"You another one of those Rising Sun brats?" a fat man, wearing an apron covered in fish guts and blood, asked him as soon as he was within earshot.

Rising Sun? Is that like the Luminous Sky Society?

Luke looked at him, confused. "Um—"

The fisherman looked back at him warily before shaking his head and muttering, "Kids these days," under his breath. Then, bending down, he threw out a plank, connecting his boat and Luke's raft. "You're wearing the robes. I may be a fisherman, but I know a cultivator when I see one. Get on."

"Thank you!" Luke looked at it and then the fisherman hesitantly before glancing at the other boats in the distance and deciding it was probably safe.

He doesn't look like he's planning to kill me, and I have enough mana to make it to the shore with my boots if it comes down to it. Luke looked at the man again. *Not that he looks like he'll be able to put up a fight anyway.*

Spreading his arms out for balance, he quickly walked onto the fisherman's boat, resisting the urge to crinkle his nose as the smell hit him, before nodding gratefully to the man.

"Hi. I'm—"

"I don't care," he interrupted. "I've had it"—he gestured to the other boats—"we've all had it with you sect brats going upriver, freeloading off our town, and causing a ruckus every night. How many times do we have to tell you that there's no treasure there? There's nothing there at all, and there hasn't been for decades." The fisherman shook his head and threw his arms up in frustration. "Bah. I don't know why I bother. It's not like your type ever listens to my type, ain't that right, lad? I'm just a dumb mortal, ain't I?"

I have no idea what's happening, but I'll roll with it.

"Uh. I'm not really sure what to say. We're not supposed to say anything about what we do. I'm sure you know how it is." Luke smiled at him, impressed with his own ability to bullshit so cleanly.

The man looked at him with clear disappointment before shaking his head. He handed him a broom. "Make yourself useful while you're on my boat. I don't care if you're a fancy cultivator or a pig, I don't give free rides." He grunted before turning away and lumbering to the opposite end of the vessel, fiddling around with the nets hanging over the side of the ship.

Luke looked around and got to work, once again letting Max's memories guide his actions.

Still no clue what's going on, but things seem to be working out.

CHAPTER 34

The Rising Sun

So, how long have you been doing this for?" Luke asked the fisherman as they rowed the boat down back to port, a long day of work behind them.

"Since I can remember," he replied, his eyes locked firmly in the distance.

"You know, if things were different, I would have been a fisherman, too."

Well, not me, per se, but this body for sure. I'd still be sitting behind a desk.

"That so?" he replied curtly. "I could tell that ya knew what you were doing."

"Yeah. I spent a lot of time on a boat growing up. They were good times," Luke said wistfully, looking across the surface of the river, tracing the paths of the boats as they too rushed toward the dock.

Is it weird that I'm feeling nostalgic about memories that aren't mine? I know I'm not Max. His soul left this body, and I took it over. His memories are just that—memories. I can barely put the few names I remember to faces. I can't even remember what the fisherman and his wife even looked like, beyond them both being old. Being here, though, on a boat, it feels right. Like I'm at home.

"Yer pop a fisher, too?"

"I don't know. I can't remember him. The man who raised me was."

"Mmm. Any man that raises ya might as well be a father." He grunted. "How'd the cultivators find ya? Or did ya find them?"

"They found me. It was pretty sudden, how it all happened. I never really thought my life would turn out the way it did. I didn't even know any of this was possible."

"No one ever does. When I was a boy, some robes . . . " He trailed off and looked at Luke awkwardly before correcting himself. "Some cultivators came by and killed a crocodile that was harassing the town. And what a beast it was, too. A hundred feet long and more than a dozen thick. We were supposed to stay in town and not disturb them as they worked. But I was a kid, and I'd heard stories. I wanted to watch them kill it." He turned to face Luke and smiled widely with joy, proudly showing off two rows of yellow teeth.

"It was brutal, but boy, was it amazing. They stood a distance away and threw these things that exploded. But that didn't do nothing to it, so they went at it with their swords and spears. Poked it full of so many holes, the ground turned red with its blood. Even that wasn't enough, so they started filling the holes they'd poked in its hide with more of that magic paper. That did it in, all right."

"That would . . . The blood didn't scare you?"

"Why would it?" He looked at Luke strangely.

Why do I keep forgetting that this isn't Earth? The people here are used to a harder way of life.

"My pa had me gutting fish and butchering chickens since I was a wee little lad." He chuckled. "Watching those robes made me want to be one of them. I'd heard that they held a trial every year, and that anyone could try it, to see if they had the talent. I begged and pleaded for days so my pa would let me go." He shook his head fondly.

"Did he?"

"Aye. He did. Gave me his blessing, too." He turned away from Luke. "The week before I was supposed to leave for the test, he died. They said he got pulled into the river by a monster fish. A buddy of his noticed that he wasn't bringing his boat back round, and when they checked, he wasn't anywhere on it."

"I'm sorry," Luke said softly. "Does that happen often around here?"

"Aye. Every now and then we'd all hear some stories. The mayor even asked the robes to look into it, but none of 'em found nothing. Said there's nothing they can do, and after a month they went back to that mountain of theirs."

"That's not good," Luke supplied lamely, fighting the urge to peer in the murky depths of the river and see for himself if the monster was under the boat. He had been worried about some powerful beast being in the water, and having his suspicions confirmed was unnerving.

"It's not for a lack of trying, mind you. Whatever it is that's pulling us under don't stick around, and you lot have more on your plate than a couple missing fishermen every year."

"I suppose that's true." Luke shrugged, wondering how much the fisherman actually knew about cultivators and what they got up to.

I doubt he knows about how we raid tombs and compete in lethal challenges for the prizes left behind in them by überpowerful empresses.

"Are . . . are ya going to fight it in the Giant Tide?" the fisherman asked suddenly. "I heard some of the Rising Sun folk talk about needing to go to the capital soon for it."

Does he mean the Gegenees? He has to be unless there's more than one kind of giant terrorizing the island. I hope not.

"I am."

"Hmm." He grunted softly. "I know you lot aren't supposed to mingle with us mortal folk, but why don't ya come around? Let my wife treat ya to some dinner." He looked around the boat appreciatively. "You did some good work today. More than I expected."

Well, this is unexpected. But . . . I kind of want to. Besides, Luke reasoned to himself, *it can't hurt to learn more about the island. There's no better way than breaking bread with the locals.*

"Your wife won't mind?"

"Zoe? Never! She'll be happier than a horse with hay to have a guest eat her food."

Luke drummed his fingers on the oar. "If it won't cause any trouble, then . . . Okay. My name is Luke, by the way."

"I'm Al . . . Now I'm guessing ya know how to tie a knot?" he asked.

Memories of old, wrinkled hands guiding him through the process flashed in his mind.

"Yeah, I know."

"Good lad."

"Have ya been to the town before, or are you like most of 'em others robes—er . . . cultivators, camping outside the walls?" Al asked Luke as they lugged his catches for the day toward the market.

Luke lifted an eyebrow at the slip. *Is calling cultivators "robes" supposed to offend me or something? He's been doing it the entire time I've talked to him.*

"Camping outside. I'm still pretty new to all of this, and I guess they don't trust me to, uh, talk to you all. I know the rules, though. Can't sell you anything, can't tell you how anything works and all that. To be honest. I'm not supposed to be talking to you at all. I'm a little surprised you haven't asked me any questions about how it all works."

"I don't need to." He lowered his voice. "I already know how."

"What?"

"My son was in the Rising Sun Sect back in the day. I couldn't go because I had to look after my ma, but I wanted him to have a better life than this." He tilted his head, gesturing toward the filthy streets and the piles of fly-covered fish all along it. "It's a good life for a small man like me, but I wanted my son to be great. To be better, to go further."

Wanted, huh? Luke thought somberly.

"When he turned fifteen, I pushed him to take their ruddy test, the one I couldn't, and he passed. He told me there was no one who did better than him." Al scratched under his eye. "I was so proud. We both were. His mother cooed for days over how handsome he looked in those robes . . . Anyhow, you wait here, I'll be back." The pair stopped in front of a store front. "I've gotta sell 'em. It'll just be a minute."

"Um, yeah. Take your time." Luke nodded to him and stepped away from the front of the door.

Turning around, he looked around the street and suddenly became aware of all the eyes on him. They were discreet and fleeting, which was why he hadn't noticed them on the way into the town, but they were there—staring when they thought he wouldn't notice and shying away when they realized they had been caught.

Is a cultivator really that big of a deal to these people? Luke mused, stepping away from the shop front, and onto the street, glancing down the length of it to see what else was down there.

Only to lock eyes with another person dressed in robes—blue robes.

Well, that was fast.

They stared at each other, both looking like they had been caught doing something that they weren't supposed to. Which in Luke's case wasn't far from the truth.

Not knowing what else to do, Luke waved at the other cultivator, who took that as a sign to stop gaping and started making his way toward him.

Play it cool, Luke. Don't act weird. You're not doing anything wrong. You're not breaking the law, even though you kind of are. Just play it cool. He hyped himself up as the other cultivator approached him.

"Who are you?" the cultivator asked.

"Um. I'm Luke. Who are you?"

The other man opened and closed his mouth before saying, "I'm Luke."

"You're what?"

"I'm Luke."

"So we're both Luke?" asked Luke.

"I guess so."

"And you're not messing with me?"

"Why would I do that? I don't even know you."

"I am you." Luke grinned at him. Other-Luke opened and closed his mouth. "That was a joke."

"I know," Other-Luke said defensively. "I don't recognize you."

"We just met."

"Are you always like this?" He cupped his forehead. "You're giving me a headache."

"No, I'm not. This is just a little funny." *And I just get like this when I'm nervous.*

Other Luke sighed in exasperation. "You're not with the expedition?"

"I'm not. I'm not from the Rising Sun, either."

"You're not?" He frowned. "Are you from the Nine Stars? You're a bit far from where you're supposed to be."

"No. I'm just lost—no real clue where I am. I do want to go to the capital for the Giant Tide, though, if you could give me directions."

"You are a cultivator, right?" Other-Luke asked.

"Yes." Luke nodded politely.

"But you're not from the Rising Sun or from the Nine Stars?"

"No."

"I don't know what to do with you," Other-Luke said flatly.

"Why do you have to do anything with me?"

Other-Luke once again opened and closed his mouth before crossing his arms under his chest, furrowing his eyebrows as he tried to think.

"That's a good point. Nobody ever said anything to me about cultivators not from our sect."

"If it helps, nobody told me anything, either."

Other-Luke looked at him blankly. "That doesn't help."

"Look, I'm trying, okay?"

"Trying what? My patience?" He snorted.

"I suppose. So, the capital—how do I get there?" Luke asked again.

"What's the rush? The Giant Tide isn't for two months. Either an Elder will fly us there or the emperor will activate the teleportation platforms."

"I don't have an Elder to fly me there."

"Look, I really don't know what to do with you, and a town full of mortals isn't the place to talk. Why don't you come back to camp with me, and I'll let Nel talk to you. This can be her problem."

Luke glanced back to the shop and briefly met eyes with Al, realizing that he was done with selling his fish.

"I still have something to do here. Where's your camp? I'll come by tonight, after I'm done."

"It's a mile north of the town." He traced Luke's gaze and glanced meaningfully at Al. "I don't know what your business is with these mortals, but keep your lips sealed about the important stuff. You aren't from the Rising Sun, so you're not my responsibility, but this town is sect territory."

"Yeah, I know."

"Good. I have to get going, but I will tell the others about you. So make sure you drop by the camp, or they'll come looking."

"What happens if I don't?" Luke asked.

Other-Luke shrugged his shoulders. "Beats me. It's not for me to decide. Don't freak out, though. If I had to guess, Nel will ask you to come back to the Rising Sun once we're done here. Some Elder might ask you to join up or something. They'll probably ask some questions, make sure you're not some evil asshole. You're not the only stray in the world, and you won't be the last."

Questions might be the bane of my existence.

"Right. I'll be there."

"Good." Other-Luke started walking away before stopping abruptly. "With the Giant Tide so close, patience has been running thin, and everyone is on edge. Any other time, the Elders would probably give you some leeway to fuck around, and they might not even care what a rogue cultivator like you gets up to, so long you're not causing trouble. Now, though, it'll probably be better for everyone, especially you, if you make things easy."

Well, that isn't ominous at all.

"Got it."

CHAPTER 35

Dinner and Dust

Luke watched Other-Luke walk away with an inscrutable expression before shaking his head slightly and heading back toward a worried-looking Al.

His thoughts churned and his mind replayed the conversation over and over with every step he took. He had expected to run into other cultivators eventually, and frankly, it would have been weirder not to run into some. Nevertheless, he hadn't expected it to happen minutes after he reentered civilization.

It would have been nice to have some more time to figure stuff out, but it's not necessarily a bad thing. I'm running low on potions and have no talismans, and on top of that I still have no real idea how to make either of those by myself. If I can set things up so we're at least somewhat friendly, they might let me buy some off them. Maybe I can even join them. I doubt that they'll be too different from the society.

Besides, other than me popping up out of nowhere, they have no reason to be suspicious or believe that I'm guilty of anything, and if I play my cards right, I can probably come up with something that will get them off my back about my origins. If they even bother asking. Which they will.

Still, it's not like cultivators showing up out of nowhere is rare, and Theos doesn't seem to have much in the way of legal documents. I doubt they'd bother to check if I told them that I was raised way out in the wild and only came to town when the person raising me died. Hell, I could even say my dad's a Hero and he sent me here for experience. That's basically what Spiros and them are doing anyhow.

No, that would be stupid—claiming a relationship with a hero is bound to raise questions. Maybe a random cultivator? Hmm. Arke is still around, too, so whatever excuse I come up with, it'll need to be something that won't stand out to her as well.

He gripped the handle of his sword as he felt a headache coming on.

It's fine. I have a few hours to get my story straight, and I will.

"Everything fine with ya? The pair of you looked awful tense for a bit," said Al.

"Yeah, everything's fine. He just didn't expect me to be here."

"Ha, I thought he was telling you to keep yer mouth shut or something."

"Well, he did remind me not to tell people anything important." Luke shrugged. "So I guess you're right."

"Nah, lad, word round town is he's quite taken with the alley cats." Al grinned and winked at him. "Pays 'em well, too, so they've taken to fighting over who gets him."

"He's . . . paying cats?" Luke turned to him. "Why would he do that?"

Al looked at Luke oddly. "No, he's been . . . ahh, it's no fun if I have to explain it to ya. Forget it." He started marching away. "House is this way."

Alley cats? Oh . . . OHH. Interesting.

Luke followed after him.

Al's house was exactly how Luke had envisioned it: a smallish one-story building made of brick, not too far from the river. A big, square chimney jutted out from its roof, with tastefully painted wooden accents arrayed around the window of the door, giving it a rather homely feel.

Chickens roamed freely around his well-manicured lawn, kept in place by a waist-high picket fence that encircled his surprisingly large property. Al gently prodded one away from the entrance and let Luke inside.

I guess with this world being as big as it is, real estate is pretty cheap.

"Blasted chickens. Zoe likes keeping the little shits around for the eggs, but she complains for days every time one of 'em ruins her garden."

"That's unfortunate." Luke grinned at him.

"I still love 'er." He grinned at Luke before leading him inside a moment later, chuckling softly. "Zoe," he shouted, "I've got a guest!"

"I'm right here, no need to shout." An elderly woman emerged from another room.

"Well, yer hearing's been going, so I have to, don't I?" he grumbled under his breath.

The woman gave her husband the stink eye before turning to Luke. Her eyes, for the briefest moment, danced over his robes, before meeting his own, seemingly unsurprised. "And who might you be, dear?"

"I'm Luke, ma'am. Al, uh, invited me over for dinner."

"Well, aren't you a sweet one. You just go on and call me Zoe, dear." She shuffled around their dining table. "You boys must be starving. I'll get the food ready. I put some water out back if you two want to freshen up."

"All right, come on, Luke. She makes it sound like a request, but what she really means is yer stinking up my house, and I need ya to stop, or else." Al pulled him aside.

Two hours later and with his belly absolutely stuffed with food, Luke waved goodbye to the couple and walked onto the street.

No wonder Al is as fat as he is. That lady can cook, and she knows it.

"Well, if it isn't the rogue," a familiar voice called out in the dark. Other-Luke stepped out from behind a house across the street.

"Hey." Luke waved at him. "I was just about to come to you. You didn't have to stalk me."

"It's not like I wanted to. Anyway, let's go. I waited for you to finish your food, and I would rather be over and done with all this." He started walking down the paved path, expecting Luke to follow after him.

Hesitating briefly, Luke did just that.

"What's the Rising Sun like?" Luke asked.

"You want to join?"

"I'm not opposed to it."

"It's not impossible, I suppose. How'd you end up by yourself, anyway? You look too young to have fled a mine, so what is it? Why'd you leave your sect and come here?"

"Why are you so sure I fled from my sect?"

"It's not like there are many other options, now are there? You have the robes, you have a sword, you know about talismans. Clearly you're not a mortal who figured out how to cultivate. Most of them keep their mouths shut and don't strut around in the open. You also mentioned knowing the rules. The only way you'd know them is if you had been told them, ain't that so?"

"Hmm." Luke hummed. *I can work with this. The mines are supposed to be brutal, so it's not a surprise that people would escape from them. I'm too young, but maybe . . .*

"I didn't escape from anywhere. My dad was a member of some sect. A different island from what he told me. He taught me how."

"I'm guessing that's his sword you have on your hip, then?"

"It is."

"Where have you been all this time?"

"Up the river."

Other-Luke looked at him flatly. "Where did you really live?"

"Up the river?" Luke said again, trying not to panic.

What's so weird about living up the river?

"That's impossible. The cyclops kills every human that trespasses in her territory."

"What?" Luke asked, suddenly feeling a cold chill down his back.

A cyclops?

"The cyclops. Sophia the Big. She came to Sylcra a hundred years ago and fought Lord Cyzicus to a standstill. After fighting for ten days, they agreed to split the island in half until one became strong enough to kill the other. Until then, the east side of the island would belong to her, and the west side would belong to the emperor," Other-Luke explained, looking at Luke incredulously. "Nothing? Everybody knows that! Even the mortals know about it. It's why they've been so pissy about us being here. They think we'll make her angry or something."

"I didn't know that, and I guess my dad didn't, either, but now that you mention it, I always thought it was weird that no one lived there. It seemed like perfectly good land."

"I can't believe you're not dead."

"Maybe I— We weren't deep enough in her territory for her to care?"

He shook his head. "Maybe. I wouldn't know—no one's stupid enough to challenge someone who could fight the emperor to a standstill. The Elders that were there said that the clouds parted and the earth shook the entire time they were battling."

"That strong, huh?" Luke asked as they walked out of the town's gates.

"Mmm-hmm. You ever wonder what it would be like to be that powerful?" Other-Luke asked suddenly. "So strong that you can just pick an island and decide that it's yours?" He sighed, looking at the sky. "What I wouldn't give to be that strong."

I don't think being strong enough to take over an island is strong at all. Not when I've seen entire worlds be destroyed. Or when people like Arke can just show up and do whatever they please.

"Not really. The only thing I want is to be strong enough to decide my own fate."

Other-Luke looked at him oddly. "Can't you already do that?"

"No." Luke shook his head. "Not until I become a god."

"HA-HA-HA." Other-Luke slapped him on his back. "You dream big for a guy who can't even make his own talismans."

"And you laugh a lot for a guy who needs to pay to have sex," Luke snapped back.

Other-Luke stopped in his tracks. "How'd you know?"

"The whole town knows, friend. You really thought they wouldn't pay attention to a cultivator? I noticed them staring the second I walked in, and people talk."

"HA." A loud laugh resounded through the clearing, and a woman in red robes descended from the sky, landing softly on the ground before them.

"Nel? What are you doing here?" Other-Luke asked the woman.

"You were taking way too long, and I thought something might have happened to you."

"I told you I'd be fine!"

"You were meeting a rogue. I thought he might be dangerous. Besides, you're my baby brother—I worry." She blurred forward and ruffled his hair.

"Then why did you send me in the first place?"

"I didn't want to go. Now, what's this about you paying for sex?"

"Uh. He's just joking. You're just joking, right?" He glared at Luke.

"I think that this is between you two." Luke scratched the back of his head.

How long has she been following us? The entire time?

Nel smirked at Other-Luke. "I'll have to talk to Mom about this."

"No, you don't! And you!" He pointed at Luke. "Why'd you have to tell her?"

"I didn't know! Sorry." Luke lifted his hands in surrender.

"That's enough," Nel interrupted them and fixed her eyes on Luke. "Is what you said true?"

"Yes."

"And you want to join the Rising Sun?"

Luke nodded.

"Okay, you're in."

"Just like that?" Luke asked skeptically.

"Well, we have to put you in the register, but as an Elder, I can bring whoever I want into the sect."

I guess it's not a surprise. Nefkha did basically the same thing.

"When you were in the east, did you notice any sheep?" she asked.

"No. It's all just grass, and these big bull-like things out there. Some rabbits and stuff, too, I guess."

"Hmm. So you really weren't lying. You didn't kill any of them, did you?" She looked at him intently.

"I tried a few times, but they were too fast."

She sighed in relief. "Good. Those bulls aren't bulls. They're the cyclops's sheep. If you're ever stupid enough to go back there, never kill one. Sophia's killed off every predator on her half of the island to make room for her flock to graze. So long as you don't kill her sheep, she'll let anyone who trespasses do as they want. Most of the time."

What the fuck? Really, what the fuck? Was I really that close to dying? A bead of sweat rolled down his face.

"I don't think I'm ever going back, but thank you."

"Smart lad. It's getting rather late. I'll fly us back to camp."

"No, thanks, I'll walk." Other-Luke stomped off.

"'Bye." Nel waved at him as she watched him go. "I'm still telling Mom, Lukeus."

Lukeus? Whatever. "I think I'll walk t—"

Nel lifted her hand in the air, interrupting him, and looked back at the town in the distance. Frowning, Luke followed her gaze.

"What are you looki—" Luke trailed off.

The ground shook. Dust rose in the sky. The world became silent. Then the screaming began.

CHAPTER 36

A Giant Cometh

What's going on?" Luke asked, a ball of nerves forming in his gut as the earth rumbled beneath his feet.

"A giant is being born," Nel answered, rising a few feet into the air but for the moment not leaving. A ring on her finger flashed, and a spear, ten feet long and made of some shining silver metal, appeared in the air beside her. Luke's eyes lingered on the mysterious glyphs etched along its length, glowing softly in the evening light.

What are those? he thought.

"I thought the Giant Tide was a few months away."

"One giant isn't a tide," she answered absently, "and there are always giants." She rose higher into the air as another tremor shook the earth.

Lukeus came running back, his eyes wide in surprise and a sword already drawn. "Is that what I think it is?"

Nel frowned and nodded solemnly. "Gather the—"

"Lily!" he screamed and sprinted back into the town.

Luke and Nel briefly shared looks of surprise and confusion.

"Idiot!" Nel cursed under her breath, but she let him go regardless, even looking slightly relieved as he ran past the gate and into the town proper.

"Is the town in danger?" Luke asked her, his mind flashing to Al and Zoe.

"No. The town is shielded. The shaking is the giant trying and failing to get into the town from underneath. It should give up soon and emerge around here somewhere."

"Shielded?"

"Yes. We'd all be dead if monsters crawled out of the earth beneath our homes." She looked at him like he was an idiot.

Relax, lady, I just got here.

"Right." Luke nodded along at her explanation, turning to watch the town. More and more dust had risen into the air, but like she said, the giant was unable to emerge into the city. "Why do they attack?"

"I don't know."

"How strong are they?"

Her frown deepened. "It depends. Most of them are at the Mortal tier, some at the Warrior, and if it's a bad year, a handful of them spawn at the Hero tier. That normally only happens at the peak of the Tide, though."

"What's this one?"

"I don't know."

I have a bad feeling about this.

"I guess we'll find out," Luke said, pulling his own sword from its sheath. His eyes darted to Nel's longer-than-average spear and back to his own average-size sword. *Is it too small?*

No. Maybe if I didn't have the boots, I'd be biting a giant's ankles, but with them, I should have adequate reach. If it comes down to that. He looked at Nel appraisingly. *She is a Warrior, so there's a good chance that it won't. It'll be interesting to see what someone who has transcended mortality can do.*

The ground rumbled again.

"Elder!" A few dozen figures came running down the street, a mixture of blue and black-robed cultivators.

"Is tha—"

"A giant, yes." Nel looked over at them. "I need all Outer Disciples to go into the town and make sure the mortals are okay. Help them with what you can. They should know not to come out of the town already, but there are always a few who think they know better. Keep them in."

"Right!" A girl nodded eagerly. "Let's go!" She took off, and the others followed after her.

"What are you waiting for?" one of them said to Luke, seeing him stand still.

"Oh, um, I'm not a—"

"He stays." Nel cut Luke off. "Go."

The Outer Disciple looked confused but obeyed her command nonetheless.

"Elder Agnella. What do you need us to do?"

"Draw your weapons and form a loose circle around the town. I want you to position yourself a hundred meters away from the walls. That's where the giant will emerge. Take these." Her ring flashed, and stacks of talismans appeared in the air around her. She gestured vaguely, and the stack of papers separated evenly before sorting itself into small piles and floating to every Inner Disciple. "Three Warrior-tier protective talismans, three explosive talismans, and one flare. If you see the giant, light the flare, and I'll come over to you. The light will draw the creature, but the protective talismans should hold long enough for me to get there. If they fail, do NOT, and I mean it, DO NOT lead the creature toward the town."

The Inner Disciples nodded solemnly and scurried off.

"What do you need me to do?" Luke asked.

"I don't know you, nor do I trust you with the safety of these people. Do what you wish, but stay out of my way, and away from the town." She stared at him threateningly.

Luke met her gaze evenly and nodded.

That was one fast shift in personality.

"I'm glad we understand each other." Her ring flashed again, and another set of talismans appeared before they floated down toward Luke. "They're the same as the ones I gave the others."

"Thanks?" Luke grabbed them out of the air and looked at her curiously. *Mixed signals much?*

"You are a disciple of the Rising Sun now, and I won't leave you to die. In the unlikely event that the giant emerges near you, light the flare and I'll come to you." She rose higher into the air and drifted a few feet away before stalling. "I'd suggest you wait for our return at the camp. The monster is attracted to people, and it won't pick a lone target over tens of thousands. Hopefully."

Then, in a blur of motion, she was gone.

Fast, Luke thought. He stared at the talismans she'd left him before dropping them into his inventory.

What to do, what to do.

Luke looked at the town and then at the camp, trying to decide between them.

Should I just do what she says? If the giant really is going to pop out at a random spot, then trying to find where it's going to emerge from is useless. I could keep an eye out for the flares and go over, but this is potentially a Warrior-tier monster. Or higher. I really hope it's not higher.

Do I really want to put myself anywhere close to it? Luke clenched and unclenched his fist around his sword before turning on his heel and walking farther away from the town.

Right now, doing as she says is probably for the best. Seeing a monster isn't worth getting on her bad side, and joining another organization has too many benefits for me to risk Nel changing her mind by acting stupid. If what she says is true about the town, then I'm not likely to make a big difference by going inside, either. If anything, it's more likely I'll disrupt whatever they're trying to do, or just end up standing awkwardly in a corner.

Not worth it.

Another tremor ran through the ground. This one was closer and stronger than any Luke had felt before. Pausing, he turned back toward the town.

His heart dropped into his stomach.

A single tree-size arm poked out of the surface of the earth. Long, thin, gray, and veiny. A head ripped its way free next. Bald, gray, with six eyes that glowed red with the light of molten stone, lacking any other features. Another arm jutted outward, breaking free of its earthen prison.

It slapped its two arms to the earth, and Luke watched with astonishment as the ground hardened and became a glassy obsidian where its palms hit grass. With an effortless heave, it pulled itself free from the dirt. Two more sets of arms followed, jutting out of its ribs, which in turn were followed by a pair of monstrous legs. Revealing its full form. It was as tall as a two-story house, and six freakishly large arms brushed the ground on its otherwise proportional frame.

Languidly, it stretched its limbs and rolled its shoulders. Like a king surveying its domain, its gaze locked onto the horizon. Its skin bubbled and churned before hardening, once-smooth flesh turning to rock.

It looked to the sky, and its eyes crinkled into a smile.

Luke took a slow and cautious step back, careful not to move too fast, lest he draw its attention to him. He ignored the beating of his heart. Its head snapped in his direction.

Luke's eyes locked with the giant's.

Recalling Nel's instructions, he withdrew the flare from his inventory and ripped the perforated tab on the paper's bottom. The talisman flew free from his fingers and floated in the air for a moment before erupting into brilliant white light, glowing brighter and brighter as it ascended into the sky. Leaving a trail leading back to Luke.

The Gegenees bent its knees, and all six of its hands sank into the earth.

What's it—

Something whizzed by Luke's head and smashed into a tree behind him, shattering its trunk in an instant and filling the air with leaves. The creature stood straight and proudly displayed five hands clutching obsidian orbs, while an empty sixth waved at Luke happily.

What the fuck. Why is it waving!

Luke ripped the tab off a protective talisman, and a large, translucent wall appeared in front of him.

The giant furrowed its eyeballs in a crude facsimile of a frown, its arm blurred, and an obsidian orb shattered over the barrier, which for the moment held firm. Its false frown deepened, two arms blurred in quick succession, and two more times the giant's artillery broke over Luke's barrier.

Seemingly having absorbed enough punishment, the barrier dissolved, and as it did, Luke activated another one. Just in time to stop another barrage.

This thing is on a whole different level, Luke thought, on the verge of panicking. The third and last talisman was in his hand, ready for the moment his current one fizzled out.

Focus. I need to focus. I don't have time to be scared, Luke thought as he slipped into the First Stance of the Sword.

Time seemed to slow as he became hyperaware of the giant's movements. Luke's eyes traced over every contour of its body and came to an obvious conclusion. He was too clunky and not anywhere near fast enough to react to its projectiles.

The monster dipped its hands into the ground again, no doubt preparing for another volley. Luke focused on his mana as he prepared to act.

Mentally calling on his status, he dumped all his stat points into Agility. Every drop of aethereal mana that the Seed had stored away entered his body at once and, under the inhumanly precise control of the Seed, spread over his entire nervous system and into his tendons. At the same time, the world itself seemed to snap into focus as colors became more vivid and every detail more crisp.

In quick succession, one obsidian orb after another crashed into the barrier, and the second it gave way, Luke ran forward, faster than he ever had before.

I can't attack it from the front, its arms give it too much reach, and not even my spear is long enough to snake past them.

The monster's arm flexed, and Luke kicked off the ground and into the air, dodging its attack with fractions of a second to spare. Channeling mana into his boots, Luke ran across the air, the First Stance alerting him to the monster's every action and guiding him through the barrage.

The distance between them shrank rapidly, and the monster cocked its head to the side in confusion, seemingly stunned that its prey was running toward it rather than away. Its eyes set into a smile.

Lifting a leg into the air, it kicked the earth. The ground twisted where its foot raked across, and a spray of obsidian balls flew into the air.

Activating his last protective talisman, Luke let it absorb the attack as he climbed higher and higher into the sky.

His mana dwindled away as the First Stance of the Sword once again whispered in the back of his mind. Directing him toward the monster's inevitable demise.

All I need to do is— The draw on his mana spiked.

Abruptly the technique stopped working, his vision swam, and his boots failed him. He was out of mana.

Shit, shit, shi—

Luke tumbled to the ground, rolling to a stop at the monster's feet.

The monster stepped back and bowed forward, observing the human that had landed before it.

Luke's eyes met all six of the giant's. It blinked slowly before stretching back up. Lifting a fist into the air, it waved goodbye with five of its hands.

A message flashed in front of his eyes.

Threat detected.

NO FUCKING SHIT.

CHAPTER 37

In the Sky

*S*eed? *Now may be a good time to offer a charge.*

It stayed silent.

Of course it's got nothing to say.

Luke looked at the giant's equally giant fist with incomprehension, his life flashing before his eyes as he struggled to think of a way to escape. Wondering if this was how he was going to die.

Honestly, it's better than dying in a car crash. Way more impressive, if nothing else. Is this really the end? Already?

No.

It can't be. Maybe the Seed is going to try and put me in a different body when this one—

A bolt of lightning shot through the giant's head, turning it to ash as it passed and pausing the creature's movements.

Or it was waiting for that.

Luke blinked in surprise as he scrambled to his feet and leaped back from the creature that had almost ended his life.

Is it dead? He looked at the monster's headless corpse, watching with disgust as squirming tendrils of lava erupted from its neck.

NOPE.

"Get away!" Nel flew to him and scooped him into her arms, carrying them both a good distance from the town and the earthborn.

Dropping him to his feet, she turned back toward the giant, and they watched in apprehension as the tendrils formed into a new head. The giant set its eyes into a smile and waved at them cheerfully.

I really hate how that thing is so happy, Luke thought. *It really makes this way creepier than it has to be. I'm already scared for my life—isn't that enough for it?*

"This is bad!" A worried frown worked its way onto Nel's face. Sighing, she held out her hand, and a spear freed itself from deep beneath the earth and flew to her waiting palm.

A second later, her ring flashed, and a talisman appeared in her hand. She ripped the end off carelessly, and Luke watched in awe as it folded itself into a bird and, faster than his eyes could follow it, disappeared in a stream of light.

What was that?

A look of resolve came over her face, and she clutched her spear tightly. The smell of ozone filled the air as arcs of lightning traveled up and down the shaft of her spear.

"I'm going to keep it busy. We can't let it run free no matter what happens. The wards protecting the town won't hold up forever. I called for help, but if I die, tell my mom I love her!"

"Wait, let's think this—"

Her foot braced against the ground, the earth crumpled, and Nel appeared in front of the creature.

She had moved so fast that even with his freshly enhanced Agility, Luke struggled to see more than a blur. What he did see left him feeling nothing but dread.

Nel's spear was caught in one of the giant's hands, and it was cocking its still partially formed head curiously. Its chest rose and fell in what Luke was sure was perverse laughter.

"ARRRHHRR," Nel screamed at it before relinquishing her spear and flying higher into the air. A bow appeared in her hand, an arrow already nocked. From high in the sky, she rained down one arrow after another. Each one wormed its way into the monster's body and exploded, leaving deep gouges in their wake, peppering every surface of the giant's body.

The monster just stood there, weathering her attacks and seemingly unconcerned by the damage that was being done to it. Its posture practically screamed boredom as it rested three of its hands on its hips, drumming its fingers against its rocky flesh while it inspected her spear. Slowly turning it over and occasionally stabbing the air with it.

Luke observed the battle from the ground, slowly beginning to realize that the monster was not only beyond him, but Nel, too.

It was too fast, and too strong. Whatever damage they did was pointless in the face of its ability to regenerate itself, and it knew it.

There has to be something I can do, right? If things keep going the way they are, it'll exhaust Nel, and then what's stopping it from killing everyone else?

Should I run? A treacherous part of his brain whispered that he had no real connection to these people. That he didn't even know who they were.

No. I can't. Not only is that scummy, but something tells me this thing likes playing with its food, and it won't let me go. It won't let any of us go.

Think. Think. Think.

The First Stance . . . it drained all my mana. It was stupid of me to use it without fully understanding how it works. It did the same when I was fighting Yjarn, but using it and the boots at the same time was a mistake. I didn't think that the drain would be greater the stronger the enemy is. What did it show me, though? Clearly there's a way to kill it. Maybe it has a core somewhere in its body. A critical point, one that it can't regenerate. Maybe its heart, if it has one, he thought.

In the distance, Luke watched as the Inner Disciples who had circled the walls earlier came running before coming to a stop as they witnessed the battle taking place.

Standing between the town and the monster, they argued among themselves briefly before one broke away from the crowd and reached into his robes. Kneeling to the ground, he attached a slip of paper to a rock and pelted it at the giant.

Luke recognized his intent almost immediately. The cultivator had thrown an explosive talisman, one of the ones Nel had given them earlier.

If her explosive arrows aren't doing the job, then neither are his explosive talismans. Luke shook his head. *At least he's doing something, though.*

The battle, if it could be called that, continued in the same vein for minutes longer. The giant seemed content to let them attack it, and that's what the disciples of the Rising Sun did.

As the minutes dragged on, however, despair settled into their hearts as they came to realize their foe wasn't something that they could defeat.

Suddenly it looked around, its eyes widened in fright. Bending its knees, its hands once again sank into the earth and came back with six obsidian orbs, before it stopped and stood eerily still.

Threat detected.

Wha—

Arke descended from the sky. Bathed in the light of the setting suns, her white wings looked as if they were on fire.

Shit.

Luke could feel his heart beating frantically in his chest as the not-angel flapped her wings rhythmically, floating between him and the giant. Just a few feet away.

What's she doing here?

"Is this paltry creature what threatens your domain?" She craned her neck and looked right at Luke. His heart almost leaped out of his chest as she addressed him.

My domain? What?

"You think quite little of me, Lady Arke." A tall and thin man, dressed in pure gold and wearing the most pretentious crown he had ever seen, walked out from behind Luke and joined her in inspecting the giant. What to Luke had been a deadly foe was to them a mere curiosity.

What— How long has she been here? How long has he been here? Luke thought frantically.

Arke laughed softly as she tracked the new arrival with her eyes. "Come, Cyzicus, you know as well as I do that my opinion of you is perfectly apt."

"Truly, you wound me." He bowed to her, then looking to the sky he yelled, "Agnella! Come down and say hi to your grandpa!"

Seriously, what the fuck is going on?

Luke's eyes darted from Arke, to the man in gold, and to Nel, who looked equally astonished by what was going on.

"I'm fighting a giant!" she yelled back.

"Oh, of course." Cyzicus waved errantly at the creature. A curtain of golden sparks sprayed out of his hands and doused the still monster. When they were gone, so was the giant, leaving a pair of large couch-size feet on the ground as the only evidence that it had ever existed. He looked back up to the sky again. "I do apologize for stealing your kill, Agnella. I'm afraid this particular creature is, for the moment, beyond your ability to destroy. You've only just entered the Warrior tier, after all." He nodded to her, looking beyond regretful for having saved her life.

"I, uh . . . Yes, Grandfather!" Nel bowed to him in the sky before she realized that she was still flying, and, blushing, she flew down, bowing to him and then Arke a moment later. "I thank you for your aid."

"No thanks needed, Granddaughter." He laughed jovially and rumpled her hair. "How goes your expedition?"

Nel blushed deeper. "Poorly. We are no closer now than we were the last time we spoke. I fear the creature may have fled farther than we dare tread into the cyclops's territory."

He frowned deeply before sighing. "No matter, then—what is lost is lost. Perhaps it's time to return home?"

"Tha—"

Cyzicus cut her off with a wave of his hand. "The Tide is near, and it is increasingly dangerous to wander in the wilderness."

"Yes, Grandfather." Nel bowed once again. "We will return home."

"Where is Lukeus? He left with you, did he not?"

"I sent him and the Outer Disciples to the town to organize matters with the mortals. In case the mortals panicked," she lied smoothly.

"Isn't she just wonderfully smart, Lady Arke?" Cyzicus beamed at his granddaughter proudly.

"Very," Arke said dryly.

"I knew you would agree! I think Agnella will be the one to succeed me as emperor once my old age catches up to me," he supplied to the uninterested not-angel, looking every bit like a proud parent. "I thought I'd introduce you, in case you're still here when that happens."

Did he just—

Luke buckled to his knees as *something* pressed down on him. He lifted his eyes and saw that, with the exception of Cyzicus and Arke, everyone was on their knees, from Nel to every Outer Disciple.

"Be careful how you speak to me, Cyzicus."

"Of course, my lady. I would never dream of being anything other than my most hospitable." He bowed down to her. "As you know, I've mobilized every cultivator on all of Sylcra in search of your thief, and we will not rest until he is found."

"And yet, he does not stand before me," she bit out.

Technically correct, Luke thought as he mulled over their conversation. *I am on my knees.*

"I cannot present to you a thief that is not here, my lady, as much as I desire to do so. Nor can I present to you a thief I have never seen, or whose abilities I do not know, or a thief that you do not know is on this island." He grinned at her.

The pressure doubled, planting Luke's face deep into the earth.

Cyzicus frowned distastefully. "I humbly ask that you not torture my subjects, Lady Arke. Especially not those who so valiantly fought a battle far above their abilities in defense for those I'm sworn to protect by the creed," he said, his voice suddenly cold. "A duty I will fulfill even if you kill me."

"You do not command me."

"I wouldn't dare. However, many grow increasingly impatient with your antics. No ship has docked on the archipelago for weeks. I cannot afford to turn them away much longer."

"You will do as you're told," she hissed.

"I do as the divines bid me."

The pressure suddenly eased, and Luke lifted his face from the ground.

She doesn't even know it's me, and I'm already eating dirt.

"Pray tell, what have the gods told you?"

"That is between me and them, I'm afraid." He adjusted the crown on his head. "You should know the rules."

"Humph." She flapped her wings, and for a moment Luke thought he would be carried away with the resulting gusts, but the wind vanished, and he heard the Emperor sigh in relief.

"Okay, the mean lady is gone now; we can all be normal." Cyzicus clapped his hands and smiled.

Luke shakily rose to his feet and looked around. She was gone. A fact that brought no small amount of relief to him.

"You!" Cyzicus grinned and pointed at Luke. "You were brilliant! Never in a thousand years have I seen a mortal charge a Warrior-tier monster so brazenly. Truly spectacular. For a moment I even thought you would succeed. Incredible. Truly amazing." He turned to Nel. "And you, so heroic!" He rumpled her hair again. "If your father was still alive, he would be so proud of the woman you've become. Come give this old man a hug!" He stretched his arms wide, and, not even bothering to wait, he closed the distance between them and captured her in a bear hug. "And you!" He pointed to the Inner Disciple who had thrown the explosive talisman. "So brave. It warms my heart to see my family surrounded by fine, upstanding cultivators."

Luke opened and closed his mouth as the emperor of Sylcra drowned everyone present in compliments.

Is this how he always is? Luke thought, amused. *I kinda like him.*

CHAPTER 38

Cyzicus of Cyzicus

"The ward stone will need to be recharged after the beating the giant gave it," the emperor explained as he led Luke and Nel into the town. Luke was left wondering why he had been chosen to come with the pair when no other disciple had.

Is my identity already exposed? Luke thought worriedly. *He did see me fly, and I doubt enchanted boots are common, but I didn't think they would link me to Carim. And I don't think he saw me pull anything out of the inventory.*

But he hasn't said anything yet, either. If he wanted to turn me in to Arke, she was right there, so that can't be it, can it?

As the ruler of Sylcra droned on and on, Luke started to suspect that an answer would come, but only when the emperor willed it, which, at the rate things were going, made Luke suspect that it wouldn't be any time soon.

"Now, normally I don't do this kind of thing, but it's good to guide the younger generation from time to time. That's what my own father told me all those centuries ago, at any rate!" He nodded to the townspeople as they parted ways for the trio. Their curious eyes locked on the three cultivators as they walked purposefully through the town.

Cyzicus suddenly stopped, squinting his eyes as scanned each building. "It has been a while, but, aha! There it is!" He rubbed his hands together and marched forward, leading them to an empty plot of land at the center of the town. Luke glanced between an equally confused Nel and the smiling Hero, wondering what he was supposed to be looking at.

"Without ward stones shielding my towns and cities, the giants would have overrun Sylcra a millennium ago. With them, every time one attacks, I get alerted at the capital. Depending on the size of the town, most of them can hold off Mortal-tier Gegenees for about a week, Warrior tiers for thirty minutes, and Hero tiers for about one or two minutes. Once I have everything sorted out, I can usually teleport people where they need to go well within that time frame," he explained casually. "Or go by myself if I have nothing else to do."

Pretty cool, Luke thought. He was moderately impressed with how seriously the emperor took the safety of his people.

A ring flashed on Cyzicus's finger, and a large golden key appeared in his hand. He jabbed it forward into the air, and to Luke's surprise a giant altar shimmered into existence.

It's just like the Hero's Tomb. Huh.

"Clever bit of runework, these things. Nothing compared to what the gods can do, of course, but quite amazing nonetheless." He strode forward and rested his hand on the altar. "Especially since it was only a warrior who built these."

Immediately it lit up a brilliant gold, and an illusory bar floated atop it, roughly half-full and rapidly filling as he channeled his mana into the ward stone.

"They keep their charge by drawing on ambient mana, but it takes weeks for it to replenish itself that way—depending, of course, on the density of mana present. This particular part of the island isn't exactly mana-rich, and with the Giant Tide so close, it's better to keep it topped up." His ring flashed again, and he produced another key, which then floated through the air into Nel's hands. "This is for you, since you're a warrior now. After every battle, I want you to recharge the wards. Although it will take you longer than it does me."

"Yes, Grandfather!" Nel bowed to him, dutifully staring at the key before her own ring flashed and it disappeared.

"There's no need for formalities, child. I moved beyond such trivialities ages ago." He shook his head in exasperation and turned to Luke. "Her mother is prickly about this sort of thing," he explained with an apologetic shrug, "and none of my grandchildren are keen on listening to me above their mothers. No loyalty, I tell you," he complained, not looking particularly upset about that particular fact.

"I see," Luke said after a moment of hesitation, not quite sure how to respond to the emperor and still trying to puzzle together what the purpose behind it all was. Worry gnawed at him as one awful scenario after another ran through his head, and he desperately did not want to have landed in another situation where someone lorded his secret over his head.

"I sense something special about you," he said suddenly.

"You do?" Luke asked, wincing internally as he donned a carefully neutral expression.

I really wish you didn't, he grumbled to himself.

"Of course," Cyzicus stated matter-of-factly. "Through the millennia, I've developed a keen sense of potential, and I've learned to recognize those who possess it. I think you have what it takes to go far in this world," he said earnestly.

"I see. Thank you?"

"I speak only the truth—there's no need to thank me, child." He scratched his neck. "What's your name?"

"Luke."

His eyes widened in surprise. "Lukeus?"

"No . . . just Luke."

"Ah, of course. I have a grandson named Lukeus, and he insists on shortening his name. I thought you might be the same."

"We've met, although I didn't realize that you were all related."

"Oh, of course. You are a member of the Rising Sun—it stands to reason that you would have. Where was I? Oh, right. You have talent. The way you attacked the monster was truly impressive. A technique, if my eyes haven't deceived me."

Nel perked up in surprise and gazed questioningly at Luke, looking impressed despite herself.

He nodded slowly.

"No need to look so alarmed, although it is quite rare to see a mortal wield one, it isn't unheard-of. Little Agnella here was just like you in that regard." He beamed at her proudly.

"Thank you, Grandfather!" She bowed again.

He smiled as he shook his head at the gesture. "As I was saying, you're quite talented. You may not know about what's happening in the world outside my little corner of it, but fate is stirring, and it has even the gods worried. Things have been stagnant on Theos for eons, but now something is simmering under the surface. Just waiting to boil over and engulf this world in chaos."

"I'm not following," Luke said after a moment.

"Amid chaos, there is opportunity." He turned back to the altar the second the bar filled completely and removed his hand. "Opportunity, for those who seek it, to rise far beyond what is expected or even thought of as possible."

I'm really not following. Luke felt a headache forming behind his eyes as he struggled to decipher the emperor's words and what they had to do with him.

At least he's not blackmailing me. That's good, right?

"I—" Luke started to say before the hero cut him off.

"You don't get it, I know. I don't expect you to; it's fine. If it helps put you at ease, I don't care who taught you that technique, and I don't care who gave you those shoes. I *really* don't. I've lived long enough to understand that becoming an obstacle for someone who stirs fate, such as yourself, is a poor idea. If history has taught me anything, it is that those that get in the way of destiny are trampled underfoot. The titans learned that lesson the hard way, and I suspect Arke will learn it again, and soon. What I do care about is that you're a talented kid, from Sylcra."

Nel's eyes widened in surprise as she connected the dots. "Grandfather! You can't mean—"

He silenced her with a wave of his hand before turning back to Luke. "In six months' time, there will be a tournament. The greatest cultivators in the world will compete, and I want you to enter on behalf of Sylcra. I had lost hope for the mortal bracket, but I really think that if you participate, we have a good chance of winning. It will take some work, of course, but with my help, and the giants to cut your teeth on, I'll be able to push you to the peak of the Mortal tier just in time. What do you say?"

Yeah, no way I would have guessed that. Luke mulled over his words. *A competition, though?*

"What kind of tournament is it?"

"The actual events change from year to year, but it's all in sport, and the prizes are to die for. For you and me both," Cyzicus said, stars practically shining in his eyes.

"Prizes?" Luke perked up.

Cyzicus grinned. "Great ones. One time the winner of the Mortal tier received a golden apple from the evening garden. A single bite adds a century to your life span and has enough mana to take you to the peak of the Warrior tier," he boasted, clearly hoping to impress Luke.

That's pretty awesome, but— "It's not a fight to the death or anything, is it? I won't risk my life for greed."

"Win or lose, you'll live. The tournament isn't to the death," the emperor assured him. "A lot of the people competing will be of, shall we say, high pedigree, and the gods don't like their kids fighting to the death for what amounts to scraps."

"Gods?" A bead of sweat rolled down the side of Luke's face. *Yeah, fuck this. I'm not getting involved.*

"Their children tend to participate, and the prizes have to come from somewhere. I believe this year it is Lord Hephaestus hosting, and he's known for his inventions."

Hephaestus—isn't he the god of building stuff? Luke thought, keeping his face carefully blank.

"Thank you for your confidence, but I—"

"You don't have to worry about offending the deities, if that's what you're worried about. Or their children, for that matter. Most of them don't even know who their parents are—immortals tend to have a lot—but that's beside the point. Look"—he took the crown off his head, dusted it, and put it back on—"think about it. That's all I'm asking. If you say no, then I'll understand. I really do think, though, that you have a lot to gain. We both do," he said meaningfully.

"I— Okay. I'll think about it," Luke said eventually.

The emperor smiled at him. "Good. I have to head back and figure out where that poor excuse for an Olympian went. I don't know what she thinks she's achieving by staying here, but the novelty is wearing thin. You know she's staying in my castle?" He floated in the air as he shook his head and muttered, "Some people," under his breath before vanishing.

"'Bye!" Nel shouted after him.

"*So,*" Luke said, turning to her. "Is that how stuff normally goes with him?"

She shrugged her shoulders. "Grandfather has ruled Sylcra for thousands of years, and he cares a lot about it. You should compete."

Luke frowned. "I thought you were against it?"

"I don't know what he saw in you, but if he thinks you have a chance at winning, then I trust him. And he doesn't ask for favors lightly."

"Do you know why he wants me to compete?"

"That . . . I'm not sure. He must have a reason, though. Even then, the benefit for you isn't small. Just the prizes alone are enough, not to mention how much you would advance under his tutelage. He hasn't taken a disciple in decades, but everyone he has taken has advanced to the Warrior tier."

That sounds great, but I'm not exactly worried about not becoming a Warrior. With the Seed to guide my path, that's basically assured. Not getting killed along the way is a much bigger concern.

"Are you going to participate?" Luke asked her.

A determined look came over her face. "I will. A champion brings great prestige to their home, and I intend to win in my bracket."

"Is that all it is? A pride thing, and some prizes?"

If it's really just a friendly competition, then it might be worth it. Fame would suck, but I can change my face whenever I want. I'm sure there's more to the mask than just three different forms in a variety of colors.

"Elder Agnella! Elder Agnella!" a black-robed cultivator came running up to them. "We've found it!"

Her eyes widened in surprise.

"I have to go. We can talk about the Olympics later!" she said, before taking off into the air, leaving Luke alone with the Outer Disciple.

The Olympics?

CHAPTER 39

The Catbird

H ey, I'm Luke." He extended his hand and introduced himself to the Outer Disciple who had delivered the news.

He grabbed Luke's hand as he caught his breath. "Axin."

"Sooo . . . what did you guys find?"

He grinned. "A griffin. It's why we're here. We heard rumors of one in the area, and Elder Agnella decided to lead an expedition to capture it."

Luke's eyes widened in surprise. "A griffin?" he asked, just to make sure he had heard him right. "That's the thing with an eagle's head and wings attached to a lion's body, right?" he asked eagerly, already imagining what such a creature would look like in real life.

This world is crazy, but they do have some cool stuff, he thought.

Axin grinned in response. "Mmm-hmm."

"What does she want it for?"

He shrugged his shoulders. "I'm not sure. We think she just wanted a steed, but they're supposed to be valuable. I just hope she catches it this time so we can go home. We've been after it for months, but it's really fast, and only the Elder can fly fast enough to chase after it," he explained, stepping back into the main street. "What's your deal, by the way?"

"It's a long story."

"Mmm-hmm." Axin grunted. "Some other time, then. I'm a bit drained for a long story."

"Yeah, I'm dead on my feet, too. Do you mind taking me to your camp? I think I'd kill for a bed and a warm blanket right about now."

And I have a lot of thinking to do. The Olympics, the Rising Sun, the emperor, Arke. There's so much going on, and it all came on so suddenly.

"Yeah, I was just about to head there, too. What was the giant like, by the way? You're the guy that stayed with her, yeah?"

Luke nodded. "I was, and it was scary. Really scary. It was at the Warrior tier. Thing almost killed me." Luke stretched his arms. "Are they all so happy?"

"It was happy?" Axin asked incredulously.

"Yeah . . . it was trying to kill me, but it was laughing and smiling and stuff."

"But they don't have mouths," Axin pointed out.

"I know, and it didn't, but it did this thing with its eyes, and it was waving and stuff. I don't know, I just thought it was weird." Luke frowned. "And creepy."

"I guess we'll find out if that's normal or not eventually. In the stories, the giants are always mindless beasts, but maybe those are just the Mortal-tier ones."

"Maybe." Luke ran his hands through his hair.

The pair heard the camp before they saw it. Sounds of laughter, and loud conversations proliferated through the night as the members of the Rising Sun Sect celebrated the giant's defeat.

When the camp finally came into view, Luke's mouth dropped open in surprise as he saw Lukeus swaying drunkenly as he stood atop the giant's foot, a mortal woman draped across his shoulder and a bottle full of booze in his hand.

I can't believe they actually dragged its feet here.

"It was the most epic thing I've ever imagined ever seeing!" Lukeus lifted his bottle into the air. The crowd assembled before him cheered, seemingly impressed by his nonsensical speech, and lifted their own bottles in response.

He was in the town, wasn't he? Luke grinned at the spectacle as he walked deeper into the camp.

Everywhere he went, the Inner Disciples had assembled in small clumps and were regaling their black-robed counterparts with already-embellished accounts of what had happened. Who, for their part, were wearing looks of disappointment, realizing that they had not only missed the chance to see Elder Agnella fight the monster, but also how Arke stopped it in its tracks and how Emperor Cyzicus had made short work of it.

Their voices sank to whispers as they recounted the events that took place after.

"Did Lord Cyzicus really call her a mean lady?" a blonde girl asked

"He did, and she got angry, and then my face was in the dirt. She was so strong, but then Lord Cyzicus was like, 'I won't let you harm my citizens, even if it kills me,' and he sounded so scary when he said it, and Arke flew away after that."

"You're telling the story all wrong. What really happened is—" Another Inner Disciple shook his head and interrupted them, interjecting with his own, more correct version of the story.

"Do you have a spare tent for me?" Luke asked.

"You can sleep in that one," Axin said, pointing to an empty tent in a group of those already in use. "It's mine, but I don't need it for tonight." He patted Luke on the shoulder and walked away with a pep in his step.

Luke followed him with his eyes as he made a beeline to a girl on the opposite side of the camp and scratched the back of his head awkwardly as he realized why the tent had been offered so freely.

I really need to start carrying more of my stuff in a physical bag and lug it around. At least until I can get my hands on one of those magic rings and use it to explain my inventory.

Settling into the tent, Luke called up his status.

Status	Skills	Quests	Inventory
Name: Lukas King			
Tier: Mortal			
Mana: 980/4,648			
Rate: 15% per hour			
Strength: 109			
Agility: 239			
Constitution: 112			
Arcana: 83			
Stat Points: 0			
Bloodline: Locked. Conditions not met. (1/10,000)			
Charges: 7/10			

It has not been a productive two weeks, he thought. *I barely improved any attributes other than Agility, and even then, most of that has been from stat points.*

It makes sense; I didn't really bother exercising when I was in the grasslands on the way here, so I shouldn't moan about it now. I probably could have figured something out, but it's not like I packed anything that would help me work out, either, so it is what it is. I'll have to make preparations so that I can continue cultivating even in the wilderness from now on, but it might be tricky.

At least all that falling improved my Constitution stat . . . He frowned.

I've been stupid with how I've been spending my points, he suddenly realized.

Saving them up for future emergencies has its place, but not to the extent that I have been. More than that, I need to start prioritizing my mana reserves.

Running out of it today nearly killed me, and if I had spent those points in Constitution and Arcana, then maybe the skill wouldn't have drained me dry. Especially now that I have the boots, not having the mana to use them is beyond stupid.

The normal drain from the stances is pretty small, lower even than my passive regen, but it ups significantly when I use it with intent to kill. I'll have to take some time to map the cost of the skill to the relative strength of my opponents. Maybe see if I can figure out how to judge the amount of mana someone has. Arya and Yjarn were both able to tell after touching me, and there's no reason I shouldn't be able to do the same.

In this particular instance, though, I think that the giant was so far above me in strength that it wouldn't have mattered. Which might be a limit of the techniques themselves. They are, after all, only Mortal-tier skills.

Just another thing to figure out.

He sighed softly as he subtly shifted his posture, listening as the activity outside gradually began to lessen and silence overtook the night.

When he woke up, it was to the sound of excited screams and beating wings as gusts of air rocked his borrowed tent.

He clutched his sword tightly, for a moment fearing Arke had returned before deciding that the odds of that happening, while not zero, were low.

If Arke was really here for me, I doubt I would have woken up.

It's kind of funny, now that I think about it. I've been within spitting distance of her twice now, and she hasn't realized that it was me. Nefkha, I could understand, didn't like the Olympians and didn't want to help them in any way, so he hid my presence, he thought as he got dressed, already having an idea of what the commotion was.

But then, why is Cyzicus so antagonistic toward her? His words were polite, but their meaning wasn't. And he's not scared of her. He acknowledged that she could kill him, but there was no fear.

Arke doesn't seem to be the type of person to take an insult lying down, and she's strong enough to kill a god. So why would she let a hero talk to her like that? Unless it's not Cyzicus that she's worried about. He mentioned the creed and referenced the rules—could that be it?

Do the gods govern themselves? Or is there someone standing above even them, someone that's making and enforcing the rules, so that everyone obeys? Either way, it would make some sense. At the very least, it explains that despite all her bluster, she hasn't actually made a show of her power yet. She's afraid.

Luke grinned at that thought as he stepped out of the tent. A grin that only widened when his earlier suspicion was confirmed.

Lying lazily in the middle of the camp was the most majestic creature he had ever seen. It was big, the size of an elephant, with golden wings tucked into its feline body, while its equally golden, eagle-like head surveyed the crowd forming around it with curiosity.

Wow.

"How'd you get it to be so calm, Elder?"

"I made it my familiar," Nel answered absently, walking around it in a circle as she stroked its fur.

A familiar? Luke thought as he inched closer to the warrior and her pet. His mind darted to the egg he had stored in his inventory as he suddenly realized that he might have a use for it after all.

It would be pretty awesome having a steed like that. Although, he thought grudgingly, *an eagle doesn't seem as cool as a griffin. But it is supposed to be an eagle descended from one who ate a titan's liver, so maybe.*

"Luke, there you are!" Nel called out to him the second he made his way to the front of the crowd. Reluctantly, she tore her eyes away from the catbird as she parted the crowd and walked toward him.

"Hi," he said. "That's a nice cat you have there."

She grinned in response. "I have something to tell you. Come." She led him out of the camp and toward the river. "I know I invited you to join the Rising Sun, but Grandfather has requested that you join him in the capital."

"What? Really?"

I guess it was too much to expect him to leave me alone. Think about it, my ass, Luke scoffed.

"It's not what you're thinking. Your participation in the Olympics is still your choice, but he thinks that your potential will be wasted doing chores in the Rising Sun. You can refuse and, if you want to, join the sect anyway. Grandfather isn't the type of person who forces others to obey his will."

Luke frowned as he considered her words.

"What's the capital like?"

"It's . . . the capital. The seat of his power. It's big and they have plays and festivals almost every day. It's lively. I don't know. You'll be fine there."

It kind of sounds like an Earth city.

"And there's really no pressure. I can just not go?"

"Yes." She sighed. "Grandfather said he recognized your type. He won't force you, and he won't try and manipulate you, either. It's why I'm asking you and he isn't. So you wouldn't feel pressured."

"Do you know what he wants from me?" Luke asked. *Because I sure as hell don't.*

She bit her lip. "I'm not sure, but," she hedged, "I've heard rumors that he's close to breaking through to the next tier, and it's not only the winner of the tournament that gets a prize." She looked at him meaningfully.

"Huh."

So if I'm reading the situation right, he wants me to participate because he actually thinks that I can win, and he wants me to win, because he needs something to break through.

Nel's eyes suddenly widened as she looked past Luke. Following her gaze, Luke was wholly unsurprised to find the emperor standing behind him, idly smelling a rose.

"So, what do you say?" he asked.

CHAPTER 40

Mana for Dummies

Luke's eyes darted between the emperor and Nel before he sighed audibly. Bringing his arms up to his head, he considered his choice and forcibly suppressed his irritation at having been put on the spot so suddenly.

On the one hand, I really should stay under the radar. On the other hand, the offer really is tempting. There's so much I still don't know, and guidance from someone at the Hero tier, who understands this world and cultivating in general, is invaluable. I'm sure I can figure most of it out eventually, but the time I'll save has to count for something. Besides, there's only so much I can piece together from context in the lowest echelons of power.

Worst-case scenario, I still have seven charges left, and if nothing else, the Seed hasn't gotten me killed—yet. Using the charges runs the risk of drawing Arke down on my head, but they did get me away from her once.

Fuck it. I already know I'm going to regret this, but—

"Okay."

"Yes!" Cyzicus yelled, pumping his fist into the air. Then, looking awkwardly between Luke and Nel, he coughed in his hand. "Right. You won't regret this, that I can promise." He grinned.

I sure hope so. Then again, if things go belly up, I probably won't have the time to regret anything, either.

"I'll take your word for that." Luke smiled back at him, for the moment, at least, letting his doubts fall to the back of his head.

"Great. Agnella, drop by the capital more often. Your grandpa gets bored sometimes, and congratulations on your new steed. A griffin is a rare and powerful mount, and she will serve you well. Tell Lukeus to stop being a scoundrel," said Cyzicus, stepping in to give her a hug before turning to Luke. "This might make you a little dizzy." He tapped him on his shoulder.

The world flickered, and in the next instant, Luke was in a different spot. A large room, with paintings depicting various monsters and the heroes defeating them littering every square inch of the wall. A white desk carved from ivory sat in the middle facing a set of large silver doors.

"What was that?" he asked, turning to Cyzicus, only to see him heaving and hunched over his knees, desperately trying to catch his breath.

"One moment." He lifted a finger into the air as he collected himself. "Teleporting people without a formation in place can be rather exhausting. Even with the relatively small distance that we covered," he said between gasps.

Heroes can just teleport around? Luke thought as he fought off a sudden wave of vertigo. Blinking his eyes, he steadied himself against a wall.

"That's an impressive ability."

"It is, isn't it? Not one without drawbacks, however, and not one that's entirely mine," said Cyzicus, his breath now coming more evenly.

"It's not?" Luke asked.

Learning more already.

"No, this particular power comes with being an emperor. One of the more useful perks of the position."

"Oh . . . I'm not sure what that means."

"Some other time, Luke. For the moment, we have a lot of work to do if we want to push you to the peak of the Mortal tier. Especially as we only have six months." He straightened his posture and, with a few quick strides, threw open the doors. "Come."

"I—" Luke said, before stopping himself and following after the emperor. He resolved to talk about his enrollment in the Olympics some other time.

Walking down the corridor, he couldn't help but be impressed by the opulence. With silver furnishings, white marble, and fancy paintings, all of which were illuminated by tasteful skylights and some sort of magic-powered lamps, it really was a home befitting an emperor. A welcome change in scenery from the poorly lit cobblestone floors and moss-covered walls of the Hero's Tomb, which Luke had grown used to, and a large step up from bumming in the wilderness.

"Where are we going?"

"First, we're going to get you a manasink. They're one of the few things that will help you cover the distance between mortal and warrior, and quite useful, even outside training."

"What's it for?"

"You'll see in a minute," he responded curtly, nodding and smiling as they passed by a small group of white-robed women. "We'll also need to get you some blue robes."

Luke waved at them awkwardly as they directed curious glances toward him.

"Already?"

"It may be sooner than normal, but with your mana sense unlocked, it's only a matter of time anyway," he explained, stopping in front of a pair of random doors deep in the halls of his castle. Resting his hands on them, they flashed silver before swinging open.

"This is my armory. Everything you see here, you can earn." Cyzicus ushered him in.

It was a large room, and it put the hero's own trophy room to shame. Like hers, there was a wide assortment of objects all floating above their own pedestals, everything from swords to pieces of armor and bottles of pills.

Not as many eggs, though, Luke thought as he stepped in.

"Earn them?"

"Yes. By killing giants. I exchange merits earned by killing them for items in this room."

"I see."

"Over the centuries I've discovered that there is little that moves the hearts and fans of the greed of cultivators other than treasure. Of course, it's only fair that those who risk life and battle on my behalf be fairly compensated," he said, walking down an aisle and coming to a stop in front of a pedestal, floating above which was a golden signet ring.

Snatching it out of the air, he flung it toward Luke.

Tracing its path through the air, he caught it deftly—surprising himself as he did.

I can't believe that up until a few months ago I used to drop everything anyone ever threw at me, and now it's easier than breathing.

"Put that on and send your mana into it," Cyzicus instructed, walking deeper into the room as he did.

Briefly agonizing what finger to put it on, Luke settled on the middle finger of his left hand and grinned when it resized to fit him perfectly. Inspecting the way it looked on his hand, he nodded approvingly.

I never really thought of myself as a guy who wears jewelry, but it looks nice, he thought as he admired the ring. Bringing it close to his face, he observed the glyph carved on its face—a circle with a square inside it.

Then, doing as Cyzicus instructed, he channeled his mana toward it, only to be rebuffed by some invisible force. Frowning, he tightened his mental grasp on his mana and pushed harder and harder until he finally managed to send a single point's worth into it. A process that left him with an ache pulsing in his head.

"Did you manage it?" the emperor asked, walking back toward him and inspecting a large, four-foot-long greatsword. Which, with the exception of being a foot longer, and lacking a blue jewel encrusted in its pommel, looked nearly identical to Luke's own sword.

"I did. Why is it so hard? Sending mana into my boots is way easier than this."

"It's supposed to be," he said, casually cutting the air with the sword and smiling as a torrent of hot air buffeted through the room. "The ring is a manasink. It's meant to train something the scholars call Arcana."

Coincidence? I think not.

"What do you know about cultivating past the midstage of the Mortal tier?"

Luke scratched his chin as he considered what to say before answering. "Not a lot, honestly. I didn't learn to sense mana all that long ago, only when I figured out the technique and someone advised me to let my body cultivate naturally until it reaches saturation, whatever that means."

"Whoever told you that did you a great favor. Cultivating aethereal mana manually is a must for most people, but you should never do it at all. Honestly"—he paused as if he was carefully choosing his words—"it's a poor way to cultivate mana."

"Really? How come?"

"It's quite simple—they don't know what they're doing. Your body is a complicated machine, and unless you understand it well, tinkering with it does more harm than good. When your body naturally processes mana, it does so with precision that a human mind is incapable of achieving. It works, but the work done is of an inferior quality. It lacks depth and stability."

"I don't get it, then. How are you supposed to cultivate if your body reaches its limit?"

"By using a manasink, of course," the emperor replied cheerfully. "Without one, when you expel your mana from your body, you face no resistance. If you empty your reserves countless times, your mana will grow more vivid and robust, but you'll die before it reaches the threshold to the Warrior tier. The act of expelling your mana into the air just isn't strenuous enough. Items like your boots are better for improving your Arcana, but not by a lot. Items like that ring are designed to give resistance, and when your mana faces resistance, it grows. Unlike your body, however, your mana never gets saturated, so you can improve it with this method indefinitely. As you improve your Arcana, the innate potential of your body rises, and as such, it will never get saturated. Hence, if you improve your Arcana, you never have to rely on the other method at all."

"Then all those people improving their bodies with mana are just doing it wrong?" Luke asked incredulously.

Did I fuck up big-time by spending points on anything other than mana? Luke thought worriedly. *No, surely the Seed is better at distributing mana than the average Mortal-tier cultivator. I've seen how intricately it moves mana when I spend stat points. Still, it's not something I should leave to chance. I'll have to figure out some way to test it.*

Cyzicus frowned. "Not exactly. If you can advance to the Warrior tier, then most if not all of your fumbling can be washed away with some diligence. It's not ideal, but it is possible. When you ascend to a higher tier, the innate potential of your body rises, and your saturation point rises far beyond the mortal limit. If you exercise dutifully, then, like packing sand between rocks, you can account for your deficiencies."

"That's something, I suppose. So you're saying that I should use the ring to push my Arcana, and raising my Arcana will raise the saturation point on my body, so just regular exercise will be enough? Meaning that I won't ever have to worry about dissolving aethereal mana with my own?"

"Correct." He beamed. "Any other questions?"

"Yeah. I've talked to people in the past about cultivating, and they said that they focus on specific attributes. Like strength and speed. How does that work?"

Cyzicus drummed his fingers along the edge of his blade as he thought about the question before finally answering with some hesitancy.

"There are certain limits that, once crossed, trigger a reaction in the very fabric of our reality. Like water, once boiled, evaporates into steam, or if cooled, turns to ice. Mana behaves similarly, but not exactly the same. Once certain thresholds are crossed, its nature changes. As for your question, it is hard to answer. Our bodies are whole, but they consist of different systems. Improving even one of those systems with mana past a certain point will change the nature of mana in your body. However, mana isn't quite that simple. Its nature is spiritual as much as it is physical. It's why withholding knowledge of it from the general public is so effective in preventing them from cultivating. If they do not know that it exists, then no matter how hard they push themselves physically, it will never accumulate in their bodies."

"You're saying that belief impacts how well someone cultivates, or if they cultivate at all?"

"Precisely." He beamed.

Sounds like hoo-ha, but it is magic, so who am I to judge?

"Why are mortals prevented from cultivating?" Luke asked suddenly. It was something that he had been curious about for a long time, and the answers he had received from the Inner Disciples had never really sounded convincing. Until now, though, he always had greater concerns than to argue about the merits of everyone cultivating or not.

As an annoyed expression made its way onto Cyzicus's face, though, Luke wondered if he should have even asked.

"The answer to that is," he said, sarcasm oozing out of every pore in his body, "that it's dangerous for there to be too many cultivators. The real reason is that the divines rule Theos, and they are afraid to loosen their grasp on it. In many ways, those who ascend past the Mortal tier, and each tier above it, are a problem of numbers. By limiting the number of those that cultivate, and by ensuring that those that do cultivate do so inefficiently, the number of those who can rise to challenge them will be fewer."

"Oh," Luke said as everything clicked in his mind.

People in power want to stay in power. I should have guessed.

"Right. Here, take this, too." He suddenly extended the pommel of the sword he was holding. "Your sword is tacky rubbish. If you want to wield a weapon made of gold, at least use one with some half-decent enchantments."

Well, this is awkward, Luke thought, clutching the pommel of his sword.

CHAPTER 41

Learning What Happens

My sword isn't tacky rubbish," Luke said defensively.

Cyzicus quirked his eyebrows. "Really?"

"Really." Luke nodded at him earnestly.

"And what about it makes you feel that way?"

"It, uh—" Luke scratched his chin as he scrambled for an explanation.

Should I tell him that the sword siphons mana? He's been helpful so far, and he indirectly saved my life. He also has some vested interest in my growth. If he knows how it works and still wants to help me, then that's a massive plus.

Except, he doesn't know about the Seed, and there's no way in hell I'm telling him about that. If he hadn't just lectured me on how ill-advised it was to manually cultivate mana, then it would have been perfect, but as it stands, he might actively discourage me from using it.

"It's sentimental," Luke answered eventually. "What's so special about that one?"

The emperor looked unconvinced, and Luke caught his eyes briefly darting to Bellerophon's sword before meeting his own once again.

"It's nothing too amazing. You're a mortal and as such incapable of wielding some of my better artifacts properly. This one"—he hefted the blade into the air—"is a Warrior-tier artifact, designed specifically to be used by mortals, and it does this."

He swung the blade in a wide arc. A blue glow appeared along the sword's edge, and when it reached the peak of its motion, the light detached from the blade and cut through the air before harmlessly splashing off a wall.

That's pretty cool, but kinda weak. Luke looked at the lacking aftermath of the attack before turning back to Cyzicus. "That's not bad, I guess."

He cleared his throat. "Nothing at the Warrior tier is powerful enough to damage my home, but I assure you the projection is quite useful. It will drain a sizable portion of your mana as you are now, however, a medium-range attack has its place in battle." He extended the handle of the weapon again.

Taking it from his hand, Luke inspected the blade briefly before funneling his mana into it. Unlike the ring he had received earlier, it absorbed it without hesitation.

It's thirsty, Luke thought as he opened his status. He had a general sense of how much mana the sword was draining, but it was nowhere near as precise as the Seed.

As his mana decreased from nearly full, then to half, and then to a quarter, he began to worry if he even had enough energy to make the blue edge appear. Then, finally, with only ten percent of his reserves remaining, the edge lit up blue, just waiting to be released the moment he broke his connection with the blade.

"It's not strictly necessary, but it does help with aim when you swing the blade," said Cyzicus.

Nodding absently, Luke picked a random section of the wall and swung down and at the same time withdrew his mana. Once again, a wave of blue light traveled through the room and splashed impotently against the wall.

"It was slower that time." Luke frowned.

"It is a matter of practice. Now, if my math is correct, the two items in total cost thirteen thousand merits." The emperor grinned as Luke opened and closed his mouth. "You didn't think they were free, now, did you?"

"Well, you didn't think I had any merits, now, did you?" Luke shot back.

"Of course you do!" he said cheerfully.

"I do?" He frowned. *Since when?*

"Let me see, participating in a battle against a Warrior-tier giant earned you two thousand merits, which is enough for the sword. That leaves eleven thousand more for that ring. I'm afraid you'll have to spend every waking moment during the first three months of the Tide fighting giants, but I'm sure you're up to the task."

The first three months? Oh, right. The Olympics.

"I haven't agreed to join the tournament."

The ever-present grin on Cyzicus's face widened. "I'm sure I—"

Whatever he was going to say was interrupted when a woman in red robes came flying into the room.

"My lord!" she said, kneeling down in front of the pair. "We've found someone possessing a body! It could be the thief."

She's found what? Luke's eyes darted between Cyzicus and the woman. For a moment he entertained the idea that all this had been an elaborate ruse to lure him to their castle, where they could deliver him to Arke.

Do they think I'm secretly strong, like Nefkha first did, and did all this to trap me?

Cyzicus sighed loudly, a deep frown appearing on his face. "Very well." His ring flashed, and something darted through the air faster than Luke's eyes could follow, sinking through the roof and presumably going outside. "Lead the way."

She nodded solemnly before turning on her heel and walking out on foot, with Cyzicus following after her, leaving Luke alone in the room cradling his new sword.

Or maybe not.

Cyzicus poked his head through the door. "What are you waiting for? Come." He waved his hand, gesturing for him to follow. "Why do you think we're walking?"

"Right," Luke mumbled, before following him.

If this is a trap, it's an unnecessarily elaborate one. His mind flashed back to how effortlessly the giant had toyed with him, and how casually the man before him had destroyed it.

I'm a small fish who almost got eaten by a much bigger fish, who was then eaten by an even bigger fish, and on top of that, there's an even bigger fish that's still trying to eat me . . . At least the Seed hasn't said anything—that's gotta mean something.

The warrior led them down a hall, and a single flight of stairs that opened up to reveal a large throne room. Kneeling at the foot of the chair was a dirty, homeless-looking man dressed in rags, which were once upon a time blue robes. His hands and feet were encased in large steel manacles, and black hair spilled over his face, preventing Luke from seeing who it was.

A gust of air shook the room, and Cyzicus appeared on his throne.

"They tell me you're the thief."

"I didn't steal anything!" he rasped, straining against his bonds.

"You stole that body. I can feel your corrupted mana from here. The stench of death lingers, as I'm sure you know."

"Its soul had already departed. I stole nothing. I only took that which was ownerless."

"Hmm." Cyzicus shrugged noncommittedly. "What tier were you? For your soul to sustain a body with that level of damage and still persist, you must have been a hero at the very least. Am I right?"

"I WAS A SAINT!" the man roared. Splotches of blood sailed through the air and splattered on the pristine marble floors.

Okay, so this isn't some elaborate trap. Good to know.

Cyzicus blinked in surprise. "Oh my. It seems as if I'm in the company of an esteemed figure. Forgive my impertinence." He inclined his head. "I am quite curious what you're doing here. If you were truly a saint, you must be quite far from home."

"Who I am and what I desire is of no concern to some petty emperor of a tiny island. Release me, and I shall grant you one boon. It will take me time to expunge the tainted mana, but I—"

"Let me stop you there. We both know the fate of your kind. I cannot leave you to prey on my people, or any people, for that matter. You should have let your soul seek rest in the Aether."

"Then why have you imprisoned me?"

"I didn't want to, but I suppose you'll find out soon enough." Cyzicus sighed, resting his chin on his hand. "It will be in your best interest to relinquish your hold on that body. Before you do, though, there are greater forces at play than even I understand. Things will not be pleasant for you if you don't," he urged.

Threat detected.

Of course.

"Ah, there she is!" Cyzicus muttered under his breath, looking at the shackled figure with pity. An instant later, the doors flew open and Arke strode in.

Her eyes instantly locked on the kneeling figure, and then with a beat of her wings she was in front of him. Cocking her head to the side, she buried her arm in his chest and then kicked the body away, uncaring of the putrid blood soaking her hand.

An ethereal figure, vaguely in the shape of a man, squirmed in her grasp. Pulsating black and red lines snaked their way through its form as Arke stared into its shadowy eyes.

That's his soul. What happened to it? Why does it look like that?

"Are you the one?" she asked him.

No, that's me.

The saint screamed silently in response. Bits and pieces of his soul began to flake off and evaporate into the air.

It's dissolving, Luke thought morbidly. *What's her plan, though? Even if he did have the Seed, what if it chooses someone else again? It chose me over her once—what makes her think now will be any different?*

The silence in the room over the next few minutes was suffocating. Arke seemed content to wait for the man to perish. Cyzicus attempted to maintain a neutral expression, but Luke saw him fidget uncomfortably more than once, clearly unsettled by what he was witnessing.

Eventually, though, the soul withered away until Arke was left holding a small pebble-size fragment of it. Scoffing, she released it into the air, where it disappeared a moment later.

"He's not the thief. Keep looking."

"This is the sixth time," Cyzicus drawled. "The sixth time you've erased a soul's existence to fuel your petty grudge. Even if you had left him as he was, his pathetic attempt at returning to life would have seen him dwindle away into a mindless animal, and he would have died. If he fed on the innocent, Lord Anubis himself would have reaped his soul. But"—he stood from his throne and walked over to her—"not even he would have been cruel enough to erase him from existence. It's forbi—"

Arke grinned, lifted her finger, and flicked. Cyzicus flew through the air and crashed through his throne.

"You're an ant. Do not presume to lecture me on matters you know nothing about."

Chuckling, he rose to his feet, dusted his golden robes, adjusted the crown on his head, and spit a globule of blood onto the ground.

"Perhaps that would be wise." He stretched his hands to his side. "But I'm not an ant that you can step on—not without consequences, at least."

She scoffed. "The faith you have in your gods is amusing, but even they cannot protect you from me."

"*Our* gods seem to be doing an okay job of it. I am still alive, after all. You, however, are walking on thin ice. Olympus spared you once, but you know as well as I do that they will not tolerate this crusade of yours for much longer. Your loyalty isn't without question, and your sister can only beg for mercy so many times."

"Tch." She looked around the room, her eyes lingering on the red-robed warrior before landing on Luke.

His heart drummed in anticipation, and his knees buckled under invisible pressure, bringing him to his knees.

This again?

"ENOUGH!" Cyzicus yelled. His ring flashed, and a bolt of lightning appeared at his side. The pressure suddenly eased. "I've told you that my subjects aren't for you to play with."

Her eyes traced the bolt of lightning apprehensively. "So you have been given teeth. How quaint." A spear made of light appeared above her head, and she rose into the air. "You're going to keep searching for that thief. No matter how long it takes."

A blinding light surged through the room, and when it faded, Arke was gone, and the once-pristine throne room was in ruins.

"My lord!" the warrior yelled, flying to the charred remains of the throne.

"I'm fine," Cyzicus said, pulling himself out of the rubble of his castle. "Luke," he called out, "are you—"

"I'm good." He climbed onto his feet, blinking spots out of his eyes as he did. "What's that about?"

I know, but it would be weirder not to ask.

Before Cyzicus could answer, though, another red-robed warrior flew into the room. He was fatter than any cultivator Luke had seen before, and sported an unflattering and patchy beard.

"My lord! Your grandson was killed!" he said, collapsing onto his knees.

CHAPTER 42

Life Goes On

Luke tensed as his eyes traveled between the kneeling warrior and the emperor.

"How?" asked Cyzicus. His voice was low but shaking with barely suppressed rage.

An uncertain expression came onto the Warrior's face as he looked around the broken room. Then, rising to his feet, he walked forward and whispered something in Cyzicus's ear, stepping back and kneeling once he had delivered his news.

Cyzicus's expression darkened as he clenched and unclenched his fist. The ground beneath his feet cracked, and a rage-filled aura wafted through the room for an instant before receding as he regained control of his temper. Luke was left wondering if had imagined it.

"Very well. Clite!" He turned to the warrior who had led him and Luke here. "I have some matters to deal with, and I shall be indisposed for the foreseeable future. Please look after young Luke. I promised him that I would see him reach the peak of the Mortal tier in six months' time, and I entrust you with that duty."

She bowed deeply. "I will do my utmost."

"Good. Luke, I'm afraid I won't be able to guide you as much as I had hoped. I cannot let this go unanswered, but you are in good hands. As for the tournament, I won't force you to compete, however, if you were to do so, we'd both gain much. Your advantages give me confidence that you will go far . . . It's right to be cautious of fame and the attention of greater powers, but do not let fear hold you back. Advancing through the tiers is difficult and fraught with danger. Cautiousness is to be valued, but cowardice is a poor response. At least for those of us who seek a place among the gods."

Did he just call me a coward? Am I being a coward? No. He doesn't have all the information I do. The lady that flicked him across the room is hunting me, and I need to be cautious. But now isn't the time to argue, and neither will I gain anything by explaining myself to him.

"I understand, and thank you for all this," he said after a moment, and half-heartedly lifted the sword and ring the hero had given him into the air. "For what it's worth, I'm sorry for your loss. I hope your grandson finds peace, wherever he is now."

Cyzicus nodded and then disappeared in a flash of light, leaving Luke alone with the two warriors. He let out a sigh in both sympathy and relief as some tension left his body. Nothing about the way the hero had acted had Luke worried for his safety, but his power alone made him feel uncomfortable. Like having a police officer driving behind you on the road, or being in the presence of someone carrying a gun. He felt bad for even thinking about it, especially so soon after one of Cyzicus's family members had died, but he was almost glad the man had left.

Frankly, a lot had happened in the past day, and Luke was already missing his time in the grasslands.

Seeing Arke twice in as many days was far outside what he had wanted and incredibly stressful, but at the same time it instilled a certain sense of confidence in him, too.

I've seen her three times since I've been on Theos, and every single time she's left. She really has no clue that I'm the one she's looking for. There's obviously something more going on behind the scenes, too. Nefkha not liking her is one thing, but Cyzicus being openly antagonistic is unexpected. So is the fact that he's so brazen in his dealing with her. Maybe Theos isn't as lawless as I thought it was.

His eyes traveled to the half-buried and formerly possessed body.

That guy, too. Nefkha was right on that front—the way the Seed implanted my soul into this body must be different compared to whatever method that guy used. His body looks like it's rotting, and smells like it, too. I didn't pay much attention to it back then because I didn't know what to expect or what questions to ask, but I'm actually alive. My heart beats, and my blood flows through my veins. Him, not so much.

Luke's eyes traced the hole Arke had left in the corpse's chest and the foul and clotted blood oozing out of it.

Still, if the guy possessing the body was a saint, which sounds like it's higher than the Hero tier, and that's the best he could do, it makes a lot more sense why Nefkha was willing to bet on me being able to help him. Still, he must have balls of steel. I didn't know what I was getting into back then, but for Nefkha to blackmail me, while knowing how ridiculous the difference between the tiers is, was brave of him. I wonder what he wanted my help with, for him to take the risk, though? Maybe when I'm a god, I'll go back there and ask. Until then, though, it's not my concern.

The two warriors talked to each other briefly in hushed voices before splitting up, with Clite coming to him and the other leaving through the front door.

"Come," she said, leading him deeper into the castle. "If you are to ascend to the peak of the Mortal tier, you have your work cut out for you."

"Um, yeah. How are we going to do that, though? Six months seems undoable." *Especially because they don't know about my sword.*

"That ring on your finger will be critical, and it will be painful, but it is possible. To start, I need you to constantly push your mana into it. Mana isn't flesh—it does not tire—so long as your will is strong, it is doable."

"All the time?" Luke asked, staring at it apprehensively.

"Yes. Starting now. We do not have time to waste. If you are not in combat, then you must use the ring. Walking isn't so strenuous a task that it is impossible."

"Right," Luke said, concentrating on his mana and pushing it toward the ring and past the resistance. He ignored the dull headache that formed as he funneled one torturous point into the ring after another.

As they approached their destination, he opened his status and was surprised to see that the Arcana stat had already ticked up by one, compared to what it had been in the morning.

This is scarily effective.

"This is the training yard." She threw open a door, revealing a small cluster of blue-robed men and women sparring with each other. All of them looked young, with the oldest among them looking like he was seventeen, and even then, Luke thought that he might just look older than his age. "These are the most talented cultivators in Sylcra. Like you, the emperor has recruited them to participate in the Olympics."

"Oh. I thought I was the only one."

Clite looked at him oddly. "You are not. Although your mastery of a technique does make you a more attractive prospect then some, the emperor is not so reckless as to send only one participant. Nor is the talent among the sects and guilds in Sylcra so lacking that you are the only option."

"Oh." Luke scratched the back of his head, blushing as he realized that he had come across as both ignorant and arrogant at the same time.

"Yes, quite."

"Do any of them know how to use a technique?"

"No. Teaching a mortal such a skill is arduous work, and often not worth the trouble. It is quicker and more efficient to raise a mortal to the Warrior tier and then allow them to pursue one when they have developed a keener understanding of the heavens."

Well, isn't that vague.

"I see. Will any of them be capable of keeping up with me, then?"

She once again gave him an odd look.

"My technique is pretty good—if they don't have something comparable, I don't see how they'll be able to put up a fight," he elaborated.

Yup, she definitely thinks that I'm an arrogant ass.

"I am unsure if the confidence you have in your abilities is grounded in reality, but I assure you that none of them will be an easy foe. They have been trained in the way of combat since they could walk, and I think whatever insight that truth buried in your skill provides will likely be of less use than you imagine it to be. And, while they lack a technique, that does not mean that they do not possess their own advantages."

"Oh."

"You look unconvinced."

"No, I'm convinced." *Kinda . . . not really. I should be able to pick apart every movement they make and weave between it, and I don't see how she expects any of them to put up a fight against something like that. Does she think I have a shitty skill, or that I'm stuck at moving at a low speed or something?*

"Very well. You will see for yourself eventually." Clite clapped twice in quick succession, and on cue, the sparring stopped, and the group of a dozen cultivators turned to face them. Their brows sweaty and their chests heaving with exertion, they inspected him. "This is Luke. He will be joining you from now on," she said in a deadpan tone.

Luke waved, and one blond-haired girl waved back, while the rest looked at him dispassionately.

"Where's Cyzicus?" asked a tall, bald kid.

"The *emperor*," she stressed, "is indisposed and will no longer be able to oversee your training."

"WHAT?" they suddenly shouted. "Tha—"

She lifted her hand, and they all quieted down instantly.

Are they scared of her?

"The emperor is indisposed, and while he is away, I am in charge of your training. Things will proceed in the same direction as before," she said, unbothered by their dour expressions. "Now, I believe it is time for your baths."

"We just had one yesterday!" the same bald kid complained.

The kid beside him elbowed him lightly and whispered, "That was three days ago."

"Are you sure?" he whispered back.

"Yes."

"Fuck."

Bath time. What the fuck?

Before Luke mustered up the courage to ask if she meant what he thought she did, the crowd broke apart and trudged their way past them.

"Um—"

The bald kid slapped him on his shoulder as he passed by him. "Just follow us. It's not what you think. I'm Jax, by the way."

This better not be what I think it is. Luke shook his head as he followed them out.

Their destination was a room with two pools, one of them full of boiling water, and the other filled with a strange blue liquid that seemed to suck the warmth out of the air.

"We're doing the hot one today," Jax explained as he stripped out of his robes.

"Why?"

"It's a way to cultivate your bodies," explained Clite, drawing a curtain between the two pools and separating them into two groups. She trapped the girls in on the opposite side, where they would bathe in the cold water.

"It looks like torture."

"It will improve your constitution."

"Are there no better ways than boiling ourselves?"

"There are many ways, and this is one of them. You will experience the others in due time. For now, exposing your body to extreme conditions is one of the best ways to advance," she said. A second later a ring on her finger flashed, and vials filled with blue liquid floated out in front of each of them. The others accepted them gingerly.

Uncorking them, they filled their cheeks with the potion inside, and then leaped into the water without much fanfare.

Snatching his own vial out of the air, Luke looked at it reluctantly before glancing back at Clite.

This can't be real.

"Fill your mouth, but do not swallow. Submerge yourself for as long as you are able, and once the pain becomes unbearable, drink the potion. Hold out for as long as you are able—you draw the most benefit from the process the longer you hold off on drinking the medicine. The vial contains a Warrior-tier healing potion, brewed to be slow acting, and it will dull your senses while keeping you alive. Only come out after you feel the effects begin to wear off," she instructed. Her ring flashed again, and a row of blue potions appeared along the edge of the pool. "Those are to help you recover after and unlike that one will heal you instantly."

This is fucking insane.

She cocked her head to the side. "Do you have any questions?"

"No. It's just that when I woke up today, I didn't think I would be boiling myself alive."

The prize for winning the tournament better be insane.

CHAPTER 43

Training or Torture

Luke stripped down to his undergarments and took a deep breath before uncorking the vial.

Doubt clearly plastered on his face, he stuffed his cheeks full of the blue liquid within, instinctually swishing it around his mouth. Immediately, even without swallowing, a surge of cool healing energy traveled through his body. Aches and pains that he didn't even realize he had faded into the background as the Warrior-tier medicine did its work.

It tastes fruity.

A drop of sizzling water splattered against the bare skin of his foot, making him frown at the uncomfortable heat. He inched forward, preparing to leap, peering into the frothy depths of the water.

If I can kill people, I can do this, too. Don't be scared. Step up, he told himself as he prepared to leap.

Then, glancing at the expectant stare that Clite was leveling him with, and the murky figures of those already in the water, he strode forward and jumped into the boiling pool. He regretted his decision as soon as his feet left the cold, tiled floor of the room.

Pain, angry and full of rage, assaulted him. From the tips of his toes to his eyes and the ends of his scalp, everything burned. Everything was agony. Only the soothing energy from the potion, roused to action, kept him sane. Warring against the blistering heat of the water, the energy from the potion radiated throughout him in cool waves, repairing the damage done to his skin nearly as soon as it happened.

Aethereal mana entered his body in droves, thick and viscous it mixed with his own like dye spreading through water before being whisked away and strengthening his flesh. If he wasn't in so much pain, Luke would have been fascinated with how vigorously his body processed the resource. With his mana unlocked, he had observed the process in the past.

It was slow.

Only some of the mana would soak into his body's tissues, and after a while the Seed would whisk whatever remained away, where it accumulated into stat points.

The process typically took hours. Now, every cell in his body hungered for the mysterious substance, ravenously devouring every speck of it nearly as soon as it entered. The mana not only saturated his skin but went deeper, burrowing all the way into his bones and organs. While his outsides took the brunt of the damage, the heat from the water seemed to seep into his bones and organs with ruthless precision.

This water isn't normal, Luke realized. He tried his best to detach himself from the pain but only succeeded for moments at a time.

Still, it wasn't fast enough. There was mana coming in, more than he had ever felt before, but it wasn't enough. He would be cooked alive before he strengthened enough to withstand the heat.

The cool, healing energy of the potion in his mouth began to fade, but stubbornly, Luke held on, intent on dragging it out for as long as he could. Since he was doing this, he was going to extract the most benefit out of the process as he was able to. To Luke, anything less than his best was undeserving of the suffering he'd endured thus far.

As the last remnants of healing energy faded from his mouth and the pain he was in surged, fast becoming unbearable, he was forced to swallow the potion in his mouth. He sagged in relief as the energy from the potion surged within him and fought back the heat of the water and repaired the damage it had done to his body. Once again he was reminded how effective the medicine was.

He didn't know how long he was like that, but soon after even the redoubled energy of the potion began to fade, and as his lungs began to crave oxygen, he realized it was time. Pushing off against the floor of the pool, he sprang out of the water onto the cold ground, landing on the cool, tiled floor with a wet smack and flopping around in pain, like a fish out of water.

His skin cherry red and steaming, his eyes locked on the potions that Clite had left for them. Stretching his hands forward, he crawled toward the vials. He left thin trails of blood along the ground as his skin, softened in the water, tore open.

Grabbing one, he fumbled around with the cap and drank it as fast as he could. Rolling onto his back in relief and staring into the sky, his chest heaved as his lungs captured fresh, oxygen-rich air.

Fucking hell.

A few seconds later, another trainee emerged from the water. Unlike Luke, he landed on his feet and walked gingerly toward the potions, casually picking up a vial before chugging it down. He watched Luke from the corner of his eye as he did.

"It gets easier. You did better than I did the first time," he said after a moment.

"Yeah," Luke panted, still in too much pain to muster anything other than a single syllable. He was more than a little jealous of how well the other guy seemed to be handling the pain.

"All right. Get up." He stretched down, grabbed Luke's hand, and pulled him to his feet. "The potions heal the burns perfectly, but the pain lingers the more you think about it. It helps to just walk it off. What you're feeling now is all in your head."

Luke nodded numbly, collected his clothes off the ground, and got dressed. His mind was blank, emptier than he could ever remember it being.

Barely paying attention to the others crawling out of the pool, he spotted a bench along the wall and stumbled toward it.

I can't believe that I just did that. I can't believe that I'm okay. He lifted his hand and turned it over. Not a single sign of what he had gone through marred his body.

"Fuck. How often do you do that?" he asked, thumping his head against the wall as he looked at the rest of them.

"Once every four days, and we alternate between the hot and the cold. The cold one isn't as bad," Jax answered him, scrubbing the water out from behind his ears.

"Mmm-hmm," Luke grunted in response and opened his status.

This better have been worth it.

Status	Skills	Quests	Inventory

Name: Lukas King

Tier: Mortal

Mana: 6,408

Rate: 15% per hour

Strength: 109 > 116

Agility: 239 > 240

Constitution: 112 > 144

Arcana: 84 > 89

Stat Points: 1

Bloodline: Locked. Conditions not met. (1/10,000)

Charges: 7/10

His eyebrows lifted in surprise.

Okay, that's not bad. At all. That's like . . . forty-five, no, forty-six points. Improvements across the board. With a whole thirty-two points in Constitution, and that's with just minutes in the water.

His eyes drifted toward the pool, a strange glimmer in his eyes.

It really hurt. But, if this is the reward, and for what—three minutes of pain? It might actually be worth it. Killing things with my sword is obviously better, but this is nothing to scoff at. Outside of a situation where I can find a weak horde of monsters to fight, this is much more efficient.

It may have gone even better if I had more points in Arcana.

"Hey, new guy?" Someone snapped their fingers in front of his face.

"Yeah?" Luke looked at the person who had lifted him up.

"You good? You've been staring off into space for a minute."

"I'm good. That was just something else."

He grinned in response.

"I'm Rex."

"Luke."

"I know. Clite told us, remember?"

"Yeah. I guess I'm still sorting myself out." Luke combed wet hair out of his face with his hand as he leaned back. "It's not as bad as I thought it would be. The rush of mana and the potion—they gave me something to focus on."

"Yeah, we know. After your fourth or fifth time, you don't even notice the pain."

"Really?" Luke looked at him oddly.

"No," he deadpanned. "If anything, it gets worse the more you do it. But you feel it, don't you? A week's worth of progress in minutes. The pain is a small price to pay."

Luke smiled in response. "That's what I thought, too—it just sounded too good to be true. How else are we going to train? Is everything as extreme as this?"

"You have your manasink, right?"

Luke nodded.

"That's a big one. We spend a few hours every day filling it with mana. I guess we're supposed to keep it up all the time, but it's easy to forget about, and the headaches never get better. We spar a lot. Once in a while they'll take us out somewhere, and we kill a monster or two. There's the obstacle course, too. What else . . . ?"

"You're forgetting the beatings," Jax chipped in.

The what?

"I said spars." Rex cocked his head to the side.

"You can't seriously think that getting your ass handed to you by a warrior is a spar."

"With how shitty you are at sparring, I'm not surprised you think that way." Rex grinned at him.

The curtains suddenly lifted, and the girls walked back into the room, covered head to toe in thick woolen towels over their robes and shivering with their arms crossed over their chests. Clite loomed behind them as they gathered in front of the pool.

She was staring at Luke with disapproval clear in her eyes.

He stared back at her with confusion.

Rex leaned in and whispered, "She doesn't like it when we sit in front of her."

"What?" Luke whispered back.

What kind of bullshit rule is that? I just took a dip in boiling water. I can sit.

She cleared her throat.

Suddenly Luke realized that everyone was staring at him.

This is bull, he grumbled internally. *And what did she do to them, to make them so obedient?*

Cheeks flushed red embarrassment, Luke quickly climbed to his feet and joined the rest of them.

Nodding in satisfaction, she led them out.

Like ducklings following their mother, they followed after her, and, not seeing what else to do, Luke did the same.

"Where are we going now?" he asked, his head swiveling between Rex and Jax.

Both of them shrugged their shoulders in response.

"Whatever she feels like, honestly. If Cyzicus was here, he'd probably take us to kill some monster or something, but I don't think Elder Clite can use the teleportation altars."

"Oh." Luke shrugged as he followed her.

A moment later, they reentered the same courtyard where he had first been introduced to the other trainees.

"I guess we're sparring." Jax grinned. "Rose. Me and you!" He pointed to a short blonde girl.

She huffed in response, her eyes traveling from person to person, before she sighed. "Fine. It's not like anyone else can keep up with me anyway," she grumbled.

The others frowned at her but didn't say anything.

Are she and Jax the strongest here? Luke glanced between the two. *Jax I can kind of understand—he's bald, tall, built like a brick, and looks older, but she looks like a stiff wind will blow her over. Then again, none of the girls in the society looked as strong as they actually were, either.*

"Rose will battle Luke," Clite interjected.

"Him?" Rose and Jax said at the same time, skepticism practically written on their faces.

Luke scratched his cheek awkwardly. "Is that a problem?"

"Why don't we start the new guy off with Rex?" Jax suggested. "Or even Tobias?"

Rex kicked Jax in the shin, sending the bald teen to his knees. "Are you calling me weak?"

"Yes." Jax grinned at him, climbing back to his feet. "Are you going to say that you aren't?"

"Enough! Luke, Rose. Choose a weapon and enter the ring," Clite instructed.

"I don't need one," Rose said, walking confidently into the sand-filled arena.

Luke followed her, wondering which of his two swords he should use, before realizing that Clite probably wanted him to use one of the dull wooden ones hanging on the wall. Setting his own on the ground, he picked one at random, immediately noting its heft. The wooden sword weighed more than twice as much as either of his golden ones.

More magic, I guess, he thought, making his way into the arena, a large, sandy pit circled with a thick, tawny rope.

Settling into the First Stance of the Sword, he eyed his opponent carefully. For her part, she regarded him with casual disdain.

Why is she so confident? How is she even going to fight me without a weapon?

"Start!" Clite instructed.

The draw on his mana suddenly rocketed, and he leaped to his side, narrowly managing to dodge a torrent of flame that erupted from her hands.

What the fuck.

CHAPTER 44

Flames of Fury

Luke's eyes widened in surprise at her attack.

"How did you—"

Ignoring him, she held her hand out, a wide grin stretched across her face as flames spewed forth from her open palm.

"BURN!" she yelled, cackling like a witch.

What the— Luke ducked to the side once again, his eyes narrowed with focus as he thought about how to get past her fire. He winced in pain as a gout of flame nicked his arm.

I really don't know how she's doing that, but it has to cost her a lot of mana. I think. Depending on how deep she is into the Mortal tier, though, she could have a lot to spare. Especially with the rings raising the Arcana stat, and with the baths boosting Constitution. She probably has a shit ton more mana than I do right now. So I can't rely on her running out. Especially if everyone's mana grows the same way mine does.

The First Stance could help, but I'll need to be cautious with how I use it. If it drains all my mana before I even get to her, then like with the giant, it'll be useless. At least she won't kill me, though. Hopefully.

My boots will help, too, but I still need a way to get in close without toasting myself alive. Just climbing high into the air might take me out of her range, but what then? Do I wait her out? No, that's stupid—I can't turn this into a game of who has more mana. I need to hit her hard and fast.

He tightened his grip on his weapon, his thoughts churning erratically, as he desperately tried to think of a solution.

Should I throw my sword? No. That's even more stupid. If I miss or she dodges, then I'm done. What else? I need to make an opening. If I had a shield, then she wouldn't be a problem, but I don't.

Think. Think. Think.

He dived to the side as another jet of flame tore through the air, in a feat of agility that surprised even himself. Rolling back to his feet, he grabbed a fistful of sand and flung it straight into her eyes.

"AHH! What the fuck!" she cursed loudly, instinctually bringing her forearm to her face to rub the debris free from her eyes. Blindly, she lashed out with gouts of flame in his general direction to keep him at bay. Seizing the opportunity, Luke started kicking more and more sand into her face.

It looks like she can't sustain the attack for long, either. It cuts through the air, but it's not a continuous stream of fire. More like a stretched-out fireball than a flamethrower. I can work with that.

A second or less. That's as long as the burst of fire lasts.

It's just long enough for it to reach me, but not long enough to change the angle and attack where I'll be. Even so, one hit and I'm looking at some serious burns.

Eyebrows furrowed in concentration, he channeled mana into his boots and stepped into the air.

Leveraging every ounce of power in his legs to close the distance between himself and Rose as quickly as he possibly could, he sank into the First Stance in midair. He panicked briefly as felt his mana start to dwindle before tamping down on his emotions.

If I lose, it's not a big deal, he assured himself.

Her every action came into focus, and he became intimately aware of every movement of her body as he did. He savored the look of shock on her face when she finally cleared the sand out of her eyes and saw that he was no longer where she expected him to be. Blinking rapidly, she swiveled her neck so fast, Luke thought that she might give herself whiplash.

When she did see him, it was too late. He was too close. His mana rapidly drained away as the First Stance revealed the intent behind her every twitch. The information the skill provided was considerably less detailed than when he had used it on Yjarn, geared as it was to guiding Luke past swords and other weapons, but it worked well enough that he could predict where and when a blast of flame would come.

Using his boots to bounce off the air, he came down at her like lightning. The skill urged him to sink his sword through her left eye and into her skull. Ignoring its direction, he came to a skidding stop in midair, his wooden sword resting lightly on her shoulder, its dulled edge flat against her neck.

If I had a real sword, one flick from my wrist, and her head would fly, he thought darkly, as his eyes met her red and puffy gaze.

"You cheated," she huffed, crossing her arms under her chest.

No.

"You threw fireballs at me," Luke said, taking a step back and then falling to the ground, having cut the flow of mana to his shoes. "How did you do that, anyway?"

"Tsk." She turned away and walked out of the ring, not answering him.

Rude.

"I didn't cheat!" he said, walking out after her.

"You kind of did," she snapped back.

"How?"

"You flew!"

"You threw fire!"

"It's not the same!"

"Enough," Clite said authoritatively. "There was no cheating. Luke used wit and the tools he had available to defeat you. Rose, you let arrogance blind you. Had you deigned to even hold a weapon and lured him in close enough that he couldn't so easily dodge, then you would have fared much better. With your flames you had the longer reach, but you lost that advantage when you let him obstruct your vision."

"Whatever," Rose mumbled under her breath, walking past Clite and standing next to a raven-haired girl.

"Theo, Jax. You two are next." Clite called the next match, and the two boys broke from the crowd and armed themselves with a weapon of their choice.

After standing around awkwardly for a moment, Luke's eyes raked over the assembled teenagers before he walked over to Rex.

"That was a good fight," said Rex. "Rose is hard to beat. Her fire makes every battle with her trickier than it needs to be."

"Thanks. How does she—" Luke made a gesture with his open palm.

Rex shrugged his shoulders. "I don't know, and does it really matter?"

Luke frowned, slightly caught off guard by his overly defensive tone. "I guess not. I was just curious. I didn't know that was even possible."

"Mmm-hmm. We're all curious about how you flew into the air, too, but no one will ask. That's kind of the rule around here. We're all the freaks and prodigies that the emperor could get his hands on so that Sylcra has a shot at winning the tournament." He stared at Luke meaningfully. "We're not here to make friends. If anything, we're all competition. Only one person from each tier will win the prize, after all."

Well, isn't he a little tense. Still— Luke looked around the room, his eyes darting from person to person, and suddenly he felt incredibly lonely. *He's not wrong. If we are going to be competing against each other, it doesn't make sense for us to reveal our tricks. Besides, it's not like I'm champing at the bit to tell them my own secrets, either.*

Speaking of flying, though . . . He looked over at Rose. *Are her flames from an artifact like my shoes? Or something else?*

Maybe, but I don't think so, he thought, his eyes lingering on a bracelet she wore before going to a ring on a left-hand finger. *Cyzicus probably has vaults full of powerful artifacts. If all it took to win at the Olympics was a rich backer, then he wouldn't bother recruiting any of us.*

The rest of the fights went by fairly quickly; unlike Rose, the others fought only with weapons. Much to Luke's disappointment. If they had any abilities beyond those that came from cultivating, they didn't display them. Still, Luke paid careful attention to each battle and listened dutifully to Clite's assessment of each one, learning what he could from their mistakes.

Each and every one of them, however, showed skill far beyond what Luke expected, and he knew without a doubt that without the First Stance guiding his moves, all of them would make quick work of him.

More than that, they were all nearing the peak of the Mortal tier, hitting harder and moving faster than Luke could even dream of doing himself.

"So what do you guys do around here when you're not training?" Luke asked hours later as he followed Jax back to the part of the castle Cyzicus had set aside for them.

Jax scratched his head. "There's not much to do," he said, but the small grin on his face told Luke otherwise.

"So you just train and then sit in your room with the ring?" Luke prodded him.

"Yeah."

"I don't buy that. Come on, what do you really do?"

"Nothing." He looked off into the distance. "Clite doesn't like us slacking off. She goes out of the way to make life harder for us if we slack off. Says that the emperor's generosity isn't to be trampled upon."

"Hmm. Is she the one that organizes all the training?"

"Sometimes. Normally it's Cyzicus, but she's always around. It was weird of him not to come today, though. He's been dropping clues about hunting some bear for a long time now, and I thought he was going to take us today. Guess not, though." He sighed, sounding more than a little disappointed.

Can't really blame him, though. Today's been kind of insane.

Luke opened and closed his mouth. "His grandson was killed."

"What? Which one? Felix? Lukeus? Algros? Telman?" Jax stopped in his tracks, rattling off one name after the other.

"I don't know. I didn't realize he had so many."

"He's an ancient emperor, and he's been alive for millennia. Of course he has a lot of family!" he scoffed. "Come, we have to find Rex—he'll know."

"He would?"

"Rex is one of Cyzicus's grandkids, too. He knows everything that happens in the capital."

"That . . . How many grandkids does he have?"

"A lot. He has three sons, and his youngest is famous for bedding a lot of women."

"Oh."

"That is an understatement. Cyzicus loves all his grandchildren, spoils them rotten. If one of them was killed, then he's going to go on a warpath."

"A warpath?"

"Yes!" He paced back and forth. "Rex is probably at the gardens. Come." He took off in a brisk run.

"What do you mean by *warpath*?" Luke asked, chasing after him.

"I mean that the last time this happened, all of Sylcra was roused to war," he said, his voice clipped.

"War? Against who?"

"The Peles."

That's helpful, Luke thought, his mind racing as mulled over what Jax had said. *Obviously a murder in the emperor's family is a big deal, but Clite just rolled with it, and Cyzicus just left.*

With everything else that happened, it didn't even occur to me that this would be a big deal, but that was beyond naïve of me. On Earth people are killed all the time, the police catch you, there's a trial, you go to jail, and then that's that. Story closed.

Stuff doesn't go beyond that. At least not anymore.

Here, though, Cyzicus, as nice as he seems, is the ruler of a nation. Killing his family is an act of war. Not to mention the fact that cultivators are, in a way, killing machines.

But who would do it? Arke?

Maybe, but what does she have to gain? Sure, he's an ass to her, but he's still helping her. If nothing else, she has to know that killing his family would end whatever relationship they do have.

"Couldn't his grandson have just died? Maybe in a giant attack or something?"

"You're the one that said he was killed!"

"Oh, right. Yeah."

CHAPTER 45

Drums of War

Do we really have to run?" Luke asked Jax after a few minutes of jogging down the castle halls. It was fun, and it reminded him of running down the halls in school, but the odd looks they were getting from the palace's staff only got more and more embarrassing the longer they ran.

"Yes! If there's a chance of there being another war, I need to know. Right now!" he yelled back, picking up even more speed.

Sighing, Luke picked up his own pace as he chased after Jax, easily keeping up with the other cultivator.

When they finally got there, the view took Luke's breath away.

The garden was ethereal in its beauty. Butterflies of every color and size drifted through the air, their wings shimmering in the light of Theos's suns. Tiny rainbow-colored hummingbirds flitted from flower to flower, and flamingos and peacocks paced languidly on freshly trimmed and perfectly manicured grass.

A winding stone path snaked between flower beds and under tall, fruit-bearing trees. A small waterfall in the distance emptied into a peaceful, lotus-covered lake, filling the area with the soothing gurgle of water and the musical chirping of birds.

Slowing down, Jax made a cone around his mouth with his hands and yelled, "REX!" at the top of his lungs.

For a moment every creature in the garden stood still and stared straight at them before continuing with their lives, curious about the humans that had broken their peace but not enough to do anything about it.

"I've told you not to do that, you loud asshole!" a voice shouted back from deep within the garden.

Grinning in spite of his earlier rush, Jax marched forward, trampling on the grass with reckless abandon and sending rabbits scurrying out of their way. Hesitating briefly, Luke sighed and followed him.

I already ran all the way here—might as well go all the way. Poor garden, though.

They found Rex leaning with his back against a tree, his finger held out in front of him and on it a large blue-and-white butterfly, slowly and gracefully beating its wings.

"The new guy said one of your brothers died."

Luke suppressed the urge to cringe at how callously Jax had delivered the news.

"No," Rex responded flatly.

What? Luke frowned.

Jax opened and closed his mouth before staring at Luke, disgusted. "What kind of sick jokes do you like to tell? You fucking asshole. How can you just say stuff like—"

Sick joke, my ass. What's his deal? Luke stared at Rex. *Does he not know that his brother is dead? But then, why would he just deny it?*

"It's not a joke, and I'm not lying. Maybe you just don't know?" he said, crossing his arms under his chest. "I know what I heard."

"I would know if one of my brothers died." Rex furrowed his eyebrow, and the butterfly flew off his finger and began flying in loose circles in front of him. "It was my cousin."

This fucking guy. Luke fumed. "Well, thanks for being clear."

"Oh." Jax's eyes narrowed. "How did it happen? Was—"

"The Rebel," Rex interrupted him.

"Fuck. Fuck. Fuck. I need to go home," Jax mumbled, pacing back and forth. "Where's Cyzicus? He needs to let me use a teleportation altar."

"Who's the Rebel?" Luke asked.

"A rogue cultivator at the Hero tier. She came to the island sixty years ago, and she's been trying to supplant Cyzicus as emperor ever since," said Rex.

First Sophia the cyclops, and now this character? What's with this island and squatters?

"Is that how it works? If you're strong enough, you just show up somewhere and take it? Don't the gods interfere?"

Rex scoffed as if the very idea of the gods doing anything at all was ridiculous, but he didn't say anything.

"Rex. I need you to—"

"Jax, calm down." Rex leaned back and closed his eyes. "Even if you do go home, what are you going to do? Fight the Rebel? Fight her warriors? You're a single mortal. Nothing you do will make a difference. At best you'll die a quick death."

"What am I supposed to do, then? Huh! Stay here and train while she butchers my family?"

"She's not going to kill your family, Jax. There's literally no point."

"She's done it before."

Okay, so clearly, I'm missing some context here.

"That was different, and you know it," Rex said. "It's been a long time since then; she probably has bigger concerns."

Jax paced back and forth. "I need to be home! I'll grab my mother and my sister and flee. Bring them back here."

"If you want to be stupid, then go. What are you hassling me for?" Rex sighed. "Look, there's literally nothing you can do, even if you go there. They're too far, and you'll need Gramps to take you there and bring you back—walking will take you months. And he can't. Besides, her plan is obvious. She killed my cousin to start the battle. She picked now to do it because she knows that the Tide is coming."

"That's her plan, then? Side with the giants and destroy the island?"

That—

"No, you idiot. She wants to kill Gramps now, just before the Tide, to force Sylcra and all her cultivators to bend their knees. Gramps is the only one strong enough to helm the teleportation network, and without it, they won't be able to protect any of the towns or cities, and if she's the only hero on the island . . ." He trailed off, nodding meaningfully at the two of them.

"Wait, let me get this straight." Luke scratched his chin in thought. "You"—he pointed to Jax—"want to go home because your family might be in danger from this Rebel. For some reason. The Rebel wants to kill Cyzicus so that everyone else on the island has no choice but to rely on her to teleport them to the different cities when they get attacked by giants in six months. To do that, she needed to lure Cyzicus into a battle, which she did by killing your cousin."

A pretty classic coup.

"Basically." Rex nodded.

"I see . . . So I guess what it comes down to is which one of them is stronger."

"I suppose it would."

"That . . . Who's stronger? Cyzicus or the Rebel?"

"That's the question now, isn't it? The last time they fought was when she led the Pelesian Army to Sylcra. Back then, she was no match for Gramps, and her army was too small to challenge the sects. But a lot can change in sixty years." He shrugged, seemingly unconcerned with the outcome.

"And where do you fit in all of this?" Luke turned to Jax.

"Clan Skyscar, my family, came from Peles as part of her campaign. My grandfather was a general in her army. But when he saw how cruelly she was fighting the war, and all the innocent blood that was being spilled, we surrendered to Cyzicus. Years after the war, she slaughtered most of us in retaliation. But if she's out of hiding, then . . ." He trailed off.

The pieces of the puzzle clicked in Luke's head.

So it wasn't Arke that killed his grandson at all. Still, what should I do? Do I stay here and bet that Cyzicus wins? What happens if he doesn't?

Does it matter? he thought numbly. *It would suck if he dies, but I don't see a way to affect the outcome at all. Obviously, it would be better if he wins, but if he does lose, what does that mean?*

He glanced between Rex and Jax.

Both of them will probably die. I can't imagine a world where descendants of traitors and the previous emperor would be spared. Realistically, I don't have a horse in the race, but will she see it that way if she wins and finds a handful of elite mortals trained personally by Cyzicus, all of them living in her new castle?

It makes more sense to leave and not risk it. I don't even know if I want to compete in the Olympics, and I literally just met all of them yesterday. Sure, Cyzicus and Nel probably saved my life, but Nel was doing her job, and he was saving his granddaughter. I just happened to be there.

The training is cool, and the ring especially is useful, but I already have it. The baths are a neat trick, and I bet they have more like them, but I don't need them. Not with the Seed.

All I really need is some monsters to kill and a way off the archipelago. The latter, I can't do anything about until the situation with Arke changes, but this whole island will supposedly be drowned in giants in a few months.

That might not be enough stat points to get me to the Warrior tier, especially when I consider I still have to unlock the Bloodline, and I still need to master the techniques, but it should be enough to let me max out my attributes. Which is a massive plus.

"Oh, they're here," Rex said, climbing to his feet as he stared off in the distance.

"Who?" Luke followed his gaze and traced it to a small speck in the sky. As the speck came closer and closer to them, he realized that he had actually seen it before. It was a griffin, and riding on its back were two figures. "What's Nel doing here?"

"I didn't realize you were acquainted."

"I just met her yesterday. Why is she here?"

"Gramps asked them to come. He wanted us to do something for him." Rex glanced between him and Jax consideringly before shaking his head and turning back toward the sky.

"Is that what I think it is?" Jax whispered under his breath, his eyes wide in awe.

It's so fast, Luke thought as the griffin cut through the air, growing larger and larger with every second that passed. It went from a spot in the sky to flying above their head in seconds and then touched the ground at their feet moments later.

The second it did, Lukeus stumbled off and fell to his hands and knees, moaning and heaving as he emptied the contents of his stomach.

"I'm never riding that thing again!"

"It's not that bad," Nel said defensively, floating off its back and landing gently on the ground. Her eyes darted over Jax and lingered curiously on Luke before she lunged forward and caught Rex in a hug. "How've you been?"

"Good," he mumbled, shoving her away.

"Are you ready to go?" she asked.

"I am."

"Good." She turned to Luke. "How are you settling in?"

"They boiled me alive." He lifted a hand and pulled back his index finger. "A girl threw fireballs at me. I saw Arke destroy a part of your castle, which was cool. She also killed some dead guy and then blasted your grandpa through his throne," he rattled off. "But I got this ring and this sword, plus a massive amount of debt. So I guess I can't complain. Thanks for recommending this place."

He flashed her the most obnoxious smile he could and gave her a thumbs-up.

"Well, I'm glad you seem to be having an exciting time. I'd love to stay and chat, but we have some work to do." She knelt next to Lukeus and slung him over her shoulder before tossing him back onto her steed. "Hop on, Rex. There's no time to waste."

"Wait!" Jax knelt and prostrated himself before her. "Take me with you! I need a ride!"

"Who are you?"

"I'm Jax of Clan Skyscar. My family might be in danger."

A glimmer of recognition passed through her eyes. "Where do you want to go?"

"North. Across the river, to Sixra. If you can't go all the way, I understand, but if you can take me across, I'll be eternally grateful," he said, his face still planted on the ground.

She looked at Rex and he frowned before nodding imperceptibly.

Sighing, she shrugged. "Fine, get on."

Leaping to his feet, Jax eagerly climbed on top of the beast without a shred of hesitation, clearly fearing that she might change her mind.

"Thank you!" He bowed.

"Can I come, too?" Luke asked suddenly.

They all looked at him oddly.

"Why do you want to come?" Nel asked.

"Well, it's that or staying here and boiling myself alive every few days." *And because I don't want to be here when shit inevitably goes down, that's why.*

"I understand not wanting to train, but I'm afraid that Aura can only carry four people. Sorry."

"That's okay! You know what, I've been slacking off a lot lately. Why don't I stay here and train, and Luke goes with you?" Lukeus eagerly climbed off the griffin. "Besides, he's Luke, I'm Luke—there's practically no difference between us. No difference at all. And honestly, we both know that I'm not the mission type of guy, Nel. This guy fought a Warrior-tier giant if what they say is true. Much better choice than me, don't you think? I think so," he said, inching farther and farther away from the catbird before taking off in a sprint in the opposite direction. "You'll do great, Luke."

I think he's growing on me.

Nel watched him run off, both annoyed and with mirth in her eyes. "Fine, you can come."

"Great." Luke grinned and cautiously climbed onto the griffin. "Where are we going, by the way?"

She grinned at him. "Grandfather wants us to deliver a message to Sophia."

"Oh."

CHAPTER 46

Sophia the Big

I just want to get this straight in case there's another Sophia that I don't know about. You are referring to the cyclops that fought Cyzicus to a standstill a hundred years ago, correct?"

The same one you told me would kill people for wandering in her territory and told me to avoid.

"Yes," Nel said, flying back onto the griffin. Before Luke had a chance to change his mind, she patted her familiar twice on the back, and suddenly they were more than a hundred feet in the air, cutting through the wind with unreasonable speed. The earth beneath them contracted rapidly as they blitzed over it.

A sinking feeling in his core came and left in an instant as they climbed to their final altitude.

"It's quiet," Luke said, blinking slowly. Surprise bloomed as he realized that he couldn't feel any wind on his face.

This is so much better than a shield and rug. He grinned softly, leaning over the side slightly and surprised to see they were already above water.

The capital must have been on the river's bank, just like most of the other towns.

"Of course it is." She scratched the griffin's neck. "She's manipulating the wind."

"Oh. How?"

Nel shrugged her shoulders. "Animals cultivate differently than humans. Especially those that can trace their bloodline to divine creatures like Aura. And she's in the Warrior tier." She grinned proudly.

"She's descendant from a god?"

Nel looked at Luke oddly. "Well, an eagle and a lion can't have babies when they're in the Mortal tier. As for her"—she shrugged—"I don't know for sure if she has divine ancestry, but I think it's likely. Whichever creature sired her line wouldn't be weak, though."

"What tier do you have to be to have kids with a different species?" Luke asked curiously, only to blush a moment later when he heard Jax snicker in amusement and Nel cough awkwardly.

I shouldn't have asked that.

"I'm not interested in that—I was just wondering," he tried to clarify.

Jax burst into laughter.

"What did Gramps want us to tell Sophia?" Rex asked, saving him from further embarrassment.

"He wants her help," she answered flatly.

"To fight the Rebel? That seems unlike him," he mused. "He's always so—" He gestured vaguely.

"He is." She nodded. "He wants her to power the teleportation altars while he puts an end to the Rebel once and for all."

"You think he stands a chance? He's . . . old," Rex said reluctantly.

She tensed. "He does," she answered, but even Luke could tell that she was uncertain. "She's worried that Grandfather may ascend to the next tier soon. If he does, then there is no hope for her victory."

But according to her own words, he needs something to get there—a prize from the Olympics. So at the very least, he's six months away from that happening, assuming the tournament doesn't go on for longer. Even then, it's up to chance. If the people he puts in don't win, then he's likely to stay stuck. Maybe. So the Rebel probably thinks he has a decent chance.

"Will the cyclops care about Cyzicus ascending?" Luke asked. "Aren't they delaying their battle until one of them grows stronger than the other? If that's the case, why would she help?"

"I—I don't know. Grandfather seemed confident that she would agree, but we'll find out once we get there. If not, then . . . I don't know," she admitted.

It doesn't make sense. Luke frowned. *Sure, it would stop the Rebel from taking the throne as easily if there's another hero powering the altars, and it would add an obstacle to her path, but that would only matter if Cyzicus lost. Does he expect to lose?*

No. That doesn't make sense. Why go into a battle that you expect to lose?

She did kill her grandson, so it could be a pride thing. The way he provokes Arke, that would even make sense, but Arke can't retaliate for whatever reason. Would he be as gung-ho about it if there was an actual chance that he would lose? Would he really risk the lives of everyone who depends on him, because he was provoked?

He scratched his cheek. *I just don't know enough. But that seems unlikely. The fact that he's sending us out already means he has a plan.*

"Where is she, anyway?" Jax asked from his spot at the very back of the griffin.

Nel's storage ring flashed, and a scroll appeared in her hand. Then, floating into the air, she turned around so that she was face-to-face with Luke.

"All right." She unfurled it, spreading it over their mount's back. "Here's the plan."

Luke felt some shuffling behind him and, craning his neck, saw that both Jax and Rex had climbed to their feet and were crouching side by side over his shoulder.

Aren't they afraid that they're going to fall to their deaths?

"According to Grandfather, Sophia built her forge here." She tapped her finger on the northeast end of the island. "We're here." She pointed at the western edge of the island, to a spot just south of the river that cut through it. "And Sixra is here." She rested her finger on a dot across the river, a good way inland.

It's a bit of a detour, but not crazy. The negative distance is minimal.

"Jax, we will drop you off at Sixra and then head straight to her domain. After I drop you off, you're on your own. We don't have time to linger, and we don't have the resources to help. I'd suggest that you take your family somewhere out of the way and keep your ear out for any news." She hesitated, her mouth opening before snapping shut. "In case Grandfather does lose, you should take your family and head here." She tapped a spot along the island's coast. "Once the situation with Arke is resolved, you should be able to charter passage to a different island. It will keep you safe from any reprisal."

"Right. Thank you!" He bowed, his bald scalp grazing Luke's back.

"Take this." Her ring flashed again, and the map disappeared. She had replaced it with a talisman. "It's part of a set. If it burns, that means that I tore my half and the Rebel won."

He took a deep breath, sighed, and bowed his head. "Thank you. May it never burn. I will not forget the favor you have shown me today."

"It's not a big deal. I understand wanting to look after your family." She smiled at him before floating an inch or so off her familiar's back and reorienting herself so she was looking ahead.

The next hour of the journey passed in silence.

Luke spent it adding one agonizing point of mana after the other into the ring. If it weren't for the fact that his Arcana stat had ticked up twice in that time, he would have been seriously tempted to throw the manasink into the river beneath them and never look at it again.

The headache the process caused just seemed to build and build, endlessly escalating, making the mere act of existing a painful chore.

It's basically free points and, more importantly, points I can earn safely. But this fucking sucks. What I wouldn't do for a nest of harpies right now. I can't believe how much I wasted that opportunity. And I fucked up with the tomb, too, I should have milked that place for everything it was worth. Progress there was good, but not what it could have been had I been a little greedier. I might have even reached the end of the Mortal tier if I didn't learn the techniques as fast as I did.

He pulled back his mana and took a deep breath, wanting to take the edge off the pain and release his frustration.

With the First Stances and some creativity, I could probably farm two or three hundred points from a single nest of harpies. If not more. I do that a handful of times, and I'll be at the peak of the Mortal tier in no time. The training isn't bad, but it's definitely suboptimal. With my sword, I could be making some serious progress, and without all the pain.

But points are points, and I can't be lazy. Not now, and not ever.

I'll have the chance to farm a massive number of them soon, so until then— He stared at the ring with disgust. *I keep going. Every tiny scrap of strength will help me survive.*

He sighed softly before closing his eyes, concentrating on his mana.

Half an hour later, a gust of wind ruffled his hair.

"OH SHI—" Nel yelled, and the next second, he was plummeting through the air. Luke's eyes snapped open, and for a brief moment, he wished they had never had. *Holy fucking hell. What the fuck is that?*

Hovering in the sky above the griffin was a massive, ugly, serpentlike thing. It had hundreds of bat-like wings arrayed in neat rows along its side, jutting out like the legs of a millipede. Its scales were a dark pink—the color of an open wound. At the tip of each wing were wicked ivory claws.

Nel summoned her spear from her ring, flew off the griffin, and charged the beast. Lightning arced along its silver shaft, ready for battle. Leaving Rex alone on her mount.

"Help!" Jax shouted, falling from the sky, the wind muffling his yell to a mere whisper. One that Luke heard. Angling himself forward, he hurtled through the sky toward him, eager to get away from the creature and more than happy to save a life.

Jax's eyes met his, and he stretched his arms wide in an effort to slow his descent. *Right. He saw me use my boots.*

Luke caught up to Jax in seconds and latched on to his robe. Orienting himself so that his feet were perpendicular to the ground, he shot short pulses of mana into his boots to slow their fall. He was careful not to send too much lest his momentum lead to him injuring himself. His body was not yet strong enough to handle the strain from stopping from an extreme velocity to nothing without serious injury.

This is bad, Luke realized as soon as he grabbed Jax, calling up his status as he checked the state of his mana. *I don't have enough for a proper landing. If I let us fall normally, until we're close to the ground, I might be able to make it, but the timing will need to be perfect. We're over water, but at this height a fall would kill us regardless, and without a boat, we'd drown once we fell in anyhow.*

We're too far away from the shore to swim. Fuck.

He craned his neck and searched through the sky. His eyes locked onto the griffin in the distance. It was panicked and moving haphazardly in wide circles around them.

That's the only way, he realized. Pumping more and more mana into his boots, he slowed their fall to a crawl and yelled, "REXXXXX. OVER HERE!"

His knees aching, he stopped their fall and bounded through the air in giant leaps, racing toward Nel's steed.

Rex turned to face them and, after a brief glance, climbed to the front of the creature. He pointed desperately behind him in an attempt to make it see them. It ignored him.

Shit. Shit. Shit. We're gonna die.

"I got you!" Nel yelled, hurtling through the air toward the pair. Grabbing Luke, she whistled loudly and flung them toward the beast. The griffin turned in the sky and swept toward them, catching the pair gently on its back.

"Where is it?" Jax asked right away, drawing his sword from its sheath as he looked through the sky.

"I don't know. It just vanished," Rex said after a moment.

"What do you mean?" Luke frowned as he knelt on the griffin's back, clutching her fur tightly.

"One moment it was there, then Nel threw her spear at it, and then it vanished."

"That's good, right? Maybe it fell out of the sky!" Jax said.

"If it was gone, Nel would have come back," Rex argued, a worried frown on his face.

Nel suddenly stretched her arm back and launched her spear into a seemingly empty spot in the sky. Red mist exploded outward as her spear sank into *something*.

The air shimmered, and the serpent revealed itself.

"Did it just . . ." Jax trailed off.

"Yes," Rex said flatly.

Why can a snake fly and make itself invisible? This is bullshit.

CHAPTER 47

Some Weird Snake

Luke opened his status, for a second tearing away his eye from the battle in the sky. Checking his mana, he dismissed it.

Status	Skills	Quests	Inventory
Name: Lukas King
Tier: Mortal
Mana: 3,991/6,624
Rate: 15% per hour
Strength: 116
Agility: 240
Constitution: 144
Arcana: 92
Stat Points: 0
Bloodline: Locked. Conditions not met. (1/10,000)
Charges: 7/10

Still have some. Maybe enough for another fall or two. He sighed in relief, returning his attention to the fight. He was glad to still have a safety net, however small it was, in case something else pushed him off.

To his surprise, Nel seemed to fare a lot better against the winged serpent than she had the giant. Something he attributed to the fact that the creature bled and, unlike the giant, didn't regenerate itself as soon as any damage was done to it.

She stood in the air, always making sure to position herself between the creature and the griffin, preventing it from breaking past her and getting to them. Not that it seemed particularly intent on doing so. Her spear crackled with white electricity and tore through the sky over and over, impaling the creature before returning to her waiting hand. The spear tore itself free with a wet squelch dozens of times every few seconds, and it moved so fast that it was a blur to their eyes.

It's like she's mashing buttons in a game. He grinned. *Nothing wrong with that, though—if it works, it works. If the thing is too stupid find a way out, then that's on it.*

The serpent was simply unable to cope with Nel's barrage. Its ability to turn invisible wasn't perfect, and Nel was unusually adept at dealing with it whenever it did try. Her eyes found the faint shimmer of its presence and the droplets of blood dripping from its body with unerring accuracy.

Nor was it fast enough to escape her spear. Not that it was willing to do so in the first place.

Despite the damage it was accruing, the monster showed no signs of retreating. If anything, it seemed more and more determined the longer the fight persisted. Even when it turned invisible, it was to try and sneak past her guard, and never to escape.

How is it even alive? Luke thought incredulously as the one-sided battle dragged on.

The serpent had so many holes poked through its body after a minute or two of the treatment that it was hard to find an unwounded spot.

"Why isn't it dying?" Jax mumbled under his breath. His hand gripped his sword so tightly that his knuckles had turned white.

"Because Nel's not hitting anything important." Rex stretched his arm out lazily, pointing to the monster's head. "It's taking her hits but protecting its eyes and head. And look at where it does hit. Her spear sinks in a little, but—"

"It's not getting past the ribs." Jax sighed.

He's right . . . "Do you think she can finish it?" Luke asked, turning to Rex.

"Maybe. It doesn't matter too much either way," he answered casually.

"What do you mean?"

"The griffin is a lot faster than that thing. She's fighting it, but we can leave any time. Just look how slow it is," he said matter-of-factly. "If we hadn't run into it, there wouldn't have even been a battle at all. Honestly, if Nel gave it the chance, it would run, but it knows that she won't let it escape. The second it turns its back, it's going to get a spear in its skull."

"Why aren't we leaving, then?" Jax asked.

Rex just stared blankly at the battle. "Creatures at the Warrior tier are valuable and rare. Our mother is also an alchemist. One of the best on the island, actually. The sheer amount of mana saturating the bodies of warriors make them an exceptional reagent, and a monster that size could be used to make hundreds of high-quality potions. I don't think I have to tell you how valuable those are," he explained. "Not with the Tide so close."

"But still, do we have the time? We have a mission to complete," Jax grumbled. "I thought delivering the message would be more important than killing some random monster living in the middle of nowhere."

"If time was a big constraint on this mission, then she wouldn't have agreed to take you. Or come to the capital to grab me, for that matter."

"Why did she come for you?" Luke asked.

Rex just grinned at him. "You'll find out if you find out. Just because we're going to a cyclops's forge together doesn't change the fact that we'll be competing in a few months."

"Really?" Luke deadpanned. *He's still on that?*

"Yes." The smile slipped from his face. "Really. My abilities and my secrets are mine. I have no obligation to tell you anything. The same way you don't have to tell me anything. If I were you, I'd be glad for that. If everyone went around thinking they were entitled to your knowledge, the world would be a bloody place."

Well, he's not wrong. It's not like I was going to tell him my secrets. I've killed to keep my own already. It's only fair that he doesn't tell me his own.

Still . . . Luke frowned at Rex. *It kind of sucks not knowing what's up. It's not like we're complete strangers, and knowing what he can do and the extent of his abilities could mean life or death. It's not like I'm asking him to explain everything he can do in excruciating detail. Whatever.*

Shaking his head, Luke focused on the battle.

It's probably something dumb anyway.

Their battle, if it could even be called that anymore, continued in the same vein for minutes. Nel was beginning to look tired from the constant exertion, but the serpent looked on the verge of death. She had begun aiming for its wings, drastically reducing its ability to maneuver in the air. Something she had avoided earlier on in a feeble attempt to protect its most valuable organs. As the battle wore on, though, she became more and more careless to the damage she was causing it, having decided that it was more important to kill the beast than it was to extract the maximum amount of value from it.

I wonder how many stat points a warrior is worth.

Instantly Luke began thinking of ways to land the killing blow on the creature. His mind churned out one bad idea after another. He discarded all of them, deciding that randomly leaping into the battle would get him killed.

If I can manage it, though, I'll make some progress with leveling up my sword. And who knows when I'll get a chance like this again?

There seem to be a lot more Warrior-tier beings on Sylcra than there were on Carim, but a hundred isn't a small number. Now that I think about it, a hundred warriors is probably a solid percentage of them. If I can chip away at the upgrade requirement, I should.

"Do you think she'll let me land the killing blow?" he asked Rex.

"What?"

"I want to kill it."

"Are you stupid?"

Luke smiled at him as he watched Rex's opinion of him sink in real time.

"I like to think I'm brave. Besides, how often do you get the opportunity to kill something at the Warrior tier as a mortal?"

"Never. It's suicide. Idiotic beyond belief. What about that makes you want to get involved?" he asked incredulously.

"Look at it." Luke gestured vaguely in the serpent's direction. "It's about to keel over and die any second now. I should be able to get close and stab it in the eye pretty easily."

"Rex is right. What you're describing is insane. What's the point of landing a killing blow, anyway?"

Well, I have this awesome sword that used to belong to a demigod that siphons the mana of whatever I kill with it. "I just want to. It'll be something to brag about in a few decades."

"Even if you could get close without being ripped apart, the odds of you being able to do any damage to it at all are next to none. It's a warrior. Even weakened, its flesh is too strong for a mortal to cut through," Rex argued.

"That could be a problem. Do you think I should test cutting its tail or something first? See if that works before committing to a killing blow."

"Are you stupid?" Rex asked again.

Luke ignored him. Crawling forward on the griffin's back, he wrapped an arm around its thick neck and unsheathed Bellerophon's Blade.

"Can you understand me?" he asked the eagle head, ignoring Jax and Rex muttering in the background. The creature ignored him. Unfettered, he continued. "I want you to fly closer to Nel—can you do that? I need to talk to her."

It cocked its head to the side.

"Please?" Luke asked again.

This is stupid. It's just an animal. Why would it even understand me? Luke sighed softly.

One of its eyes met both of Luke's.

Then, to the surprise of everyone, it banked hard and fast. A moment later, it was hovering next to Nel.

"Aura! What are you doing?" she asked, not taking her eyes off the beast. Her chest rose and fell in exertion.

"I asked her to." Luke swung his leg over the side of the griffin's neck, getting ready to sprint into the air at a moment's notice. "I want to kill it."

"What?"

"I know it sounds ridiculous, but I want to kill it."

Nel opened and closed her mouth in shock. "Why?"

Luke ignored her question. "I was thinking, I'll have Aura fly past that thing, and I'll jump onto its back and stab it through the skull."

"You'll die" she said as her spear pulled itself free. Catching it with casual ease, she flicked it back at the monster.

"It'll have no way to attack me if I'm on its back, and if you keep it distracted, it should be fine."

"That's stupid, and you have nothing to gain. Killing it won't get you its corpse. I'm not going to give it to you after all this work."

Its corpse? What? Ew.

"If you let me do it, I'll participate in the Olympics."

She gave him the stink eye before biting her bottom lip in thought. "Fine," she agreed grudgingly. "I need a moment. When I say go, jump! You'll know where to attack."

Her ring flashed, and four more spears, identical to the one she was already using, appeared in the air beside her. All five of them whirled in the air around her, and her face went red with exertion as each of the spears became brighter and brighter, lighting running down their shafts.

One after the other, they ripped through the air, each one aimed at different parts of the creature's head. It dodged two of them while one lodged itself in its neck, higher up its body than any spear had hit before. Not wasting a second, she launched another. Aimed right at its eyes.

It dodged.

"GO," she shouted, launching the last spear. It flew through the air, and the griffin took off after it and arrived in the air above the creature moments before the spear struck the monster.

Luke jumped, sword drawn.

Her spear grazed the top of the creature's neck, leaving a deep gash along its skull.

Luke's eyes glimmered as he realized what she had done. Diving forward, he pushed downward, using his boots to give him extra leverage in the air.

His sword buried itself straight into the creature's brain, all the way until his hands were buried in its gray matter. Luke's momentum, combined with his sword's inherent sharpness, let it slip through the remaining tissue like a hot knife through butter.

It bucked.

Nel appeared underneath it and drove a spear through the roof of its mouth. Hooking it like a fish and heaving it into the air.

Mana, thick and viscous, burned its way through the sword and up Luke's arms. His world became white with pain, as agony greater than any he had felt before raced through him. He felt his Arcana stat surge rapidly as the very act of absorbing Warrior-tier mana stressed his mana far beyond what should have been possible at his tier.

The Seed came alive within him and swallowed it all. Saving him from death.

+316 Stat Points

Worth it, Luke thought, falling belly first onto the creature's bloody body as darkness clouded his vision.

CHAPTER 48

Points, Points, Points

Luke gritted his teeth, fighting with every ounce of will he could muster to stave off the impending darkness. He measured each breath in order to not reveal the pain he was in and bit his tongue to prevent himself from screaming in agony.

Don't make a scene! Don't make a scene! Don't make a scene!

He shouted the mantra over and over in his head, hoping with every fiber of his being that he would be able to stand.

His mind flashed back to his giggling fit in the tomb and the drama that had ensued after.

Screaming is much worse than that. Hold it together, he thought desperately.

He feared that if he passed out or acted weird in any way, it would lead to questions—questions that he didn't want anyone even thinking about, let alone asking. To him, it was already bad enough that Cyzicus considered him some kind of prodigy, but adding a tendency of passing out after killing monsters to the list of his oddities was not something he was inclined to do. Who knew what kind of conclusions the old man would draw, and as uninterested as he seemed to be in Luke's secrets, he would never forget the fact that a god had been killed for what he possessed. Anything that made him seem suspicious was a negative.

I can't believe I agreed to join the Olympics. I already know that's gonna be a can of worms, but if Arke thinks I came back to life the same way the saint guy did, then I should be safe. My mana is normal, while his was foul. If that's the only thing she has to go off, then I have nothing to worry about.

Clenching the handle of the sword with an iron grip, he pushed off against the disgusting blood-covered head of the winged serpent. Lazily pulling his blade free from the monster's brain, he climbed to his knees and then to his feet as carefully and naturally as he could so that nothing would seem out of place. His face pale and his blue robes covered in blood and bits of flesh, he smiled.

"What a rush! Whoo!" he cheered, tiredly lifting his sword in the air and meeting the eyes of his companions with a cheeky grin. He hurt in places he didn't even know it was possible to hurt and was doing his best not to show it.

Jax and Rex stared back at him blankly from their place on the griffin's back.

"Why did you do that?" Rex asked, confusion practically written on his face.

"Why do I have to tell you?" Luke grinned cheekily, taking satisfaction in the affronted look the teenager leveled at him.

That's right. Taste your own medicine, you asshat.

Nel wrinkled her nose in disgust. Her storage ring flashed thrice in quick succession. A single talisman, a set of blue robes, and a bucket of water appeared floating in the air with her. She tore the perforated tab off the talisman and slapped it onto the floating body of the beast, prying her spear free from the still floating corpse as she did. She was using her powers to keep it, and consequently Luke, in the air.

"Take your robes off. I won't ride with someone as filthy as you," she said, floating the bucket of air over Luke's head.

He looked down on his clothes before nodding gratefully. Flicking the blood off his sword, he returned it to his sheath. His eyes widened slightly in surprise as he noticed that it had undergone a slight change. A hair-thin azure vein now ran down its center—one that definitely hadn't been there before. Not wanting to draw any attention to it, he slid it into the sheath on his hip next to the sword Cyzicus had given him before shrugging them both off and balancing them on his feet so that they wouldn't get blood on them.

I'll take a closer look at it later, Luke thought as he stripped out of his robes. *Is it weird that this is the second time some red-robed superhuman gave me a set of robes and told me to change in front of them?*

As soon as he did, cold water engulfed him and swirled around his body. Trapped in Nel's telekinetic grip, it picked up all the debris and filth from his body. Then, with a flick of her finger, it went over the side of the beast, shattering into a fine mist, the second she broke her mental grip.

Okay, that's cool. Embarrassing, but cool, he thought, glancing at Nel, who was biting her cheek in concentration. *We probably could have just gone down to the water, though.*

Done with his impromptu shower, he eyed the distance between himself and the griffin with trepidation.

Nel lifted her eyebrow, curious as to why he wasn't climbing on.

Right. The shoes. They expect me to air walk, he thought miserably. Grasping his mana, it took every ounce of willpower he had not to shudder and collapse in pain. Channeling it into his boots, he took one excruciating step through the sky after another toward the Elder's familiar.

I didn't think absorbing Warrior-tier mana would be this awful, he thought, settling awkwardly onto the griffin.

Nel shoved the creature into her ring, and a second later, they were silently cutting through the air again.

Luke opened his status.

Status	Skills	Quests	Inventory

Name: Lukas King
Tier: Mortal

Mana: 3,114/9,504

Rate: 15% per hour

Strength: 116

Agility: 240

Constitution: 144

Arcana: 92 > 132

Stat Points: 316

Bloodline: Locked. Conditions not met. (1/10,000)

Charges: 7/10

Yeah, he thought excitedly. *That was worth it. Forty points just from absorbing it, and over three hundred stat points. That's . . . good. Really good. Like, really, really good. Totally worth the pain.*

Have I? He did some quick math in his head. *Four hundred and four points today. If I subtract that from my total points, that's almost half the points I had yesterday.*

If I can continue at this pace, I could max out all my main attributes in like a week. Which is unlikely. I don't even know if I can survive this level of torture every day. But the six-month deadline seems a lot closer now than it did before.

Being boiled, killing a Warrior-tier monster, having all that mana suddenly running havoc in my body— He frowned. *The rest was fine, but the mana, it felt like it would have killed me if the Seed didn't draw it in. And even then . . .*

He closed his eyes and focused inward, suppressing a wince as the mere act of observing his mana sent phantom pains shooting through his body.

It already hurts less than it did a few minutes ago, but I don't know if I'm doing any permanent damage. At the very least, I should hold off on killing another warrior until the pain fully goes away.

Fuck. I can't believe I actually killed that thing. I mean, sure, Nel did basically all the work and I just finished it off, but still.

Just a few weeks ago, I couldn't have even imagined doing that. I was worried about fighting mid-Mortal-stage monsters. A few months ago, Nefkha had me scared to death, and now I'm a mortal who killed a warrior. One that's riding a griffin with the daughter of an emperor, on the way to meet a cyclops called Sophia.

His eyes suddenly widened.

"Hey, Nel," he called out. "Are you a princess?"

"What?"

"Are you a princess?"

She sputtered in surprise. Behind him, Rex and Jax snickered before Jax burst out into full-blown laughter.

"You just figured that out?" Rex asked him disbelievingly. "You really are an idiot."

"And you're a prince . . ." Luke trailed off, filling his cheeks with air before breathing it all out. "That's pretty unbelievable."

"Why?" Rex asked, his voice gaining an odd edge.

"Well, you're so . . . pissy."

"I'm what?"

"I think you heard what I said."

"I think the new guy has your measure," Jax said mirthfully.

"So what's it like, Nel? Cyzicus seems like a fun person to hang around with."

"I suppose that in a way, I am a princess," she said reluctantly, "but Grandfather doesn't grant any of us any additional privileges or duties. To me or any of my siblings or cousins. He loves all of us, but he's the sole voice of authority in Sylcra. He does enough to make sure that we have the guidance we need to live up to our full potential, but . . ." She trailed off.

"He doesn't care if we spend our lives cultivating every second of every day or living like a mortal," Rex finished. "He'll come visit regardless."

"That's pretty nice of him," Luke said.

"It's practical," Rex corrected. "He won't waste time making someone do something they don't want to. If he really wants something, he'll tempt you, try to cajole you, and bribe you, but he'll never force anyone's hands."

Hmm.

"Do you know why he hates Arke so much? The way he talked to her yesterday, and then this morning. He made her so angry she blasted him through his own throne. I don't get why he would do that. Provoking someone stronger than him doesn't seem wise."

"That . . ." Nel hesitated. "I don't know. He isn't one to hide his intentions, though. He always says what's on his mind, and being an emperor, it isn't just about being at the Hero tier. The gods have rules, and they protect their territories. They won't allow anyone, not even Arke, to upset the balance they have created."

"What about the Rebel, then?"

She frowned. "That's different. I don't know what tier Arke is, but the Rebel is a Hero. Grandfather is expected to deal with her, and those below the Hero tier, by himself. If he can't prevent someone at the same level as him from snatching his domain, then he shouldn't have it in the first place. That's how it's always been. They'll intervene if the threat is beyond him, though. In a way, he has more to fear from the Rebel than he does Arke."

Hmm.

"Yesterday, he mentioned something about the titans and Arke," Luke supplied. His mind churned as he thought about what it could mean. *A lesson they learned the hard way, and one Arke will learn again. That's what he said.* "Do you know anything about that?"

"There was a war," she said eventually, "between Olympus and Othrys. Gods and titans."

Is a titan different from a god? Luke mused. *Is that what Arke is?*

"Arke fought for the titans at first, but she turned traitor and joined Olympus. That's all I know. Why it was fought, and how it ended—it's one of the few things that Grandfather won't speak about." She frowned.

"How long ago was it?"

"Long," said Rex. "Tens of thousands of years ago, if not longer. None of that stuff matters anymore, though." He yawned, looking over the edge of the griffin.

Maybe not to you.

"This griffin of yours is faster than I thought," Rex said. "I can't believe we already crossed the river. The journey is supposed to take days."

Nel preened and scratched her familiar's neck lovingly. "She is, isn't she?"

"She is. If you ever manage to breed her, you should give me the cub. Or is it an egg?"

"A cub, I think," Nel answered. "And if I do manage to breed her, it would be a miracle, and I would never give her baby to you."

"Who then? Lukeus? All he'd use it for is to bed every prostitute on the island. Probably not even for the first time!" he whined.

What a legend.

"If you want a griffin so bad, why don't you go and catch one yourself and then convince it to bond with you?" Nel said teasingly.

"Fine. I don't know why I expected something different from you anyways," he grumbled. "It's getting dark. Let's make camp."

"No. There's still some light. Let's go a little farther," Jax urged.

Luke tuned them out as they continued to argue about whether to make camp now or in a few minutes and instead called up his status.

I have points to spend, and I have to be smart about it.

CHAPTER 49

Learning a Craft

So. Mana is obviously the key. The more I have of it, the better. The stances, my boots, the sword—I need it for all of them.

My Agility is already high enough that I don't feel the need to bump it up just yet, and so far Strength, while useful, hasn't been a game changer. My sword is sharp enough, and the techniques lethal enough, that I don't strictly need the advantage of pure strength.

Which makes what I have to do pretty obvious: all the free points in Arcana and Constitution. Ideally, I should make them equal and grow them in tandem. Being more durable is never the wrong choice, and as my Constitution improves, so will my Strength and Agility. Definitely not to the same extent if I improved those stats individually, but it's not a bad trade-off. And if I spend all my free points, then I'll have, let's see . . . He scrunched his eyebrows as he did the math in his head. *Around forty thousand mana.*

That's . . . pretty fucking good. I won't have to worry about the boots running out on me, at the very least. And I'll be able to get more than a single swing from the sword Cyzicus gave me. A mid- to long-range attack will definitely be useful, especially one that doesn't need any ammo.

Luke opened his status, wary of the pain he was still in and acutely aware of the fact that Rex was just inches behind him and Nel was in front of him. Since both of them could probably detect his mana, he decided to raise his Arcana attribute by a single point. He planned to drip feed himself the stat points over a period of a few days or weeks to make the gains less noticeable.

He regretted his decision immediately, as a searing heat spread throughout his body.

Nope! Not doing that anytime soon. He closed his status. *I'll try again tomorrow and see how that feels.*

They flew for another hour before setting up camp.

"I'm going to go hunt something," Rex said the second the griffin touched down in a clearing. "Can I borrow a bow?"

"I have food," Nel offered, pulling a bow and a quiver full of arrows from her ring as she did.

He grimaced. "Your food is bland." Then, collecting the weapons, he wandered into the forest.

Kinda rude. As expected.

"I should probably go with him," Jax said, striding into the dark woods after Rex and leaving Luke alone with the warrior.

Nel, like Luke, carried all the essentials of comfortable living with her everywhere she went, fully realizing the benefits of having easy access to portable storage. A few minutes after the two boys slunk away, she had the whole campsite ready: tents, bedrolls, pillows, chairs, tables, and a half dozen other random items meant to make life easy all laid out in a loose circle around a large bonfire.

Unlike Luke's inventory, though, food left in hers would spoil, whereas in his, time seemed to stop, allowing him to remove what he wanted in exactly the same state he had put it in.

Even so, Nel had found a way around it—tagging her food with preservation talismans.

"The talismans don't keep food fresh for long, but it's fine for a day or two," she explained, noticing Luke's gaze.

"Can you teach me how to make one?" he asked, watching her pull one off a container full of rice and tossing it, where it hung suspended over the fire.

She frowned at him. "A preservation talisman?"

"Talismans in general. I don't know how they work, like, at all."

"That . . ." She glanced at her food, and then back at him again. "Yeah, we have time. I'd advise against spending too much time on learning how to make them, though. Your time will be better spent using the manasink and cultivating than it would on these. We usually let those that have lost hope of ascending to the Warrior tier make them."

So Trixie was right about that, too. I wonder if she's still stuck in the tomb? Arya and Spiros would have made it out by now. Especially if Len and Yjarn managed to clear the empress's bar. Although, I wonder where they went? Spiros probably stayed in Carim. I don't think he'd leave his sister and cousin behind, but what about Arya? It didn't seem like she had anything tying her to the island. I don't think she mentioned her family a single time we were there.

Nel's storage ring flashed, pulling Luke out of his thoughts, and a handful of blank slips appeared on the table along with a thin wooden cylinder and a thin leather-bound booklet.

Grinning in excitement, he picked up and inspected the wooden cylinder. *Is this supposed to be a pen? It doesn't have ink, but it kind of looks like one.* He rotated it in his hand, noting the small glyphs engraved down its shaft.

"The process isn't complicated. You draw a symbol and then channel your mana into it to power it. That book has the common talismans, and those slips are what we use. All the ones I gave you are designed to activate when you tear them, so we make the paper easy to rip in advance."

He grabbed the book and flipped it open.

Explosive. His eyes traced over the complex but beautiful series of lines that made the talisman and the label underneath it. *It doesn't look anything like the talismans I've used in the past, though.* He flipped through the book one page at a time. *Protective, preservation, fire, and contraceptive? The fuck?* His eyebrows shot up in surprise at the last item. *One thing is clearly not like the others.*

"Do I channel my mana into this to make it work?" He picked up the pen and twirled it between his fingers.

"Yes. The stylus isn't really needed—anything that you can write with works—but it's enchanted to write so long as you put mana through it. It's not as messy as charcoal, and it doesn't smudge, either."

Cool.

"So you draw one of these symbols"—he tapped the book and lifted up the pen—"with this, and then you fill them with mana?" *That's way easier than I expected.*

"Yes. The hard part isn't drawing them, though, it's charging them."

"Hmm," Luke grunted, flipping the book back to the page with the protection charm.

Might as well start with the lifesaver.

Grabbing a slip, he drew the symbol. His boosted agility allowed him to draw the glyphs on the page perfectly, quickly, and easily. "Why not just make a stamp?"

Nel swallowed her food. "It doesn't work. Anyone can use a talisman, but only the person who draws it can charge it. Here." Her ring flashed, and a piece of paper landed in front of him. The glyphs for an explosion talisman were already drawn on it. "Try putting mana in this one, and then the one you drew."

Picking hers up off the table, he concentrated on his mana. It was still achy, but the pain had faded rapidly, and his Arcana stat had ticked up another seven points while they were still in the air, much to Luke's relief, and surprise.

With a flex of his will, he moved his mana toward the paper, and like she said, it felt no different than venting it into the air.

"Huh."

He picked up the one he drew and pushed his mana toward it. Instantly, he felt it latch onto the ink, much like it did when he was funneling the energy into his boots. With an effort of will, he began to push more and more into it. To his frustration, only a small fraction of his mana appeared to be absorbed by the glyphs, with the rest dissipating into the air. Frowning, he increased his output from tens of points to hundreds, expecting the increased amount of mana to make a difference in the rate it filled. It didn't.

Nel grinned, swallowing another mouthful of food. "Did you try to put mana in it faster?"

"Yeah."

"That won't work," she said matter-of-factly. "How fast you can push mana into them isn't related to how quickly you release it. It's a fixed rate over time. The only way to improve is by constantly filling one after another. Eventually your mana learns how to get in there faster, but it takes time. Every new talisman also needs to be learned from scratch, so even if you learn to make a protective talisman in a reasonable amount of time, if you ever decide to make an explosive one, then you'll be starting from square one."

Well, that sucks. He reduced his mana output to one point of mana every couple seconds, matching the rate the talisman was absorbing it.

"What about Warrior-tier talismans? And would this one hold up to that giant's boulders?"

"No. Definitely not." She shook her head from side to side. "If I were you, I'd get out of the way if a warrior attacked you. Maybe surrender if you can. And Warrior-tier talismans are the same glyphs as those, but just filled with Warrior-tier mana instead. So only someone at that tier can make one."

So it's not all bad news. If I learn how to make these once, I can just continue making them forever. And the paper, other than being perforated, looks pretty standard, too. I have more than enough of it in my inventory.

"Are these the only talismans you have?"

She frowned. "I don't think you realize what I just gave you. Those are all the talismans the Rising Sun has access to. If you were a member of the sect, then you would have had to spend thousands of merits to even learn one of them. It's only because you'll be representing Sylcra in the tournament that I even allowed you to see them."

"Oh."

"Quite. I'd also caution you against mixing and matching the glyphs. Unless you somehow learn how to read and write in the ancient tongue, you'll likely blow yourself up."

"The what? And what?" Luke looked at the talismans with a sudden sense of apprehension.

"It's the language of the divines. Every word has power, and carelessly toying with it will get you killed."

"That's good to know. I'll be sure to be careful," he said evenly, eyeing the book.

The ancient tongue. So that's what these symbols are. You write them down, and reality bends. That's . . . kind of wild.

"Good." She waved her hand, and the talisman she had drawn flew away from him and back into her hands. Closing her eyes, she funneled her mana into it, and after a few seconds, it blinked white, and the symbols drawn on it changed, condensing into the familiar pattern of the other talismans he'd used.

So that's how it works.

"You can have it, and these," she said, flinging it back to him, along with a handful of other talismans from her ring. "They're all Warrior tier, so you'll have something to rely on if things get dangerous."

"Thank you."

"Don't mention it." She waved him off.

"NEL!" Jax came running back into the camp, his clothes tattered and covered in blood. "They took him. They took Rex!" he panted, hunching over his knees.

Of course they did.

A spear appeared in Nel's hand, and she rose up in the air.

"Where?" she demanded.

Jax pointed to the direction he had emerged from.

Not wasting a second, or even bothering to ask who or what had taken her brother, she flew into the tree line, moving so fast she looked like a blur in Luke's eyes.

"What happened?" Luke asked, standing up and drawing his sword from his sheath in anticipation.

Jax didn't answer and just stood there, his chest rising and falling as he caught his breath, staring off in the direction Nel had gone.

"What happened?" Luke asked again, tightening his grip on his blade. His heart beat in anticipation as he realized that something was wrong.

"Nothing . . . Nothing happened." Jax looked at him. His eyes cold, he withdrew his sword from its sheath and inched toward Luke.

Man . . . Fuck this. I should have stayed in the capital.

CHAPTER 50

Traitors and Traps

The fire crackled as the two blue-robed figures stared at each other.

"Why are you doing this?" Luke asked, carefully keeping his tone casual as he pocketed the batch of talismans Nel had left him. Leafing through the bunch, he separated a single protective talisman from the others, folding his fingers around it so that he could easily tear the perforated tab. Just in case.

Rose could throw fireballs. Jax didn't show any abilities like that, but he was still handpicked by Cyzicus. It's best if I don't take any chances.

Jax stayed silent. His sword and shaved head both shone in the orange glow of the campfire as he circled around Luke.

"It's not me, is it? Like, we just met, and I really don't think I did anything to offend you . . . I'm pretty sure about that, actually. Honestly, I thought we were getting along pretty well," Luke continued.

I'm also pretty sure that you don't know anything that would make you want to kill me, either. There's no way in hell you know about the God Seed. It could be my sword, but so far, no one's noticed anything odd about it. Not Cyzicus, not Nel, and not even the society when they got their set of harpy wings.

Jax frowned and kept circling him, seemingly looking for an opening to attack.

Why is he being so cautious? When we sparred before, he was nowhere near this hesitant. I don't even have my sword drawn, for fuck's sake.

"Why aren't you saying anything?" Luke asked, drawing his own sword from its sheath. "If you insist on dying by my blade, can you at least do me the courtesy of telling me why I had to kill you."

"Those are bold words," Jax finally said, his voice low and strained. He sniffled. A tear welled up in his eye and rolled down his cheek.

Huh.

"Are you crying?"

What the fuck is going on? Like, seriously? Luke thought.

"No!" He lifted his arm up and rubbed the tears off his face.

. . . fuck this. Disarm first, questions later.

Seizing the opportunity while his opponent was distracted, Luke slipped into the First Stance and closed the distance between them as fast as he could. He kept a careful eye on his mana as he did, in case there was a sudden drain. It never came.

I've won, he realized, a single step away from his foe.

Jax was too slow to respond, and his intentions were clear as day in Luke's mind with the aid of the technique. Luke snaked past his guard in a single smooth stride. Whacking him in the face with the flat of his blade, he struck his sword arm with an open palm, belatedly realizing that Jax hadn't even tried to fight back.

This is . . .

Jax's blade ripped free from his hand and sank into the earth near their feet. Luke, copying Yjarn, lunged forward and kneed him in the ribs with every ounce of strength he could muster. Jax stumbled back, wheezing for air, and clutched his sides. Luke hooked his shin across Jax's ankle and sent him falling ass first onto the ground.

That was easy. Luke frowned, his chest rising and falling and the tip of his sword pressed down on his opponent's neck. *Way too easy. Why didn't he fight back? Is he trying to make me kill him? Why?*

"What's going on?" Luke asked again.

Jax turned his head to the side as tears streamed down his face.

"Look. You're kind of putting me in an awkward situation here. I don't know if I should kill you or give you something to wipe your tears with," Luke said, standing over Jax, uncertain as to what to do. "There's obviously something going on, so why don't you just tell me and we can figure it out, yeah?"

Jax started sobbing. Curling up into a fetal position, he started rocking back and forth.

This is awkward . . . so awkward.

"Is this because of your family? You were worried about them, weren't you? Did something happen to them?"

He still didn't speak.

What should I do? Luke scratched the back of his head.

"What really happened to Rex? Where did you send Nel?"

" . . . "

"Fucking hell, man, will you say something? Listen, you rolling in the mud bawling your eyes out isn't helpful. I need you to get your shit together and tell me what happened. Who took Rex? Why were you trying to pick a fight with me? Why did you give up so fast? I can't help you if I don't know what's happening," Luke pleaded, increasingly frustrated as everything he said fell on deaf ears.

This is starting to creep me out.

Luke frowned as he tried to puzzle out the situation. A sinking feeling spread through his chest as he realized that they were in the middle of nowhere, while someone was nearby and hunting them. All the while, he didn't know who or what they were, how to stop them, or even if he could. Only that a single encounter had seemingly sapped one of his companions of the desire to live.

Rex and Jax shouldn't be weak, but Rex got caught while Jax escaped. So at the very least, it's not some warrior or hero out there—unless they're playing some cruel game.

Should I just leave him and go?

But where? After Nel? Or should I just run away, disappear into the wilderness and wash my hands of all of this? He was tempted.

He hadn't expected to be embroiled in this mess. He had wanted to kill some giants and rake in a large number of status points. Not get caught in the middle of a power struggle between two Hero-tier cultivators vying for a throne. No matter how nice one of the two had been to him.

"Kreeee!" The griffin clambered to its feet and began pacing around the clearing. Stretching its wings to make itself look big, it hissed, staring at the direction Nel had left in.

"He went this way." A voice echoed out from the forest. Tensing, Luke grabbed Jax's sword and chucked it far away before hiding behind a tree, leaving Jax alone in the middle of the camp.

Why's he not hiding?

A group of three bald men wandered into the clearing.

"Is that a—"

"It is. Don't do anything to provoke it. Griffins aren't supposed to be violent. If we ignore it, it should ignore us. They must have used it to fly over the river," said the leader, interrupting the other.

"Right. Is that him?" One of them pointed a spear at Jax. "Why is he just lying on the ground?"

"He's the one, boss. The needle pointed straight at him."

"Hmm. You're Jax right? Alexander's son, if I'm not mistaken. Your father was a good man—shame what happened to him. He wasn't stupid, though. So I have to ask, did you really think you could get away?" the leader asked, crouching down in front of Jax. "Where are your friends?"

"You already took him," Jax said, glaring at him.

They know each other?

"Let's not lie, kid. Do you think we don't know what goes on in the capital?"

"If you knew what was happening in the capital, you wouldn't have come here," Jax answered cryptically.

"Hmm. Is that so?" The leader paled and stood up urgently. "They might have a warrior with them. Send a message back to camp—we need reinforcements." He barked orders as he pulled his sword out of his sheath and rested it on Jax's neck. "Here's the deal, kid. You tell me why you left the capital, and I'll let you live. You can even come back to the clan. How does that sound? You had a little sister, right?"

"I'm not going to tell you anything."

"That's not true. You should know as well as I do that your mind will break. Why not save us the hassle, and yourself the pain, and tell me what I want to know? Besides, what has Cyzicus done for you, huh! What's he done for us? We won his war, and how does he treat us? Leaving us a barren strip of—"

A flash of light emanated from deep within the foliage, and a shock wave traveled through the air moments later. Seconds after that, Nel burst into the clearing with Rex, unconscious and drenched in blood, slung over her shoulder.

She's not dead. Luke sighed in relief.

She took one look at Jax lying on the ground and at the others standing around him, and her ring flashed, a spear appeared in her hand, and the next second it pierced through Jax's head.

Wha—

"Run!" the leader screamed. It was pointless. Her ring flashed three more times in quick succession, and a spear impaled itself through each of their hearts, killing them before they could take even a single step outside the clearing.

"We need to go. Now," she said coldly. Seemingly staring straight at Luke.

Luke stepped out from behind the tree. Nervous sweat poured down the side of his face as he looked at Jax's corpse.

She just killed him. Fuck.

"We don't have time to dawdle. One of them released a flare. If we stay here, we'll be overrun."

"Uh, right," Luke said nervously, watching her gently set Rex on her steed. She walked forward and ripped her spears free from Jax's skull and the three corpses and waved her hand.

Everything in the whole clearing packed itself up and returned to her ring.

Luke's eyes darted between Jax's corpse, Rex's body, and Nel, before he nodded.

Something tells me that I don't exactly have a choice.

Sheathing his sword, he climbed onto her griffin, and then they were in the air moments later.

"What happened?" Luke asked again.

"Traitors," she said, her voice seething with barely restrained anger. "Traitors happened." Turning Rex over, she forcibly opened his mouth and poured a bright-blue liquid down his throat.

"I see. Is he going to be okay?"

"Yes," she said. Her ring pulsed, and a bow appeared in her hand. She handed it and a quiver full of arrows to Luke. "They shouldn't be able to keep up, but if you see anything," she stressed, "kill it."

"I will."

She nodded in satisfaction.

Luke hesitated. "Who are we running from?"

"We're not running, but Clan Skyscar . . . Jax's family. They came here with the Rebel, but when it became clear that their leader would lose, they turned their backs on her. It seems like they decided to get back into her good graces by betraying us." She sighed. "Jax was unlikely to have even known about it, but his clan is in possession of a blood compass. They used that to lay an ambush."

"A what?"

"It's what it sounds like—an artifact that points you to your descendants. They're rare; not even Grandfather has one, but they allow you to keep track of all the members of your bloodline."

Luke frowned. "You couldn't have let him live? Killing him like that, when he meant us no harm . . . it—"

She shook her head. "No. He died the moment his clan decided to throw their lot in with the Rebel. If he came with us, they would know exactly where we are, and if we left him, they would know where we were going . . ." She glared at Luke. "He wasn't hiding with you. Don't pretend that it wasn't you who put him on the ground, and that you wouldn't have killed him as well."

Luke sighed. "After you left, he drew his blade. He made me think he was going to attack me, but when I attacked, he didn't even attempt to fight back."

Nel frowned. "It seems he was loyal then, but the second his clan turned traitor, his fate was decided. It's unfortunate, but—"

"Yeah." Luke ran his hand through his hair. "No choice. I get it."

This world is a shitty place. I already knew that.

"How far are we from the cyclops?"

"Two days."

CHAPTER 51

A Big Forge

You killed him?" Rex asked Nel the second he woke up, hours after the deed had been done. Despite his question, though, Luke could tell that he already knew the answer. He had been expecting that outcome, probably since the moment he got taken and discovered why. After all, a hostile reunion with Jax's treacherous clan couldn't have ended much differently.

It's not like a warrior would ever lose to a mortal. Even Jax knew he was going to die, Luke thought bleakly. *He still chose to come back and warn us, though. Even tried to have me kill him. Did he want me to do it before Nel came back with Rex? Spare them the pain or something?*

What a guy. Luke sighed, once again feeling a heaviness in his heart. The harsh reality of Theos bore down on his shoulders. It was far too easy to forget that death lurked around every corner and in every shadow in this world. Not that it was hard to understand why—immortality was a prize many would die for.

"There wasn't another choice," Nel said. Her tone was flat as she stared off into the distance.

"You could have left him alive! He was my friend . . ." Rex whispered, guilt etched on his face as he angrily brushed a tear away with his sleeve.

"That wasn't an option. Look—I . . . I didn't want to." She sighed. "But there's a lot at stake. I'm sorry, but I really didn't have a choice. Not then, at that moment. I—I shouldn't have brought Jax with us. He would have been safe at the capital. I should have known that the Rebel would put pressure on the different factions, and that the Skyscar clan would be among the first to bend their knees. I knew about the blood compass, but I didn't think . . . I shouldn't have brought Luke, either, but what's done is done." She sighed, leaning forward and wrapping her arms around her familiar's neck. "I can't change the past, and there's no room for regret now," she said, her voice low but steady. "I really am sorry things had to be this way."

She's acting tough, but killing him got to her. I doubt she's used to doing this sort of thing, but she's too smart not to see the situation as it is. Not killing him was asking for trouble, and she can't afford to be merciful. Not when it would cost not just her, but everyone who's relying on her, too. Luke scratched the back of his head and slowly shuffled back an inch, adding what little distance he could between him and Rex as the boy's face twisted in sadness and his shoulders heaving as grieved the loss of his friend.

If I were in her position—I would have done the same. That doesn't make it any easier to live with, though, Luke thought, remembering those he had killed in the past. *Life in this world, it's not like Earth. Theos is harsh. Nel knows that, I learned that, and Rex will understand—eventually.*

"Is going to the cyclops really that important?" Rex asked.

"It's the only way," she said confidently. "Despite their battle a century ago, Grandfather is convinced that she is content with her half of Sylcra. He plans to give her the east side of the island permanently in exchange for her help. His hope is that, at the very least, she'll power the teleportation altars while he and the Rebel battle, but what he really wants is for her to join him in crushing the Rebel once and for all. The two of them against one hero will result in an easy victory."

"He'd give half the island to a monster?" Rex scoffed.

"Cyclopes aren't monsters," Nel said hesitantly. "They're an old race. Ancient and powerful. Perhaps a little misunderstood. Besides, practically speaking, half the island already belongs to her . . . This would just make it formal. And yes, Grandfather would. An uninhabited part of the island is a small price to pay for the lives of his family."

Oh, right. This Rebel probably plans on killing all his descendants. Wouldn't make sense to let them live and plot revenge, and with Arke preventing anyone from leaving, she probably can, too. Unless Cyzicus has a way to teleport people off the island like Alexia did. Hmm.

"We won't need to do any of this if Gramps just becomes a saint," Rex argued.

"I'm sure that if Grandfather had the luxury of time, he would not consider ceding half his territory to her a viable option. Unfortunately, the Rebel has struck, and he can't hide. Not when we're so close to a Giant Tide. He's unable to break through as he is, and unless Sylcra does well in the Olympics, it's unlikely that he ever will. Which means this is the best he can do. Besides, Sophia has proven to be an agreeable neighbor. Not once has she ventured into our territory, and she's only killed humans who provoked her first. This is the best option."

"Still . . . I don't like it. To rest our hopes on someone we don't know."

"Grandfather has known Sophia for longer than you and I have been alive. Besides, your approval doesn't matter. Unless you can think of a better solution, this conversation is pointless."

Rex frowned in response.

"What are cyclopes like? I've never met one before," Luke asked.

"Like humans, but bigger, and they only have one eye. I've never met one, either—all I know is what Grandfather told me. Supposedly there aren't many of them left anymore. The titans hunted and killed most of them, and those that remain mostly live on the fringes of civilization, alone and in isolation. Like Sophia."

"Why in isolation?"

Nel shrugged. "I don't know. They probably just like being alone."

Well, I can't really argue with that logic, Luke thought as he opened his status and added a handful of points to his Constitution and Arcana stats. He suppressed a wince as a twinge of pain ran through his body. The aftereffects of killing a Warrior-tier monster still caused him some pain, but whatever damage had been done was fading quickly.

By Nel's estimate, they would reach Sophia in a little over a day, and he wanted to be as strong as he possibly could when they got there, which meant spending all his stat points before then. Realistically he knew that even the peak of the Mortal tier was woefully weak compared to the forces they would be arrayed against, but even so, every point of Strength he could gain would increase the odds of his survival.

So long as he had enough mana, he was confident in defeating most mortals, and an increase in Constitution was always welcome.

"How old are you?" Luke suddenly asked.

"Me?" Nel said, craning her neck and looking at Luke.

"Yeah."

"I'm nineteen. You?"

Nineteen. Luke's eyebrows shot up in surprise. "I'm sixteen," he lied as he considered her words. In truth, he didn't know how old he was, or rather, how old Max's body was. The memories he had inherited from Max didn't depict anything from before the fisherman had found him, but both his adoptive parents were sure that his actual age wasn't far from what they had guessed. Now that he'd learned that it was possible to track people's bloodlines, though, he was more than a little worried that someone would show up and claim some relation to him.

If that happens, though, at the very least they won't be able to call me out on my personality. More importantly, whatever method that's used to track me by blood probably can't be deceived by changing my appearance. That's a problem for future me, though, and only if it ever comes up. I can't imagine someone abandoning a kid in the ocean and then trying to come back into that same kid's life more than a decade later. At the same time, gods are real now, so nothing is really outside the realm of possibility.

That said, I doubt the Seed would have chosen a body that came with baggage that I can't deal with. Besides, whoever my relatives are, they let Max die once. They can't care too much about me if they let that happen.

"Becoming a warrior at that age, that's . . . impressive." *Arya, Yjarn, and basically all the other Inner Disciples at the society were into their twenties, and most of them were nowhere near the threshold. For her to already be a warrior . . . Cyzicus doesn't do things by half.*

"Mmm. I suppose. It would have been embarrassing if I hadn't become a warrior by now. Honestly, I wanted to delay a little longer and build a better foundation, but Grandfather said that the earlier you advance through the tiers, the easier it is. On the other hand, having a flimsy foundation makes you weaker than you otherwise could be. Striking a balance between potential and strength is tricky."

"Isn't potential the obvious choice?"

"Not necessarily. The higher you get your attributes before you break through, the more potent they are after, and whatever attribute you break through with gets a massive boost in efficacy. So ideally, you'd want to be as close to the peak as possible with all of them before you cross the threshold. Actually doing that is hard. There are *some* shortcuts you can take, like being boiled alive"—she grinned—"which massively boosts your general Constitution, but they aren't easy, and tricks like that stop working after a while, anyway. The way it was explained to me is that you want to train in the most efficient way possible and get all the easy and least time-consuming benefits and then push past the barrier as soon as you can. The earlier the better."

"Huh," Luke grunted. *With the Paragon's Path, I should be looking at a very solid boost if that's the case. I wonder if there's an equivalent path for people who ascend through the tiers as fast as possible? The speed run to my Paragon. Seems unlikely, but who knows. At the very least, I doubt that the Paragon is the only special path.*

Opening his status, he dumped another handful of points in Arcana and Constitution, clenching his jaw as a wave of agony coursed through his body, hoping, as he did, that no one would question why his mana was increasing so suddenly.

I'm not touching Rex or Nel, so it should be fine. I'm pretty sure they can't see how much mana I have, and neither of them has touched me. So long as the griffin doesn't start talking, I'm golden.

Clang. Clang. Clang.

Luke heard the cyclops before he saw her or her home. The crisp noise of metal striking metal reverberated through the air at regular intervals and became louder and louder the closer they got.

At least we know she's home. Luke winced as he stuffed his index fingers into his ears. The sound of clashing metal had grown so loud it started to physically hurt his head. *And if all cyclopes like making this much noise, it's no wonder that they live in isolation at the fringes of society. This is insane.*

Not long after they heard her, they started to fly over a junkyard full of what appeared to be the abandoned remains of her projects. Giant pieces of metalwork littered the grass as far as the eye could see, from helmets with brilliant red or blue plumage, chest pieces big enough to be houses, metal hills that Luke thought could be shields, and even swords so big they looked like they were made to cut mountains in half instead of people.

A good portion of her creations were covered in rust that leached onto the ground around them like a disease, while others were so polished that the reflected light of Theos's suns blinded them if it caught the right angle.

Suddenly the hammering stopped.

"WHO?" Sophia asked, her voice tearing through the air so loudly that their teeth chattered with the accompanied vibrations.

"I am Agnella, daughter of Kyzikos and granddaughter of Cyzicus," she yelled out.

"I am Rex, son of Kyzikos and grandson of Cyzicus."

Luke's eyes darted between the two.

"I am Luke," he yelled, scratching the back of his head in embarrassment and doing his best not to look at Nel and Rex as they gave him looks of exasperation.

"Lady Sophia, we have come to discuss a matter of grave importance, and humbly request an audience with you," said Nel.

Clouds boiled in the sky, and the ground shook. A single eye, made of light, blocked out the sky above their heads. It blinked.

"NO."

Welp. Something tells me we're not going to be taking no for an answer.

CHAPTER 52

A Stubborn Cyclops

The trio sitting on the back of the griffin exchanged awkward glances as the sound of hammering metal resumed.

"We have to talk to her again," Nel yelled over the noise.

"Are you sure she won't just blast us out of the sky?" Luke asked, knowing that it was a pointless question. He could tell that Nel wouldn't back down. Not with her home and family on the line.

"No." She patted her familiar, and they were once again cutting through the sky toward the source of the noise.

That's just great. Let's totally go and bother the super-powerful being that can proba-bly kill all of us as easily as she breathes after she told us to leave.

The closer they got, the louder the sound of her forge became.

"Are those—" Luke said dumbly, looking at the shock waves moving through the air in time with Sophia's hammering.

"Yeah," Rex said. "The air is distorting with the strength of her strikes."

How strong does someone need to be to make the air shatter? He felt his mouth go dry at the thought. *And we're going to talk to her, when she's already said she doesn't want to.* He stared at Nel's back as they traveled farther and farther into the one-eyed giant's domain. A small, primal part of him screamed in his mind that what they were doing was insane. Every instinct he had said that it was madness to test the patience of someone who was so much stronger than them.

"So, what's the plan now?" he asked.

"Grandfather suspected that she wouldn't agree right away, and he gave me some gifts to pass on to her," Nel said reluctantly.

"Oh. That's good." *Any plan is good.*

"Mmm-hmm."

"What gifts?" Rex asked.

"I don't know. Grandfather instructed me not to look."

"What?" Rex said incredulously. "Why can't we look?"

Her cheeks turned red. "The gifts are in a storage ring, and it's enchanted so that I can't—"

"Um. We might have a problem," Rex interrupted.

Sophia had materialized. Or perhaps she had always been there but was only now allowing them to see her. Whatever the case, her sudden appearance left Luke in awe.

She was well over a hundred feet tall, with long blond hair that reached her waist and pale skin that seemed to glow from the inside. She was dressed entirely in black leather, but what manner of beast could provide so much of it and in a piece big enough to dress a giant was a mystery.

She's pretty, Luke thought numbly as he stared at her. He had expected her to be big, given her epithet, but he hadn't expected her to be proportional. As it was, she looked like someone had taken a lithe human woman, subtracted an eye, and made her bigger. Much bigger.

"Why are you still here, descendants of Cyzicus?" she grumbled, blinking her large blue eye slowly as she slung her hammer over her back. The gust of air from the casual movement pushed the griffin back a dozen feet in the air.

I'm not a descendant of Cyzicus—I think—but either way now doesn't seem like the time to correct her. Especially if being related to him makes her less likely to kill us.

"We offer you these gifts," Nel yelled back. Reaching into her robe, she pulled out a ring, stared at it nervously for a second, then telekinetically lifted it off her open palm and moved it through the air toward the giant.

Sophia cocked her head to the side. Lifting her hand, the action once again stirring the wind to an unreasonable degree, she curled her fingers toward herself.

Immediately Luke's mind flashed back to his death. His heart beat in anticipation as a force he was helpless against seized him with no regard to his will and tugged them forward along with the offered ring.

The storage ring landed on her finger and rapidly began to increase in size. Grinning eagerly, Sophia slid it on to her finger.

"That Cyzicus. He's always been a charmer," she said, her cheeks turning a rosy pink.

He's a what? Cyzicus, you sly old dog! Luke grinned as he watched Nel and Rex share an extremely awkward glance. Clearly, neither of them had expected that response from her, even if it was much better than either of them had expected.

The trio watched with a mix of curiosity and apprehension as the cyclops closed her eye in concentration. A moment later, a hissing noise followed by a click came from the ring. It flashed three times. A letter, proportional in size to her, appeared in her hand, followed by the largest teddy bear Luke had ever seen and a single, equally large, blue flower.

Sophia's face grew even redder, and her breath sped up in anticipation. Tucking the flower behind her ear, she unfolded the letter. Her eye darted across its surface with startling speed, and a smile grew on her face.

"EEEP," she squealed, cupping her cheek with an open palm. "He finally agreed. I knew he would!" She bounced up and down excitedly.

"What does the letter say?" Nel asked cautiously.

She grinned at them and turned the letter toward them. It read,

My darling Sophia,

The time has finally come for me to take you as my bride. My granddaughter, Agnella, grows more capable every day, and I suspect in a few short years she will be strong enough to succeed me as empress of Sylcra, allowing me to finally be free from the burden of my throne and for us to be together.

Alas, not all is well. That wretched woman, Tyrisa of Peles, has crawled out of the mud in order to steal my precious kingdom. As you know, she is quite the slippery one, and I must thicken my skin and ask for your help.

I can kill her, of this I assure you, but it will take me time. With the Giant Tide so near, time is a luxury I do not possess much of. It would gladden me greatly if you could join my grandchildren and return with them to the capital so that when the time comes, you can aid my warriors in fending off the Tide for another cycle. It is an exhausting task, but I have trained my subordinates well; they will not require much direction or aid—merely your mana to move them through space, and perhaps they will ask you to defeat a Hero-tier giant if one is born.

I know you hate the humdrum of civilization and prefer to avoid the company of many. If the idea of residing in the capital, for however short an amount of time, is not to your taste, I beseech you to join me in battle, for I am confident that the two of us together will triumph over this wicked woman who dares presume that she can take what is mine.

I apologize for being curt, but my blood boils with rage when I think of her. Just a short while ago, I received news that she killed my grandson Algres. While he was a no-good scoundrel, ruining my good name just like his father did before him, he was still family. I cannot leave his death unpunished.

I am leaving now to find and kill her. I suspect she lurks in the Northern Marshes, hiding among the Hydras like the snake she is. I aim to end this feud between the two of us before it devolves into a war. It is the only way.

I gladly await your arrival by my side, or news that you have entered the capital.

No matter what choice you make, I would like to bequeath to you half of the island of Sylcra and name you empress of all land to the east of Syle.

With love,

Cyzicus

"Is he serious about making you empress?" Rex said dumbly after reading the letter.

"Why is that a surprise? He's been saying that since I became a Warrior."

"Yes, but—"

"But what?"

"I thought he was just doting on you because you're his only granddaughter. I didn't think he actually meant it. I thought it would be our uncle Al who became emperor."

"Uncle Alkis?" Nel scoffed. "Why would he be emperor? He has no hope of breaking into the Hero tier, and he's a no-good scoundrel. I don't think anyone has even seen him for decades. Grandfather would be insane to trust him with the throne. Maybe if it was Cousin Yannis, but even he has no hope of breaking into the Hero tier."

"I gu—"

"Guys," Luke interrupted them, tapping Rex urgently on the shoulder. "While I'm sure that Nel succeeding Cyzicus is fascinating, we have *bigger* things to worry about."

They both immediately straightened up and met Sophia's large blue eye.

"I have no interest in going to the capital," she said flatly. "I shall head west and meet Cyzicus in the marshes."

"Thank you, Lady Sophia." Nel bowed her head slightly.

"No need for that, little empress," she chided, floating into the air as she did. Her form began to ripple, and to their astonishment, she began to shrink—and fast.

I wonder which one is her actual height, Luke thought as both she and her clothes rapidly shrank. *At least the thing with Cyzicus makes more sense now that I know she shrinks. The logistics otherwise—* He shook his head slightly. *Keep it clean, Luke. No need to go there. No need at all.*

Once the transformation was complete, she stood in the air, meters away from them. The ring Nel had given her flashed a handful of times, and both the letter and the teddy bear disappeared, leaving only the blue flower tucked behind her ear, which had shrunk with her.

Is this it, then? Mission complete. She has the letter, and she's going to help Cyzicus. If he's right about how this will play out, then the two of them together should be able to beat the Rebel.

Which means I can go back to the capital and train for the Olympics worry-free until the Tide.

Sophia lifted her hand and balled her fingers into a fist.

Metal shredded the earth beneath them and rose into the sky.

She pulled her hammer from her back and struck the air. A shock wave traveled out, and the metal split into countless metallic ropes.

"What are you doing?" Nel asked, her eyes wide, as she patted the side of her griffin, desperately attempting to make the creature fly away. It didn't.

The ropes latched onto their hands and feet and imprisoned them in space.

"What are you—" Nel asked again, struggling against her bonds.

The cyclops flew forward and placed a single finger on her lips.

"Hush, child. I mean you no harm," Sophia said, a soothing but creepy smile on her face.

Luke attempted to break free of his bonds, but he might as well have been an ant struggling inside a glass jar. He was too weak. They all were.

"What's the meaning of this?" Rex asked angrily, glaring at the cyclops with blistering rage. "The letter said that you and Gramps wanted to get married, so what's this about?"

Sophia smiled. "As I was saying, I don't mean to harm any of you. If, however, she is meant to succeed Cyzicus"—her lone eye locked onto Nel's—"then I cannot risk her coming to harm. I shall join your grandfather in his hunt, but if he really means to retire, then nothing can happen to his heir. As such, you three will stay here while the situation outside resolves itself."

"I appreciate your kind gesture," Nel said urgently. "But there is more going on outside than just the war. The Olympics are in six months, and I need to train—"

"Enough," Sophia said. "I care not for the gods or their games. You will stay here, and you will be safe. As for your training . . ." She bit her lip, her eyes darting between the three of them. "I will give you four—no, ten sheep," she said grudgingly, as if she had done them a great favor. "It's the least I can do for my new family."

The fuck am I supposed to do with a sheep? Luke thought incredulously.

CHAPTER 53

Sheep Go Baa!

The three of them plus the griffin struggled in their metal bonds as they were dragged toward the earth and then pulled in. The ground parted, inches from their skin, as darkness engulfed their senses.

"This is where you will stay," said Sophia as they emerged into the light seconds later.

This looks . . . high-tech, thought Luke, blinking the spots out of his eyes as they adjusted to the sudden brightness. *Definitely a change from all the marble, wood, and bricks everyone else uses.*

The floors and walls were made of a silvery metal, and strips along the edges cast a clinical white light into the room. One end of the room opened up to an artificial grassland where, as promised, ten elephant-size, bull-like sheep were grazing, idly staring at the new entries with bits of grass in their mouths and sharp horns glinting ominously in the light. They promised a skewering to whoever came close.

Along one wall were shelves, stocked with all manner of books, scrolls, and bottles. Along the opposite wall, an assortment of dumbbells and other workout equipment. Three large beds were nestled deep in a dimly lit portion of the room, a fair distance away from the opening with the sheep.

"I'm assuming you three have manasinks already?" Sophia asked as she walked into the grassland. She glanced briefly at them, her lone eye expertly finding the ring on Luke's finger before darting to Rex and then Nel. "Good." She nodded. "The sheep are trained, and there's a machine that will milk them. All of them are in the Warrior tier, so if you're a mortal, don't drink too much." She turned back and eyed Luke and Rex. "And once you do drink it, make sure you burn the mana off by using the weights in the corner or something. Don't drink more than half a cup, and you should already know not to cultivate the mana manually," she advised them. "Agnella, you can drink all you want. It won't be as beneficial for you as it is for them, but mana is mana. One of the sheep—that big black one, actually—is at the peak of the Warrior tier, so if you drink its milk, it should give you some benefit. What else . . ."

Drink milk? Does it have mana in it?

"We can cultivate with milk?" Rex asked, for once seeming equally as clueless as Luke.

"Not just any milk. My sheep are special." Sophia beamed. "Cyclopes of ages past have bred them specifically for cultivation. I had to give them a special regime of potions, and—" She shook her hand through the air. "It doesn't matter. All you need to know is that their milk has mana and putting the mana in the milk is a labor of decades. Especially to get it to the right quality and density. At my level, what they make now isn't exactly useful, but if the baby sheep drink the milk of the elder sheep, they get stronger faster, and hopefully within the next century or so, I'll have a flock of a dozen Hero-tier sheep."

So the milk does have mana. And Warrior-tier mana from the sound of it . . . that's good. Really good. If it's anything like the monster I killed earlier, then I'll have to be careful, but this could take me to the peak.

"Lady Sophia, I thank you but—"

She cut Nel off with a wave of her hand. "I know what you want to say. I get it. Being imprisoned isn't any fun, even if the box you're in is a really nice one. Cyzicus has told me about this woman before, and I've learned a few things about her myself. I know firsthand how many of your brothers and cousins she's killed, and I know how hard it was for your grandfather to have his enemies kill his own family and not be able to do anything about it. It nearly broke him." She sighed. "He spent a decade hunting her, but she was always too slippery, and with the Tides, he could never be too far from the capital. At the Mortal tier, and even the Warrior tier, battles are easy. Two opponents face off, and the weaker one dies. At the Hero tier—things are different. Any cultivator at that level worth their salt isn't easily cornered. We have too many ways to run. To hide and remain hidden. It's . . . If a hero doesn't want to die, it's nearly impossible for another one to kill them."

"Then how does he plan on killing her now?" Nel frowned.

She grinned. "Well, unfortunately for her, she can't leave the island. Emperors are the only ones that can teleport in and out undetected, and she isn't one. If she tries, that crazy lady Arke will kill her. Like she's done with anyone else who's tried. There's some kind of ward around the archipelago and each island, and it alerts her when anyone crosses. Which means she's trapped. And with two cultivators of similar strength hunting her . . ." She chuckled. "There's not a chance of her leaving alive."

"Oh . . ."

"Indeed. As annoying as it has been having that woman on the island, I guess it had some unexpected benefits."

"That winged lady—why does everyone hate her?" Luke asked, seizing the opportunity to ask the one question that had been bugging him for a long time.

"HA. She's an Olympian now, which is bad in and of itself, but before that she was an Othrysian. There's nothing worse than being an Othrysian," the cyclops said, her hands balling themselves into a white-knuckled fist.

"That doesn't mean much to me," Luke confessed.

Titans versus gods, obviously I've heard of it, but how much is the same and how much is different? Troy is real, and Spiros might be Paris. Even Cyzicus and Arke could be mythological figures as far as I know. Does that mean that Zeus and Poseidon are brothers? What about Hades? Cyzicus mentioned him, but how does a god of death factor into things? Was Aeolus some kind of death god, or is control over souls something you just get once you cultivate high enough? Like a warrior being able to fly. There's still too much I don't know, and no good way to find out.

"I'd be surprised if a young one like you did know, and you're much too weak to have a reason to know any of this anyhow." She stretched out her arm, and on cue a single sheep broke free from the crowd and trotted toward her. "Othrys was the home of the titans, and Othrysian is what they called themselves. They were a band of gods that ruled Theos for ages. It was a dark time. They were cruel. They butchered mortals like they did chickens and pigs. Their degeneracy knew no depths, and their greed knew no heights. They inspired hate, were careless with their power, and . . ." She trailed off, a dark look in her eye, and her face settled into a deep frown. "It doesn't matter. When you live like they did, justice comes to you. No matter how powerful you are, there's no one in this world that is truly invincible, and they learned that the hard way. After they fell, the Olympians took over, and things have generally been better. There are still assholes, mind you, but Zeus won't kill millions because he tasted some bad wine, and if someone does act out, he'll get off his ass and deliver some justice. At the very least, the council is good at keeping each other's worst impulses at bay. That's about all you need to know."

So not too different from the tale I know. There seems to be less baby eating at the least.

Why couldn't there just be a library somewhere that I could just read this all in? It would make life so much easier. At least then I would know what I should know and what I shouldn't.

"As for Arke in particular, her actions aren't in good form. She's far stronger than anyone on the archipelago, and using strength to twist everyone's arms into compliance is what the titanomachy was fought for. To see her act like this . . ." She shook her head. "It's not what anyone wants to see. Mind you, she hasn't done anything too egregious. I've heard rumors of what she's been doing to the possessors, but those folk chose to be cursed anyhow, and only a fool will try and fight for them."

Isn't that what Cyzicus got blasted for?

"How long are you going to keep us here?" Rex broke Luke out of his musings.

"Until she's dead." She cupped her chin. "With me and Cyzicus working together, that should take about . . . a week? Maybe two?"

Luke sighed in relief. *A week or two in a bunker while the war sorts itself out isn't bad. Not bad at all, actually.*

"Worst-case scenario . . . we die, and you can leave when one of you becomes a Hero and figures out how to dismantle my wards."

What?

"But that's unlikely. With Cyzicus and me working together, and Arke keeping her from fleeing the island . . . there's little to no chance that she's able to pull her tricks like last time."

"Let's say you and Grandfather fail? How would I get out of here?" Nel asked.

"It won't be hard," she assured her. "The wards aren't meant to keep friends in; they're meant to keep enemies out. You'll be able to feel them as soon as you ascend. Quite frankly, if Cyzicus thinks you have the ability to ascend to the Hero tier, your chances are better here than nearly anywhere else on this island. There are people who would give me their firstborn for what I'm giving you. Take what you can from it—I'm not so generous that I'd let you back in here again when you inevitably realize what exactly you're getting."

"Very well." Nel bowed down. "I thank you for your kindness, and I wish you and Grandfather the best in your battle against the Rebel . . . and in your marital pursuits."

Sophia smiled softly, slapping the sheep gently and watching it as it wandered away. "So formal." She shook her head. "I can see what Cyzicus sees in you—you have some potential, girl. Not just to the Hero tier but beyond." Her eyes briefly darted over Luke and Rex. "You two aren't bad, either."

"Aren't bad?" Rex muttered under his breath. Just loud enough for everyone to hear with their enhanced senses.

I'll take it. Who the fuck wants to be overtly special in this world? I already have one god-killing asshole after me, and I could definitely do without anyone else thinking the same.

"I'm afraid I should get going. The faster I deal with this would-be usurper, the faster I can have you lot out of my home." She lifted her hand, wiggled her fingers, and disappeared.

"So . . ." Luke said, looking between the two siblings. "Who wants to try sheep milk, and do you think she has cookies?"

"Why would she have cookies?"

"You don't like cookies?"

"I like cookies, I just don't see why a cyclops would have them lying around."

"Hey, watch your tone. That 'cyclops'"—Luke made some air quotes—"is your new grandmother, a hero, and an empress."

Rex stared at him blankly. "Just because she might get married to Gramps, doesn't make her my grandma."

"Well, actually, it kind of does," Nel said, walking toward the sheep. "You know how Grandfather is—he'll insist on it. Family is important to him."

Rex frowned and walked after her, choosing not to say anything.

"Have you guys heard of this special milk before?" Luke asked, following them.

"No."

"Yes," Nel said. ". . . kind of. I've heard of special techniques that imbue parts of animals and plants with mana. Some animals do it naturally, and others can be made to. The apples from the evening garden are supposed to be like that. There are some snakes that imbue their venom, too, but that's less useful."

"Huh. So how do we do this?" Luke asked as they gathered around a sheep. All three of them craned their necks and watched it chew.

Rex bent down on his knees and looked underneath it.

"What are you doing? You don't even have a bucket." Luke quirked his eyebrow.

"I'll just use my mouth."

The fuck? There's supposed to be a machine that does this, isn't there? What's he thinking?

"Baa." It leaped over their heads and darted away.

Yeah, I would run, too, Luke thought, his eyes briefly meeting Nel's. Both their gazes filled with revulsion.

CHAPTER 54

Numbers Go *Brrr!*

Luke watched the sheep's figure fade away into the distance with an expression of mild relief.

"Why would you think that getting its milk—directly"—he shuddered—"is a good idea?" Luke asked, turning to Rex and crossing his arms under his chest.

"Well, do you have a better idea?"

Is he for real? He can't be, Luke thought, resisting the urge to facepalm. *She literally told us that the sheep are milked by a machine. How did he forget?*

"I can't imagine having a worse idea; there isn't anything I can think of that would be worse," he lied, knowing objectively that there were worse ideas but unwilling to even entertain them.

"Well, if you're so—"

"That's enough." Nel massaged her eyebrows. "That's incredibly stupid, Rex. Living in the capital has rotted your brain, and look—" She nodded her head toward a sheep in the distance.

Luke squinted his eyes, straining to see what she was pointing at.

Oh. That's clever.

"It's just a sheep," Rex said, his eyes incapable of seeing the thin tubes jutting out from the ground and latching onto the sheep from a distance.

My vision really has gotten better, Luke realized. *Guess those points in Agility weren't a complete waste.*

"There are tubes sticking out of the ground attached to its belly. That's probably what Sophia meant when she said there's a machine to milk them," Luke explained, already looking around the room to find where the extracted milk was being sent.

"Oh," Rex mumbled, his face rapidly turning red as he remembered that specific piece of information. "I uh . . . Normally I—" he hedged, almost sighing in relief when Nel interrupted him.

"Over there." She pointed to the wall of shelves.

I can't believe I thought he was kinda smart when I met him. The kid just likes being edgy. Go figure.

Early Warrior, Mid-Warrior, Late Warrior. Not bad. Luke nodded appreciatively, his eyes darting between the three nozzles sticking out of the wall. A small metal plaque above each one told him exactly which was which.

Not bad at all.

"Who wants to go first?" Nel asked, glancing between him and Rex.

"New guy, you're up." Rex grinned at him.

"Why me? Don't you think it should be Nel that goes first? She's the strongest out of all of us."

"I'm sure it's safe," she assured him. "I just . . . I don't like it."

"What?"

"Milk. It's gross. It—"

"It's milk," Luke said.

"That's why you should drink it," Nel argued lamely.

"That . . . Fine." He shook his head, not interested in arguing with the siblings about it. *It's not like I wasn't going to drink it. What's the big deal anyway? Milk is milk—sure, sheep milk is kind of out there, but is cow milk objectively better?*

Grabbing a glass from a nearby shelf, he put it under the nozzle labeled Early Warrior.

If this stuff is anything like the stat points from killing the flying serpent, then it's probably best not to overdo it. I doubt it'll be anywhere close, but starting with the least potent one is just common sense.

White liquid gushed from the tap as soon as he slid the glass underneath it, the flow cutting itself off as the glass filled halfway.

Is that it?

Staring at glass apprehensively, Luke brought it to his lips and gave it a quick sniff, nodding approvingly when no foul odor climbed up his nose.

Well. Here goes nothing.

He opened his mouth and swallowed the meager amount of liquid as soon as the taste hit his tongue.

Not bad. Not bad at all. He smacked his lips as the fluid settled into his stomach. Closing his eyes, he felt his mana, frowning as he tried to feel it in his system.

Where's the mana?

Suddenly it hit. Mana appeared within his body, seemingly out of nowhere. It felt heavy and uncomfortable in him, but luckily the Seed had no problem whisking it away to wherever it stored stat points.

+3 Stat Points
+3 Stat Points
+3 Stat Points
+2 Stat Points

Eleven points for drinking one glass of milk. That's . . . He eyed the empty glass, its walls stained white with traces of the fluid, with greed. *I need more. A lot more. All of it. Forget maxing out my main attributes—if I drink enough, I might even be able to unlock my Bloodline. All without lifting a finger.*

He looked at the tap labeled Late Warrior. *Especially if I get some of that.*

"So how is it?" Nel asked.

"Not bad, not bad at all. Lots of mana." Luke nodded before turning to Rex. "You should probably drink it in small sips instead of a big gulp—the mana feels a little heavy. I think I wasted some of it, too," Luke lied confidently, understanding fully that the Seed didn't waste mana. "It's probably more effective drinking that after a good workout."

"I'll be fine," he claimed. Grabbing a glass, Rex put it under the tap and, imitating Luke, chugged it all in one go.

Only to stumble to his knees moments later. "Ugh."

"What happened?" Nel knelt down next to him, putting a hand over his chest as she did, no doubt sensing his mana.

"I'm fine . . ." He grunted. "I just need to—"

"Told you," Luke said casually, frowning slightly when Rex shot him a venomous glare in response.

Right, his sister just killed his friend a couple days ago. Probably not the best time to make fun of a guy for being dumb, Luke realized as he scratched his chin awkwardly. *I bet the pain doesn't help much, either—it's nowhere near as bad as killing the serpent was, but it's still a punch in the gut. And he doesn't have the Seed to take away the burden . . . I'll talk to him later.* Luke turned away and looked back at the milk dispensers.

I can't just chug that stuff down without caution. At least not without looking like an idiot. It's pretty clear that the best way to cultivate is by destroying our muscles and then drinking the milk to recover. That said, what's the worst that will happen if I do?

Nel and Rex will think that I'm cultivating manually, which, while suboptimal, is something that people do. They'll probably get a bit snobbish, but should I care about that?

At worst, they'll think I'm either stupid or impatient, but the gains . . . It's worth it. I'll just have to be careful not to overdo it.

Rex stumbled to his feet. "How are you perfectly fine?" he asked Luke.

"Uh . . . It's just pain. I guess I'm used to it?"

"Boiling ourselves was a little bit of pain. How do you even brace for *that*?" he demanded.

Luke scratched the back of his head. "Are you seriously comparing being boiled alive to drinking milk? How are they even remotely on the same level?"

"With the wat—"

"Rex, not everyone has the same sensitivity to mana," Nel explained, putting a cup under the Late Warrior tap. "It should get less painful the more you do it, though."

Frowning, she downed the liquid in a single gulp, wrinkling her nose in disgust as she did.

"Blech." She shuddered, holding the empty cup in front of her, and frowned. "It's something," she said eventually. "Better than nothing, but the mana my body draws is already at the Warrior tier. I'd have to drink barrels of it to get the same benefit as you two." She sighed.

"Oh. That sucks," Luke said, sliding his own glass back under the tap and grinning a little when the machine filled it back up right away. "I think I like it here." He chugged it down. He suppressed a grin as another round of stat point notifications filled his vision.

Nel frowned at him. "I know we have a lot, but don't waste it needlessly." She looked around the room. "I should be able to set up a training regimen for you two. Something more optimized than just blindly drinking the milk and hoping for the best," she said, walking around the room. She ran her hands over the spines of the various books and inspected the potion vials.

"What are you thinking?" Rex asked her.

"There's enough healing potions for hot and cold baths here, and those are a must. And they'll be a lot more effective with mana from the milk in your system. I'll have to dig some holes, but it shouldn't be a problem. I'll make an exercise routine for you as well. It won't be as well tuned as what Grandfather had you doing in the capital, but I'll do my best. The closer you two are to the Warrior tier, the better your odds will be in the Olympics, so we definitely can't slack off. Oh, and . . ." She rambled on, and Luke zoned out, only half paying attention to what she was saying.

Stuffing my stomach with as much mana milk as possible would be nice, but there's no reason I can't follow her training and drink as much of it as I can at the same time. Besides, there's only ten sheep here, and there's three of us. There probably isn't a limitless supply of the stuff anyway.

Luke put his glass under the tap again. Once again it filled his glass. Chugging it down eagerly, he put it back underneath the dispenser.

"What are you doing?" Rex asked.

"Seeing how much milk we can expect every day. If we're going to be here for a while, then at the very least we can figure out how much we have."

"That's a good idea!" Nel beamed at him, grabbing her own glass and putting it back under the tap. Drinking the contents reluctantly, she repeated the process one more time before the Late Warrior tap refused to spit out any more of the liquid.

That's not bad. At all, Luke mused once they had everything tallied up. The Early Warrior tap gave nine cups of milk, each one good for nine to twelve stat points. The Mid-Warrior gave six, each one good for around twenty-three stat points, and while Luke didn't get to test the Late Warrior milk, he expected it to give him around fifty stat points.

"How are we going to split them?" he asked right away, his eyes meeting Nel's.

I don't think she's going to screw me over here, but if she decides to take a bigger share or gives Rex more, then there isn't much I can do besides whine about it.

"The early and midstage milk isn't useful to me," she said after a while. "You two can split that evenly, and I'll take the late stage."

He cupped his chin as he did the math in his head. *That works—it's not the absolute best way to split the milk, but it's not the worst, either. If we did a fully even split, I'd only get an extra twenty or so points a day. It's a good chunk of change, but I'm still getting more than a hundred points as is. Considering the fact that neither of them has the Seed to store excess mana, they'll probably be getting a small fraction of that.*

"Okay," Luke agreed and stared expectantly at Rex, half expecting him to make a fuss and demand a bigger share.

"I'm fine with it too," he said after a while.

Huh. Sweet.

Luke opened his status.

Status	Skills	Quests	Inventory
Name: Lukas King
Tier: Mortal
Mana: 45,150/45,150
Rate: 15% per hour
Strength: 116
Agility: 240
Constitution: 301
Arcana: 300
Stat Points: 101
Bloodline: Locked. Conditions not met. (1/10,000)
Charges: 7/10

The Seed is busted, and coming on this trip was definitely the right move, he thought as he read his stats and did his level best to suppress a grin as he thought about where to put his newly gained stat points. Near giddy at the thought of all the points he would be raking in over the next few weeks, he had to take a few breaths just to calm himself down.

I'll get another twenty thousand points worth of mana if I put them all in Constitution and Arcana like I have been, but my Strength stat is starting to fall behind.

Whatever. He dismissed his status and yawned, his eyes gravitating toward the beds. *I'll figure that out tomorrow after I get some sleep. Two whole days on a griffin's back without rest is exhausting, even with three hundred points in Constitution.*

CHAPTER 55

That Was Easy

Frowning in irritation at the falsely bored expression on her face as they sparred, Luke ducked underneath Nel's lazy swipe. He correctly recognized her attack and the mischievous glint in her eye for what it was—a trap. Not one he was keen on falling into—he wanted to cut loose, not get a beatdown from someone a tier higher than him. Unfortunately for him, Nel liked to keep Luke on his toes, and he had been caught unprepared more than once in the past.

By now, though, he knew better than to try and meet her blow for blow when she made her intentions that obvious. The last time he had made that mistake, she had sent him hurtling through the sky, the Warrior's monstrous strength letting her toss him around with contemptuous ease. Her grin as she batted him around like a ping-pong ball still gave him the chills.

He had his boots, which gave him some options when that happened, but another lesson he had learned was that fighting her in the air was a terrible idea. Not only was she infinitely more mobile, flitting around both faster and with more grace than he could even dream of in more directions and with a lot more leverage than him to boot, but whatever method the shoes used to keep him anchored in the sky wasn't infallible. Every time she maneuvered them up there, she would trade a few blows as a courtesy until she decided that she had humored him enough.

When that happened, his blade would meet the shaft of her spear, and the next thing he knew, he would be pushed back toward the ground. No amount of mana pumped into his boots would let him stop her from driving him into the earth.

Not wanting to pick worms out of his teeth, he stepped back, narrowly avoiding another swipe of her spear.

She grinned. "Will you not attack?" she asked, amused that he had seen through her game twice in a row.

"It wouldn't be fun if I didn't."

Luke's frown vanished, instantly replaced by a challenging grin as he stepped forward, slamming his golden blade into the shaft of her spear with every ounce of strength he could muster. He did his best to ignore the ringing in his arms as he pitted himself against what was for all intents and purposes an immovable object.

She flicked her wrist and blasted him back. His feet dug trenches in the grass as he pumped mana into his boots to slow himself down, only to charge her again a moment later.

"Why do you even fight her?" Rex said, resting with his back against the griffin's side, biting into the core of an apple as he watched them. "You know you can't beat her, so what's the point?"

I mean, he's not wrong, not really. She's so far above my level that I might as well be trying to draw blood from a rock. Even with all the improvements I've made. And it's not like she's skillfully picking apart my movements and showing me weaknesses in my form. Honestly, she's just beating me by virtue of being both stronger and faster. But—

"Don't worry about it," Luke yelled as he charged her again, only to once again be sent hurtling back.

There's something liberating about being able to go at it with one hundred percent of my power and not have to worry about hurting anyone.

Luke had never really had the chance to just go all out and test the limits of his physical abilities. In the tomb, it was either life or death, or no killing allowed. In moments where his life was on the line, the correct response was to fight smarter, not harder, because nearly everyone in there hit harder than he did.

Fighting a monster comes close, but it isn't the same. A monster would kill me if I made a dumb mistake. Whenever I've fought one, I wasn't holding back, but I wasn't exactly letting loose, either. It was strategic, and every move was calculated to bring death as efficiently as possible.

And sparring against someone at the same level is the worst. You always need to be careful not to push too hard so you don't actually kill or injure the person, and you have to be even more careful so you don't get injured in case the person sparring with you slips up.

This, though—he grinned as he charged Nel one more time, leveraging every drop of his hard-earned strength to strike her—*is what it's all about. Pedal to the metal, full throttle, maximum power. Zero restraint, because I don't need to. There is no real chance of me hitting her, and if I did, she'd probably be fine anyway.*

Nel shifted her posture slightly as Luke closed in on her.

Fuck.

"Wai—" he yelled as she lunged forward. His eyes widened in shock.

The next second, he was lying flat on his back with the tip of her spear pointing at his neck. Arcs of electricity traveled up and down its shaft and buzzed annoyingly in his ear.

"You win." He relaxed onto the ground, sighing softly when she removed the deadly weapon from his throat.

"I did not win. That implies we were competing in the first place, and I assure you, any competition between us will have to wait until you become a warrior yourself. Your progress, however, has been nothing shy of amazing. I can see why Grandfather went to such great lengths to recruit you," she said, extending her hand.

Fuck yeah, it is. This place is practically heaven for someone with my advantages. As for Cyzicus recognizing that, I don't think so. He probably just recruited me because he saw that I knew a technique.

Luke opened his status as he climbed to his feet. Strictly speaking, he didn't need to even look at it anymore. At least not for the time being. He just liked seeing it.

<table>
<tr><td align="center">Status | Skills | Quests | Inventory</td></tr>
<tr><td align="center">Name: Lukas King</td></tr>
<tr><td align="center">Tier: Mortal</td></tr>
<tr><td align="center">Mana: 351,102/499,000.5</td></tr>
<tr><td align="center">Rate: 15% per hour</td></tr>
<tr><td align="center">Strength: 999</td></tr>
<tr><td align="center">Agility: 999</td></tr>
<tr><td align="center">Constitution: 999</td></tr>
<tr><td align="center">Arcana: 999</td></tr>
<tr><td align="center">Stat Points: 4</td></tr>
<tr><td align="center">Bloodline: Locked. Conditions not met. (123/10,000)</td></tr>
<tr><td align="center">Charges: 7/10</td></tr>
</table>

The mana milk, combined with frequent baths in boiling and freezing water, head-splitting usage of the manasink, and regular sparring and exercise, had made for a very effective method to cultivate. So much so that just over four weeks had been enough to take all his attributes up to the peak of the Mortal tier.

A single point in any of those stats would let him ascend to the Warrior tier, were it not for the Path of the Paragon.

As it was, despite all his progress, he was less than a third of the way through to advancing to the next level of cultivation.

And depending on how long it's going to take me to master the stances, I could be bottlenecked for a while. At least I'll have a solid shot at the Olympics now. I don't know exactly what to expect, but I doubt my competition will expect someone teetering at the edge of the Mortal-Warrior threshold in all major attributes. With the obscene amount of mana I have, I can even use the shoes, the stances, and the sword Cyzicus gave me more than once or twice a day.

If Rex can be taken as an average participant, then most of them shouldn't be a problem. That is, of course, assuming that he isn't hiding anything. He looked over at his fellow mortal from the corner of his eye. *He's definitely hiding something, but that only matters if we can ever get out of here.*

"Sophia said that she'd be back in a week or two, right?" he asked Nel.

She nodded.

"We're two weeks over then. Let's say she doesn't come back. How long would it take you to break into the Hero tier?"

She frowned, opening and closing her mouth as mulled over her answer. "Ten years at the current pace."

"Is that a number you're confident in?"

"It could be sooner."

That's not too bad. Ten years in here with these two—I probably won't go all the way insane. I'll definitely unlock my Bloodline, assuming the sheep live that long.

Progressing with the stances would be a little harder. Something tells me that if I want to improve them, I'll actually need to use them to kill at some point. Not just use the information they give me to make my opponent surrender.

"What are you thinking?" Nel asked.

"That it wouldn't be that bad being stuck here for a bit longer. If someone hasn't come and gotten us yet, then that probably means that things aren't going too well outside. It might be better to get used to the idea now."

"Perhaps," she said, her tone suddenly clipped. Her eyes for the briefest second darted over Luke's shoulder and then back.

What's she loo—

"LUKE, LUKE, LUKE. How could you have such little faith in me?" a voice echoed around them.

Is that—?

Cyzicus tapped Luke on the shoulder, making him jump into the air in fright. "Ahh! Why can't you come from the front?" Luke said, clutching his chest with his hand.

"GRAMPS!" Rex came sprinting forward. "How long have you been here?"

"A couple hours, give or take."

This guy . . . Luke resisted the urge to facepalm at his antics, as he turned to face him. Wow . . . *He looks terrible.*

Cyzicus's long hair was in a mess. He had deep bags underneath his eyes, and while his gold robes were pristine, his posture screamed exhaustion and even his smile felt hollow.

"Have you defeated the Rebel?" Nel asked.

He lifted the crown from his head and scratched his hair. "Not yet." He frowned. "It took a while to find her, and once we did . . ." He slipped his crown back on his head. "Once we found her, the coward that she is, she didn't even attempt to fight." He shook his head in disbelief. "She activated a talisman and disappeared. Once we caught up with her again, it was the same thing. Again and again and again we find her, and she runs."

"I see."

"Did you come here to get us out of here? Your . . . friend"—Rex stared intently at his grandfather—"has kept us locked up for over a month."

"I hadn't noticed." He smiled, looking at them with a grin on his face before walking up to Rex and rubbing his hair affectionately. "I do apologize for that, however. Sophia is rather willful, and she doesn't have too many friends. Sometimes her judgment is a little suspect. In this case, however, I do believe she made the right call. At the least, you two have benefited greatly."

"Where is she now?" Luke asked.

"Hunting after Tyrisa as we speak. I'm afraid circumstances have changed, and I can no longer be an active participant in her demise. Sophia will keep her occupied until such a time that I am able to rejoin the battle. If it comes to that. She has been remarkably . . . brutal, shall we say, in her pursuit. To be frank, I'm not even sure Tyrisa will live long enough for me to rejoin the battle."

"What changed?" Nel asked.

"The Tide. I've been told that it will begin three days from now, and as such, I am required at the capital. It was my hope to have Sophia take my place there if matters dragged on for long enough, but she refuses to be among any company greater in number than five." He shrugged.

"What?" Nel's jaw dropped open. "Why would the Tide come earlier? That's not supposed to happen! The cur—" Cyzicus cut her off with a glare. A pulse of pressure radiated out from his body before subsiding. Nel turned pale before glancing awkwardly between Luke and Rex. "I, uh. That . . . I—"

The curse? Is that what she was going to say? Luke looked between Cyzicus and Nel before his eyes met Rex's. He looked just as confused as Luke felt.

"Luke. Rex. I'm afraid both of you have become privy to something that you need not be concerned about. As you have no doubt deduced, there is more to the Gegenees invading Sylcra than meets the eye, but I will caution you to look no further into the issue."

"I couldn't care less," Luke responded right away. Meaning it, too.

Cyzicus beamed. "Good. Rex?"

His eyes darted between Nel and his grandfather, before he nodded reluctantly. "Fine."

"Very well." Cyzicus clapped his hands. "Let's steal some sheep and get out of here."

"What?" Nel, Luke, and Rex said simultaneously.

CHAPTER 56

Stealing Some Sheep

The emperor blushed. "It's not like that—perhaps the word *steal* isn't optimal. Sophia said I can have some as a wedding gift," he said, fiddling with his crown, more bashful than Luke had ever seen him before.

"That's nice of her . . . Congratulations on your engagement, by the way." Luke smiled at him.

"Thank you very much." He nodded, and then, puffing out his chest, he walked toward Nel's familiar and started petting it. The creature immediately began to preen and hiss in satisfaction under his ministrations.

Luke suppressed a smile, as Nel frowned jealously before donning a carefully blank expression.

"How are we going to take the sheep to the capital?" she asked.

"I gave Sophia a teleportation altar—we'll just use that. You three can come with me, but if you want to fly back, then that is fine as well." He made a show of looking around their temporary lodging. "Where's Lukeus?"

Nel shifted slightly. "He's at the capital."

"He didn't come with you?"

"No . . ."

He frowned slightly before nodding. "Very well." His gaze traveled across the room, scouting out the sheep. "Agnella, why don't you and your brother gather the sheep?" His ring flashed, and a handful of talismans appeared in front of the two. "Tag them with these, and they should fall asleep. The altar is . . ." He closed his eyes in concentration, the ground split in the middle of the grassed area, and a dais emerged from somewhere underneath. "There."

"Okay," Nel said, snatching the talismans from the air. She glanced meaningfully at Luke before nodding. Her own ring flashed a moment later, and a small carpet appeared on the ground. Rex winced as he stepped onto it, and a moment later they were gone.

A bead of sweat rolled down the side of Luke's face as the emperor's undivided attention fell on him. Cyzicus's ring flashed, and a talisman flew free from his hand and formed a translucent bubble around the pair, and the world instantly fell silent, leaving Luke alone with the sound of his breathing and his heart beating in his chest.

"Uh . . . what's this?" he asked, noting how strange his voice sounded in the absence of any other noise.

"No need to fear, young Luke. It just blocks the sound. I'd rather keep this conversation between me and you. Agnella has very good ears and a habit of eavesdropping. I don't usually mind that sort of thing, as I'm not one who lurks in the shadows, but it isn't right of me to make the decision for you."

"Right." *That doesn't sound ominous at all.* "What did you want to talk about?" he asked, ignoring how dry his mouth suddenly felt.

"Why are you here?"

"Huh?"

"Why are you here?" Cyzicus asked again, crossing his arms over his chest.

Luke's eyes met the emperor's expectant gaze as he thought about what to say.

"Like here in Sophia's home? Or—"

He nodded.

"Honestly . . . I kind of heard what was going on with the Rebel, and I didn't want to get caught up in it. Not that I don't appreciate the sword and the ring, and your advice—it's just that . . . I don't know you that well. I don't know the Rebel, and I didn't want to get caught up in whatever your conflict is," Luke rambled, fidgeting with the pommel of his sword.

"That's remarkably honest of you. Perhaps even wise. I likely would have made the same decision as you were I in your position, if I am honest. Involving oneself in a conflict beyond your tier with little information and no personal stake is . . . unwise. Logic does dictate to not involve oneself."

"It does do that."

"Can I give you some advice?" Luke nodded at him. "The world is a frightening place. I know that better than most. A few decades ago, a woman came onto my island and challenged me for Sylcra's throne, killing my family to provoke me into battle. A battle she lost and fled from. Now I find out that not only is she back, but she's killed even more of my family. Arke is a being who could kill me easier than I killed that giant you attempted to fight. There are gods roaming the world that could sink this whole island to the sea floor just because they want to. I could execute you this very second, and there wouldn't be any consequences for me. Do you understand what I'm trying to say here?"

"Not at all."

"HA. I like you." He grinned. "Let me make it simple, then. Fearing the tyranny of the strong is no way to live. Not that caution doesn't have its place—believe me, it does. But you can't allow it to dictate your every decision. You can't let it paralyze and infect your thought process. It's hard to remember sometimes, but greed isn't the only emotion that exists. There are far more people, from gods to mortals, that are willing to lend you a hand and pull you up than there are people who will kick you down. It doesn't have to be me, but you need someone you can let your guard down against. Find people you can trust to have your back, and then build upon that bond until it is stronger than any temptation that exists in this world."

"I—"

"You don't look convinced."

"It's just—I understand where you're coming from, I do. But life, it's . . . cheap. I've—I've killed people for some pretty stupid stuff. And it sucks, but it is what it is. I didn't have a choice. But how do I make sense of the fact that I could have been the one who died if I was any less cautious? If I hadn't been slightly faster, or smarter, or quicker? How do you trust someone when someone infinitely stronger than I am can lock two people in a room and tell them only one can leave?"

"You're talking about Alexia's inheritance, right?"

Luke's eyes widened in surprise. "How did you—"

He snorted.

"Kid. I knew her, and I know her tomb opened up recently. An emperor's inheritance isn't something to sneeze at. To be honest, I've known you were from Carim since the moment I laid eyes on you and saw those boots on your feet. I made them, after all. I always wondered what happened to them."

"Oh." *Even in death, Yjarn managed to fuck me over. Great. Just great. All that work to get off Carim, and my identity is already halfway exposed.*

"Mmm-hmm. Listen, Alexia had her heart in the right place, but there's a reason the Atlantians killed her. She didn't have the most"—he looked to the side, carefully choosing his words—"she didn't have the firmest grasp on reality. She was a bloody genius—rose from the Mortal tier to the Hero tier in fifty years—but she was a troublemaker. She felt that her struggles gave her the right to do what she wanted to whoever she wanted, and she got killed for that. If I'm being honest, I can't even blame the Atlantians for cutting her down after what she did. If it wasn't them, at the rate she was going, it would have been someone else."

"What did she do?"

"It's not important." He shook his head. "Now, where was I? Right, Luke. You seem to have a good brain in your skull, so I'll explain this in simple terms. People like Arke, Alexia, Tyrisa, they are a small number, and they don't tend to live long. Theos isn't kind to their ilk. Those who make more enemies than friends always—and I mean always—end up dead. Cultivating does that. Someone pitifully weak one day can come back in a millennium a million times stronger. Injustice doesn't last. The Olympians overthrew the titans for much of the same reason, and even the titans built their rule on the backs of those they freed from the tyranny of the ancients before them. It's a cycle."

"I see."

"Do you?" He raised an eyebrow. "Why do you think Arke hasn't killed everyone on the entire archipelago? She's strong enough, if I had to guess—it would take her an hour if she went from island to island. So why hasn't she? You were there when she redecorated my throne room, but I got up with only scuffs on my clothes and a few loose strands of hair. That's it. I didn't even get a bruise. Do you know why?"

"Are there laws stopping her from killing you?"

"Some, but that's not why she didn't do it. I have friends, Luke. It's that simple. Friends I've shed blood for. Friends I'd die for. Friends who've done the same for me. I suppose I also have a good reputation as a fair and just ruler." He scratched his chin. "The laws . . . they're suggestions. As an emperor, I do have the protection of the council from threats beyond my means. That's true, and I'm sure it factored into her decision to tolerate my continued existence. The laws are, however, only enforced when someone cares enough to do so. There's been more than one hero whose death has gone unavenged because they had more enemies than they did sense. Likewise, Arke stands on flimsy ground when it comes to Olympus. One slip, and she's going the same way as the titans, and unlike me, there are very few who would be sad to see her go. Don't underestimate the value of not being alone, Luke."

Luke closed his eyes and sighed softly. "I'll keep that in mind."

"Good." Cyzicus grinned. "Have you given thought to participating in the tournament?"

"I have, and I'll do it. I worked something out with Nel in exchange, and I won't go back on my word."

"Wonderful!" Cyzicus cheered, a wide grin stretching his lips taut against his teeth. "I believe that Agnella has finished gathering the last of the sheep. Let us return to the capital. I cannot put into words how much I'm anticipating a night of rest in my own bed."

"Um . . . Before we go. I wanted to ask you for a favor. Me being from Carim—can you keep that between us?"

Cyzicus's eyes narrowed. "Why?"

"I'd rather not—" Luke shook his head. "I have some secrets that I don't want people tracing back to me. That I fear being traced back to me. And fear—well, fear is the mind killer. Other than you, there shouldn't be anyone who has reason to suspect that I'm not from here, and you're right—I need to start trusting people at some point. I can't keep letting paranoia guide my every decision, and I can't take the knowledge you already have from your mind. So I'm just asking. Will you do me a favor and keep my origins quiet?"

Cyzicus grinned as he drummed his finger along his arm. "Fear is the mind killer. How apt. Very well." His ring flashed, and a small marble-size glass ball appeared pinched between two fingers.

"What's that?"

"This is an oath orb. I'm flattered that you think well enough of me to take me at my word, and I look forward to building trust between us, but I believe it's best not to leave room for doubt so early in our relationship." Cyzicus closed his eyes, and the orb lit up a brilliant red. "I, Cyzicus, emperor of Sylcra, swear that I will not and have not disclosed the origins as I know them of Luke, inheritor of Alexia, to anyone without his consent, both in spirit and in word." He opened his eyes, and the glass bead dimmed and shot through the air toward Luke. "Channel your mana into it, and say you accept my oath," he instructed. "Keep the titles I used the same, but if you don't like something about it, just say so, and we can change the wording."

I'm not a lawyer, but honestly, it seems decent.

"I, Luke, inheritor of Alexia, accept the oath sworn by Cyzicus, emperor of Sylcra," he intoned. The orb blinked red three times in quick succession, and he felt a bond form between him and it. The terms of their contract settled in his mind, and he knew that the instant the other man broke his word, so would that link in his mind. "What happens if the orb breaks or you break the terms?"

"That orb won't break. It's a Saint-tier artifact. As for me breaking my word? I can't. I'll have to ascend past the Saint tier if I want to, and between you and me, that's unlikely to happen. There's a chance I'll become one, but my momentum has long since been expended. As such, even if I do, you'll be fine."

"Thank you."

"It's fine." Cyzicus waved him off. "I saw you sparring with Agnella; you've come a long way. I have high hopes for you in the Olympics, and if you do well in them, I stand to gain much. As wonderful as I am, I'm not helping you out of pure altruism."

"Right. I'll do my best."

"Good lad. Now, let's get back to the capital. You have some giants to kill."

CHAPTER 57

The Giant Tide

They appeared in the same office Cyzicus had first teleported Luke to when he brought them into the castle. This time, though, he didn't look nearly as strained by the expenditure. If it weren't for the slight rise and fall of his chest, Luke wouldn't have even been able to tell that he had exerted himself.

Where did the sheep go?

"Where's Aura?" Nel asked.

Oh, right. The griffin is missing, too.

"I sent her and the sheep to the garden. I'm not much for formalities, but I do have enough sense not to discuss bad news in the company of livestock. Especially not in my own office," the emperor said, walking over to his chair and falling down heavily atop it. "Truly, home is home." He sighed. His eyes darting to a clock on the wall, he scratched his chin and sighed. "Even so, there is much work to be done." A ring flashed on his finger, and a streak of light shot out and escaped through the walls.

He waved his hands, and the white marble floors twisted and congealed, and the room rearranged itself. His desk expanded and stretched out through the room, and sculpted marble chairs rose from the floor around it.

"Have a seat. There's much we need to talk about." Cyzicus said.

"Talk about what?" Rex asked, settling into the chair closest to him.

"The tournament. Things haven't gone quite to plan, and with the Tide so close, I wish to get you all on the same page," he said. Almost on cue, the double doors to his office were thrown open, and Clite walked in. Nearly a dozen blue-robed and a couple red-robed cultivators trailed behind her.

"I thought he left?" Rose grumbled, slinking into a seat, her eyes meeting Luke's and her eyebrows rising confrontationally. "And where's Jax? That moron left with you, didn't he?"

"He did?" Cyzicus turned to Nel.

Luke shifted uncomfortably in his chair, the stone suddenly seeming a lot more uncomfortable than it was moments ago. A heaviness settled over the room and its occupants as each and every one of them focused on Nel.

"I killed him," she said eventually.

"What?" Rose blurted, amid the startled looks of the other tournament hopefuls. "Why would you do that!" she screamed, rapidly blinking the tears out of her eyes.

Rex looked away from her. "Hey. It wasn't—"

"Rex," Nel interrupted him, before looking Rose in the eyes. "He wanted to come with us so he could escape with his family. Unfortunately, Clan Skyscar has betrayed the throne, and they laid an ambush for us. They used a blood compass—"

Luke tuned out the conversation, merely paying attention to everyone's expressions as they listened to Nel recount what had happened at the start of their journey.

"That is quite the unfortunate turn of events," Cyzicus said, his tone unnaturally even. "Clite, look into his family, and see if we can do anything to help them. At the very least, we can bring his mother and sister into the capital. Their clan will know where they are, but I can't imagine what use such information will have."

Clite nodded. "It will be done."

"Good. Don't force anything, but once they get here, please have someone explain the events as they happened, and make sure they are minded by someone loyal. Tell them that they are being watched, too. I don't want someone fooling them into betraying us. Keep an eye out for anyone who approaches them as well, especially anyone who shouldn't know about them being here. If they don't want to take refuge though, then don't insist. We already killed the woman's son, and there is no need to be heavy-handed." Cyzicus sighed, taking the crown off his head and scratching his scalp. His gaze darted from one person to the next. "Any other surprises I should be aware of?"

No one said anything.

"Very well. There are two things I must discuss with all of you. The first is that the Giant Tide will begin three days from now, and not in three months as was originally forecast. A summons has been sent, and soon all available cultivators will be arriving at the capital to fight them. As you are no doubt already aware, I'll manage the teleportation altars, and with the wards surrounding all human settlements, we'll know the giants are attacking as soon as they emerge from the ground. There will be many mortals caught unaware by the arrival of the Tide, so there will be extra missions for those of you willing to aid them in between moments of your training. The Tide, while important, and I imagine nearly all of you will be contributing to it, isn't your main concern. That is the tournament, which will begin in five months as expected." His ring shone on his finger as he withdrew a sheet of silver paper from it.

Mesmerizing runes shone on its metallic surface, drawing the eyes of everyone in the room. Setting it down on the table, he looked across at each of them.

"It is, of course no secret, that I desire for Sylcra to win. There have been rumors circulating as to why that is the case, and in the interest of honesty, I'll just come out and say it. There are prizes not only for the people that win, but also for the kings or"—he nodded to himself—"the emperors that send forward the candidates. While the prize the winners will take is still to be announced, the prize I shall receive has been known to me for decades. It is an elixir, one that will allow me to break through my bottleneck and ascend to the next tier. I don't think I need to tell you why I desire such a thing." He smiled sardonically.

"Did they say what the trial would be?" Rex asked.

"No. However, Lord Hephaestus, this year's game master, has announced some changes. Typically the tournament has two brackets, the Mortal tier and the Warrior tier. That will not be the case anymore. Only those at the Warrior tier will be able to compete."

"What?" Rex stood from his seat and stared at Cyzicus in alarm. "After all that, we can't even compete? How can he just—"

"It is quite the change, yes. Unfortunately, Lord Hephaestus claims that he doesn't have the time for two tournaments, and as such, there will only be a single bracket for warriors. Moreover, he doesn't, and I quote, 'want it to be boring'—as such, only warriors under the age of eighteen are allowed to participate unconditionally. Those who are between twenty-one and eighteen are still allowed to compete but only if they advanced to the warrior tier less than six months before the start of the tournament."

Nel's face set into a frown. "I can't, then?"

"No. As it stands, none of you are eligible," Cyzicus said, interlocking his fingers. A tense silence raged in the room.

"Why did he change the age for warriors? It's always been those who are twenty-one or younger. What's this stuff with six months?" one of the red-robed cultivators who had walked in with Clite complained.

"According to the missive that was sent to me, he only wants the most talented cultivators in the world claiming his prize. Those that have sat in the Warrior tier for months or even years longer than their more talented counterparts shouldn't be given the advantage. As such, Agnella, Hector, Jules—all three of you are no longer eligible. I of course recognize all the work that you have put in, and as such, each of you can take one item from my vault," Cyzicus conceded, nodding apologetically at them.

Well, that sucks for them, but it's not like the training was useless. Being stronger is a prize in and of itself, especially if they had a hero personally guiding their development. Getting a free treasure on top of that—it's generous of him.

"As for the rest of you, you will have to break through to the next stage in the coming months to be eligible. I know some of you are closer than others to the peak of your tier and that some of you were relying on your bloodlines, unique constitutions, and skills to overcome the gap in raw attributes. It is a valid approach, but with the new information that has come to light, I'd suggest you focus on ascending to the next tier as quickly as possible."

That might be a problem, Luke thought worriedly, for the moment filing away the information Cyzicus had let slip. *With the giants and my sword and maybe some access to the sheep milk, I shouldn't have a problem with unlocking my Bloodline, but the First Stances are a whole other problem. I haven't managed to improve them one bit since I left the tomb. I'll talk to Cyzicus or Clite about them, though. Maybe even about the Paragon's Path.*

According to the Seed, I'm not the only one who's done it before, so it should be okay to bring it up with him. I still don't know how valuable something like my sword is, so it's probably a bad idea telling anyone about it. Considering that Sophia went through decades of effort to get the sheep to make mana milk for essentially the same benefit my sword provides is telling. Sure, they work differently, and the sheep are probably better because you don't have to kill things to get mana, but the sword has its own advantages.

"What if we can't make it to the Warrior tier?" Rose asked.

"If you can't make it, you can't make it. I won't punish you." Cyzicus smiled warmly at her. "This is outside all of our expectations. All I can ask is that you try your best. If even a couple of you can make it in time, I would be satisfied. And of course, while I wish for us to win, I do understand that you will be competing against opponents just as, if not more, talented than you. While I will be disappointed, I'm not unreasonable," he said, getting up from his seat. "Clite, I'll leave them in your care once again."

"As you will, my lord." She lowered her head.

He grinned. "Always so formal. We've known each other for centuries—I really thought we would be beyond such things decades ago." He patted Luke on the shoulder and nodded to Rex and Nel before walking out of the room.

. . . Was he checking how much mana I have? Luke thought, having felt the faintest ripple in his own mana.

"I'll be going as well," Nel said.

Sharing a glance, the two other warriors shrugged and followed after her.

"So where have you two been all month?" Rose turned them.

"We were on a mission for Gramps."

"I guessed that much. Where did you go? Was it worth Jax's life?" she whispered.

"There's another hero fighting against the Rebel now," Rex said.

Yeah. Another hero, who he was already planning on marrying. Luke frowned. *The "mission" probably wasn't even about getting Sophia to help. I've seen those talismans they use. And he can teleport wherever he wants. The only reason he wouldn't ask Sophia herself would be if delivering the letter wasn't the main concern.*

Nel, Lukeus, and Rex. Those were supposed to be the three who went on the mission, and all three are his grandchildren.

Sophia just happened to imprison us in her super-secure facility, with ten sheep and all the training equipment and stuff we could ever want and enough mana milk to make our time there worth it.

That son of a bitch—he was just trying to keep his family safe by making them keep a low profile at his girlfriend's house. Hell, he even did it in a way they wouldn't oppose. All of them thought they were doing something important and went along with it.

And Jax? He just died because no one knew the actual stakes.

He glanced between Rex and the crying Rose, wondering if Rex had even realized what exactly had happened. How meaningless his death had actually been.

That's not true. If Cyzicus actually brings his family to the capital and does keep them safe, then . . . even then, it's not worth it. A kid died. Miserably and without hope. Just because we were all acting on incomplete information.

"That's enough sitting around. If any of you are to become warriors within the next five months, then we can't afford to slack," said Clite, her eyes meeting Luke's with a knowing glint.

CHAPTER 58

Defending a Town

Luke soaked in the pool of frigid blue liquid, which was most definitely not water, and did his best not to immediately swallow the healing potion in mouth. With his improved Constitution, it wasn't hard. It was still uncomfortable, and the liquid was cold enough to be damaging, but it wasn't pure agony like the boiling water had been a mere month ago. Instead, the training had become a test of his mental fortitude.

Closing his eyes, he just observed, concentrating in spite of the chill and paying particularly close attention to the mana that was entering his body. Before he had reached the peak of the Mortal tier, his body would have soaked it up like a wet sponge, but now it just stayed there until the Seed roused itself and sucked it away. Absently, he dismissed the stat point notifications.

Waves in the water alerted him to the others shifting about and leaving. The first person triggered a domino effect that made the rest leave.

A few more minutes should be fine, Luke thought, and, separating a drop of the healing potion in his mouth from the rest, he swallowed it. A single question was on his mind.

Is everything capped?

It was a question he had asked himself on more than one occasion ever since he had hit the peak a few days ago. This time, he wanted an answer.

As more and more mana built inside him, he moved his own mana to capture it, intending to do the one thing that he had been warned not to do—cultivate manually.

It should be fine, he assured himself, vowing not to do anything too drastic in case it worked.

He didn't think it would work.

The Seed distributed mana in a way that no single part of his body was ever left behind, and it improved all parts of his body equally. Luke had never noticed a time where his right arm was stronger than his left, or one of his eyes or ears less sensitive than the other. Even exercises that should have fundamentally improved one part of him over the rest didn't seem to. It was the same whether he assigned points with the Seed or let his body deal with the mana. They both preserved the natural balance in his body's abilities naturally. It was likely for that reason that Cyzicus expressly discouraged manually kneading mana into various body parts.

Still. People do it and are fine, and unless you have a manasink, it's the only way to cultivate.

Besides—he clenched his fist—*I already have a solid base. I doubt I'll break something if I use a tiny little bit of mana to improve something.*

Mixing the aethereal mana with his own, he briefly considered where exactly he should put it before deciding on his eyes.

He had witnessed the Seed at work in the general area when he used it to boost his agility enough times that he was confident that he wouldn't ruin anything on the off chance that it did work, and with his Arcana as high as it was, he could move it around with a fair bit of dexterity.

As he moved the mixture of his own mana and the Seed's to his eyes, though, he immediately realized that it wouldn't work.

While he had never cultivated manually before, he had gone through the motions, doing everything besides pushing it into his tissues and at the last second surrendering his control of the aethereal mana to the Seed.

In those tests, his body felt porous and permeable. Full of tiny little holes that the gathered mana would sneak into. Now it was akin to a smooth surface that actively rebuffed mana. Not wanting to give up quite so quickly, he tried other parts of himself, from his skin to individual organs, but all of them felt the same.

In a way, that's good. No, it is good, Luke consoled himself, happy in the knowledge that the Paragon's Path considered every single part of him to be at the peak of his tier. *If I had been able to cultivate at all, then that would mean that the Seed was leaving blank spots. The fact that I can't . . . Well, that just means there's nothing left to cultivate.*

Swallowing some more of the potion in his mouth, he relinquished his hold on his mana. Once again, he let the Seed carry it away.

He opened his status. There was one more thing he wanted to test.

Turning his attention back to his mana, he added a single point to his Bloodline, watching closely to see how exactly it was spent. Then another two points, and then three, and four at a time when even that didn't work.

Is the mana even going to my body? Luke frowned, swallowing the last little bit of the potion still in his mouth.

It has to be. Is this another situation like the one with awakening my mana? I keep adding points until something triggers it? Fuck, I better not have another episode of some kind.

He shook his head. *Whatever. I know something is going to happen at ten thousand points. I'll keep trying until then, but my real focus needs to be the techniques. I'll get the points eventually, but if I don't master the stances, then I'm stuck.*

Climbing out of the water, he brushed the hair out of his eyes, frowning slightly as the slimy liquid slid off his body, leaving him covered in the icky substance. They didn't use water for the cold pool because it froze, but the more he used it, the more he wished it was water.

"You were in there for a while," Rex said the second he stepped out, a hint of something in his eyes.

Luke shivered as he walked to the healing potion, wincing in pain with every step he took. "Yeah, well, you know how it is," he answered vaguely. He grinned slightly as he threw the other cultivator's words back in his face.

Picking up the heated towel left there for him, he wiped himself clean, enjoying the warmth of the towel as he stepped under the shower and ignored the weird looks the others were giving him. He had been in the pool substantially longer than any of them, so it wasn't unexpected. Especially considering that, a month ago, he was the first one who had climbed out of the hot water.

The Seed really is ridiculous.

I went from having the shallowest cultivation among them to the highest, and these guys look like they barely improved. Is it Arcana that's making them lag behind? Even with the manasink, the amount they can increase the attribute is probably nowhere near close to what I can do with the Seed. And if my guess about everyone starting out with a single point in it is right, they probably don't have more than a hundred or so points in there, if that. Depending on the relationship between a person's saturation point and Arcana, that could be it. Especially if it's a one-to-one ratio . . . No, that seems too small. It's likely a one-to-two or a one-to-three ratio. Not that I can blame them—using a manasink is torture. At least when you work out, it's your body that's in pain, and it's easy to ignore. A headache, though, that shit's inside your head.

On top of that, any mana their body doesn't use gets wasted. So anytime their Arcana isn't up to snuff, they just waste the mana.

Getting dressed, he waited with the others for Clite to come and retrieve them, wondering what she had planned for the day. The last two days he had been here, she seemed content to leave them alone, only showing up at the beginning of the day and at the end, saying the oncoming Tide was keeping her busy.

A minute later, the curtain between the hot and cold pools parted and she emerged with all the girls. Then, without wasting time, she led them away from their usual courtyard and out toward the back of the castle. Stopping at a seemingly random room, she ushered them in.

That's a lot of weapons, Luke thought as he stepped in. Hundreds of spears, bows, swords, shields, and bits of armor littered the wall, sat in barrels and shelves arrayed in neat rows. Easily enough weapons to supply an army.

Rex gulped audibly next to him. "Are we going to fight the giants today?" he asked.

"You will be," Clite said. "If I'm not mistaken, Lord Cyzicus gifted you each a manasink and an artifact. However, it is unwise to go into battle with anything less than a full set of arms. These are all Mortal-tier weapons, enchanted with basic durability and nothing else. They will suffice for Mortal-tier giants. I want each of you outfitted in basic armor, with at least one sword, one spear, and one shield. If you have skill with a bow, you may forgo a spear for it and a quiver," she instructed, stepping to the side and indicating for them to enter.

Ignoring the nervous faces of those around him, Luke confidently strode into the room. Making a beeline for the shield section, he picked a medium-size one. Casually feeling its heft in his hand, he tapped it with his knuckles and nodded in satisfaction. He still had a handful of shields and some training spears in his inventory, but he'd never had a chance to pull them out—not without exposing the fact that he had some kind of storage space. This one, though, was a lot better than anything he had on hand.

Picking out a long metal spear, he headed over to the armor section.

This is the real deal, huh. Sylcra is really at war with the giants, and they dress like it, too. He felt his heart beat in his chest. A part of him was nervous. Another, much bigger part of him was excited.

Shrugging into the chest plate and then strapping the grieves onto his wrists, he realized why that was. He wasn't weak anymore. Compared to heroes, warriors, and whatever the hell Arke was, he was a gnat. Against even countless mortal opponents, though—he wasn't someone they could take lightly. More than that, he was confident in holding his own. With more mana than he knew what to do with, techniques guiding his movements, and his boots giving him mobility, he had come a long way since he came to Theos.

An army of giants wasn't even something he considered to be a threat to him anymore.

If my enemy is a mortal, I can kill it. An army of mortals . . . they're just points. He grinned.

"You're not nervous?" said Nikitas, one of the other guys in the group training for the tournament. It took Luke a moment to remember his name. The shorter boy hadn't made much of an impression on him. He had dark hair and average looks, and nothing about him stood out.

"Should I be?"

"Probably." He shrugged, picking a helmet off the rack. "The Tide isn't a joke. A lot of the people we're fighting with are going to die. Not us—they've spent too much money, so we'll be fine . . . probably. But a lot of people will."

"Right. Well, let's do what we can."

"Yeah," he said, and picking a quiver full of arrows off the ground, he slung it over his back and walked away.

Once they were all outfitted, Clite led them out behind the castle.

There were more cultivators gathered than Luke had ever seen before. Nearly a thousand warriors and tens of thousands of blue-robed cultivators stood around Cyzicus.

He was seated on a floating throne, a holographic map of the island hovering in front of him. Red dots, signifying giants, and green dots, signifying cities, littered the half of the island occupied by humans.

Every few seconds, a cluster of blue-robed cultivators, dressed in armor, would step forward onto a platform and a warrior would fly in and join them.

"Come," Clite said, and they cut a path through the assembled force and made a beeline toward Cyzicus.

He looked exhausted. Sweat poured down the sides of his face and drenched his robes. His chest rose and fell in exaggerated movements. His ring flickered, and a large crystal appeared in the air and dissolved into his crown. Instantly his complexion became better, and he perked up in his chair.

Their group made their way to the platform, Clite stopping a group of cultivators from moving forward with a wave of her palm.

Cyzicus didn't even glance at them as the world around them flickered, and he whisked them away.

Here we go. Luke blinked away the nausea as they appeared in the center of a town. In the distance, stones hurled from by enormous hands shattered against a translucent barrier.

"YOU'RE HERE," yelled a scared-looking fat man, raising his hands into the air in relief.

CHAPTER 59

Culling Enemy Numbers

We are." Clite nodded to the man before taking off at a brisk pace toward the barrier that surrounded the town, not even sparing a second glance for him.

"We're saved!" he yelled, pumping his fist into the air and twirling in a slow circle. The Olympic hopefuls squinted their eyes at his antics as they stepped off the platform, amused grins on their faces as they passed him.

"Don't get your hopes up yet," Rose mumbled under her breath, pouring water over his enthusiasm, only to wilt when Clite turned back and shot her the coldest stare Luke had ever seen.

"Is there anyone outside the walls that needs to be rescued?" she asked.

"No one, milady. The emperor's messenger came to us two days ago, and we were able to get everyone inside. I even ordered riders to go out and collect all the travelers."

"Good." Clite nodded. "What do your rations look like?"

"Enough to last us three weeks."

Her ring flashed, and a large wooden crate, littered with talismans, appeared behind them in the street.

"With that, you should have enough for five. I'll make a note that you received the extra supplies, and someone will be here with more before they run out. If something unforeseen happens, you know how to signal us, right?"

"We will light the three-color fire from the tallest tower," he said, thumping his chest.

"Good."

Luke craned his neck as they marched after her, tracing the paths of the shattered remains of the nearly countless boulders rolling down the curve of the spherical barrier all the way to the walls jutting out from the horizon. He could barely see the bobbing, stonelike heads of the Gegenees peaking over it as they whaled at the barrier. Waves of light pulsed through the bubble with every impact, but for the moment at least, it held strong.

A red bird flew through the raining stone and flew unimpeded through the shimmering barrier and landed imperiously on a brick-and-mortar building.

That can't be a normal bird, thought Luke. *And it seems like the barrier only stops the giants.*

The townsfolk pointed at them and whispered as they walked down the cobblestone path. Some of them whooped and cheered, while others glared. A little girl clutching a doll to her chest waved, and out of the corner of his eyes Luke saw Rose wave back. A streak of bright-red flame, trailing her hand, made the girl's jaw drop to the floor . . . and quite suddenly reduced the number of hateful stares. Her mother came forward and carried her off, disappearing into the crowd.

"What's with the mixed reactions?" Luke asked.

"Probably the stress." Rex shrugged. "I'd imagine if a bunch of giants showed up where you live and started throwing stones, there would be some conflicting emotions. Most of them probably not friendly."

"Yeah, but we're here to help, right? Why are some of them mad at us?" he whispered.

"I don't know. People are weird."

Can't really argue with that logic, but still, why are they mad? He scanned the crowd, picking out the angry faces from the rest. *There's not a lot of them, but it can't be because of the giants, can it?*

"Do you have any idea how we normally fight giants? Like, is there a certain formation we make, do we just go in swords swinging, or will she"—he inclined his head toward Clite—"do something?"

"This is my first Tide, too, you know? Just because I'm related to the emperor doesn't mean I know everything," Rex replied before hesitating slightly. "From what I've heard, normally we'd go—"

Clite cleared her throat, her voice echoing sharply in their ears. "If you would wait a minute, I shall explain your roles to you."

Rex looked at him helplessly.

There were more giants than Luke had anticipated. Hundreds of them, each one at least ten feet tall and covered in earthen armor. They were much smaller than the one he had seen a month ago, and less intimidating, too, lacking the spark of intelligence and shrewd cunning that had made the Warrior-tier one so menacing. Their bodies were bulkier and lacked the sinewy muscles of their stronger cousin. Their skin was coarse and rocky, and their six eyes dull, lacking the menacing glow Luke was familiar with. Even their proportions felt wrong. The torsos were too short, making the arms look like they had been forced to fit.

As he watched, a few more tore themselves free from the ground before clumsily ambling toward the town. Digging their long limbs into the upturned earth along the way, they would pepper the barrier around the town with steaming boulders formed of coagulated mud and pebbles that they picked off the ground. A far cry from the obsidian cannonballs he had weathered before with the help of Nel's talismans, but still lethal.

Clite assessed them impassively. Then, stretching her hand out, she touched the barrier with a rune-covered gray stone that appeared in her hand. It glowed a greenish yellow the second it crossed the boundary. Nodding slightly, she turned to face them.

"Six of you will circle around the town, three in each direction, and kill any and all strays. Those of you with bows will stand back and provide cover. All the giants assembled are at the Mortal tier, and most of them will be easily dispatched by your arrows. The rest of you will split into two teams. One team will fight from the wall and slay the giants from the cover of the ward. The other team will be dropped behind the spawn point and will be responsible for culling their numbers from within," she commanded. Her ring flashed, and a set of talismans appeared in the air in front of them.

Sorting through them quickly, he slid them into his pockets. Thoughts churned in his head as he pored over the battle plan.

It sounds . . . dumb. Most of us will have the barrier to retreat behind if or when they need to. I'm not a tactician, but sending a handful of us on the other side has to be the stupidest thing I've ever heard. There's hundreds of them and a dozen of us if we count Clite. Actually, if Clite attacks from the rear, it should be fine.

"What will you do?" Nikitas asked, already pulling his bow free from its place on his back.

"I need to recharge the barrier. I expect that by the time I finish, all the giants will be dead. If you cannot do at least that much, then attending the Olympics would not be worth your time."

What?

"How would that even work?" Luke wrapped his hand around the pommel of his sword, glad to see that he wasn't the only one wearing a look of doubt among the crowd after hearing her plan. "First off, they're still spawning. Second, doesn't it make more sense if everyone attacks them from within? That way, we all have somewhere to retreat to, if things go bad."

"At the current rate, the barrier will give out within the hour. I need to recharge it, else the collateral damage will be beyond what I'm willing to tolerate. Moreover, these are all Mortal-tier giants, and they are not cunning adversaries. Their advantage lies in their numbers and their stamina, not in their cleverness. They have a single-minded determination to kill as many humans as possible; as such, they will target the town above all else. So long as you don't wade too deep into their ranks, you won't have to engage more than a handful at a time. If you retreat, it is unlikely for them to give chase—unless, of course, you retreat toward the town," she answered patiently.

"How long will they keep spawning for?"

"They will spawn until you kill the prime."

There should be a book on this, Luke thought. *She's got to know that we don't know anything about these things, and it couldn't hurt to have some idea of what we're doing here besides killing giants.*

"The prime?"

"The prime is the first giant to be born. So long as it lives, the giants will come."

"So which one is it, then?"

"There is no way to tell, beyond being present at the moment of its birth. Even then, at the start of an attack, more than a hundred emerge from the earth at the same time. If you kill all of them, however, you won't need to know which one was first."

Sounds legit.

"I see." *If that's the case, then there's only two spots to be in, and I know which one is better.* "Can I be a part of the group that attacks from the back?" Luke asked, grinning slightly at the odd looks he received from the others

"I'd like to join him," Rex said a moment later.

"Very well." She nodded and then, turning toward the rest, assigned them into groups before they could decide their own.

"I'll see you there," Luke said to Rex, already channeling mana into his boots. Before the emperor's grandson could respond, Luke leaped into the air and ran through the sky at blistering speed, clearing the distance from the wall to the end of the Tide in mere seconds. Carefully, he dodged the boulders that were thrown his way with the aid of the stances.

A grin split his face as he realized just how many points he had ready to be harvested. Landing gently behind their ranks, he considered how to attack.

Range would be nice, he thought as he pulled his spear free from the strap on his back and planted it firmly into the ground. *But points are nicer. The shield will just get in the way. I shouldn't need it with these giants anyhow. Which leaves me with these bad boys.* He unsheathed both of his golden blades, Bellerophon's xiphos in his right hand and the emperor's gift in his left. He picked a target out of the horde and ran toward it. His heart beat in anticipation as the wind ruffled his robes.

Climbing two steps into the air, he swung his blade in a wide arc on his unsuspecting target, cutting with all his strength down the crook of its neck and into its back, effortlessly sinking his blade a foot into its body.

+3 Stat Points

That's it?

Luke kicked off its back, and the creature landed face-first on the ground. The heavy thump of its fall attracted the gazes of two more giants.

Less than I wanted but . . . there's plenty. He narrowed his eyes.

Slipping into the First Stance of the Sword, he instantly became familiar with their movements. The truth embedded in the motions guided his actions, and for the first time, he let it run free, uncaring as the technique hungrily devoured his mana by the hundreds.

There were no rules getting in his way. There would be no stopping his blade at the last second. It was just him and some things that needed to die.

He stepped to the side and gracefully batted away a boulder with the flat of his blade, uncaring of the hot debris that splashed over him. He was a paragon at the peak of his tier; warm pebbles didn't concern him or his Constitution. Sprinting forward, he charged his second blade with mana and slashed. An arc of blue light whooshed through the air.

Three of the giant's arms fell to the ground. Muddy red ichor oozed from its wounds as it tilted its head in confusion. Fractions of a second later, its head joined its amputated arms in the dirt. Its six eyes blinked slowly before they closed for the last time.

The whisper of the First Stance became a song in his head as he inched closer and closer to the truth buried within.

One by one, giants fell to his two blades.

Clite appeared a distance behind him. Holding Rex and Nikitas by their arms, she dropped them to the ground and flew away. Her gaze lingering on Luke momentarily, she dropped a handful of Mortal-tier explosive talismans in their midst. The explosion itself was ineffectual, but the chaos caused the creatures to trip over and trample themselves.

"Is he stupid?" Nikitas turned to Rex and, pulling back the string on his bow, he loosed a single arrow into a giant barreling toward Luke. It sank straight into one of the giant's six eyes and killed it instantly.

Rex watched with a frown. His jaw clenched and a vein popped on his forehead as Luke unleashed death on the giants, teasing three or four at a time from the crowd and slaughtering them in seconds before returning to get more.

"No. He's strong," Rex said eventually. "Stronger than us."

"I can see that. Where did Lord Cyzicus find him, anyway?"

"Gramps didn't find him. Lukeus did."

"Ahh. Well, that explains it. Monsters attract monsters."

"That they do."

CHAPTER 60

Songs of Truth

He had stopped walking on the ground. The giant corpses of his defeated enemies that littered it made finding stable footing a challenge. The deep gouges they left as they dug into the earth for more ammunition also didn't help matters.

Instead, he relied solely on his boots and trusted in his plentiful mana to see him through the battle. Walking over five feet in the air, he darted from foe to foe.

Nikitas and Rex had found the area where most of the new giants were spawning and had worked out a method to kill them while they were still finding their bearings, leaving Luke alone to thin the crowd from the back end.

A role he was happy to fulfill. So long as he listened to the song of the First Stance, he was nearly untouchable.

An arc of light escaped the edge of his golden blade and chunks of loose gravel scattered as it intercepted two different projectiles headed his way. Another swing of the same blade produced a subsequent wave of light that split the neck of the creature that had thrown them.

An unsatisfied frown settled on Luke's face as he was forced to kill another of the monsters with the wrong sword and consequently miss out on the stat points. He had learned, however, that it was better to kill right away the ones smart enough to try and fight him from a distance. Their harassment was mostly ineffectual, but sometimes a projectile would come at him that was inescapable. Whether it was through luck or skill on the part of the giants or a weakness of his own skill, he didn't know.

What he did know was that whenever it happened, it interrupted the flow of his technique, pulling him free from the rhythm of the battle and leaving him with nothing but his own ability. Something that led to more than once close call before he could reenter the stance.

The more he killed, though, the more he began to realize that *something* was missing. After the initial rush from finally unleashing the technique to its full potential faded, an inkling that something was wrong permeated his thoughts. It started as a small voice at the back of his head, but as the minutes passed, and the giants fell, the sense grew.

The inaudible song of truth began to feel incomplete and hollow. It was flawed, and Luke thought he knew why.

He killed one more giant before retreating to the spot where he had left his spear.

"Are you tired?" yelled Nikitas, rapidly firing two more arrows and killing the stragglers that had chased after Luke. He nodded in appreciation as he opened his status.

<table>
<tr><td colspan="2">Status | Skills | Quests | Inventory</td></tr>
<tr><td colspan="2">Name: Lukas King</td></tr>
<tr><td colspan="2">Tier: Mortal</td></tr>
<tr><td colspan="2">Mana: 361,421/499,000.5</td></tr>
<tr><td colspan="2">Rate: 15% per hour</td></tr>
<tr><td colspan="2">Strength: 999</td></tr>
<tr><td colspan="2">Agility: 999</td></tr>
<tr><td colspan="2">Constitution: 999</td></tr>
<tr><td colspan="2">Arcana: 999</td></tr>
<tr><td colspan="2">Stat Points: 96</td></tr>
<tr><td colspan="2">Bloodline: Locked. Conditions not met. (131/10,000)</td></tr>
<tr><td colspan="2">Charges: 7/10</td></tr>
</table>

"No, I still have some juice left," Luke said.

"Then why are you here?"

Returning the sword Cyzicus had given him to his sheath, he pulled his spear out of the ground. "I just wanted to test some stuff out while I have the chance. Do you know much about techniques?"

"Is that how you walk on air?"

"You can just say no if you don't." He twirled the weapon around in his hands, taking a moment to get accustomed to its shape and weight, before slipping into the First Stance of the Spear. Picking a giant out of the crowd, he leaned back and, with a textbook perfect stance, launched it at the creature. It whistled in the wind with the force of his throw, and he grinned in satisfaction when it pierced all the way through the monster's torso before burying itself at an angle in their midst, perfectly delivering on the vision of death fed to him by the technique.

"That was nice. Is that a technique?"

This guy. Luke shook his head and ignored the question.

Unhooking his shield from his back, he slid his arm into the strap and rejoined the fray with a slow jog, entering the First Stance of the Sword as he moved toward his spear in the thick of the army, surrendering himself once again to the truth at the heart of the skills.

Now, how do I use all three weapons at the same time? Using a shield and a sword is easy enough. Using a shield and a spear is also possible, but it isn't the best way to engage the giants. The best way in this situation is definitely one sword and one shield. The bigger reach from the spear won't do me much good against a horde. I also only have two hands, and as much as I want to, I don't think putting my sword in my mouth is the solution I'm looking for.

So the question I really should be asking is how to best use the technique. How do I make it flow even better?

It's clear that no matter what stance I use, the result is the same. I feel their bodies like I do my own, and I can read their posture like a book. Every twitch, every breath, every thought that they express through their stance I can predict and react to.

The description of the skills says there is a truth infused in them. I know that whatever it is, it's the same for all three stances.

In a way, they aren't even three different techniques. It's one, just reskinned into different contexts, and different forms. With all three weapons drawing on different aspects of it, but for what is ultimately, the same goal. Killing—

Understanding sparked on his face.

That's why the song felt wrong . . . I wasn't trying to kill; I was trying to harvest points.

And it's not just killing, either. Killing with efficiency. There is no playing around. The three techniques always guide me toward the fastest way to end someone . . . His thoughts strayed as, one by one, more and more giants fell to his hands.

It's honestly freaky how easy killing something is with them.

Something tugged at his consciousness. Something big.

He deflected a boulder with his shield, pivoted midair, and sank his sword into a giant's throat. Batting away the outstretched hands of another giant with his shield, he stabbed into a third giant's heart.

Killing is easy.

His eyes widened as his mana started draining by the tens of thousands. A prompt from the Seed flickered in his vision before vanishing. He felt the far-off but ever-present resistance fade away into nothing as something clicked into place. Even without opening the skill tab in his status, he knew that the percentages of each technique were rapidly shooting up.

Killing is easy. That was the truth the empress had constructed her three stances around. Luke struck down another giant, surprised to find himself agreeing.

In a different life, a split-second accident had seen him die. Arke had killed Aeolus effortlessly, in a single exchange. He, Mykonos, June, and Spiros had found it simple to kill that snake. The harpies had posed little to no challenge when pit against Laxas's and Arya's preparedness.

He had killed Nafik and an unknown number of foes in the tomb. Even leaving Yjarn immobilized and on the verge of death had been a simple—if heart-rending—affair.

Things were the same on Sylcra, from Cyzicus killing that Warrior-tier giant to Nel killing Jax. It was all the same.

As one giant after another fell to his blade, he realized that the truth was irrefutable. No matter how hard he searched his memories, he couldn't find one instance of when killing something had been hard.

Even when it was him almost being killed. All it meant was that killing him was easy. It meant that survival was hard.

A barrier he didn't even know existed faded.

Merging Skills.

First Stance of the Sword 99.9 . . . % (Mortal)

First Stance of the Shield 99.9 . . . % (Mortal)

First Stance of the Spear 99.9 . . . % (Mortal)

Merged.

First Truth of Death 0.1% (Warrior)

For the briefest fraction of a second, a tapestry unfolded within his mind's eye. A large, sprawling thing, filled with uncountable colors, rested at the edge of his awareness. On it were inscribed all the truths in the world, waiting to be discovered. He shied away from it, knowing instinctively that it wasn't something a mortal should gaze upon. Doing so came with a promise of madness.

He dismissed the messages and cut the flow of mana to his boots, dropping onto the ground to avoid a giant grabbing at him, only to climb back up a moment later with an upward swipe aimed at its belly, nearly splitting the giant in two above its waist.

Did I just . . . I did. He grinned, realizing that he had successfully, after weeks of no progress, managed to clear yet another requirement for surpassing the Mortal tier, leaving only his Bloodline as the last hurdle.

How is it different, though? And do I just . . .

The world gained a gray tint.

Ghosts appeared in his vision, shadows of every giant that was targeting him, moving half a step faster than the actual creature, laying bare not only their future positions but the best way to kill them.

Practically it's not the biggest difference, but future sight . . . that's a game changer. And the way the ghosts are only from the giants actively trying to kill me—that's huge.

He frowned as his mana dropped nearly sixty thousand points in the span of a second.

It's costly, too. Guess my mana troubles are nowhere near over, but I should have expected that from a Warrior-tier ability.

He released his hold on the upgraded skill and once again entered the First Stance, grinning as the world regained its former hue and a song singing the death of his opponents came alive in his head. He continued his slaughter.

"I think somebody killed the prime," Rex said, his face twisted in disgust as he climbed over the mutilated remains of the dead to reach Luke. "A new one hasn't spawned in a few minutes."

"There's not many of them left, either." Luke climbed a dozen feet into the air and surveyed the battlefield, suddenly aware of just how close he was to the town's wall.

Half an hour later, Luke saw an archer shoot down the last of the Gegenees, and almost on cue Clite appeared in the sky above them.

"Good job. You did well for your first time fighting back the Tide. I will warn you, though, not to get complicit. Today is merely the first day of a long series of battles. The strength of the giants will continue to rise the longer the Tide persists. Mid- and peak-stage giants will become more and more common, and eventually even Warrior-tier giants will begin to spawn. Do not let today's victory make you arrogant."

"We won't," Rose grumbled.

"Good." She nodded. A moment later, her ring flashed, and a talisman flew into the town. The gates flung open, and dozens of the townspeople walked out and began loading the dead onto carts, moving them into a large pile to be cremated.

"How are we getting back to the capital?" asked Nikitas.

"Lord Cyzicus is connected to the altar we arrived through. Once we all climb onto it, he will teleport us to the castle," said Clite.

"Oh. Well, that all works out pretty nicely, then." Nikitas grinned.

It did work out pretty nicely. A few more of these, and I should have no trouble breaking into the next tier. If the giants do get stronger, then it's even better in a way. The faster I can gather points, the closer I come to not having to fear Arke. The closer I get to holding my own fate in my hands.

Mortal, Warrior, Hero.

At the Hero tier, seemingly everyone can become an emperor. And if the way Arke treats Cyzicus is any indication, then emperors get some level of protection from the gods.

If I can get to that level and shake Arke off my tail in the meantime, then I can take it easy. Maybe even do what Cyzicus is doing and sponsor mortals to fight for me in the Olympics and use the prize to cultivate to higher levels.

He gave the Seed a mental nudge. *Any ideas on how to get her off my back?* he asked it, not at all expecting it to reply.

Quest Alert: An Angel's End

Oh, shit.

CHAPTER 61

An Angel's End

<table>
<tr><td align="center">Status | Quests | Inventory</td></tr>
<tr><td align="center">An Angel's End:</td></tr>
<tr><td align="center">When a foe is too strong, you must borrow the strength of others. Heracles, son of Zeus, has been trapped on the island of Sylcra for weeks. Separated from his allies by Arke, and surrounded by an army of Gegenees, he grows weary. Recover his storage ring and deliver it to him so that he may call upon his fleet and in doing so break the blockade imposed on the Dolion archipelago.

. . .

Time Limit: 9 days, 8 hours, and 15 minutes.</td></tr>
</table>

Luke almost tripped over his feet as he read the Seed-issued quest. It was different from every other mission the Seed had given him due to two simple facts: it came with a deadline and a map.

Marked on which were two locations, one represented by an icon of a ring, and the other by a humanoid stick figure, making what he had to do rather simple.

I get the ring, I give it to Heracles, and I'm well and truly free.

Heracles, who is probably Hercules. As in the greatest of Greek heroes. Right up there with Achilles, Perseus, and Theseus. A man who, if I'm remembering this right, became a god at the end of his myth. That doesn't matter, though. What matters is what he can do for me. If he can break the blockade, then that means there are people coming and going from the archipelago.

If there are people coming and going off the island, then Arke won't even know if her thief is still here. At that point, it doesn't matter if I stay on the island or not. That tiny seed of doubt, that I may have snuck off somehow, would ruin her search. People are already reluctant when it comes to helping her, and this would be the icing on the cake.

As a son of Zeus, Heracles must have enough clout that he can ignore Arke without any real consequences, and I can't imagine her risking Zeus's anger. Not when even Cyzicus is confident in the fact that she won't hurt him, and I doubt he has anywhere near the backing the child of a literal god does.

Which ties everything up neatly. I get him his ring, go back to the capital, and compete in the Olympics. Once they're done, I can stick around. Or, if I hear any whispers about the situation in Carim, I just sneak off and use the mask again. Well, that and find some way to disguise my sword. If I go by another name on top of that, then there quite literally won't be anything anyone can do to find me.

Hopefully.

How should I play this, though?

Let's see. The ring isn't exactly far from Heracles. Minutes if I had a griffin, but maybe a day if I have to run on foot.

Luke ran his hands through his hair and, numb to the activity around him, he stepped onto the altar.

Getting there is going to be awkward. Maybe. There's no way I can get there by myself—like, at all. If there's a town nearby, I could ask Cyzicus to teleport me. I'll have to come up with some reason to tell him why, though, in case he asks for an explanation.

If he says no, or if he's just too busy, then I'll just track down Nel. Her griffin is fast enough that we'd be there in a day. I'd still need to find some way to convince her, though. Maybe even ask Rex about it. Whatever I do, though, I can't afford to waste time. I don't know what that countdown is, but I really don't want to find out what happens when it goes to zero.

The rest depends on the exact circumstances.

Best-case scenario would be that the ring is just lying around on some random patch of grass. Worst case, someone or something has it. Either way, there's nothing I can do about it until I get there.

The world around him flickered, as the teleportation altar lit up underneath his feet. Clite ushered them off it the second they arrived back in the capital, led them through a door and back toward their quarters in the castle, and scurried back from the way they'd come after bidding them a hasty *well done.*

She's in a hurry.

"Hey, Rex," Luke called out.

He poked his head out of his room. "Yeah?"

"Can I come in?"

"Why?" Rex crossed his arms under his chest.

Luke sighed, his eyes darting between him and the other trainees, as he considered what to say.

"I need a favor."

"Is it stupid?"

"Not to me, and it's important."

He looked at Luke searchingly and nodded. "Fine."

Waving dismissively to the others, Luke followed the emperor's grandson.

"What do you want?" Rex asked impatiently.

Luke scratched the back of his head as he looked around Rex's room, for the moment ignoring the questions. Like his, it was rather spartan, but elegant. Abstract paintings hung on the walls, and a giant four-poster bed was laid out in the middle. The only difference was a rack full of weapons along one of the walls and a bookshelf on the other.

"Let's say I needed a way from here to the western end of the island. On the other side of the river. How would I go about doing that?"

Rex frowned. "What do you want to go there for? Now isn't really the time for casual sightseeing."

"I'll get to that in a minute. Is there a way?"

"How fast do you need to be there?"

Luke blinked in surprise.

"In about a week or so. The sooner the better. Do you think I can ask Cyzicus to teleport me to some city near where I want to go? Somewhere he was already planning on sending help."

"If you really need to be there in a week, then waiting for a specific place to be attacked by giants won't work. They attack randomly, and if I'm not mistaken, nobody lives where you want to go anyway. That entire area is a desert." He strode toward his shelf and laid out a scroll on his bed. "See. The entire north half of the island is basically a disaster area. Sophia owns that half." He ran his hand over the east side of the island. "So that entire area is a no-go. The north is basically a swamp, and it's dangerous. And the west end is just a desert. The middle part was given to Clan Skyscar. Actually, that section is mostly fine, but they get attacked a lot by the creatures of the swamp."

"How would you suggest I get there, then?"

"I know a way."

"What is it?"

"Why do you want to go there?" Rex asked.

"I need to do something."

"What?"

Luke stayed silent.

"If you're not going to say, then I'm not going to help."

"What's your idea? If it's just asking Nel, then I could do that myself."

"Nel's not in the capital anymore. She went back to the Rising Sun, and she'll probably stay there for the rest of the week."

"Oh."

Think. Think. Think.

Luke pinched the bridge of his nose.

This is a bad idea.

"If I tell you, this stays between us." *The last thing I need is you spreading my BS around.*

"Sure."

"I'm serious. This doesn't leave this room."

"Fine. It won't. You have my word."

"Good. What do you know about Zeus?"

Rex's eyes widened in surprise. "Wha—" He sputtered. "Do *you* know who he is?"

Luke nodded slowly.

Rex opened and closed his mouth and began pacing around the room nervously.

"Why—How . . ." He grabbed his hair. "How are you involved with the king of Olympus?" He collapsed onto his bed before sitting up and staring at Luke with his eyes wide-open and whispering, "Is he here?"

"Not as far as I know."

"Who the fuck are you? Are you one of his kids?"

Am I? "Um—"

Fuck. I didn't even think that was possible. But weren't most Greek myths him just disguising himself and having kids that went on to do some cool shit? Obviously he's doing that here, too.

"Don't answer that. I don't want to know . . . Are you, though?"

"I don't know who my parents are."

"You told Lukeus your father raised you."

"I lied. Cyzicus knows where I'm from. Let's move past this. You said you had a way?"

"Zeus?"

That was definitely a bad idea, but ugh. Fuck it.

"Let's just say I'm doing someone a favor, and I'm not allowed to talk about it. *Okay?*" Luke stressed.

"Fine . . . This is . . . It's bigger than I thought. All right. I'll have to talk to Clite and make something up, and—all right. Meet me in the gardens tomorrow at sunrise. I'll have something figured out by then."

"A week. That's how fast I have to be there. Are you sure you can get me there?"

"Not a problem. Now go. I have to figure some stuff out."

"Wait. Cyzicus won't care, will he?"

"It'll be fine. Gramps is busy—I'd be surprised if he even notices—and at the end of the day, you're not that important to him. If it weren't for the Olympics, nobody would care about you anyways."

Luke shrugged. "I know."

Nobody's made it a secret that the only reason I'm here is to compete on Cyzicus's behalf.

"There you are. Come," Rex said, the second Luke stepped into the garden.

"Are you okay, man?" Luke asked, raking his eyes over Rex, who looked like he'd just fought off an entire army by himself.

"Hmm? Yeah, I'm fine. Nothing to worry about. I managed to figure out our transportation problem."

Our? That better not mean what I think it does. Luke sighed and followed him. *He looks way too excited.*

"So, it isn't quite as fast as Nel's griffin." He grinned, ushering Luke into a clearing at the very end of the path. "But a chariot is a lot more comfortable."

"Whoa."

Parked on the grass was the fanciest chariot Luke had ever seen. Big enough to carry a dozen people, with intricate engravings all along its dark wood and thickly padded leather seats.

"Is that a—" Luke said, his eyes immediately darting to the front of the chariot, where twin ropes snaked out and connected securely to a harness. Attached to that was a giant chestnut Pegasus, its wings folded neatly to its side, its mane billowing even without any wind, and shiny metal shoes glittering softly where they touched the ground.

"Mmm-hmm." Rex nodded smugly. "Meet Nutbutter."

"Is that her name?"

"His name, and yes." Rex went up and rubbed the creature's side, only to hop back, scared, when Nutbutter neighed loudly and stamped his feet on the ground.

"Didn't I tell you not to do that?" Lukeus said. Rubbing the sleep out of his eyes, he clambered out from the depths of the chariot and lovingly ran his hands over Nutbutter's side before grasping his face with both hands. "Who's a good boy? You are!" He kissed the horse's nose. "That's right. Apple."

"Right." Rex rushed to the side of the cart and eagerly fished out an apple. "Here."

"Hi." Luke nodded to Lukeus.

"We meet again," he responded dryly. "I'm surprised you survived the cyclops."

"Oh. You don't know—"

Rex tossed a stone at him.

"Know what?"

"Nothing. So I can borrow Nutbutter, then?"

"Borrow?" His eyebrows shot up in surprise. "Whatever gave you that idea?"

Luke looked at Rex.

"Oh. We're all going together."

"We are?"

"We are." Lukeus nodded. "Nutbutter only lets me fly him. Anyways, what's this I hear about you doing a favor for Zeus?"

"Dude. I told you not to tell anyone!"

"Sorry." Rex lifted his hands in the air. "He's the only one who can fly Nutbutter, and he beat it out of me."

"So. Zeus? What's that about? We don't leave until I know why and where."

"Okay." Luke nodded reluctantly. "I'll explain."

CHAPTER 62

Is That It?

Luke scratched the side of his neck hesitantly. He had spent a lot of the previous night thinking of responses for just this kind of scenario. Unfortunately, at the moment, none of them felt up to snuff. He had to say something, though.

"So here's the thing . . ." He drummed his fingers along the grip of his sword.

Lukeus crossed his arms and raised an eyebrow.

"I can't tell you much. But the gist of it is that I need to find something and give it to someone."

"Find what and to who? And why you?" he asked.

"There's a son of Zeus on the island," Luke said, watching Lukeus's expression carefully. "I have to get him his storage ring. As for why I was chosen . . . Uh, I don't know," he answered honestly. "But believe me, I can't, and I mean it, tell you guys any more. If that doesn't satisfy you, then I guess that's it. I'll find some other way."

"No. That's enough." Lukeus nodded. "I've heard about this kind of thing before."

"You have?"

What kind of stuff has he been hearing?

"Mmm-hmm." Lukeus grunted.

"That's nice . . . So are we good to go?"

If he bails the same way he's done every time up till now, I'm gonna be pissed.

"Yeah, we're good. Honestly, I'm kind of excited to meet Heracles again. I had no clue he was already on the island. Otherwise, I probably would have gone and gotten him already. Can't believe he's been stuck out west this entire time." He shook his head ruefully. Patting the Pegasus on his nose one last time, he walked back to the side of the chariot and climbed in. "I should have known he'd find some way to sneak past that winged lady. The guy doesn't know when to give up."

Luke's thoughts ground to a halt as he tried to process the information.

I didn't mention Heracles, did I?

"No need to look so shocked. Honestly, this is probably a mistake. You see, you're Luke and I'm Luke, and you live in the castle and I live in the castle, so it makes sense that you got the message and not me. But me and Heracles are friends. I've known the guy for years now, actually. It was probably supposed to be me that went and got him anyway. It's a little weird that the message went to you—normally they don't make mistakes like this—but . . ." He lifted his hands in that air. "It happens."

Message? What's he even talking about?

Luke turned to Rex, only to see that he looked equally surprised at the revelation.

"Right. Let's set off." Lukeus clapped his hands together before pointing at Luke. "Do you even want to come? I can probably take care of it myself, but I'd appreciate some company besides Rex. He's kind of boring."

"I'm not!"

Well. This is working out better than expected. Do I want to go, though? Is it even possible to outsource a quest? Should I risk it?

"Would Cyzicus care if I left?"

"The old man's so busy, I doubt he'll even notice. Besides, we'll be back before that dumb tournament, too, so it shouldn't matter."

"All right, then. Let's go. You, uh, packed everything we'll need, right?"

"Did you, Rex?" Lukeus asked.

"I did. Enough food, lots of beer, and some clothes."

Seeing as everything was in order, Luke took one last look around the garden before climbing onto the chariot. Sighing in pleasure, as he wiggled onto the softly padded bench. The leather conformed to his body in the perfect way, and at just the right temperature.

"Is this enchanted?"

"Of course. I had it specially made by the best crafters on the island. I owe the old man a fortune in merits, but I had to have it, you know? And Nutbutter doesn't like to be ridden, either, so I kind of needed one after my last one broke. Bumming rides from Nel was getting old, too. This is actually my first time riding this one, though," he said, taking the reins and tugging on them gently.

The Pegasus immediately took off, galloping a short distance before extending his wings and taking to the sky with a single flap. All without a single jolt being felt in the chariot.

Luke stared, mesmerized, as his muscles rippled underneath his fur. "How did you tame him?"

"Hmm." Lukeus glanced out of the corner of his eye and scoffed. "You don't know? I don't know why I'm surprised." He grinned. "You don't even know how to make talismans."

"His education is lacking, but that's only expected from someone who didn't grow up with the finest tutors, brother," Rex said. A mischievous grin teasing his lips, he leaned back and crossed his arms behind his head.

"I suppose that is fair. Taming animals is rather simple if you have a—"

"Despite his lackluster education, he is stronger than you," Rex interrupted him.

"If he's stronger than me, he's stronger than you. And while he's definitely stronger than you, he can't be stronger than me." Lukeus shook his head.

"Why don't you fight him and find out? Luke hasn't lost a single spar. That's probably why the gods picked him to find your friend and not you."

This guy.

"Like I said before, I'm sure that was a simple mistake. As for your little club, the only reason it even exists is because I don't want to participate in that dumb tournament. Gramps wouldn't need you if he had me."

It does? Luke looked at Lukeus doubtfully. *Is he actually strong?*

"That's not true," Rex argued.

"Oh, it is." Lukeus grinned.

"Why don't you want to compete?" Luke asked.

"Because I'm not entertainment." He puffed his chest. "There are plenty of fools, like you two, who will jump when someone stronger says up, but *I* have my pride."

"What are you talking about?" Rex said. "The Olympic tournament comes with a lot of prestige. Most people can't participate even if they want to. Some of the people who win even end up as emperors. And the prizes!"

"Yes. Many deluded prodigies end up competing, and after they cultivate enough, they can go beg some god for an army to take over some land for the amazing opportunity to pay them taxes. It's all very dandy. If you're a real man, why not load a ship with your friends and set sail for lands unknown? Clear out the monsters yourself, name yourself emperor, and at the end of it, keep all your money."

"You can do that?" Luke's eyes lit up.

"Don't listen to him." Rex shook his head. "No one does that. It's nearly impossible. Sailing without a destination is suicide, and if you do find an uninhabited parcel, chances are it's crawling with monsters. Not to mention that if you leave a piece of wilderness alone for long enough, you'll have Hero-tier or higher beasts cropping up. You'd have better chances conquering an existing empire."

"Gramps did it," Lukeus argued.

Rex shrugged. "He's also the one that says doing it that way isn't wise."

"We'll see."

"Arrogant much? You haven't even become a warrior yet."

Lukeus grinned in response and turned away. Grabbing the reins with one hand, he started to play with them, making Nutbutter swerve from side to side.

"What are you doing?"

"In my old chariot, if I did that, you'd have fallen out. This new one is nice, but I don't get nearly as much *feel*. It doesn't matter. Luke, do you know where to go? Like, exactly—'west' is pretty vague."

"Yeah." Reaching into his robes, Luke pulled out a map he had drawn the night before.

"Hmm." Lukeus scanned the map, pulling his own out of his robes and comparing the two. "Impressive drawing. We should be there in three days." He leaned back, marking the two points on his own, and handing Luke back his map.

"If we don't get attacked. Luke, do you remember the sky snake?" Rex asked.

"I don't think I'll ever forget it. That thing was disgusting."

"It was stupid of you to kill it. You should have let Nel do it," he said, looking straight at his brother.

Lukeus raised an eyebrow. "Sky snakes are Warrior tier. Who are you trying to fool, Rex?"

"Nobody. I told you Luke was strong, didn't I?"

Luke sighed. *What's he trying to do?*

"I just . . . executed it. Nel already had it defeated. What were you saying about taming animals again?"

"Oh. Yeah. I don't know how most people do it, but I just use my Bloodline. It's pretty simple."

A Bloodline? Luke perked up. *Not exactly what I was hoping for. . . But*— "What is that, exactly?"

"Uh. It's basically just an ability. Kind of showed up when I unlocked my mana. When I put my hands on an animal, I can make a bond with it, if it likes me. This little rascal"—Lukeus reached around and put his arms around Rex's shoulder—"has it, too."

Luke's eyes glimmered. *So I finally learned your secret.*

"Are you bonded to anything, Rex?"

"Rex. Bond. Ha. The only things he's been able to make bonds with are bugs."

"That's not true!"

"Are bugs impossible, too?"

"No."

"Well, I don't see your griffin anywhere. Or your Pegasus. Have you ever even bonded to a cat?"

"I'm just waiting for something inter—"

"You don't have to give me excuses, little bro. I'll always love you."

"Shut up. I'm taking a nap," Rex said, rolling over on his side and shielding his eyes from the morning sun with his arm.

"Ah, come on. You know I was teasing you, right? You take everything so seriously."

"No. I. Don't."

"I don't know. What do you think, Luke? You've spent a lot of time with him lately."

"I think this is gonna be a long trip."

"You're not wrong."

Kind of wish I was. That might be more pleasant. And less cringe, he thought, focusing his attention on the ring as he began the torturous process of filling it with mana.

Having a higher Arcana stat hadn't made the experience of filling it any easier, but he had discovered something rather fascinating about it—namely that every eighty-seven points of mana he put into the ring gave him one stat point.

The relationship between stat points and mana invested hadn't been clear in the beginning. Back when he had gotten the ring, there was still room to grow, and growth seemed to vary, and he would gain points in his Arcana seemingly at random.

Since he had maxed it out, though, it had been the same number of points every time. He didn't know exactly why, but his best guess was that since his Arcana didn't grow any more, it took the same amount of effort to accumulate the same amount of aethereal mana within him.

However it worked, Luke was happy that it did. If he pushed himself, he found that he could put in the required eighty-seven points in roughly fifteen minutes, averaging four stat points an hour. What excited him even more, though, was that a few weeks ago, it had taken him seventeen minutes to add the same number of points to his ring.

If I can keep bringing my time down even more and add it to all the other training and the points I get for killing stuff, then I should be able to reach the Warrior tier soon. Maybe even in a couple of months. And if there's a lot of the giants wherever Heracles is, I could do even better. Maybe even get there in a few weeks.

The rest of their trip passed without much fanfare. They managed to cross over the river without being assailed by any beast, and they made quick time, stopping only at night to camp and taking quick hour-long breaks every once in a while for Nutbutter.

The Pegasus, while strong and quick, was neither as fast nor as hardy as Nel's griffin. He required both a lot more food and downtime. Something that Luke was fine with.

The three of them were having a good time, and he had come to appreciate the small moments of inactivity, and with the points he was able to accumulate with the ring, it didn't feel like a waste of time.

"Is this where his ring is, then?" asked Lukeus. A deep frown marred his face.

Luke looked at his map and then peeked his head over the side of the chariot. "I think so." He winced.

"Does this Heracles fellow really need his ring? I can convince Gramps to give him another one," Rex said.

"We have to get it," Luke said resolutely. "And it isn't that bad."

"Are you seeing the same thing I'm seeing?"

No. I see true freedom. "Yes. Now, let's not be babies about this, okay? We have a job to do."

"Well, technically, you got the message, so am I really needed?" Lukeus asked.

CHAPTER 63

Sneaking into Holes

Really?" Luke frowned. "You're going to back out now?"

"Can you blame me? Are you seeing what I'm seeing?" Lukeus pointed to the dark and gaping hole in the sandy dune. It contrasted sharply with the glimmering golden sand that stretched to the horizon.

An uncountable number of fluorescent eyes shone in the cloudy blackness and traced the path of their chariot in the sky. Alert, ready, and hungry.

I don't exactly want to go in there, either, but sometimes you just have to do what you have to do. And I have to go in there.

"It'll be fine . . ." Luke hedged, ignoring the skeptical looks the two brothers were giving him. "What are they, anyway?"

"I think they're bats," said Rex.

"No, bats sleep during the day. Those things are definitely awake." Luke shook his head. "The way their eyes glow, it's kind of catlike, actually. Do you know any, uh, cat monsters that live in deserts?"

"Sphinxes?"

"They're like harpies?"

Rex cocked his head to the side. "I think so . . ."

"They aren't, you idiot," Lukeus scoffed. "It doesn't matter what they are. We'd be insane to go in there. Even if they're weak, there's too many of them. Why don't we check on Heracles and see if he's okay first? We might not even need his storage ring. Why do we need his ring, anyways?"

That . . . Heracles isn't far, but the quest was pretty clear: get the ring, give it to him, and he calls his fleet. It didn't say we can't go there and talk to him first, but—

This fucking sucks.

"The . . . message was pretty obvious. We get the ring first."

"Nuh-uh." Lukeus tugged on the reins, and Nutbutter flapped his wings, flying them higher in the air, but contrary to his claim, he didn't immediately start flying toward where Heracles was, either. Merely circling high above the cavern.

"I have a plan. Sort of," Luke said eventually.

"I can tell you right now, if your plan is me going inside that thing, you can forget it."

"I think I agree with Lukeus. Going down there seems like suicide."

"Not if we find a way to get the . . . *things* out. We have explosive talismans, right?"

"I have a bunch," Rex said.

"Warrior or Mortal?"

"Both." Lukeus grinned.

"And protective talismans?"

"My grandfather rules this entire island. My father, mother, sister, and half my servants are warriors. What do you think?" Lukeus said, pulling a thick stack of them out of his pocket. "We're rich."

"I thought you guys didn't get any special treatment?"

"Not from Gramps, but our mother runs an entire sect. Besides, spoiling us with power is one thing, and keeping us safe is another matter entirely. Having enough talismans falls firmly in the latter category."

"It makes things rather simple, then. Whatever's in there isn't likely to be a hero, so with the talismans, none of us should die instantly. There's a lot of *things* in there, but I bet a few explosive talismans will have them scurrying like rats."

"What if they fly? Nutbutter is quick, but I'm not going to risk him on something like this. Let's just go to Heracles—he's an hour that way. We still have plenty of time until your deadline runs out. More than enough to come back for the ring if we need to."

Luke frowned. Lukeus's words made sense, but he couldn't help but feel that doing the quest out of order was a mistake. The Seed itself was quiet, but then again, it had never actually told him how to do a quest. There was no step-by-step guide. The only information it gave him was what he needed to do.

More than that, this was the first time the Seed had offered him a mission that required him to make an active decision and convince other people to go along with it, and he wasn't sure he liked it. Joining the society for his sword and entering the tomb had required little to no maneuvering on his part. Nefkha had come to him, while signing up for the expedition was simple.

The journey to Cyzicus had taken some twists and turns, but ultimately Cyzicus himself had shown up and taken him there. The Seed seemed content to usher him along with only a passive role in events. It made his entire adventure kind of easy.

Now, though, well, not only did he have to make a decision, but he had to convince people that it was a good idea.

It's stupid. Checking on Heracles does make more sense; it really does. But I can't shake the feeling that not following the quest to the letter is going to be bad.

The Seed—it predicts and knows things that I can't even fathom. It might as well be omnipotent as far as I'm concerned. But how smart is it, really? Can things go wrong if I fuck something up, or would it take that into account before issuing the quest and plan for it in advance?

So far, it seems to plan for success rather than failure to get me out of situations. I would have been well and truly stuck if I didn't learn the techniques in the tomb, after all, and other than the charges, I don't see how I would have gotten out of that. Then again, the mere existence of charges kind of seems like an admission that shit can and does go wrong. More than that, there's a reason the Seed is still around. Because the people who've had it keep dying.

Now, the question is, did they die because they can't do the quests it offers them, or did they die in spite of succeeding?

For Aeolus, it was obviously the latter, but the Seed's mentioned past users. If Arke wasn't lying when she gloated way back when she killed him, gods dying is rare, but it still happens. What are the odds that everyone who has the Seed becomes a god and dies?

No, it's more likely that they fail early on and use the charges to carry them through tough situations, and when they run out and get cornered again, it's game over.

"What are you thinking?" Lukeus asked.

"I'm thinking that there must be a reason we have to get the ring *before* we go to Heracles. The . . . message . . . said he was trapped. What if whatever's in the ring is the only thing that would stop us from being trapped, too?"

"That's possible, I guess. Heracles isn't the type of guy to get trapped, though. Not easily, at least. I can't imagine anything under the Hero tier managing that, though. Even then . . . the stuff he carries around makes what we have look like trash. Last time we talked he was bragging about having God-tier talismans."

"Right. Well, he would have needed to sneak past Arke to get here, wouldn't he?"

"Oh." Lukeus paled.

Rex leaned in, a frantic expression on his face. "Arke, as in that crazy angel that's been wandering around the island? We're freeing Heracles from Arke?" he whispered.

Luke ignored him. "Anyways, this is my plan. We climb high into the air, and I'll jump off the chariot and into the hole with a bunch of talismans. It's probably for the best if all of us *don't* go in there, just in case. I can walk on air, so I should be able to make my escape if it comes down to it. Unless either of you can fly, too, I think I'll just go alone," he said, looking pointedly at Lukeus.

Lukeus shifted slightly but chose not to say anything.

Whatever. Leaving them here means that I can pop all the talismans into my inventory, preactivated. An instant force field, combined with my skill, combined with a fuck ton of mana . . . It should be enough to get in and out at the very least.

"What do you want us to do?"

"Just stick around. You'll be far enough away not to be in any danger, but if you see me in trouble, I'd appreciate it if you could bail me out. Just, uh . . . if you see me making a break for it, swoop in with this fancy chariot and scoop me from the sky, and we can ride into the sunset."

"You're taking a pretty big risk here." Lukeus patted him on the back.

"I think I have good odds, to be honest."

"Well. If you're confident you can do it, I won't stop you."

Luke looked at him blankly. *Somehow, I'm not surprised that you won't.* "All right, hand over your talismans."

"Here." Lukeus handed him his stack, easily two inches thick, all Warrior tier, and already sorted.

"Thanks." Luke stuffed them into his pocket before looking at Rex expectantly. "You want mine, too?"

"Yes. Have you seen what I'm diving into? I'll even give back what I don't use." *Not. Who knows when I'll get the chance to get my hands on so many again?*

Rex looked at Luke with pain in his eyes as he reached into his robes. Instead of handing them over, though, he split his stack in two and then gave Luke the smaller half.

"Why are you being so stingy with them?" Lukeus frowned.

"What if we need some later?"

". . . that's a good point. Can I have some of mine back, too?"

"Umm." Luke climbed to his feet and subtly began channeling mana into his boots. "Why don't you share the ones Rex kept? They seem like enough to get you out of a pinch. And you're pretty strong, right? Stronger than me, so it shouldn't be a massive issue, right?"

"He only kept twenty of ea—"

Luke jumped straight into the air and landed in the sky, waving slowly as the chariot vanished from beneath his feet.

Okay, that was kind of cool. He grinned and, stuffing his hand in his pocket, he slowly walked above the gaping hole in the ground.

Now for the protective talismans. I should keep a dozen or so as they are, in case I need to share them with someone later or use them with people around. The rest, though—

He concentrated on his inventory and ripped the tabs off the bottom, activating them and then sending them straight to his storage.

Explosives are a bit more tricky. I can't imagine a shorter fuse being useful all the time, but it can't hurt. Definitely helped in the tomb.

He ran his fingers through them and stashed some of them in his pocket and then placed the rest in his inventory, staggering some of their fuses at different times before putting them in but leaving the majority of them untorn.

Unlike the protective ones, the explosives were more useful when attached to projectiles, and he didn't want to preemptively activate too many. With the amount of them he had, though, he still managed to get a decent number in both categories.

How should I do this now? Drop straight in or lob some explosives in from the side? Or I can stand right above and hope they just fly past me.

Actually, I don't even know if the things can fly.

Standing off to the side but still in the air it is, then. High enough that if they run out, I'm out of their reach, but low enough that if they do fly out, they go past me and not at me.

He nodded to himself before cutting the flow of mana to his shoes and letting himself free-fall through the sky, mostly using his arms and the air rushing past him to guide his path through the sky. Something that he discovered came a lot easier than he'd imagined it would be.

I can't believe a month ago, I was scared about climbing too high and falling when I ran out of mana. Now I probably have enough that I never need to walk on the ground again.

All right. Be proud later. Right now, I need to focus.

As the dunes grew larger and larger in his vision, Luke righted himself in the air. Then, running thirty feet above the ground, he stopped a hundred yards away from the gaping hole in the ground.

Summoning into his hands a hefty, fist-size rock he'd picked up in the wilderness, he affixed an explosive talisman onto it before sending it back into his inventory. Repeating the process a dozen more times, he tossed his makeshift weapon in his hand, getting used to its weight as he prepared to unleash hell on the unsuspecting cave dwellers.

I kind of feel sorry for those chumps.

Waving cheerfully to the chariot, now a small speck in the sky, he ripped the tab of the talisman and tossed the rock into the hole.

The second it left his hand, another projectile appeared in its place and trailed after its brother in the sky. Again and again until he had thrown half his arsenal.

The ensuing explosions sent sand blasting into the air, and the whole world seemed to rumble. Waves of cold air rushed out of the hole and flattened his hair.

A roar echoed from within the cavern.

I'm fucked, Luke thought. His eyes widened in fear as they beheld the horror he had awoken.

CHAPTER 64

Eyeful of Ugly

Why did I think that lots of eyes means lots and lots of small monsters and not a shadowy abomination with a bajillion of them? I just killed a snake with a thousand fucking wings. I should have known. I really should have.

The creature that emerged from the cavern was best described as an eldritch horror. Countless hairlike black tentacles spilled out from a thin spinelike membrane. Luminescent eyes covered nearly every surface of its shapeless body, and humanlike teeth blinked around them at random and made unnerving clicking noises when the bottom jaw-lid met the upper. Merely looking at it was painful, and Luke wasn't sure if it was because the *thing* was doing something, or if it was a natural consequence of witnessing something truly *disgusting*.

He didn't have time to find out, either. It was looking right at him, and despite the fact that it was so alien, Luke could tell exactly what it was feeling: hunger and anger. Both of which were feelings that filled him with levels of fear he had scarcely felt before. Nor did he want them to be directed toward him.

Briefly he entered the First Stance, only to exit it immediately. He cursed under his breath at what it had shown him.

Yeah, I'm not destroying every single eye it has. Even with the skill helping me dodge, it has too many tendrils to make close combat worth the risk.

It pulsed in agitation, and then its eyes began to ooze fluid. Tears of pain or mouthwatering drool, Luke didn't know, but he took it as a sign to get the hell away.

Fuck Aeolus. Fuck Arke. Fuck Heracles. Fuck the Seed. Fuck everyone. How did my life come to this? he cursed as he took one giant leap after another, shooting himself higher and higher into the sky but carefully keeping the monster within his sights.

Hoping beyond hope that if he ran fast enough and far enough, the thing would leave him alone. For the moment, at least, it seemed content watching him from a distance. Its expression changed, going from hungry to regretful as Luke crept away from it. Ever so slowly, it began to inch back toward its cave.

The ring. Fuck. I can't let it go back in. Not without trying. Luke's jaw set in determination.

Pulling one explosive talisman out of his inventory after another, he tossed them at it with unerring accuracy.

Its form shifted, and the talismans whizzed past its body and sank into the sand. Golden crystals sprayed into the air, and Luke grinned as they sprinkled into the creature's eyes.

It writhed in pain, and its eyes immediately gained a bloodshot hue and lost some of their light.

Okay. It's creepy as fuck, but not too durable. If sand in its eyes can still hurt it, then this . . . nightmare is likely still in the Mortal tier. Hopefully. I can work with that.

Yeah.

Maybe.

He risked a glance toward the chariot flying in the sky. It was still a mere speck. He knew, though, that if Lukeus wanted to, he could come to his aid in moments. Whether he would or not Luke couldn't be sure about, however. The emperor's grandsons had both proven to be unreliable and strange. He hoped that they did, though.

All right. I can work with this, he affirmed to himself, a vague semblance of a plan beginning to take shape in his mind.

"Hey!" he shouted at the creature and flung another explosive talisman at it. This time he waited long enough that it would burst in the air when passing by its hair-like tentacles.

The creature had learned from his actions and become wise to his plan, and instead of contorting itself to let the stone pass it by, it attempted to bat the talisman away.

It didn't work.

Luke, too, had learned.

Bloody bits of its tentacles and eyes splattered against the sand when they exploded the moment it touched them.

"RRRREEEEEEEEEEEEEEE."

He winced. His ears throbbed in pain from the noise, and his control over his mana slipped, causing him to miss a step in the air. It took every ounce of his concentration to regain control over his fall, just barely avoiding what was sure to have been a gruesome end. A bead of sweat rolled down the side of his face as he redoubled his effort to put as much space between him and it as he could.

What the fuck was that? I've never heard of anything being able to mess with someone else's mana before.

Out of the corner of his eyes, he saw that Lukeus had come closer, no doubt realizing that the creature wasn't what they had thought it was.

A determined frown set itself on Luke's face as he pulled out even more of his Warrior-tier explosives. He knew what he had to do, and he desperately hoped that either Rex or Lukeus was fast enough on the uptake to realize the opportunity he was going to give them.

He aimed just behind the writhing mass of eyes and flesh and let the talisman loose. Curtains of sand rose into the air and fell on the creature.

Another enraged shriek tore through the air. Luke gritted his teeth as his mana once again fell out of focus. This time, though, he was expecting it and he managed to recover control in moments, only falling a dozen feet before regaining the lost distance.

Why isn't it following me? He cursed under his breath before tossing even more talismans at it. Once more it let loose its cry. This time Luke didn't even twitch. Repeated exposure to the noise seemed to have made the attack lose efficacy.

"Hey, you . . . thing!" he yelled. "What are you, too stupid to come and get me? HUH! I should have expected that from such a cowardly creature."

"REA—HA-HA-HA-HA." Its tentacles coalesced into crude approximations of wings, all of them arrayed haphazardly and in a way that should not have supported flight. It rose into the air anyway.

Fuck. Fuck. Fuck. It flies, too? What is this thing?

Luke turned around and spirited away. Calling a handful of talismans into his hands, he ripped the tabs off and let the wind carry them away toward the monster, activating a protective talisman moments before they were set to blow. The resulting explosion felt hot against his back, even through the force field.

The monster flew right into them, either not recognizing the attack or not caring. Luke grinned as the explosion tore its wings to shreds, hampering its already unsteady flight and sending it tumbling to the ground.

Capitalizing on the opportunity, Luke drew the sword Cyzicus had given him. Filling it with mana, he slashed forward repeatedly. Each swing severed strands of its eyeball-covered tendrils.

Emboldened, Luke spammed the sword's abilities, sending one arc of light after another into the creature.

"Keep it there!" Lukeus yelled as he flew by.

Out of the corner of his eyes, Luke saw Rex jump out of the chariot. Rolling onto the sand to break his fall, he dived into the monster's cave.

Yes! Luke grinned as Lukeus came back around. Standing heroically in his chariot, with a bow drawn, he loosed one arrow after another into the monster. Each one exploded the second it hit it.

The monster writhed pathetically on the ground as both Lukes attacked it relentlessly. Eventually its thrashing slowed, and the monster began to lose its form. Its wings unraveled back into tendrils that were quickly separated from its body by the duo.

That's right! This is what high ground looks like! Luke grinned.

"REEEEEEEEEEE."

"Wha—" Lukeus yelled. His face became pale. Nutbutter neighed in fright, and Luke watched with dread as the two crashed into the ground.

The nightmare seized the opportunity and instantly burrowed into the sand leaving them alone for the moment.

Shit.

"Are you okay?"

"I'll be fine—check on Rex!" Lukeus yelled back, crawling out of the chariot with his sword drawn.

Nodding, Luke dropped from the sky and sprinted full speed toward the monster's cave, keeping an eye out for the creature in case it reemerged.

Rex came stumbling out of the cave seconds later.

Heracles's Storage Ring

The sign floated in Luke's vision above him. He grinned.

Now all we need to do is get out of here. Take the ring to him, and I'm Arke-free.

"All right. Get on," Luke said, crouching on the ground in front of Rex, indicating he should climb onto his back. He half expected him to protest, but to his surprise, the boy didn't argue at all. "You have the ring?"

"I do." He chuckled. "It's not the only thing I got, either." He shuffled around and held his arm in front of Luke.

"Is that—"

"Yes."

"You took its egg!"

"I did," Rex said gleefully. "You know how I can't bond with creatures. Well, I can, but only when they're inside an egg."

"You want that *thing* as a pet?"

"Isn't it awesome?"

"You're fucking insane."

"Maybe."

"RHEHHEEEEEEEEEEEEEEEE."

Luke winced as the monster let out its loudest scream yet.

"Ahh. What is that?"

The sand parted in front of them, and its eyes, all nine thousand of them, locked onto the egg in Rex's hand. The jaw-lids frothed in anger around its eyes, and its spittle flew in every direction.

"Throw the egg. Throw it now!" Luke yelled.

"What! NO! Do you have any idea how powerful a dreadglare is?"

"Yes!"

"I'm not tossing it. I thought Gramps had killed every last one of them. I'll never find another one."

"Dude. If it's an egg you want, I have you covered. I have a great egg, from a crazy-powerful beast. It's better than a Pegasus and a griffin combined. Please, just throw that away, so that thing leaves us alone."

"I won't, and I'm not stupid, Luke. I'm keeping it."

"You tried to drink milk from a sheep directly! You are very stupid! Trust me, drop it."

He frowned. "That's uncalled-for."

No. No, it is not. I promise you. It is not.

An arrow shot out from the distance and blew up inside the creature. A lone eyeball sailed through the air and splattered on Luke.

"What happened to Nutbutter?" Rex whispered.

"Wha—SHIT!" Luke cursed and ran toward Lukeus.

The Pegasus had survived the fall, but his wings were mangled. Any other time, it likely wouldn't be a big deal. Even a Warrior-tier healing potion would see the familiar restored to prime health.

Right now, his injury likely meant death.

Luke's mind raced as he attempted to think of a solution.

We have to kill it before it kills us. But how?

"Lukeus!" Rex yelled. "It's hero time!"

Huh?

"What's hero time?" Luke asked.

He didn't have to wait long for an answer. Rex ripped the tab off a talisman behind him, and a shimmering golden barrier engulfed them.

Through it, Luke saw a similar barrier appear around Lukeus and Nutbutter.

Oh . . . Luke grinned. His eyes widened in delight as he saw Lukeus remove a slip of paper from his robe and affix it to an arrow.

Time seemed to slow as he pulled back the drawstring. The arrow cut through the air like a bolt of lightning, shining so brightly that, even with his enhanced Constitution, Luke was forced to look away.

When it struck the dreadglare, the world turned white. A shock wave sent the bubble they were in careening into the sky.

When his vision returned to normal, it was to the sight of raining sand. The dunes that had moments ago covered the horizon were gone. In their place was a scorched wasteland. Lukeus had glassed the desert. The beast was simply gone—every last bit of it turned to ash.

The only proof of its existence that was left were the small splatters of blood and eyeball matter staining his robes—and the egg that Rex was clutching in his hands.

"Were those Hero-tier talismans?"

"They were," Rex said. Even without seeing his expression, Luke could feel the grin on his face.

"They are pretty strong."

"They are."

"I can't believe you're keeping that egg."

"I can. With this thing, the Olympics are as good as mine for the taking."

"Maybe." Luke landed gently on the ground and walked over to Lukeus. "What tier do you think that one we just killed was?"

"Definitely a mortal. If it was at the Warrior tier, we would all be dead."

"Why is it so strong?"

"I don't know. Demons usually are, though."

"Demons?"

"Demons."

The fuck is a demon?

CHAPTER 65

Son of Zeus

Unease built up inside Luke as the hot, glassy sand crunched under his feet with every step he took, once again reminding him how ridiculous the world of gods was. To think someone he had been traveling with for the better part of three days was carrying around enough explosives to level a town and the means to survive such an event from within. It was sobering.

It was one thing to know that gods and other more powerful people could erase his existence whenever they desired it, and that he was largely helpless to the whims of the more powerful. It was another to know that their descendants, or anyone with a certain connection, could take his life by simply tearing a perforated tab off a paper.

He sighed deeply, shaking the thoughts from his head. Lukeus, Nel, Cyzicus, Rex—they were all good people, despite the power they possessed.

An image of Jax, impaled clean through by a spear covered in lightning, flashed in his mind.

But that didn't mean they wouldn't kill him. He sighed again.

Don't go down that rabbit hole, Luke, he told himself. *That way is a life lived alone with no friends. What happened to Jax sucked. Actually, that's an understatement. But it was also a result of an alarming number of things going wrong. How was Jax supposed to know his clan had betrayed Cyzicus? Or that they would be monitoring his movements as he approached his own home with alarming speed?*

Focus on the now.

"You all right?" Luke asked Lukeus. Idly inspecting him for wounds, he nodded approvingly when he found none. As violent as the explosion was, he wasn't sure if the other cultivator had been far enough for the talisman to protect him completely.

"Not a scratch." He dusted off his robes and turned to the charred remains of his chariot with a frown on his face. The protective talisman he had activated had not covered all of it, and all that remained was stray bits of wood, along with a small number of their provisions that had fallen out—a few jugs of water and some jerky. "The defenses built into it broke most of my fall, and the talisman worked fine." He frowned as he knelt beside Nutbutter.

The chestnut Pegasus neighed pathetically on the ground. His wings were mangled, his hind covered in scratches, and his legs were contorted at awkward, unnatural angles.

The chariot probably crashed into him when it went down. Luke winced in sympathy.

"Do you have any potions with you, Rex, or were they all in the chariot?" Lukeus asked, combing his hands through the horse's fur.

"Chariot."

"Shit," he muttered under his breath.

"Here. I have some of my own." Luke pretended to reach into his robes and retrieved a Warrior-tier potion from his inventory. He had nicked a bunch of them from Sophia's lair. She had left them, presumably so they had something to heal injuries with. Not that any of them had suffered any.

"Thanks," he said. "Open up, Nutbutter, this will make you all better, okay?" he cooed, lightly scratching his chin. The Pegasus did as he instructed, and he poured the liquid down his throat.

They watched intently as his wounds slowly sealed over and his wings partially mended themselves.

"Do you have more?"

"Yeah." Luke once again pretended to reach into his robes and produced another potion, carefully ignoring the odd look Rex gave him and pretending that nothing was out of the ordinary.

The robes were baggy enough, and their material thick enough that they could reasonably hold a couple of the tiny glass vials without it being obvious, and Luke would hold to that story.

And knowing Rex, he's more inclined to think that I'm hiding being a warrior than I am secretly having a Primordial-tier artifact implanted in my soul that comes in with a built-in storage space.

If I can actually go ahead and break through in the next few weeks or days, then that would be even better. I really don't care if he thinks I broke through a week or two earlier than I actually did. Unlike Yjarn, Cyzicus and the people here seem to know enough about how people usually cultivate faster, and they aren't tempted by it.

Hell, they're probably looking down on me, thinking that I cultivated manually with all the mana that was in the sheep milk and didn't let my body deal with the mana naturally. Which, honestly, I'm okay with. Being seen as less of a prodigy isn't terrible.

"He won't be able to fly anymore," Lukeus announced, climbing back to his feet.

"Like, ever?" Luke frowned.

"What? No! He'll be fine eventually. He just needs time to recover. A few weeks at minimum."

"What now, then?" Rex asked.

Luke looked to the sky and used the suns to reorient himself. Pulling the map he had drawn out of his pocket, he unfurled it between them.

"We're a day's walk away from him, and we still have a few days left until the deadline I got runs out. Why don't we get out of this charred area and set up camp? Take some time to catch our breath, and we'll leave tomorrow morning."

Rex shrugged.

"A little rest will be good for Nutbutter. We'll have to carry him, though. I don't want him putting weight on his legs yet."

Luke furrowed his eyebrows as he looked between the brothers and the giant Pegasus. Lifting him wasn't going to be difficult considering their strength, but he was the size of an elephant. There wasn't exactly a good or comfortable way to carry him.

Rex started to strip out of his clothes.

Wha— Why am I even surprised? Luke pinched his eyebrows and mentally prepared himself for another round of insanity and wondering what exactly had driven Rex to do what he was doing.

"Why are you taking off your clothes?" Lukeus asked before Luke could.

"We have to lift him somehow. We can use our hands, or we can make a . . . satchel." He shrugged at his uncertain word choice. "Yeah, a satchel to carry him in. If we tie all three of our robes together, we should have enough material. It should be easier that way."

"You're right." Lukeus nodded and began stripping out of his own clothes.

"You know what? I wasn't really thinking when I suggested we move out of the charred area. It'll be a lot easier if we just made camp here. This bit of desert is just as good as that bit of desert."

"No, you had it right the first time. Let's not get lazy, now." They both laid their robes on the ground and began tying them together, emptying their pockets and storing their belongings in their pants.

"I really don't think this is necessary."

"Take off your robe," Lukeus insisted.

This can't be for real, Luke thought. Seeing the look in the other boy's eyes, though, he decided it wasn't worth the energy arguing against them.

Shrugging out of his robe, he tossed it to them. "Happy?"

"Yes," Rex said.

"Was there anything else in the cave besides the ring and the egg?" Luke asked later that evening. They sat huddled together around a fire, built from the remains of Lukeus's chariot.

"No." Rex shook his head. He was inspecting the egg in the orange light of the flame, clearly wondering how he was going to hatch it. "There was this, sitting on a pile of raised sand, and the ring was next to it."

"Speaking of that." Lukeus frowned as he looked at the egg. "Don't hatch it without talking to Gramps first. There's a reason he killed all of them. We needed a Hero-tier talisman to get rid of one of its kind at the Mortal tier. The damage one of those could do at the Warrior tier or—gods forbid—the Hero tier is devastating. Demons aren't like normal animals, and our Bloodline isn't infallible. We don't enslave animals—if it's not happy being bonded to you, it will break free," he warned.

"I won't." Rex nodded and placed the egg on the sand beside him.

"Good."

"Can I see the ring?" Luke asked, extending his hand and doing his best to suppress the urge to throw the egg straight into the fire. If he never saw such a horrifying creature again in his life, he would die a happy man. As it stood, though, now wasn't the time to try and convince him.

"Sure." Rex handed it over. "You won't be able to get into it, though. I've tried already. My mana can't touch it."

Lukeus palmed his forehead. "You idiot. That ring belongs to the child of a god. Why were you trying to get into it? Do you have any idea of the types of protections it could have? Even Nel's ring shocks you when you mess around with it—why did you think his ring would be any less dangerous?"

Rex blushed scarlet but didn't say anything.

"I thought mortals couldn't use storage rings—can we?" Luke asked as he turned it over in his hand. For something belonging to a god's child, it looked rather simple. All it appeared to be was a band made of a dull gray metal. It didn't even have any runes etched onto it, and if it weren't for the letters floating above it in his vision, Luke wouldn't even know there was anything special about it.

Lukeus shrugged. "You can look inside them sometimes, but every ring is a Hero-tier item. At minimum. We don't have mana dense enough to use items crafted at that tier properly. Even ones that are specifically designed to be used by mortals are unwieldy at best. We'd be like toddlers trying to swing a sword."

Luke listened to his explanation with half an ear. It was fascinating, but he had a better way of learning about objects.

He closed his hands around it and reached out to the Seed and tried to move it to his inventory, curious to see what the Seed had to say about it.

It didn't go in.

That's new. Luke scratched his chin thoughtfully. Glancing at Lukeus, he ignored his warning and tried to touch it with his mana. Nothing.

Huh.

"All right. Let me see it, too." Lukeus held his hands out.

Luke flicked it to him.

They woke early the next morning, before the suns had even risen. None of them had slept well in the arid cold of the desert.

Being at the peak of the Mortal tier, it seemed, didn't mean that the sand suddenly felt good against your skin, or that it was any easier falling asleep in a foreign environment.

I'm better off than those two at least. Luke grinned internally, his eyes lingering on Rex and Lukeus's feet, which sank into the sand with every step they took, while he walked comfortably and smugly in the air. All the while summoning small morsels of food and cold water into his mouth as he lugged Nutbutter from behind the other two in a triangular formation.

Sweat glistened off their bare backs, as they carried the creature through the desert in a hammock fashioned from their robes. The Pegasus could walk now, but not without a limp. Which to Lukeus was enough of a reason to not make him walk at all, and his wings were still too weak to support them in flight.

With four days still on the counter and Heracles only hours away, Luke found that he didn't mind the extra night they had to camp out in the desert. Especially not when it meant that they would get to him in the early hours of the morning the next day, and not in the dead of night.

Like with Sophia, they heard him before they saw him—grunts of exertion, the whooshing of a weapon displacing the air, and the wet noise the weapon made when it struck flesh.

"Stay here," Lukeus said to Rex as he and Luke gently lowered Nutbutter down into the sand before taking off in a dead sprint toward the noise. They came to a quick stop as the desert suddenly gave way to a cliff, at the bottom of which a war played out between one man with a club and an army of giants.

CHAPTER 66

Onward to Heracles

That's a lot of giants," Lukeus said.

"Bit of an understatement," Luke said. His heart beat in anticipation as he took measure of the giant army. There was, simply speaking, a nearly uncountable number of them. An entire sea full of them, and in the air above the horde, a lone figure. "So that's him, then?"

"It is," Lukeus said casually, his voice at odds with the look of awe on his face.

Heracles was more than a mile away and floating in the sky—a hallmark of the Warrior tier. With every swing of his spiked metal club, gusts of wind cut through the air. With every roar that escaped his lips, he felled dozens of the monsters. To say that the son of Zeus fought well was an understatement.

A long metal cable clamped onto his ankle kept him anchored to a giant hunk of metal, both of them glinting brightly in the morning light. His restraints kept him trapped but granted him enough leeway to dodge the endless barrage of obsidian and rock that was being thrown at him. Not that he was. Every rock they threw, he batted back into the army with double the force. Cratering the ground and flattening the giants.

His chest heaved, and he suddenly shot toward the ground. Shoving aside the creatures with nothing but his shoulders, he stretched his metal chain taut and looped it around the metal slab that kept him anchored. The body of every giant in his path split clean in half.

Damn.

"Do you think you can fire an arrow with the ring attached to it, all the way to him?" Luke asked. "I don't think I'd survive if I tried to walk over there. Actually, never mind—I can probably go high enough so that—"

Lukeus pulled back an arrow and let it fly into the crowd of giants.

Luke watched in pain as it fell short and landed in the middle of the army.

"Don't tell me you—"

"Relax. I was just seeing if I could make the shot." He flashed his finger. The metal band was still on it.

"Phew." Luke sagged in a mixture of relief, and a small bit of sadness.

It would have been a pain in the ass to get the ring from the middle of an army, but the points wouldn't have been bad. Not at all.

"I can make the shot, though," Lukeus offered.

"While I believe you, I don't think we should risk it. I'll climb high into the air and drop it on his head."

"I think we should fire it. See that?" Lukeus pointed behind Heracles, to a vague outline of a giant sitting lazily on the corpses of its Mortal-tier counterparts with all six of its hands holding the back of its head. One that was stories tall.

"A Warrior tier," Luke said, frowning in worry when he saw it. Things just got a lot more complicated.

Fun.

"Mmm. If you think that thing won't be able to hit you, then go for it. You should know, though, that not every Warrior-tier giant is the same. The one Nel fought outside the town was a regenerator type. If this one's the same, you'll probably be fine. If it's a thrower type . . . it won't really matter how high you climb. It will hit you. It could also be a flyer type. If it's one of those, forget dodging—it'll get up there and rip you limb from limb."

Yeah. I'm not going to be able to outrun a warrior in the sky.

"What do you suggest, then?"

Lukeus didn't respond. Pulling an arrow free from his quiver, he nocked it and pointed it toward Heracles before lowering it to the ground.

"Do you have paper?"

"Uh. Yeah." Luke reached into his robes and withdrew the map he had drawn. "Here."

"Pencil?"

"No," Luke lied, knowing full well that he had a bunch of them in his inventory. If it weren't for the fact that they had all seen what was in their respective pockets earlier, he might have risked it, but as it stood, he wouldn't try. Lukeus might overlook it, but that was one of the few things that he couldn't plausibly deny. Especially not with Rex just a few feet behind him and watching him like a hawk.

"Tch." Lukeus frowned before pulling his arrow loose from the bow and dropping it onto the ground. He lifted his sword from its sheath and made a small cut on his index finger. With surprising dexterity, he tore a small bit of the paper off and wrote over Luke's sketch with blood:

It's Lukeus. I got your ring. How do I get it to you?

Nodding in satisfaction, he set the arrow on his bow and let it fly.

It made it halfway there before it was knocked out of the sky by a stray boulder.

"Any other ideas? And why isn't the big one doing anything?"

"I'm thinking." Lukeus sighed. "As for the Warrior tier, could be any reason. They're smarter than the normal ones. Most likely, it tried fighting him, lost, and is licking its wounds. Probably waiting for Heracles to get tired. If it is licking its wounds, it's not a regenerator."

Welp.

"Do you have a way to call Nel here?"

"I could . . ." He frowned. "But let's not go there just yet. I don't want to distract her." He massaged his forehead and sat down on the cliff, dangling his feet over the edge. "All right. This is what we'll do. I'll distract the big one, and you get the ring to Heracles."

"That . . . that seems like a terrible plan."

He scoffed. "Most of those giants are pathetically weak, and I bet you can cut a path through without too much trouble. Rex told me what you can do, and I've felt how much mana you have. It should be more than enough to power whatever technique you use for long enough for you to make it. As for me, I'll need to break through to the Warrior tier, but it should be fine."

"You're going to break through to the Warrior tier? Do we have time for that?" Luke asked incredulously.

"Mmm-hmm." He closed his eyes. "I'm not likely to be a match for the giant either way, but if I ascend, then I should be able to hold its attention for a few minutes. Long enough to keep it off your back. Once you get inside Heracles's range, he'll keep you safe. His ring should also have enough goodies for us to get out of here, too. That guy has enough money to buy Sylcra and probably enough talismans to raze it to the ground."

"Not that I doubt you, but isn't there a single warrior we can call?"

"Only one that I can think of that will make it here on time is Nel, and she's busy. Gramps can't send anyone unless he teleports them, and it won't be easy sending someone here. If we weren't in the middle of a Tide, he'd probably come himself, but there isn't anyone else who can power the teleportation platforms in his place. The only thing he'd move for is a Hero-tier giant. As much as he loves us, I don't want to put him in a position where he has to choose between us and the rest of the island."

"All right, how long do you need to break through?"

"I just did," Lukeus said.

What?

Dusting off his pants, he turned to Rex. "Me and Luke are going to head out for a bit." He chucked his bow and shrugged off his quiver. "We shouldn't need it, but I want you to stay here and give us cover. If you fire an arrow into me, I will stick that same arrow up your ass."

"I only did that once, and why am I staying?" Rex asked indignantly.

"Because you're the weakest one here, and I don't have anyone else to watch Nutbutter," Lukeus answered. Sliding the ring off his finger, he handed it to Luke. "If you drop that, you're going to be the one to get it."

"I will not."

"Good." He slid his sword out of its sheath and tossed it on the ground. "Step on it."

"Huh?"

"I can only carry you on stuff that has my mana infused in it, and the only thing I have that's infused with my mana is that. Step on. I want to get this over with."

"Oh." Luke nodded and did as Lukeus asked.

A second later, the pair was shooting through the air.

"You broke through! When!" Rex yelled after them, his jaw hanging open in surprise.

"Don't worry about it," Lukeus yelled back, climbing higher and higher into the sky. "I'll drop you off high and go down first. I'll try to get the thing's attention, and once I do, I'll try and get it as far from Heracles as I can. That'll be your chance to get him the ring," he explained.

Luke nodded numbly as he stared down at the army. There truly were a lot of them.

"I guess he didn't kill the prime."

"No, no, he didn't. He probably didn't even know that the prime was a thing," he muttered. "If I had to guess, though, the prime is the Warrior-tier one. It's not always the case, but when a Warrior tier pops out, it's usually also the first one that comes."

"We should also be prepared for something to happen when I give him the ring. If Arke really left him tied up like this, then she probably has some way to find out if he gets free."

"You think the key to his manacle is in his storage ring?"

"You don't?" Luke frowned.

"No. I don't know what's in there, but I doubt the key is. It's fair to assume that Arke didn't know the Tide was going to start early, because we didn't know it would. She put it in a cave with a demon, miles away, too. There's no way for Heracles to know it would be there, unless he has some way to track it, but I doubt it. I'm assuming she meant to keep him here and away from the rest of the island while she searches for the thief. The time limit we got is probably when Heracles would have fallen to the giants."

"Or it could be when Arke is going to come and check on him."

"If Arke checked on him, everything would be fine, and no one would have sent us. No, she probably put him here and forgot about it entirely. As far as I know, she hasn't even been on Sylcra for weeks. Gramps said she found a clue on some other island."

"A clue?" Luke frowned.

That's a little worrying. Whatever it is, though, it can't be a good one, considering I'm still alive. She's also been chasing red herrings this entire time. The method people use to possess bodies isn't the same one that the Seed used on me.

It's highly unlikely that Nefkha talked. Could it be one of the people from the inheritance that said something?

No.

I was definitely suspicious, but I wasn't a serious consideration. It was more that I just grew faster than they did. But even then Yjarn and Arya, or even Spiros—none of them were slower than me. Hell, Arya was faster the entire time, and Yjarn learned it literally hours after I did. That's not even mentioning Len. That guy figured it out when everyone thought he was dead.

If there were a whole bunch of people suddenly appearing on a bunch of islands on the archipelago . . . that would do it. There was a teleportation point on Carim, but not everyone would have stayed on it.

Luke isn't a rare name, and I look different. My sword has also changed a bit, and gold swords aren't particularly rare, either.

More than that, I have Cyzicus's vow that he won't tell anyone about me being from Carim.

Whatever. I just need to get Heracles the ring, and I'm home free.

"This is where we part ways," Lukeus suddenly said, pulling Luke out of his thoughts. They were miles up, straight above the son of Zeus.

Luke took a deep breath and channeled mana to his boots. Stepping off the warrior's sword, he said, "Good luck."

"You, too. Try not to get hit."

"I won't."

Lukeus grinned and shot toward the ground. Pulling a small bunch of protective talismans free from his robe, he aimed straight for the Warrior-tier giant.

It didn't take long for it to notice the emperor's grandson.

The pair clashed in the air, and like he promised, Lukeus tackled the giant away from Heracles.

Gritting his teeth in determination, Luke pulled his mana from the boots and hurtled toward the ground. It was time for him to keep to his end of the plan.

CHAPTER 67

Dropping in Unannounced

Most of the boulders in his way weren't aimed at him. That didn't stop them from relentlessly crashing against the barrier of his protective talisman three and four at a time seemingly every second. Just the sheer volume of them made the sky above Heracles lethal to be in, and Luke was grateful that he had dozens of talismans burning a hole in his inventory. Each of them ready and more than capable of stopping the Mortal-tier attacks quite easily.

How is he even alive? Even a warrior should have fallen after days of this, Luke thought as he looked below at the figure of Heracles, barely visible through all the debris flying through the air. He had been awed by his martial prowess just from seeing him fight off the giant horde from a distance. Being in the thick of it left him reeling.

Correcting his course with his boots, Luke summoned a handful of untorn talismans into his hands. Calling them directly from his inventory was more convenient, but he suspected that the son of Zeus would have questions if he used one of them that way in front of him.

Counting down in his head, he replaced his talisman with another one moments before it was set to expire, rapidly slowing his descent as he did so and stopping a hundred or so feet in the air above the man.

"Hey!" he yelled, waving his arms wildly.

"I'm kind of busy here. You with that other guy?" Heracles said, his voice booming like thunder. A deep, guttural, and manly sound if there ever was one.

"I am. My name's Luke, and I have your ring," he said, tearing the end off another talisman.

"You do?" Zeus's son asked, genuine surprise leaving his voice.

"I do."

"HA-HA-HA-HA-HA-HA. At last! Throw it to me."

Luke slid the metal band off his finger and dropped it. Almost immediately, it was caught by some invisible force and stilled in the air. For a moment it just hung in the sky, right outside the bounds of Luke's barrier. An instant later, the air cracked, and the ring slapped into Heracles's waiting palm, leaving a thin trail of rapidly fading lightning in its wake.

Fancy, Luke thought, impressed in spite of himself.

A talisman appeared in his hand, and a fraction of a second later a bright golden barrier rippled outward and washed over and past Luke. He watched, stunned and with his mouth slightly ajar, as every giant in the area was suddenly pushed back hundreds of yards by the shimmering light, and the sky cleared of their earthly orbs, leaving him and Heracles alone in the sky, standing under the warm glow of his talisman.

"I thank you!" Heracles said, rising into the air so that the chain was taut against the slab of metal anchoring him to the ground. He frowned angrily as he tested his bonds before carefully schooling his expression.

"Don't worry about it." Luke shrugged as he scratched his head. *I'm not exactly being altruistic here.*

He took his first good look at the legendary son of Zeus. He was younger than he would have thought, appearing no older than twenty. His hair was a matted and sweat-soaked blond. Thin whiskers peeked out from the edge of his lips and the side of his cheeks. Deep bags under his eyes rimmed his startling, bloodshot blue orbs. Thin strands of electricity seemed to shiver within them as he stared right at Luke. All told, he looked just like he had been fighting nonstop for days but still managed to appear handsome, not disheveled and insane like Luke expected a man in his position to be.

He grinned as he slung his club over his shoulder like a baseball bat. "Do I know you?" He cocked his head to the side. "You seem familiar."

"This is the first time we've met," Luke said, tearing his eyes away from him he scanned the crowd of giants for any signs of Lukeus. He'd lost sight of him earlier when he was working his way through the barrage of boulders.

He found him immediately. The newly ascended warrior fell through the barrier and crash-landed on his side. Stumbling to his feet a moment later, he walked back to the edge of the golden barrier and postured in front of the Warrior-tier giant he had been keeping occupied, making one obscene gesture after another at the creature with a wide grin on his face.

The giant tilted its head to the side, and its eyes crinkled in confusion. Shrugging all six of its limbs, it sat down in a squat and stared right at Lukeus.

That is so creepy, Luke thought as a shiver ran down his spine. *There's something wrong with these things.*

"Is that Lukeus?"

"It is."

"And you said you were Luke?"

"I am."

"Mmm." Heracles scratched his chin idly. "Who sent you?"

"Hmm?" *The Seed, obviously . . . but I can't tell you that, now can I?* "I don't know," he answered eventually.

"Come on, you don't have to be like that. Was it Dad? Uncle P? Uncle H? Hermes? Ares?" He paled. "Please don't tell me it was Apollo," he pleaded, a desperate edge in his voice.

"I—uh." Luke's mind went blank as the son of Zeus rattled off one god after another. "I really don't know. I'm not trying to hide it from you or anything," he said, lifting his hands into the air in defense.

He frowned. "You don't know, huh? That sounds like something all of them would try and do. Fucking mysterious assholes," he grumbled.

"They're assholes for helping you out?"

"No. They're assholes because their help doesn't come free. Last time I got in a bind, Apollo made me clean—" He stuck his tongue out and shivered. His face gained a green hue as he seemed to remember something thoroughly unpleasant. "I don't want to talk about it," he said eventually.

"That's fine."

"I should probably do something about that one, huh," Heracles said, squinting in the direction of the Warrior-tier giant. His ring glowed on his finger, and a bow appeared in his hand. He drew the string back, and Luke watched in fascination as an arrow entirely composed out of blue energy materialized.

It shot through the air silently, past Lukeus and through the barrier, before sinking into the giant's chest. The monster didn't even realize it had been hit before its entire upper body vanished in a spray of bloody mist.

Holy shit.

"That never gets old." Heracles grinned. "It's one of my sister's old bows. I don't even know what tier it is, but I killed a Hero-tier sky kraken with it on the way here. That little thing is puny compared to it," he said, gesturing to the remains of the giant.

"I bet it is." Luke nodded slowly.

"Hey, Heracles, you asshole! I had that!" Lukeus came flying through the air and tackled him, only for Heracles to stop him dead in his tracks, a single palm cupping his forehead.

"Little Lulu's all grown-up, isn't he," he said, ruffling his hair.

"Don't call me that," Lukeus snarled. "I'm not a kid anymore."

"I can see that. The way you tackled that giant was something else. I remember you being such a scaredy-cat . . . You've come a long way."

He blushed bright red and turned away. "Why'd you come to Sylcra, anyway?"

"We were getting bored on Lemnos, and then I remembered that Sylcra was pretty close, and you guys had a pesky giant problem. I figured, why not? It had been a while since I last saw you and Nel, and I bet you could use some help, and the rest of the crew could blow off a different kind of steam"—he wiggled his eyebrows—"and kill some stuff. They've grown weak after years in paradise. When we got here, though, there was a huge line of ships waiting around the entire archipelago."

Lukeus nodded. "Arke. She has a blockade surrounding the entire island. Won't let anyone come and go."

"So that's what that was. Huh. Well, I figured I'd go and check it out, so I flew ahead, and this crazy-strong winged lady stopped me. Then I was like, do you know who I am? And she was like, yes, I recognize the arrogance of Zeus's spawn when I see it. So I was like, then you should know not to stop me, and long story short, she let me through."

"She let you through and tied you to that rock and then took your storage ring and tossed it somewhere?" Luke asked.

"Well, I may have cussed at her a bit. And I told her that there wasn't a chance in Hades that my whole crew was going to wait outside, and I was just about to signal them to fuck the blockade and come through anyway when she put me to sleep. When I woke up, I was chained to that thing, and then a few days later that big giant popped out of the ground, and since then, more and more of these things have been popping out. I gotta tell you, Lulu, I don't know how you all live on this island if those things come every ten years."

"We manage."

"I bet." Heracles nodded. His ring glowed softly, and a talisman appeared in his hand. "Jason, it's me, Heracles. I'm still alive, but some crazy lady with wings imprisoned me. I need you to gather the entire fleet, break through the blockade, and free me. If you could get every other ship waiting to dock to move in as well, then that would be best. This lady is strong, but she won't kill everyone if you all move at once." He spoke to the talisman, a grin stretching his face, as he ripped the bottom half-free, and it flew off into the sky.

Fuck, yeah, Luke cheered internally. *Problems solved.*

"What was that?" Lukeus frowned.

"That was what it sounded like. If that lady really thinks she can keep me locked up without reason—with some flimsy excuse and not get payback, then she has this coming." He grinned.

"Heracles, this is my home," Lukeus said slowly. "Arke is strong. Why would you put her against us like that?"

"Are you—"

"I'm not defending her, or saying she was right to keep you trapped here, but there's more at stake than her ego and yours. If she decides to go berserk and kills everyone here, then sure. The gods will avenge us, but we'd still be dead," he said.

Heracles looked affronted by the very idea. "That won't happen," he said resolutely. "I know her type. She bullies the weak and runs scared with her tail between her legs when someone with more leverage and stronger backing comes along. Why is she here, anyway? Did you do something?"

"No. Some soul escaped with something and she's hunting it down."

"She put a blockade around the entire island to catch a zombie?"

Lukeus shrugged.

"That's ridiculous."

"I know. Everyone knows." Lukeus crossed his arms under his chest.

"Do you have a way to break free of that manacle while we wait for your . . . friends to join us?" Luke asked him, hoping to change the subject.

He frowned. "I do." His ring glowed once again, and his club vanished. In its place a small knife appeared in his hands, made of the same shiny metal as the cable and the giant chunk of metal keeping him tethered to the ground. "This should be able to cut it without destroying the island, but I'll need a few hours. The barrier is good for a day or two, so we should be safe in the meantime."

In that case— Luke turned to the horde of assembled giants just outside the golden barrier. "Take your time. I'm going to go kill those. It seems like a bad idea to leave them lying around, even if they are in the middle of a desert."

"Oh, those aren't a big deal. I have a bunch of Saint-tier talismans, we can have them—"

"No," Luke said. "I have a sword. It's good enough."

"Are you sure? That's a lot of giants."

"I'm sure," Luke insisted before turning on his heels and walking toward the edge of the barrier. "If you really want, we can blow them to smithereens when it's time to leave, if there are any left. Until then, I got it."

There's no way in hell I'm going to let this many points be wasted. Not when the Warrior tier is right there for the taking, he thought, barely managing to rein in the grin on his face.

CHAPTER 68

Deciding Not To

Hours later, the nine suns of Theos sank below the dunes on the horizon and Luke teetered at the edge of the barrier as he cut down one giant after another. His back was drenched with sweat, and splatters of mud and viscous ichor caked his face. The putrid stench of death curdled in his nose, but it was worth it. Monsters fell to his blade like flies, and with each one that he felled he was one step closer to the next tier.

+ 3 Stat Points
+ 4 Stat Points
+ 3 Stat Points

The notifications are getting annoying, though. He grinned happily as he pulled his sword free from the chest of a monster. He watched with a sense of satisfaction as its limp body fell against the barrier, only for another giant to move forward and trample over it. *But—it's definitely a good problem to have,* he thought, his chest heaving and his breath coming in short bursts.

He was sure that his actions looked strange to the others, and he could feel their gazes lingering on his back, but he wouldn't have it any other way. There were so many giants that even after killing well over fifteen hundred, he had barely made a dent in their numbers. Sure, they could have destroyed them all with some high-level talismans, but they were stuck here until Heracles cut himself free anyhow.

It might even be worth it telling them how my sword works if I can stay here all night long and harvest them to my heart's content. Hell, forget maxing out my Bloodline, I might even be able to make a solid dent into the Warrior tier. He shook his head slightly at the thought. *No. I still haven't seen anything like my sword except for Sophia's sheep, and even that's like comparing apples to oranges. Something that used to belong to a near god could be immensely valuable. But . . . I'm also a few feet from the son of the literal king of gods, Zeus. The same Zeus who happens to be the same god who killed my sword's last owner. Do I really have to be worried about being robbed if everyone I hang around with is richer than me?*

Decisions, decisions, decisions. Whatever. I'll have to research it more. Another thing on the list. Who am I kidding—that's been on the list.

He killed another giant and momentarily deactivated his technique.

While the First Truth of Death functioned similarly to the First Stance's, it was both more effective and the passive mana drain was nearly negligible when weighed against his regeneration—at least when his enemies were low-tier brutes that moved slowly, and he wasn't using the future sight. More than that, the draw remained steady; no more were there sudden surges every time he landed killing blows.

Even so, something, an instinct, told Luke that it wasn't a good idea to grow completely reliant on it. As such, he had taken to intermittently killing the giants without it being active, while trying to maintain the same easy grace he had with it on.

It wasn't easy. The giants were still no match for him, but without the near-precognitive sense built in that let him react to attacks as soon as his opponent committed to them, he ended up taking damage. Mostly from stray boulders that the technique would have guided him past.

Idly he opened his status, stepping back completely into the barrier as he took stock of his free points.

Status	Skills	Quests	Inventory
Name: Lukas King
Tier: Mortal
Mana: 487,906/499,000.5
Rate: 15% per hour
Strength: 999
Agility: 999
Constitution: 999
Arcana: 999
Stat Points: 4
Bloodline: Locked. Conditions not met. (4,812/10,000)
Charges: 7/10

Spare four, he dumped the rest into his Bloodline. Carefully, in one-hundred-point increments, lest he cross some threshold and have another episode reminiscent of his giggling fit, but as far as he could tell, the stat was a black hole. Sucking up the points, much like the Arcana stat had when he was still new to the world.

It made him nervous.

Not that it would stop him, though.

I will have to find somewhere private when I do break through, though. Maybe even hold off on any points in Bloodline so I don't cross five thousand here. I don't think anything is going to happen, but better not risk it.

"Are you done?" asked Lukeus, walking over to him.

"No."

"You're actually pretty good," he praised him.

"Thanks." Luke grinned. Cocking his head to the side, he wondered where he was going with it. Looking over his shoulder, he saw Heracles still grinding away at the cable. Thin strands of metal were splitting off like loose hairs, but there was still a while to go.

"Do you thi—"

Danger Detected.

Luke lifted his hands in the air and stopped him.

Shit. Shit. Shit, he cursed repeatedly. His heart sank in his chest as nervous energy bubbled inside him.

The night was getting brighter. Something dark shadowed the ground before it exploded over them.

Wooden chips and people rained from the sky. Shimmering bubbles appeared around them as they fell, and they bounced off the ground in the middle of the giant horde. Screams rang through the air as they tried to fight.

Pressure greater than he had ever felt fell on his shoulders and planted his knees first on the ground.

"She's here."

"YOU DARE!" Arke appeared with a single beat of her wings, grasping Heracles by his throat as she carried him in the air. The partially cut cable turned taut. A smile full of sadistic glee came over her face, and she lifted him even higher. He screamed in agony as his leg ripped free from its socket and hung awkwardly in his skin. "You dare," she hissed.

Heracles carefully schooled his expression, grinned, and then spat in her face.

She lifted him higher. His limbs stretched in ways that should have been impossible before the slab of metal that had kept him tethered rose inches off the ground, held up entirely by the strength of his tissue.

Out of the corner of his eyes, Luke saw Lukeus pull a talisman free from his pocket and set it free. It made it a dozen feet into the air before a spear of light impaled it onto the ground.

Immediately Arke let go of Heracles. A sword materialized in her hand, and with a single swing she cut the cable connecting him to the hunk of metal.

The ground cratered and the world shook when the metal touched the ground.

"Did you just remember who I am?" he asked her.

"You're awfully proud for someone who hides under his father's name," she taunted him. "But I don't think you quite understand what you cost me today."

"I don't really care."

"I know." She nodded, rubbing his cheek with her thumb. "It's unfortunate that I can't punish you more than I have. I much prefer not torturing bystanders."

"Wha—"

A rock appeared in her palm, and she stuffed it into his face.

"My dear. It's much too late to regret your decision now. You should just watch," she said. "It's more fun that way." Constructs made of blinding light appeared in the air and restrained the son of Zeus—a ring on each ankle and each wrist, pulling every limb in a different direction.

His ring began to glow, and a talisman appeared in between them. Another spear of light impaled it, stopping whatever function it was supposed to have.

She snorted. Pulling the ring from his finger, she tossed and turned it in her hands before carelessly flinging it through the horizon.

Her wings flapped, and the next moment she was standing in front of Luke and Lukeus.

"Hmm. A nobody . . . and look at that, Cyzicus's grandchild."

Fuck. Fuck. Fuck. Waves of anxiety rolled through Luke as he tried to think of a way out of this situation. With every ounce of will he could muster, he craned his neck to see the woman who had haunted and hunted him, standing before a paralyzed friend.

Walking in slow circles around Lukeus, she nodded in satisfaction. Rings of light appeared around him and lifted him in the air.

"What's—the—point of THIS?" Lukeus yelled as he struggled within his bond.

"The point? The point is that your meddling cost me millennia!" she hissed, spittle flying from her mouth and onto Lukeus's face. "Millennia I have spent relentlessly searching. Risking death countless times for the smallest of clues. Traveling to places from where no one returns. I. KILLED. A. GOD. All in pursuit of—" She took a deep breath. Closing her eyes, she hung in the air, trying to reclaim her exposure. "The point is I'm angry. The point is that his arrogance has cost me!" she yelled, pointing at Heracles. "And I need to make him pay. I need to make you suffer." She smiled.

A sword made of light appeared in her hand, in between him and her.

"WAIT," Luke yelled, struggling with every ounce of his will to climb to his feet and failing miserably.

"Who are you?" she asked.

"I'm . . . nobody. But let's think this through, all right? I've heard more than enough about your, uh . . . plan to find the thief. I think we can both agree that it wasn't the best, right?"

The pressure doubled. Then it tripled.

He felt his body ache and his bones began to fracture as an invisible, unstoppable force pressed him into the ground.

"Take care with how you speak."

Danger Detected.

No shit.

Her sword vanished, and Lukeus appeared beside him.

A shadow appeared above their head, and before he could react or get out of the way, a slab of metal fell onto them and flattened them to the ground.

"GRrkek," Lukeus wheezed.

"A fitting punishment, is it not?" Her voice echoed in Luke's ears. "They gave you the tools to free yourself from my trap, and now they shall be crushed under it. It won't make up for what I've lost, but it's better than nothing. Don't you think, Zeusson?"

> Host in imminent danger.
>
> Would you like to use a charge to escape?
>
> Yes/No

The message blinked in front of him, and for some reason, instead of feeling relief at a prospective way out, all he felt was *anger*.

Everything hurt, he was likely about to die, but for some reason he really, really did not want to hit yes.

Was this how it was always going to be? Would he escape now, like he did from Carim? Would she trace him to wherever the Seed took him again? Would he have to start over from scratch and repeat the same process over and over and over until he finally ran out of charges and she ripped the God Seed free from his soul?

No. He directed his thoughts to the Seed, and the message disappeared, but strangely enough, the option to use a charge didn't.

I run now, and this whole quest would have been for nothing. Running from Carim would have been for nothing. Killing all those people in the tomb would have been for nothing.

Closing his eyes, he strained against the metal barrier with everything he had. Using his inventory, he sent a vial of Warrior-tier healing potion straight into his mouth and tuned out the world around him. Desperately raking his mind for a solution, he latched onto his only hope.

> Quest Alert: Advance to Warrior

He grinned into the dirt as the Seed confirmed his own thoughts. There was another way. Maybe. She wanted to see them suffer, so he'd make sure he suffered for as long as possible.

Focusing on his manasink, he started shoveling mana into it.

Eighty-seven points of mana convert to one stat point. Eighty-seven points of mana convert to one stat point. Eighty-seven points of mana convert to one stat point.

He repeated the mantra in his head over and over and over again, ignoring the agonizing pain in his head in favor of his only hope for staying alive: forcing one torturous point after another into the ring.

He felt like a sword was stabbing into his head, and his vision turned red as blood spilled from his eyes. He didn't stop. He didn't give in.

Some barrier seemed to break in his mind, and suddenly the pain gave way to numbness. Mana poured out of him, and into the ring in an unstoppable torrent. It grew hot on his finger, but he didn't stop. Right now, it was his only hope.

It felt like hours, but it was over in mere seconds.

Status | Skills | Quests | Inventory
Stat Points: 5,611
Bloodline: Locked. Conditions not met. (4,812/10,000)
Charges: 7/10

He dumped them all into his Bloodline. The world turned white. The pain ebbed away. A giant sat on a throne and looked at him with surprise.

"You live, then."

CHAPTER 69

It's an Ancestor

I live . . . what?

Luke attempted to look around in the whiteness, only to find that he couldn't.

I'm not really here. Is this a dream?

"What is this? Who are you?" he asked. His eyes landed on the giant hunched forward and sitting atop an obsidian throne.

Is he Max's dad?

He was muscular and nearly naked. Dressed only in a loincloth, white hair fell down his shoulders and covered his face. Only his eyes, two solid blue orbs, were visible through his wild mane, and folded frame.

"This is my home, and I am Prometheus," he said, his voice deep but parched. As if he hadn't had anything to drink in ages.

Shit. Oh, damn. This is . . . Luke's eyes widened in surprise.

Bloodlines. I assumed they came from somewhere. I knew they would. It's in the name but—a titan, he thought, carefully keeping his expression neutral. *Who is Max? Why would the Seed pick his body? Why was someone related to a god even being raised by a mortal fisherman?*

And Prometheus on top of that.

In the myths he's one guy who's pretty consistently good, at least from what I remember. Gave fire to mankind and some other stuff . . . but there's something wrong here.

The egg I got, for the burning eagle. It's born from one that ate Prometheus's liver. Has been for millennia, according to the description the Seed gave me. That can't be a coincidence.

"I wonder, have you heard of me? Does my name still mean anything?" the titan asked, inching forward in his throne with desperation.

Luke frowned, not having expected that question. But something about how he asked told Luke it would not be good for him if he answered wrong. "I've heard stories. Vague ones. I'm not sure if they—"

"You have?" He leaned to the very edge of his seat in excitement. His hair still obscured his face, but Luke could practically feel the smile on his face. "What do they say? Do they sing about my sacrifice? Of how I valiantly fought against my own family on Zeus's behest? How I taught him and his brothers the secrets of divinity?

How I guided his children to the same feat so that he could stabilize his rule? Or how I negotiated with the Othrysians for their surrender? Or how I created the greatest kingdoms Theos has seen for them to rule? Have you?!" His eyes shone.

"I ha—"

"YOU LIE," he roared, and for a moment the whiteness shimmered and cracked, giving Luke a tiny glimpse at something disgusting before it repaired itself. Prometheus leaned back into his throne heavily, his chest rising and falling rapidly. Tears, stained with blood, dripped down the length of his hair and fell onto his chest. "I'm sorry. They've erased me, haven't they?" he said miserably. "One mistake. That's all it was. I thought I could do it. I really did. I thought I could break the limits of divinity. Ascend even higher. Is that so bad? Is that *sooo* bad? We all wanted it." Bits of blood-soaked spittle flew through the air.

What is he even talking about? Luke thought, becoming more frightened and more unnerved every second he spent in the company of the titan.

The world rumbled and shook. The giant figure of Prometheus slipped from his throne and collapsed on the ground. He coughed, and splatters of blood littered the once-pristine whiteness. Blackness crept outward and infected the world from where they fell like cracks through glass.

"What was that?" Luke asked, resisting the urge to turn on his heel and run. Only the knowledge that there was nowhere to go kept his feet rooted to the illusory ground.

Prometheus groaned miserably. Every fiber of his being oozing misery.

"It is too soon for us to speak, and our . . . connection already grows faint. My prison is most detestable." He lifted his arm and waved. Color crept into the world to reveal a hideous sight.

A crazed expression peaked through the titan's hair, revealing pale skin and rows upon rows of sharklike and yellowed teeth where his lips should have been. His muscles shrunk and revealed an emaciated frame. Scarred skin hung loosely on thin bones, with dried blood caking his entire midsection. His throne was nowhere to be seen as the fake surroundings melted away and revealed his true state.

"Tell no one that you carry my blood," he rasped. "I do not know which of my descendants sired you, but your bloodline is pure. Pure as if you were my own." He took a deep breath. Blood, black and foul, spilled from his nose. Chains clanked and scraped against the stone as he wiped his nose with his arm. A river of red tears spilled down the side of his face.

He looks wretched.

In the distance an eagle cried, and a gust of wind ruffled the titan's hair. He closed his eyes in resignation.

"DO NOT PITY ME!" he roared, turning away in shame.

"I—"

"The warden comes to feast upon my flesh. A fate I must suffer, still," he whispered. "Do not seek me. I will find you once I am free. I am sorry. Madness takes me sometimes. You must never—"

He closed his eyes. A flaming beast slammed into him, its beak ripping into the flesh of the giant. He howled in agony.

"Never what?" Luke asked, but it was too late. His vision went dark.

When he opened his eyes, he found himself back underneath the slab of metal alongside Lukeus. He gasped for breath at the crushing pressure of the stone and the accompanied agony that all returned at once.

His mind reeled as he tried to come to terms with what he had seen and the magnitude of it and what it meant, before he discarded the chain of thought entirely and opened his status.

Advance first. Figure out what the meeting with the crazy titan means for my life later.

Status	Skills	Quests	Inventory

Name: Lukas King

Tier: Mortal

Bloodline: Eyes of Insight

Mana: 809/499,000.5

Rate: 15% per hour

Strength: 999

Agility: 999

Constitution: 999

Arcana: 999

Stat Points: 423

Charges: 7/10

He ignored the line about his Bloodline on his status. As much as he wanted to learn what it meant and what it did, he had bigger and quite literally more pressing problems. If he lived, he would have plenty of time to figure out what the Eyes of Insight were and how he could use them.

As things were, however, he'd be crushed to death if he didn't get stronger immediately. He needed to break through to the Warrior tier. Adding one free point to each of his stats at the same time, he sighed in bliss as, for the first time in over a week, his attributes increased. He was just now realizing how much he had missed the sensation of his body improving. This time, whether it was because of how long it had been or because he was finally crossing into the next tier, the improvements felt even more profound. His strength surged manifold, his body toughened far beyond what it ever had before, and his nerves lit up with activity, his thoughts slowing to a crawl and his vision, hearing, and other senses sharpening, each far beyond what a single stat point should have offered.

His status flickered away.

Aethereal mana gushed into him, and his own reserves began to surge before suddenly coming to a halt. He felt something change within his mana.

It rippled and coalesced, the change starting from his heart and spreading out through the rest of his body in an instant. It still felt ephemeral, like it always did, but this time it felt more real somehow. Both closer and deeper.

It was as if he had been seeing it through a window this entire time, and now it was *right there*. Without any obstruction. Just waiting to be used.

It was a subtle change, but a profound one, and as it flowed within his body, he could feel it brush against the fabric of space itself. Pushing against it the same way his hand might push against a rock.

So that's how warriors fly. He grinned in spite of his circumstances. *I feel lighter, too*, he thought. The weight pressing down from above felt less crushing, and the sting of the ground against his face was just a tad more shallow. Just a little more tolerable.

I have a few more minutes to live at least.

Focusing on his hand, he channeled mana toward it, and then out. In a sensation similar to his boots, it caught in the air. He pushed against it, fruitlessly. The block of metal pinning him was too heavy for him to lift it off him.

"Luke!" Lukeus grunted from beside him. "Are—you still alive?"

"I am."

"Good." He went silent. "Any ideas on how to get out?" he gasped.

"Do you have any more of those Hero-tier talismans?"

"Two of each."

"Good. Let's—"

"Heracles won't survive." Lukeus shut him down immediately.

"She'll protect him, but we'll die if we don't," Luke pleaded.

"What then? We can't beat her," he whispered.

"What th—" He groaned in pain, and suddenly the load on Luke got heavier. Lukeus had stopped resisting.

"Lukeus. Lukeus!" Luke yelled. "Stay with me!" Desperation mounted inside him as he tried to think of a solution.

None came.

He gritted his teeth as he lifted with every ounce of his strength, already knowing that it was futile. His mana was already beginning to run thin, and the second it ran out, he would be crushed along with Lukeus.

Shit. Shit. Shit.

Is this it? What was that quest? I broke through to the Warrior tier. Now what?

. . . Do I use the charge? a traitorous voice inside his head whispered, urging him to give in and escape from his suffering. Blood spilled from his mouth as the last dredges of his mana kept him alive.

Reluctantly, he reached out toward the Seed, hesitating in what he thought might be his final moments. He really didn't want to run again.

Just a few more seconds. Yeah. Right at the last moment. When there's absolutely no other choice. That's when I'll use a charge, and not a second before.

Thunder boomed, and the telltale noise of rain splattering against the ground filled his ears, making his breath hitch.

It wasn't cloudy before, was it? he thought deliriously.

"ARKE!" a voice resounded through the air.

The metal slab shifted and the pressure on Luke eased before it vanished entirely, revealing the silhouette of a lone figure standing over Lukeus. A vial appeared in its hand, which it poured into Lukeus's mouth.

"Zeus," Arke said softly. "I wasn't—"

"Silence," he whispered. Immediately, her mouth snapped shut. "Are you okay?" he asked Luke. Another vial appeared in his hand, and he held it out toward Luke. His gray eyes beamed down at him softly and with kindness.

This is insane. Prometheus and now Zeus?

"I'm okay," Luke said numbly. Gingerly accepting the offered vial with shaking hands, he opened it and downed it in a single gulp. He was in too much pain to even lament wasting on minor wounds what was possibly the highest-tier healing potion he had ever touched.

He marveled as his broken skin stitched itself back together and the coppery taste of blood in his mouth receded.

"Lord Zeus, I—" Arke started to say.

"You were going to kill two of my son's friends in front of him." Zeus looked at her with a blank expression. His eyes snapped to Heracles, still restrained in the air with a rock in his mouth. Noticing her gaze, she immediately let go of his son.

Her jaw clenched, and she straightened in the air. Her earlier nervousness seemed gone. "They broke my laws. It is my right to punish them."

"Who broke your laws?" he asked, his voice barely above a whisper.

"They di—"

"Who," he interrupted her again. His voice nearly inaudible over the sound of thunder.

"My lord—"

"If I am not mistaken, it was Heracles who commanded his fleet to press past your barrier. Was it not?"

"It was, my lord," she said.

"So why was it that you would punish these two?"

Her face set into a frown.

"My lord. Heracles is your son—"

"Are you suggesting that because he is my son, I will punish you?"

"Of course not, my lord. Your justice and integrity are without question."

Zeus combed his hands through his beard. "That is true. Punish him. Right now."

"What?" she asked dumbly.

"Father, this is—"

"Silence," Zeus said. "This woman thinks I'm an unjust king. I must prove that I am not. She will punish you for breaking her law, and after she has done so, she will return with me to Olympus and explain to me what her law is and why she made it, in accordance with the creed and the oaths that bind us."

"My lord, by the authority vested in me by the council, I am allowed to—"

"Do you think I don't know the rules of my own council?"

"I don't, my lord."

"Then why are you telling them to me?"

"I—"

An arrow shot forth and bounced off Zeus's shoulder.

"Sorry!" Rex shouted from the edge of the barrier, wings made of eyes in mouths flapping behind his back.

This guy, Luke thought with a grin as he fell face-first onto the ground, unconscious.

CHAPTER 70

A Sunny Day

When Luke woke up, he was substantially more comfortable than he had been when he fell unconscious. He took a deep breath and just enjoyed the smell of food in the air. Of freshly baked bread, spices, cooked meat, and berries. Feeling lighter than he had in a long time.

If everything panned out according to the quest, then that means Arke is gone. Maybe even for good. He grinned, unable to keep the expression off his face, no matter how hard he tried.

"Are you awake?" Lukeus suddenly asked from the bed next to his. Luke blinked in surprise.

"I am . . ." He flipped over to his side and saw the freshly advanced warrior propped against the headboard of another bed three down from his in a row of them. "Why are you here? Where are we?" Luke frowned, not recognizing his surroundings at all. The fully wooden floors, walls, and ceilings felt both cozy and alien, and even the lighting—brass lanterns spouting a continuous stream of smokeless yellow-blue flames—was entirely new.

It's definitely not the castle, that's for sure. Or if it is, it's some kind of infirmary that I haven't seen before. Not having any windows is an odd choice, though. Are we underground? How long was I even out? Did Zeus teleport us?

Lukeus laughed out loud. "Did you think we were dead?"

"What . . . No, I fell unconscious after you did. Did you think we were dead?" Luke asked.

"No," he said unconvincingly, shifting slightly in his own bed. "What's the last thing you remember?"

"I'm pretty sure I remember Rex hitting Zeus with an arrow after he rescued us."

Lukeus paled at the mention of a god. "Zeus! Zeus rescued us?"

"Yeah." Luke shrugged. "It was a surprise to me, too. He kind of just showed up at the end there. Saved our asses."

"What was he like?"

Luke shrugged. "He seemed normal. Arke was super scared of him, though . . . Do you know what happened to her? I think I heard something about Olympus, but it's a little fuzzy."

Lukeus shrugged. "I woke up a few minutes ago myself. Don't even know where we are."

"Oh." Luke shuffled back into his bed and pulled the blanket tight around his neck. "It's probably fine. It's warm, it smells good, and nothing is attacking."

"Yeah, probably . . . I'm sorry," Lukeus said suddenly.

"For what?"

"I should have set off the talismans like you said, blown the metal right off us. Giving up—"

"Oh . . . that," Luke interrupted him. "It's fine. We're alive, so it's not worth thinking about. Honestly, it might have been what Arke wanted us to do." *Besides, who knows how long Zeus was there, and if he was listening to us? If anything, Lukeus's reluctance to put Heracles at harm might have been what made him step in.*

"What do you mean?"

"Well, think about it. She obviously didn't want to kill Heracles herself, but what if it was us who did it, and she just didn't save him? Would she have been able to get away with it then?"

"Maybe. She seems a little dumb for something that convoluted, though."

Luke snorted.

Lukeus grinned. "I can't believe you told her that her plan was stupid. I didn't dream that, right?"

"I don't think I actually called it stupid," Luke protested.

"You might as well have. What were you even thinking?"

"I don't know. I was just trying to get her not to kill you."

"What—by getting her to kill you instead?" He guffawed before cocking his head to the side in confusion. "Did you say Rex shot Zeus? Like with an arrow?"

"Mmm-hmm."

"That idiot." Lukeus shook his head. "We should go and find him before he shoots another deity."

"We should probably find out where we are, too." Luke sighed as he reluctantly rolled out of the bed. Only to panic when he realized that both his shoes and his weapons were missing. Cursing under his breath, he shot to his feet, his eyes widening when an accidental bump of his hip sent the bed loudly skidding through the room and into the bed next to it.

Oh, right. I'm a warrior, too, now. He frowned, recalling the rest of the madness that had occurred.

Numbly, he opened and closed his fist, taking a moment to just get used to his new strength and just meditating on both how different and abundant his mana felt.

I feel good. Strong. He grinned. *Really strong.*

The door swung open, and a man, a single foot tall, old, grizzled, dressed head to toe in steel armor, and carrying an axe that was three times his length, stepped in. He took one look at the pair, and the mess Luke had inadvertently made, and stroked his bushy red beard in resignation. Crossing his arms under his chest, he mumbled something intelligible and shook his head.

Luke blinked in surprise at the sight, exchanging an awkward glance with an equally confused Lukeus.

Is he a leprechaun? Or a dwarf? Why am I even surprised? If cyclopes can exist, so can whatever he is.

"Who are you?" Lukeus asked, floating into the air and then gingerly landing on his feet. Luke frowned when he saw that the emperor's grandson still had his shoes.

So they just took mine. Artifacts only, then?

"If yer both awake, the captain wants to see ya," the man said, ignoring his question.

"The captain?" Lukeus frowned. "Where are we?"

"And where's my stuff?" Luke asked.

"Beats me." He shrugged. "All I was told to do was stand out here and wait for you fancy bums to get your lazy asses out of a stupor. Apparently you lot drank some very high-tier healing potions and went under. Now, like I said, the captain is waiting," he grumbled, turning on his heels and marching away.

"A stupor?" Luke muttered under his breath. "How long do you think we were out?"

"No clue." Lukeus patted Luke on the shoulder and followed him.

Luke rubbed his eyebrows in frustration.

They better give me back my shit . . . Shit! Zeus killed Bellerophon! Did he take my sword? If there's anyone that would recognize it, it would be him. Luke frowned. *What about my boots and other sword, then? Cyzicus said he made those. There isn't much of a reason for a god to steal them from me. Which hopefully means that he didn't.*

His eyes traced Lukeus's frame, and he glanced around the room one last time before following him, slightly mollified by the fact that the other warrior didn't have any of his weapons, either.

If both of our things are gone, then it's pretty likely that Zeus didn't take them. Maybe they were disarming us? But then, who are they? Heracles's people?

They would have to be.

Eyeing the dwarf with meticulously hidden suspicion, Luke scanned their surroundings, carefully making a mental map of the wooden maze they found themselves in, in the unlikely event they had to make a run for it. As they walked by a kitchen, sleeping quarters, and groups of some of the strangest people Luke had ever seen, though, he increasingly didn't know what to expect.

So, he opened his status, curious to see how it had changed by his ascent into a higher state of existence.

His heart immediately sank in his chest as numbers, smaller than they had been in ages, appeared in his mind's eye.

Status | Skills | Quests | Inventory
Name: Lukas King
Tier: Warrior
Bloodline: Eyes of Insight

Mana: 351/351

Rate: 17% per hour

Strength: 14

Agility: 11

Constitution: 18

Arcana: 39

Stat Points: 9

Charges: 7/10

His attention lingered on his tier and his Bloodline. He realized what had happened, and some of the tension left his chest.

The Seed adjusted to my progress in the Warrior tier and scaled the numbers accordingly. I should have had over four hundred stat points remaining, but I only have nine. What is that a hundred times' decrease in relative value, if I adjust for any points gained while I was out?

Hmm . . . If it's mapping my progress the same way it did in the Mortal tier, then I have to get all my stats back up to a thousand to advance.

All my other attributes, besides Agility, shot up a little bit, too. Probably a mix of the healing potion and recovering from the damage done drawing in a bunch of aethereal mana and being crushed.

The gain in Arcana is insane, though. If I only increased my Agility by one point, and my theory about a hundred times' decrease in value is right, then that means a thousand points in the Mortal tier translates to ten points in the Warrior tier. For me to gain that much Arcana, then, I basically raised it by two thousand nine hundred points in one sitting—a lot, at least by my old standards. But I also gained like five thousand stat points with the ring, so it's not that crazy.

Considering that boiling myself alive only gives—gave—like fiftyish, that's pretty solid. Even though boiling myself alive is honestly a lot more pleasant than that, he thought grimly, remembering the mind-breaking pain, and idly rubbing the finger he had worn the manasink on. He frowned, unsurprised to find that it was missing as well.

They really took everything. He glared at the back of the dwarf's head and giant—relative to his size—axe bobbing with every step he took. *And they better give it back.*

His mind flashed back to the flying serpent he had killed with Nel's help over a month ago.

If I remember right, that thing gave me like three hundred points. It felt like a lot back then, but if I were to kill it now, I would only get three points. Which puts it at the level of a harpy or any of those other low-Mortal-stage monsters.

Except, that thing didn't die like a harpy. Not at all. It was nowhere near as strong as that first giant I saw, but it could take a beating. And turn invisible . . . which, speaking of—

He searched through the Seed's interface, looking for a description of his Bloodline and frowning slightly when nothing showed up anywhere.

Still. Eyes of Insight . . .

The dwarf threw open a door. Beams of sunlight shone down the pair of confused warriors as they stepped into the open sky.

"LUKEUS!" Heracles came barreling toward them and caught the emperor's grandson in a bear hug.

Luke relaxed slightly at the familiar face, glad to have his suspicion confirmed. His eyes wandered his strange new surroundings, darting from the brass railing along the edge of the crowded deck, milling with activity, to the massive array of at least fifty sails loudly flapping in the wind behind them.

A giant wooden wheel mounted imposingly on a raised platform was in the center of the deck, and a giant holographic map of what he recognized as Sylcra floated above it. On it thirty tiny red boats were shown scattered around its western edge—each one marking the position of a ship in the fleet, with nearly all of them, save the one they were on, sitting near the mouth of the giant river that split the island in two. Hundreds of miles behind their own position.

Captain suddenly makes sense. We're on a ship, he realized. *A big one, at that.*

"Kejhh," Luke wheezed as Heracles let go of Lukeus and pounced on him, the man's great strength catching him entirely by surprise. He struggled in his grip for a second before giving up. Like with Yjarn all those months ago, Luke was too weak to even wiggle in his hold.

As Heracles stepped back and beamed at him, though, Luke found that it didn't bother him quite as much as it had before.

"Glad you're all right." Luke grinned back at him, genuinely happy to be in friendly company.

"Ahem," someone coughed loudly, drawing their attention.

"Where are my manners?" Heracles stepped back and slung his arms around the pair. "Lukeus. Luke. Meet my good friend Jason. He's the cocaptain of this fine vessel." He nodded to a tall, brown-haired man who was leaning against the ship's rails. He was dressed entirely in white, accessorized entirely in gold, and strangely enough wearing a single sandal on his right foot.

Jason . . . cocaptain? Luke cocked his head to the side. A faint memory tickled his brain.

Jason waved. "Captain, just captain," he corrected him quickly and completely ignored the chagrined frown on Heracles's face. "Rex tells me that you're the ones responsible for getting this oaf free. You have my thanks." He inclined his head, and his face stretched into a wide grin.

Oh. Luke grinned as he looked around the legendary ship with renewed wonder. *That's pretty cool.*

"Where are you taking us?" Lukeus asked, wincing as he stretched away the pain of Heracles's hug.

Jason quirked an eyebrow. "He didn't tell you?"

"I told them we came to kill giants." The son of Zeus shrugged. "What, did you think we're going to leave Sylcra without doing so, especially after all the trouble we went through to get here?"

"Indeed." Jason nodded. "The *Argo,* sails to the Capital."

Ahh . . .

Luke looked between the three of them and raked his eyes across the deck of the ship. *You know what? This might actually be fun*, he thought, taking a deep breath and just enjoying the feel of Theos's nine suns shining gently on his skin.

It really might . . . Depending on what my next quest is, of course.

About the Author

Arthur Wordsmith is the author of the Theos series, originally released on Royal Road. He believes that books have the power to entertain, take people to different worlds, expand their minds, and connect them with their deepest selves. As a writer, he aims to create works of fiction that do exactly that. Visit his website at www. arthurwordsmith.com.

Podium
DISCOVER
STORIES UNBOUND
PodiumAudio.com